Best

~~~

ENDORSEMENTS

"Who would murder a woman of such moral rectitude as Mother Rosaria, mother superior of a Middle Western monastery? What was the motive and who is the guilty party?

"In *Magdalena's Conflict* Sister Camille discovers the answers to these questions with the aid of a family friend, Lieutenant Kummer. In doing so, Camille must also face her inward struggle as a modern woman enclosed in medieval robes and regulations of the pre-Vatican II church.

"In part 2 Camille must readjust both her life and her name to deal with another mystery.

"*Magdalena's Conflict* is of special interest to mystery lovers with a great curiosity about what happens behind the cloister walls, and to those who choose to leave them."

—Laura Leonard, author of *Saving Damaris*

"The details in, *Magdalena's Conflict* have a heartfelt quality that makes them vibrate rather than simply be present on the page. The tensions between, the cloth, the vows, restraints, routines, and the flesh intrigued me, including ordinary conflicts of personality."

—Clair Gustafson, Retired Diablo Valley College Instructor

MAGDALENA'S CONFLICT

FRANCES BRIES WOJNAR

Library of Congress Control Number: 2005902051
ISBN :   Hardcover   1-4134-8939-7
        Softcover   1-4134-8938-9

Magdalena's Conflict is a work of fiction. Names, characters, places, and incidents are the product of the author's imagination. Any resemblance to actual persons living or dead, events or locales are entirely coincidental.

This book was printed in the United States of America.

To order additional copies of this book, contact:
Xlibris Corporation
1-888-795-4274
www.Xlibris.com
Orders@Xlibris.com
28063

ACKNOWLEDGEMENTS

Thanks to Edward Wojnar, my husband, who freed me from many household chores and encouraged me to follow my inspiration; to my weekly critique group: Dorothy Brendlen, Inga Ferris, Jacque Hall, Laura Leonard, Evelyn Sanders, and Bertha Thomas; to Joan Killian, Cee Moorhead, Pat Reep, Tom Savignano MD, who edited and made recommendations; to Raymond Ogbemure Ph.D., who role-played psychotherapy with Sister Camille and me; to the California Contra Costa Sheriff's Office: Detective Knudsen, Homicide Division; Lieutenant Fukarama, Crime Lab; Brian Peterson MD; and Deputy Flanagan, County Morgue; and to John Rumpakis for suggesting the book title. Special thanks to Al Villaire, who spent many hours helping me with my computer and preparing this manuscript on CD.

MAIN CAST OF CHARACTERS

Sister Camille: Piano Teacher
Mother Rosaria: Mother Superior at St. Clotildes
Sister Angelica: Niece of Mother Rosaria

Sister Cordelia: Mother Superior at St. Clotildes
Sister Eugene: Directress of the Chateau Academy

Miss Drekle: Cook
Zelda Simmons: Cook
Joe Simmons: Plant Engineer

Lieutenant Hank Kummer: Detective in the Stone Hill PD
Sergeant Gary Flanagan: Detective in the Stone Hill PD

MONASTIC TERMS

AMDG—Latin initials for "All for the greater honor and glory of God"

Angelus—prayers recited at 5:00 AM, 12:00 PM, and 6:00 PM

Canonical hours—matins, lauds, prime, terce, vespers, and compline; the divisions of the divine office recited at specified times during the day

Canon law—code of laws established at a council in Rome in 1919

Cell—a sister's bedroom

Choir—cloistered part of the chapel, usually consisting of choir stalls

Cloister—an enclosure where the sisters live

Compline—see canonical hours

Great Silence—total silence from the end of evening recreation to the following morning after Mass

Guimpe—the white linen head covering under the veil

Infirmarian—the sister who takes care of the sick

Little Hours—the canonical hours: prime, tierce, sext, and none

Lauds—see canonical hours

Matins—see canonical hours

Monastery—an enclosed dwelling for monks or sisters

None—see canonical hours

Novitiate—a designated time and area where postulants and novices study and work before making final vows of poverty, obedience, and chastity

Prime—see canonical hours

Postulant—an aspirant who enters a novitiate to become a sister

Procuratrix—general housekeeper

Refectorian—the sister in charge of the refectory

Refectory—the sisters' dining room

Sext—see canonical hours

Vespers—see canonical hours

PART I

Suspicion in the Cloister

PROLOGUE

Leslie Allen sat in the backseat of the Olds Rocket, arms folded against her chest, her facial muscles pinched as if to ward off the oncoming scene. "Why did I accept an invitation to visit Susan Le Clair's home in Dubuque this weekend? I could have stayed at the Chateau with the other boarders," Leslie mumbled. "If only I could wipe out this weekend, erase it." She pushed the windblown mop of black hair out of her mascara-streaked eyes, held it a second, then let it fly. "What does it matter how I look?"

The convertible sped along the Great River Road toward the Chateau in Stone Hill, Wisconsin. Susan Le Clair, Leslie's classmate, sat in front with her mother, Madge Le Clair. With the top down, the wind gusts made it impossible for Susan and her mother to continue their conversation. Since Saturday, her mother could talk of nothing but Leslie's problem.

They turned off the highway away from the Mississippi River and climbed to the top of the tree-lined bluff. An imposing limestone Georgian mansion dominated the top of the knoll. There the Chateau, an academy for girls who wore navy blue blazers, and Saint Clotilde's, a monastery for nuns, stood in full view.

Spacious, trimmed lawns dotted with colorful perennials, vine-covered trellises, and trees gave the appearance of exclusive private grounds. In prior visits, Leslie felt like an enviable, privileged student when she entered the circle drive. Today, this buoyant feeling deserted her.

In the seconds before Madge LeClair parked and turned off the ignition, Nat King Cole's voice on the radio blared, "They tried to tell us we're too young."

The words "too young" echoed in Leslie's mind. She leaned over the front seat into Susan's ear, "I hate that song!"

Without a word to the girls, Madge LeClair opened the car door and slammed it. Leslie watched her friend's mother adjust her skirt downward in ladylike tweaks then remove the silk scarf from her head. With deft movements, Madge patted unseen waves into place and strode, heels clattering on the pavement, up the marble steps to the carved walnut doors. A smiling portress sister appeared, inviting her inside.

The girls clambered out of the car, dragging their suitcases from the trunk. For a moment, Leslie's knees went limp. She almost buckled to the ground and could have thrown up if she put her mind to it. "Your mother's so upset. What do you think will happen now when she tells Sister Eugene?"

"Well you know, Sister Eugene and my mom are good friends," Susan said. "They graduated together."

"Yeah," Leslie nodded, jutting her lower lip out, "but my life is none of your mom's business. And it doesn't give her the right to blab my problems. If Sister Eugene won't let me graduate, I'll run away before I have to call my mother."

"Don't do that, Leslie. Then you'd have another problem you don't need now."

The girls picked up their bags and sauntered around to the north side of the academy. They passed a workman dressed in overalls.

"Who is that?" Leslie asked.

"I think he's the plant engineer. It seems strange to see him here on a Sunday morning. I wonder what he's doing," Susan said.

"I think he's drunk."

Entering the student entrance, they heard piano music flooding the stairwell from the level above.

"That's Sister Camille. Why don't you talk to her?" Susan suggested.

"No, not yet," Leslie stalled, biting her lip already raw. "I don't see how she can help. She's one of the youngest nuns here and doesn't have any clout." Leslie dug her fist into the blazer pocket for a handkerchief. Pulling it out, she blew her nose. "This is going to be a bad day no matter how I look at it." She choked back the urge to sob and wiped tears that welled in her eyes.

"Just give her a try, Leslie."

The girls walked up the steps, plunked their suitcases down outside the studio where the rippling piano melodies continued. Susan knocked on the door. Sister Camille's bouncy steps approached picking up the rhythm of the music she just played.

Sister opened the door, her deep-set blue eyes registered surprise. Her attention seemed elsewhere, as if she wasn't ready to hear Leslie's sorry story.

"Good morning, Sister," the girls recited in chorus.

1

"Good morning," Sister Camille greeted the girls. The long black habit silhouetted her tall youthful figure. The snug linen head covering under the veil accented her high cheekbones. Sister disliked having her piano practice time interrupted but managed to hide her annoyance.

"What brings you back from the holiday weekend so early?" Her eyes darted from Leslie to Susan. Her hand disappeared within the deep folds of her habit bringing out a man's pocket watch hanging on a shoestring. She glanced at the timepiece hoping this visit would take a few minutes, so she could get back to that difficult section of the Brahms intermezzo.

When she practiced, everybody in the academy heard her. To students and faculty alike, it seemed a good time to share problems or to ask her help. Sometimes she wished she was an art major. What bliss an artist had painting without making a sound.

"It's only ten o'clock. Did you have a nice holiday?"

"It was okay. Nothing special. We had a picnic at Eagle Point Park on Memorial Day." Susan spoke in a monotone and then looked toward Leslie, who was twisting her handkerchief into a tight roll.

"Leslie, you look like you haven't slept all weekend. What happened?"

Leslie didn't answer.

Susan said, "My mom's talking to Sister Eugene now." She whispered. "Leslie's worried she won't graduate."

Sister turned her full attention toward Leslie, also her piano student. "This sounds serious. What is Mrs. Le Clair telling Sister Eugene? Why are you so worried?"

Leslie's lips quivered as she tried to fight back tears. Sister took her arm and guided her to a chair, knowing her practice period was forfeited.

Between sobs, Leslie said, "I'm going to have . . . a baby."

Sister Camille heard the blubbering words and caught herself from exclaiming Oh my God in censuring tones. It wasn't what she expected to hear that Sunday morning. She had been taught an unmarried, expectant girl was a disgrace. To have this happen to a graduating senior at the Chateau would, in the mind of Sister Eugene, the directress, ruin the academy's reputation. Finding her voice, she said, "Oh, you poor, dear girl. We must talk."

Getting her voice back, Leslie continued, "Mrs. Le Clair found out. I'm sure she's making trouble for me."

Susan interrupted, "Look, if it's okay, I'll leave you, two, and check in. Keep up your courage, Leslie." Susan patted her chin upward with the back of her fingers toward her friend.

Sister followed her into the hall, "Susan, did you come here directly from your car?"

"Yes, Sister," Susan nodded with assurance.

"Have you talked to any of the students on your way?"

"No, Sister."

Sister Camille smiled. From her student days, she remembered how the sisters drilled their students in the correct address for a sister. A simple yes or no would have been disrespectful. It had to be, "Yes, Sister"; "No, Sister."

She said, "Good. This is very important, Susan. Don't say a word about Leslie's condition to anyone. Do you think you can do that?"

"Yes, Sister."

"If this gets out to the students and parents, Leslie won't have a chance."

"You can count on me, Sister."

Returning to her pupil, she asked, "How do you feel, Leslie? Are you ill?"

"I feel terrible. I was so sick Saturday." Leslie paused to wipe her eyes and nose. "Mrs. Le Clair made me see her doctor. That's when she found out I was pregnant. The doctor told her. I had a suspicion, but I didn't want to believe it."

Sister Camille sat on the piano bench. She leaned forward and spoke softly. "How far along are you?" She wouldn't use the word "pregnant." That word, along with other private body terms, was taboo in a nun's vocabulary.

"It happened at the end of Christmas vacation. That would make me about four and a half months, if I counted right. My uniform's just beginning to feel snug, but I don't show." Leslie ran her thumb around the inside of her waistband still showing a gap.

"If Sister Eugene sends you home, I think there'll be too much gossip." Leslie had a chance to graduate because of the newly elected superior, Mother Rosaria. She had held the office only a few months, and major changes were already visible in both the monastery and the academy. She took a special interest in the working girls like Leslie who received scholarships and worked in the dining room.

"I hope you're right, Sister." Leslie's eyes looked brighter.

"We'll have to keep this quiet. It wouldn't be prudent for the rest of the girls to know. At least we can do that much."

"Thank you, Sister, for listening. I feel better already."

"You're so young, Leslie; you might want to think about adoption when the baby comes."

"Please, not yet. I'll have plenty of time to think about that. Now, I just want to get my diploma."

After Leslie left, Sister Camille sat at the desk with her hands bracing her head. Brahms no longer invited her back to the piano. Rather, she closed her eyes picturing how Sister Eugene and Madge Le Clair were discussing Leslie's situation. At least, Leslie's outlook looked better with Mother Rosaria having the final decision.

Sister Camille had often discussed these changes with her friend, Sister Angelica, who was also Mother Rosaria's niece. They had discussed how her aunt was treating all the sisters the same, with no special permission for private food or receiving visitors during prayer times, and about the power Sister Eugene wielded in the community.

"You've got to hand it to Sister Eugene. She makes the Stone Hill newspapers. Her students win county and state speech contests. That's how we got donations to build the addition to the gym," Sister Angelica had said.

"Don't forget the music contests. Our music students win too."

"But have you noticed the friction between Mother Rosaria and Sister Eugene?" Sister Camille had asked.

"I heard Sister Eugene say she lost her authority as the directress of the Chateau because Mother Rosaria wants to make her decisions."

"That happened last month. Mother Rosaria hired a replacement in the chemistry lab. Sister Eugene had promised the position to someone else."

*   *   *

In her piano studio, Sister Camille lifted her head from her hands. A red line showed on her forehead where the starched headband pushed up. Bringing it down to look more nunlike, she decided to cancel the rest of her practice.

Ordinarily, Sister Camille walked down the backstairs to return to the monastery. Today, she stayed on the second floor and walked past Sister Eugene's office. Edging near the closed door, Sister pictured the directress sitting like she just had tea with the Queen of England. Good manners were the hallmark of every Chateau girl, no matter what momentary crisis threatened.

Sister Camille stopped when she heard Mother Rosaria's name and scolded herself for eavesdropping. But she already knew the story and excused her nosiness.

Through the transom, she heard Sister Eugene speak in a clear voice, "That girl, Leslie, is just a street girl who earns her tuition by working in the dining room. She shouldn't be allowed to graduate. She's not a Chateau girl, and never will be. These walls have seen the last of Leslie Allen."

These walls, Sister Camille puzzled, trying to fill in the missing blanks, then remembered that last year's graduating class picture hung on a wall in the directress's office. Maybe she meant Leslie's picture wouldn't hang where the class of 1951 picture hung.

Sister Camille pictured the directress fingering the crucifix that hung below the starched wimple, staying its tendency to bounce on the breasts that were flattened by a tightly laced lining under the habit.

The inner office door opened. Sister Camille disappeared into the nearby hallway.

*   *   *

"Madge, I'm glad you came to me first. This must be kept just between us. I'll talk to Mother Rosaria immediately."

After Madge left, the directress rushed down the hall to the classroom of Sister Cordelia, the former superior. Both were Chateau graduates, which made them part of a select group sharing a strong bond.

Out of the corner of her eye, Sister Camille watched Madge Le Clair walk down the steps. She took in every detail of the blue crepe suit flattering Madge's size-10 figure. White kid pumps and purse completed the outfit. For a moment, her eyes shifted down the length of her own figure. She wondered just for a second how the suit would fit her.

Down the hall, she heard the directress say, "Have you a minute, Sister Cordelia?" Sister Cordelia said, "You look worried. Come sit down."

"You won't believe what I'm going to tell you." Sister Eugene told Leslie's story.

"What? One of our seniors? Dear God, this is awful. Even though it's the end of the semester, you can't let her graduate with the rest of our seniors," Sister Cordelia said.

"I want to suspend Leslie today. I should be able to as the directress of this academy, but now I have to contend with Mother Rosaria. How far do you think I'll get with her? She has such high ideas about restoring our holy founder's principles. I'm so tired of hearing about that. She even wants me to plan my schedule so that I can recite the divine office in choir. What am I going to do?"

"Oft expectations fail, and most oft where most it promises," Sister Cordelia said, fond of quoting Shakespeare. "If it comes to a vote, you'll have mine."

"We're in for some grueling years," Sister Eugene said. "Just the other day, my sister came to visit. She had to wait until the end of vespers to see me. When I showed Mother Rosaria the box of cherry chocolates she brought, Mother suggested I pass them around at recreation. She didn't even offer me one piece. She treats me like a novice. And we still have three years and nine months left of her term as superior. Pray, Sister, that she'll cooperate with me. I want to see the end of Leslie. Today!"

Sister Camille returned to the cloister, to her cell located around the corner from the superior's office. She was fortunate to have this location, not that she was a busybody, but she was in a prime spot to pick up on Leslie's tale. Sister prayed, "Thank you, dear Lord, for Mother Rosaria's leadership at St. Clotildes." The superior's transom was ajar.

Further down the hall, the double doors marked Cloister, No Admittance opened. The sign was for visitors who used the parlors nearby. Sister Eugene knocked on the superior's door and responded, "In his name," a monastic response to "enter."

At first, there was silence, then Mother Rosaria said, "But graduation is only two weeks off. I must talk to my council. I'll call a meeting tonight."

When Sister Eugene left, Sister Camille heard her whisper to Sister Cordelia, who just happened to meet her. "Why can't Mother Rosaria accept my decision to dismiss Leslie? She wants to have the council decide. You'll have to help me through this."

2

M other Rosaria watched her council assemble for the unscheduled meeting. Sister Cordelia, the deposed mother superior who had completed her term of office three months before, entered the door. Her erect posture and stern voice challenged the boldest. As senior English teacher she was able not only to quote Shakespeare but often transposed the author's words to fit the situation.

Next Mother Rosaria saw her aged friend and mentor, Sister Bernard, who had earned a master's degree, cum laude, in chemistry from Notre Dame many years ago. Now she suffered from severe arthritis and found schnapps to be the best medicine for her pain.

Because of Sister Bernard's hearing loss, she turned to face Sister Cordelia. "Who is Leslie?"

"Sister, you'll never believe this." Sister Cordelia stooped low, cupping her hand close to Sister Bernard's ear. "Leslie's one of our senior boarders. She's going to have a baby." Sister Cordelia paused with unwavering eyes on the aged sister then added, "She should be expelled, today."

Sister Bernard heard every word but didn't react to the intense emotion on Sister Cordelia's face. Instead, she pulled a man-size handkerchief from within a deep fold of her habit and belched quietly into it. Her poor digestion created a ripe-marinade odor. Sister Cordelia waved the fumes away and took her place near the head of the table.

Sister Diana, the assistant to the superior and art teacher, joined them. She had painted spiritual bouquets and bookmarks with pastel roses and blue forget-me-nots. These were given to friends and clergy on special occasions. The large windows of her art studio looked out on the circle drive that led directly down a steep ravine to a highway running parallel to the Mississippi River. The lush greenery covering the limestone bluffs on the Iowa side of the river often inspired her student paintings.

The last to enter was Sister Martha, the kitchen supervisor, who would soon relinquish her assignment for the summer to Sister Camille. Sister Martha had come to St. Clotildes from an orphanage with meager expectations. If a tasty course ran out at mealtime, she'd eat an extra slice of bread, claiming it was good mortification for the soul.

As the curtain of silence dropped around the table, Mother Rosaria took her seat at the head. Bowing her head, she invoked the Holy Ghost for wisdom to present the delicate Leslie Allen case to her council.

The sisters sat with their eyes cast down. Long voluminous sleeves covered their hands. With their hooded heads bowed, they resembled an artist's rendering of ancient druids in tones of gray and black. The intensity paralleled the chanting and measured stirring of a caldron.

Today Mother Rosaria hoped the melting pot wouldn't be too hot, too damaging for the subject of their meeting.

"Thank you, dear Sisters, for coming on such short notice. I want your counsel regarding one of our graduating seniors, Leslie Allen." She summarized the situation related by Sister Eugene as if it was an ordinary topic. When Mother Rosaria finished, a gasp echoed around the table. Heads bobbed momentarily then dutifully resumed their bowed posture in expectant silence.

Mother Rosaria waited a moment and then said, "None of us wants to have a scandal in our academy."

Heads nodded in agreement.

The superior continued, "There are only two weeks left before graduation." She emphasized "two weeks" in a questioning tone of voice.

The heads remained still.

"I would like to hear your sentiments. The question is, should we send Leslie home today or allow her to graduate? Sister Diana, what is your opinion?"

Sister Diana asked, "Does Leslie look pregnant?"

"No, Sister, she doesn't."

"Well then, how is it going to affect Leslie if we send her home without a diploma? This would deny her entrance into college and into the work field. Although we can't condone her behavior, it's only two weeks." Sister Diana said, "Christ said, 'Whatsoever you do to the least of my brethren, you do it to me.' I suggest other senior privileges be denied her."

Sister Bernard spoke next. Though up in years, she evaluated situations without emotion. With her handkerchief still in hand, she wiped her mouth. "Hump, I remember when Madge was a student; she used to exaggerate then to gain attention and was always a show-off. How will this child get a job if she doesn't have a diploma?" Sister Bernard waited a second and then added, "Doctors have been known to be wrong in their diagnosis." She didn't volunteer any more.

"Sister Cordelia, what are your sentiments?" Mother Rosaria asked.

Elected mother superior twice before, Sister Cordelia wore an air of one in authority. When she entered a room, her substantial hips and heavy gait announced her presence.

"I believe we should expel Leslie Allen from the Chateau today without a diploma as punishment. She's committed a mortal sin by anyone's standards. That girl is evil, and she's contaminating our girls' morals." Her voice raised a decibel, "Shakespeare said, 'Good counselors lack no clients.' We're here to counsel!"

Sister Martha gasped, her dentures clicked into place. "I wouldn't even think of taking a shower without wearing a shift. The rule of Saint Augustine warns: 'We should not behold our bare bodies and be ever careful how we get into and out of bed.'" Sister drew her lower jaw down and rubbed the corners of her mouth where a few whiskers grew.

The superior knew Sister Martha had lived a protected life and wasn't surprised that she missed the main point. She also knew some sisters had little knowledge about the facts of life.

Sister Cordelia interrupted, "I think it would be scandalous if she graduates. We have to think of the reputation of our academy. What kind of a message will this give to our alumni and students?"

The voting proceeded. Leslie Allen received three votes to graduate and two against, which allowed her to graduate.

"Thank you, dear Sisters, for your consideration in this serious matter," Mother Rosaria said. "We took in Leslie knowing she was an abused child. I don't believe we should hang the guilt of mortal sin around her neck. Christ gave us an example toward sinners in his treatment of the woman taken in adultery.

"If we look for absolute justice we could find an answer, but I fear we'd be obeying the letter rather than the spirit of the law. I would rather err on the side of charity." She spoke with a gentleness that suggested strength of character as well as tenderness. "As mine is the swing vote, I cast my vote in favor of allowing Leslie Allen to graduate." She concluded, "I know each of you thought very hard about your answers. You have my respect no matter how you voted."

*   *   *

The meeting adjourned. Sister Cordelia left the council losing no time to find Sister Eugene who waited in the directress's office for the verdict. Out of breath from rushing up the stairs, she gasped. "Leslie will graduate!"

Sister Eugene reeled back on her heels. A quick breath released through her teeth made a wheezing sound. "Mother Rosaria overrides every one of my decisions. Where is my authority? This puts me in a fine predicament. What am I going to tell Madge Le Clair?" She forced her usually controlled voice louder. "I promised her Leslie would be sent home. I don't like the way decisions are made. You'll have to help me through this, Sister." She continued nodding her head.

"I wonder what our parent guild is going to say." Sister Cordelia added, "It still surprises me how the community voted for Sister Rosaria to be superior with her bad health. Maybe that will be in our favor."

3

The five thirty rising bell rang on graduation morning. Sister Camille wakened with a feeling of annoyance. Was it because of a recurring dream of being chased up an alley in Chicago? It didn't make sense because the alley always went in the wrong direction. She tried to laugh it off as she knelt to say the regulation prayers prescribed by the rule and then scrubbed her face with Ivory soap. Her skin reflected a youthful glow.

Some nuns created an aura of serenity, not Sister Camille. She often questioned religious practices that others accepted on blind faith. Once she argued with Sister Angelica, "Does God wait to help only those we pray for? What about those who don't get prayers?"

She remembered her high school basketball team praying before games. Both sides of the court knelt in prayer. "I can't picture God deciding which team should win. But we say it's the will of God if we lose or win."

Sister Angelica accepted Sister Camille's outspoken comments as her little sister who had much to learn. She'd answer, "You made a vow of obedience to God, and then you tell him how to proceed."

"No, I feel some of these sixteenth-century-old pious practices don't make sense," said Sister Camille.

After she dressed, Sister Camille closed her cell door without so much as the sound of the lock movement, a mark of tranquility during the great silence, and walked on her tiptoes to the chapel. While preparing for the morning meditation, she thought of the opposition Mother Rosaria experienced from some of the sisters. Tension continued to play out during the week of commencement preparations. She had overheard a discussion earlier that week between Mother Rosaria, Sisters Cordelia and Eugene while she dusted the parlors.

Through the open window, she heard Mother Rosaria say, "I've often thought if the bleachers were backed against the academy building, the audience would have that beautiful, panoramic view of the Mississippi River." Her arm swept the width of the scene. "The spring foliage on the Iowa bluffs would make a beautiful background for snapshots."

With an accommodating smile, Sister Eugene said, "But, Mother, we've always had the bleachers by the tennis courts, facing the academy. It's tradition. It would be difficult to explain this change. The alumni expected their rituals." She muffled a low laugh, nodding to Sister Eugene to reinforce her opinion. Sister Cordelia picked up on her nod quicker than a relay runner. The directress said, "What do you think, Sister?"

More experienced at putting on these events, the two sisters wanted to be sure the new superior understood. "Well, as you just said, Sister, placing the bleachers facing the academy is our tradition."

High on a ladder, a workman was hooking up the electrical system. The superior called up to him explaining the new plan. Climbing down the ladder, he shoved his cap up and lit a cigarette. "I've already spent a half a day getting my electrical lead from that pole. Sister Eugene gave me orders this is where she wanted the stage built. If the stage is moved to the front of the building, I'll have to start all over." He rolled his eyes heavenward, shaking his head as he stepped toward the ladder to fold it. "I wish you, Sisters, could make up your mind."

"I'm sorry for the mix-up," Mother Rosaria said.

As Sister Camille listened, she felt Mother Rosaria was treading on shaky ground. The handyman couldn't stand much tension. She remembered one time he hit the bottle at the spring festival, leaving the sisters in the lurch. Then a month later, he appeared at the May crowning with a talking jag that embarrassed everyone.

A little farther down the campus, a carpenter drove a sixteen-penny nail into a support on the temporary stage. He stopped as Mother Rosaria approached. She asked, "Would it be a lot of work for you to change the location of the platform?"

He looked surprised but tried to be his usual agreeable self. It was his nature. A solid Catholic family man who had two daughters enrolled at the Chateau, he enjoyed working for the sisters. In a respectful tone, he pointed out, "It'll take the rest of the morning to knock down this base, but I guess it could be done. My son can help if I need him."

As these bits of conversation reached Sister Camille's ears, she applauded her superior for standing up to Sisters Cordelia and Eugene.

After Mother Rosaria left, Sister Camille heard Sister Eugene say to Sister Cordelia, "Now it's our traditions? I fear for the future of the Chateau the way she's changing things."

Within a few days, graduation preparations were completed in the new direction, and the diplomas were hand lettered in calligraphic style by Sister Diana. On the afternoon before the ceremony, Sister Eugene requested Sister Camille to search the music library for a record or tape of the song, "On, Wisconsin."

That evening, Sister Camille showed Sister Eugene how to use the tape recorder. They rehearsed timing the state song with the entrance of the speaker, the eminent writer and philosopher Lewis S. Chatner, who held the illustrious William Goldberg chair at the University of Wisconsin. Sister Camille practiced the professor's role, walking up the steps to the microphone on the dais and synchronizing her movements to the Wisconsin song.

*   *   *

Like an answer to the good sisters' prayers, graduation day dawned sunny and pleasant. Baskets of flowers formed a bower where the graduates marched. The guests arrived and sat on freshly wiped-off chairs. After the chaplain finished the baccalaureate Mass, Mr. Chatner rose to address the graduates, parents, and friends. When Sister Eugene turned on the tape recorder, it needed time to warm up. She turned up the volume to the maximum. Sharp electronic noises sounding like *ght, ight, e'll* filled the air. Each syllable grew louder until "win the game" shrieked through the speakers. Sister Eugene turned off the recorder and fingered her rosary beads as though nothing had happened.

The once-placid audience stirred in their seats, unsure of what would follow. Mr. Chatner adjusted his microphone and squinted toward the sky. "There must be a message out there someplace," he quipped.

This brought a ripple of amused sounds from the audience. Sister Camille bent over, holding her handkerchief to her face to muffle a giggle. Was Sister Eugene's last minute request for the tape worth it?

After commencement, Sister Camille went to the kitchen for the first day of her summer assignment. She folded back her long sleeves, pinned the top of an apron in place over her starched wimple, and greeted the cook, Zelda Simmons.

Instead of a cheery greeting, Mrs. Simmons said, "I'm giving you two weeks' notice, Sister. Joe and I will both go."

Sister Camille knew the story about Joe. Mother Rosaria had given the plant engineer notice after he failed to arrive at work after a week's absence. She said, "I hoped you'd stay on, Zelda. I looked forward to working with you this summer. Have you told Mother Rosaria?"

"No, I haven't. Would you?"

"I'll let her know after dinner."

"It's not because of you. You've always been fair, but Joe has to find a job. We want to work together." Zelda pressed the stem of a gold watch that hung on a chain around her neck. A small photo of Joe showed inside the lid. In one of her chattier moods, she had told Sister Camille that he had brought the watch back from Singapore when he was a merchant marine. Mrs. Simmons snapped it shut when the noon Angelus began to ring. "It's time to dish up."

Sister Camille helped the cooks ladle platters of Mississippi catfish, carrots, and potatoes on the cart for the sisters' dinner.

*   *   *

Meanwhile suitcases, trunks, desks, chairs, and chests from the boarders' quarters filled station wagons and cars. Leslie Allen caught Sister Eugene on the run. "Oh, Sister, I couldn't leave without thanking you for everything. These years at the Chateau have been my happiest times. I learned so much from you and all the dear sisters."

Sister Eugene's eyes scolded, "Keep your robe closed, Leslie. Someone might see you."

*   *   *

On the monastery side, the sisters in the refectory, not involved with postgraduation activities, ate their dinner in silence. The reading began with *The Roman Martyrology* followed by "Of Judgment and Punishment of Sinners" from *The Imitation of Christ* by Thomas a Kempis. After dinner, the sisters processed to the assembly room reciting the psalm, *De Profundus* ("Out of the Depths Do I Cry to the Lord").

Only those sisters at the rear of the procession heard Mother Rosaria slump. Those nearest said all they heard was fabric crumpling softly on the hardwood floor.

4

After the dinner recreation, Sister Camille stood in formation to hear the announcements. The sisters aligned themselves on two sides of the room in silence as if on troop inspection. With their heads bowed and hands buried in sleeves that hung below waist level, they resembled an illusion of phantoms in hooded black robes. In the same posture, Sister Diana, the assistant to the superior, stood at the head of the assembly to report on Mother Rosaria's condition.

"Dear Sisters, Mother Rosaria has suffered a heart attack. Dr. Spence warned she could have another one with her history of heart disease. He's ordered complete bed rest. Mother won't have to go to the hospital if she follows his orders. Sister Mercy is with her now. Please keep Mother Rosaria in your prayers."

From the ranks, Sister Cordelia spoke up, "May we visit Mother?"

"The doctor ordered complete rest. Please do not disturb her." Sister Diana gave a blessing, which signaled the end of the formal announcements. The sisters were free to leave the assemblage.

Sister Camille remained in place, unable to breathe. She shook her shoulders to force a deep breath and looked around for reactions. Not only did she worry about Mother Rosaria's health, but Zelda Simmons had given notice added to the crisis. She decided to wait till later to report the Zelda's notice to leave their employment. Sister Diana had enough on her mind, and the cook wasn't leaving for two weeks. Walking up the wooden stairs covered with black treads, she lifted the hem of her habit to avoid collecting dust. On the way, she met Sister Angelica. She whispered, "It would be so easy for someone to put something in Mother Rosaria's medicine or not give her the right dose. Worse yet, someone could withhold her meds."

"No one would be that evil," Sister Angelica scolded as she passed.

In the chapel, Sister prayed God would spare their superior. If Mother Rosaria didn't survive, it would be back to the old regimen. Preparing herself for meditation, Sister closed her eyes and thought how Mother Rosaria supported her piano practice. She once told her superior, "I can lose myself in the harmonies of the great composers. The logical development of their works inspires me to reach a higher appreciation of God's creation. I can communicate with him better when I practice, than at meditation. And when a composition winds down to the finale, I become aware of my surroundings. Often times I don't want to land."

Mother Rosaria had said, "That's an added gift you have. You must thank God for your talent; cherish it and continue to develop it."

These were her ideas of freedom and spirituality that some of the sisters had disapproved. For the first time since she entered the community, Sister Camille felt surer of her vocation. Mother Cordelia had considered her music a hobby. She had told Sister Camille she was singular because her devotion to music didn't conform to the other sisters' activities. The former superior also believed manual labor was the best discipline for spiritual direction, especially for the young sisters. "Idleness is the devil's workshop," she'd caution.

Dr. Spence checked his patient the next day and found Mother Rosaria on the mend. On Sunday, he allowed her to sit up and receive visitors.

That evening after kitchen cleanup, Sister Camille went to her cell. She drew water in her pitcher from the communal bathroom to use later and folded the white seersucker spread from her cot. In the hallway outside, she heard the sickroom door open and close. Turning to leave her cell, she heard whispered voices through the open transom.

"It only takes a little while to be effective."
"Are you sure?"
"Yes."

Sister's hand froze on the doorknob. Had she heard right? Was fear playing tricks on her? She recognized the voices. After their footsteps died away, she slumped down on the chair, head in her hands. She couldn't move.

The next morning, Sister Mercy took the cart to the kitchen to collect breakfast courses for Mother Rosaria and her infirmary patients. Receiving no answer at the superior's door, she entered and raised the shades. The still figure on the bed caught her attention. She turned on the overhead light and then lifted her patient's cold hand. Feeling no pulse, she rushed to the chapel where the sisters recited prime. "Sister Diana, something's wrong with Mother; I need to call the doctor. I think she's . . . gone."

"Call him," Sister Diana whispered and rushed to the sickroom. She found Mother Rosaria lying on her side, her glazed eyes staring wildly at the door as if pleading. Mother's wrist felt cold and stiff. Finding Sister Bernard in the hall, Sister Diana said, "Call the sisters from the chapel."

She returned to the sickroom and placed her fingers on Mother Rosaria's eyelids to close them.

The sisters knelt around the bed in hushed silence. Sister Cordelia started the rosary, "I believe in God . . ." The tower bell tolled, announcing a death in the monastery.

Dr. Spence arrived with his usual hurried step. He grabbed the stethoscope from his bag and checked his patient's carotid pulse. Then he lifted one of her eyelids. The sisters saw him shake his head in disbelief. He returned the stethoscope to his case after checking her heart. "No heart activity. I'm as surprised as you, Sister." He led Sister Diana into the adjoining office. "This can happen with a history of heart disease. I'll sign the death certificate."

"Thank you, Doctor. I know you did all you could for Mother Rosaria. It must be God's will."

Because of short interval between the time of death and burial according to custom, the body required minimal embalming. In the coffin, freshly cut lilies lay all around the body dressed in the holy habit. The bier rested in the middle of the chapel where two sisters recited the Psalms in alternate verses. Chanting would continue throughout the day and into the night until the requiem Mass the next morning.

Sisters Camille and Angelica spent the hours from midnight until two in the morning chanting beside the coffin. In the cold silence, the time seemed endless. Sister Camille fidgeted with her book, often losing her place in the Latin phrases, and changed her position from kneeling to sitting. Once she walked to the coffin, searching for answers. She glanced toward Sister Angelica, reading the prayers with her head bowed and poised, as a sister should. Sister Camille wanted to talk rather than chant. Why didn't she? How many rules would she break? Instead, she returned to her chapel stall. Will the truth ever be known?

When the five rising bell rang, Sister Camille sprang up. Trained in promptitude during her novitiate, she knelt and prayed, "The angel of the Lord declared unto Mary . . ." Her novice mistress taught her that a fervent novice should put aside all activities, even sleep, to attend the bell. After the morning prayer, she freshened her face with a washcloth dampened from the water in the pitcher then recited the prescribed prayers while pinning each piece of the habit into place as she dressed. Today, she counted nine pins holding the four pieces of headgear together: white-headed pins for white pieces, black-headed ones for the black veil. Sometimes she felt like a pincushion. Due to high humidity, she could still feel the sweat in the folds of her habit from the night before. When the meditation bell rang, Sister Camille knelt in her assigned stall in the choir near the coffin.

Deprived of sleep and sick with worry, she tried to hide her feelings behind the mechanical movements of the morning prayers. Sister knelt, stood, and sat at the appropriate times and chanted, responding with her side of the choir during prime, "O Lord, make haste to help me." Then turning toward the opposite choir, the sisters bowed in unison chanting, "Glory be to the Father . . ." The sisters chanted little hours in the morning. Vespers and compline were chanted in the afternoon, and matins and lauds completed the final prayer of the day.

At ten thirty, the sisters gathered again in the chapel for the requiem Mass. Besides the community of thirty-one nuns, Mother Rosaria's sister from Chicago, two nieces from Milwaukee, and a nephew attended the service. The chaplain gave a short homily.

"We'll miss Mother Rosaria's gentle disposition and open-minded approach to spiritual life. She was ahead of her time and supported many of the changes proposed."

After Mass, the sisters and visitors marched in solemn procession with the remains to the cemetery. Only the rustling of beads and movement of wool serge could be heard. In the leaden silence, Sister Diana intoned the *Miserere*.

Sister Camille followed the Latin, but her mind was elsewhere. Why did God permit Mother Rosaria's life to be snuffed out so soon after being elected superior? Responding, "*Et cum spiritu tuo*" at the gravesite, Sister raised her head and searched everyone's face, looking for something that didn't fit into the setting. In murder-mystery stories, detectives and private investigators attended funerals of victims searching for clues. She wished one of Mother Rosaria's relatives would insist on an autopsy and also wished for the courage to tell them what she'd heard the night before Mother Rosaria died. Would anybody believe her? She knew they wouldn't. After the *De Profundus*, the coffin was lowered on belts into the grave.

Sister Camille returned to the kitchen after the service to help with dinner for the guests and sisters. Making out the weekly menus, ordering groceries, and assisting the lay cooks at mealtimes were a pleasant change from her teaching piano students. Though she never fancied herself a cook, she liked to experiment with new recipes. The ladies in the kitchen seemed to enjoy the change and supported her creative menus.

Miss Drekle said, "Isn't it too bad that Mother Rosaria died? She was so young."

"Well, we have to die sometime," Mrs. Simmons said. "The sisters ain't no different." She opened the oven door and stabbed a fork into the cooker filled with fried chicken. Checking her watch, "The chicken's done. I'll turn the oven down. Here's Sister Camille."

Miss Drekle walked over to her. "I'm so sorry for your loss, Sister. How's Sister Angelica?"

"Sister Angelica's doing remarkably well. She hasn't reacted to her aunt's death yet. I'll never get over it." She turned away to hide her tears.

"Why's that?" Mrs. Simmons looked sideways at her.

"Because Mother was on the way to recovery for two days then died so suddenly."

"You can't never tell about hearts." Mrs. Simmons spoke with authority. "My mother had a bad heart and went the same way." The trio stopped talking and dished up dinner when the noon Angelus rang.

After dinner cleanup, Sister Camille put her apron in a cubbyhole marked with a cross and the number +41. Instead of a name tag, this number marked all clothing, prayer books, and silver setting at her place in the refectory. The sisters referred to these items as "our" pencil, "our" fork, "our" veil. The holy rule prescribed this practice to encourage detachment from worldly possessions.

Sisters Camille and Angelica had gone through the novitiate together. The trial period included six months of postulancy, then a year of the white veil, which isolated them as novices from outside intrusions including visitors and mail. Three years of temporary vows of poverty, chastity, and obedience followed. At twenty-six, Sister Camille was the youngest professed sister. Meeting Sister Angelica in the hall, Sister Camille said, "Let's go for a walk."

"I'd like that. I hoped I'd find you."

They walked back to the cemetery. It had a parklike serene atmosphere with benches and tiers of rose bushes in full bloom at the entrance. Stately spruce trees formed barriers on three sides of the lot. A parking lot bordered the graveyard to the north and Fifth Street to the south. The approach road up to the Chateau connected to Highway 67 that ran along the Mississippi River's edge.

Sister Angelica bent down to smell the flowers. "The red and pink roses make the cemetery so attractive this time of year," Sister Angelica said in her usual sunny manner as though it were any other day. "All the blossoms and new growth make our grounds so beautiful." She looked at the fresh grave with a single bouquet of white carnations. "Everything seemed to be going so well until . . ." Sister Angelica stopped.

Though the community had buried her aunt that morning, she tried to make everyone around her feel good. Sister Angelica felt a need to praise, to say thank you without a good reason. Her ready smile reflected the joy of being a sister. It was her nature. She made the sign of the cross. Looking back to the grave, Sister Angelica choked back tears. "I know I should be more stoic and in control of my feelings. I should offer my sorrow up, but . . ." She couldn't go on. Searching for her handkerchief, she buried her face in it.

Sister Camille put her arm around Sister Angelica's back.

"I just wish I'd done more for her," Sister Angelica said.

"Mother Rosaria once said the religious spirit should be noncontrolling."

"She's right, too," Sister Angelica replied, "but why are we so tense? Why can't we be more relaxed in our lives? I remember Mother said obedience to customs and rules didn't make a follower of Christ. Rather it was the acceptance of Christ, who inspired our way of life."

"I don't think many of the sisters could understand that. Our lives are controlled by rules. Jesus never preached such inconsequential restrictions," Sister Camille said. "Mother Rosaria treated us like accountable adults. Now that she's gone, it'll be back to the old ways. Let's hope the new superior will be from the younger ranks and not so eager to shove her weight around."

"Do you really think it's possible to have someone younger for a superior?" Sister Angelica asked. "Most of the sisters are in the sixty-to-eighty-year bracket." She turned toward her companion. "Is there something else troubling you?"

Sister Camille didn't answer right away. Instead, she reached down and pulled up a blade of grass, held it between her thumbs, then threw it down. Because the contour of their veils blocked side views, Sister Camille took Sister Angela's hand and turned to face her. "Have you thought there might be foul play involved in Mother Rosaria's death?"

"Oooh, yes. I have this awful feeling." Her voice trailed off to a whisper.

Sister Camille repeated the conversation she'd overheard through the transom. "And if she were poisoned?" They looked at each other, not wanting to answer the question.

Sister Angelica whispered, "It's a terrible thing to imagine. I feel guilty just thinking about it, but what can we do?"

"I know a friend of my family, Henry Kummer. He's a detective on the Stone Hill police force. Maybe I should talk to him. At least, he could give us advice." She reached into her pocket and pulled out a watch, a cue they didn't have much more time left before the vesper bell. The two sisters knelt by the fresh grave and prayed in silence.

Sister Camille said, "Mother Rosaria went about her work in silence and never complained. And if there's foul play, whoaaa." She looked round to see if anybody had come into the cemetery enclosure. "Let's consider the consequences." She started to talk faster. "If Mother Rosaria were the victim of murder, how much cooperation would we get from the sisters? Do you know any one we can talk to?"

"I can think of just one, Sister Bernard. We had a good talk when the white-veil novice ran away during the night. She wasn't afraid to talk about it. The others wanted to sweep the incident under the rug."

"She's good," Sister Camille said. "But whether we're right or wrong, it's going to be very difficult to remain at St. Clotildes if we report our suspicions. There'll be so much scandal and bad feelings toward us. I don't want to contemplate what that would be like."

"If your friend feels we have a case, then the police will step in. We'd be treated just like the other sisters," Sister Angelica reasoned.

Sister Camille took a labored breath and rubbed her brow. After a few moments, she raised her reddened eyes. "Let's look at it another way. If we do get the law involved, and the evidence proves murder, one of our sisters may go to prison. Think of the publicity that would cause. What will happen to the reputation of the Chateau? Do you think we can take this on? Only when Mother Rosaria's body is disinterred and tested will there be proof, and that's no small project."

"Besides, you'd have to get permission to call the detective. You know incoming and outgoing calls might be censored."

"Darn it. Why do we have to have so many controls on every little thing we do?" Sister Camille brought her fist down on the arm of the bench.

"You know we have to deny ourselves if we are going to grow in spirituality. We're taught a true religious should surrender her mind and will to the superior who is chosen by the Holy Ghost."

Sister Camille knew Sister Angelica wasn't finished.

"Only then can we reach the highest degree of perfection."

"Right now, I don't care about that. I'll never reach it anyway. My mind can't seem to accept some of the rules, like walking with decorum and guarding my eyes when another sister is just inches away, even how to hold our office book while chanting so the oils from the fingers won't stain the pages. I feel like a robot with all these rules, rules that were probably made up by men. Sometimes I think they had a grudge against women. I don't think it's healthy. The scriptures don't teach this, and even Saint Paul wasn't this demanding."

Sister Angelica laid her hand on her companion's hand.

Sister Camille pulled it away. "Do you remember when we studied ethics? We learned that a rule could be broken for a cause that was for a greater good. I believe this is such a case." Sister Camille looked into her companion's prim face.

"Then call your detective," Sister Angelica said.

$$5$$

S ister Camille walked with quick steps down the hall toward the phone booth in the academy to call Detective Kummer. She tried to block out her feelings of guilt. If she hesitated one second, her conscience would kick in and chide her for using the phone without permission. Now that vacation had started, there'd be no students hanging around the phone booth, a lucky break. Her heart thumped like a jackhammer, and her hands shook as she lifted the receiver.

The repeated buzzing at the detective's home increased her breathing rate with each ring until she wondered if she'd be able to form the words to speak. When no one answered, she placed the phone back in the cradle and closed her eyes. Waiting a few minutes to get hold of herself, she put her mind into automatic gear. What if she called the police station? Never having called the police, she feared their response might be too forceful with no leeway for discussion.

After another failed attempt, she reconsidered and agonized over the possible consequences. How would this call affect her life and the community in which she vowed to live her life in obedience, poverty, and chastity? If only she could erase what she had heard. The longer she waited, the more the conversation seemed like a dream. With no one besides Sister Angelica to speak for Mother Rosaria, Sister Camille felt she must put her doubts to rest.

In the small theater off the auditorium, she found Sister Angelica painting over a stage flat used for the senior play. Sister Camille dropped down in a front seat with her legs spread out in an unsisterly posture then drew her feet together. "What if I'm wrong?"

"Shu-ush," said Sister Angelica, dressed in a striped wraparound apron. The sides of her veil, pinned back for work, revealed an attractive profile.

"What if Dr. Spence was right that Mother Rosaria died of natural causes?" Sister Camille whispered.

Sister Angelica laid her brush aside and walked over to her. "You think too much. We must pray. The Lord will show us the way. That's all we have to do. I started a novena to Saint Jude, the saint of impossible causes, last night. You should too. We simply can't undertake this on our own."

Sister Camille wanted to ignore her friend's pious suggestion. Sometimes her little sermons irritated her. She believed in prayer, but not as a solution for everything. Like the time Mrs. Cooper brought her daughter, Natalie, for her piano lesson.

Mrs. Cooper had said, "Now, Natalie, say a prayer with Sister, so you'll have a good lesson." Sister had shaken her head. In a quiet but firm voice, she said, "Not here, Mrs. Cooper. If Natalie hasn't practiced, prayers aren't going to help." The surprised parent didn't argue.

Today, Sister didn't want to hear a treatise on prayer and insisted, "God helps those who help themselves. We have to hurry. We're the only ones who suspect anything. If we don't act, evidence will be destroyed. Mother Rosaria's already been buried a whole day."

She left the theater and returned to the phone booth and left a message for Detective Kummer at the police station.

After supper cleanup, Sister Camille folded her apron and lowered the sleeves and hem of her habit that were pinned up for work. She checked the menu for the next day and saw that all the grocery orders were delivered. Breakfast serving bowls were out and the coffee urn set for breakfast. She left the kitchen and stopped at her cubbyhole to collect the linen pillowcases given her to embroider during evening recreation. After they were completed in cross-stitch, French knots, and featherstitches, these pieces would be given along with a loaf of monastery bread at Christmas to a doctor, or some other benefactor. Entering the assembly room for recreation, Sister Camille dipped her fingers into the holy water font on the wall and blessed herself. She sat next to an older sister who recounted an incident of the order's foundation. Sister Camille had heard her tell the story of hardship so many times she could repeat it word for word. Sister made the customary "Oh" and "I see" responses. Would she be given to repeating the same old events when she grew older? Her head snapped to attention when the phone rang as she was picking out a spool of ecru embroidery floss from her sewing basket.

Every evening, the phone system was switched from the main entrance of the Chateau to the monastery. She tried to appear calm as she left to answer it.

"Henry Kummer, Stone Hill Police." His deep voice sounded friendly. "May I speak to Sister Camille?"

For a second, she couldn't focus then realized no one was around to overhear her conversation. She tightened her fingers on the phone and responded, "This is Sister Camille. You probably don't remember me, Officer Kummer, but I knew you when your family lived across the street from my parents in Georgetown. My name was Magdalena Brenner then."

"You must be Dr. Brenner's daughter. I heard you entered the Chateau. You've joined a wonderful institution. It's considered one of the best schools in Wisconsin."

"I'd like to meet you, Officer Kummer. Would it be possible for you to come to the Chateau soon? I have a critical matter to discuss with you."

"Is this urgent, Sister?"

"Yes, it is," she answered without explanation.

"How about tomorrow morning? Would eighty thirty be too early?"

With the time agreed upon, Sister hung up and stared at the wall. It took a few seconds to become acclimated to her surroundings. Finally she took a deep breath, congratulating herself, grateful she took the call. It would have been difficult to explain why a policeman had called for her.

Buoyed by his quick response, she smiled. Henry Kummer wouldn't dally around. Eight thirty wasn't a usual time for visitors, especially on a weekday morning, but she'd find a logical reason not to arouse suspicion. All calls and visits had to be cleared through the superior or, in this case the acting superior, Sister Diana. She would be easier to deal with than Sister Cordelia. Even outgoing and incoming letters were censored. Sister Angelica contended that these little practices developed submission and humility.

Wednesday morning, Sister Camille stood among eleven sisters with thin, tired voices chanting the hour of none. "The Lord bless you from Zion; may you see the prosperity of Jerusalem all the days of your life." The opposite choir answered, "May you see your children's children. Peace be upon Israel! Glory be to the Father . . ." During the last Gloria, Sister Camille heard the front doorbell ring and figured it was Lieutenant Kummer. The wall clock showed eight-twenty. She'd have at least twenty minutes before her first summer piano student.

When she entered the parlor, Detective Kummer rose and shook her hand. Dressed in a black and grey hound's-tooth sports jacket, combined with gray gabardine trousers, he looked to be about thirty-five. His broad shoulders gave him the appearance of an athlete.

He studied her face. "I'm glad you called. Your voice sounded urgent on the phone. How can I help you?"

"I need your advice, Officer Kummer."

"My friends call me Hank. Why don't you?"

"All right, Hank." She smiled for a second and then turned serious. "You may have read in the paper that our mother superior died on Monday. We buried her Tuesday." Sister paused and took a big breath as if to prepare the detective for her shocking statement. In that long moment, she thought, should she go through with it? She said, "I have this terrible gut feeling, Hank," she paused again, "I think Mother Rosaria died of unnatural causes."

The detective remained silent, waiting to hear more.

Sister felt his silence but pushed on. "Mother Rosaria collapsed Friday after dinner. Dr. Spence diagnosed her condition as a heart attack. Mother improved daily through Sunday, then Sister Mercy, our infirmarian, found her dead Monday morning."

"Why are you suspicious?"

Sister Camille said, "Because I think I overheard a conversation between two sisters outside her door Sunday evening."

"What did you hear?"

Camille lowered her tone to a whisper and repeated what she had heard. Sister searched his face for a reaction.

Hank bent his head, brushing his upper lip back and forth on his clasped hands. Looking up after what seemed an interminable pause, he said, "I'm sorry to hear about your loss, Sister. You say you 'heard.' Did you see the sisters?"

"No. I didn't, Hank."

His response was slow in coming again. Finally he spoke, "The conversation you think you heard is hardly evidence to suspect a murder."

Sister Camille cautioned, "We have to keep our voices down. These parlors are linked together, and someone might hear us."

The detective leaned forward and spoke as though they were seated around a casket. "Sister Camille, what you're telling me is mere speculation with not one shred of evidence that would convince a judge to order an autopsy. Convictions are based on evidence not suspicions. Do you read mystery stories?"

"I used to."

Hank shifted his position on the antique chair. "Well, tell me, Sister, just how do you think Mother Rosaria was the victim of foul play."

"Resentment has been building against her since she was elected mother superior three months ago. She wanted to change practices, practices the older sisters had become comfortable with. Mother Rosaria cautioned that there would be more changes, not only from our community but also from Rome. Some of the nuns blamed her. I think they'd want her out of the way."

The detective reached into his pocket. "You think a sister murdered her?" Detective Kummer's piercing eyes widened. He pulled out a bag of Amphora tobacco and a pipe from his pocket. Concentrating on lighting it, he stared at his friend through clouds of smoke.

Sister Camille felt his uncomfortable stare. "Don't you see?" She leaned forward. "It would be so easy. Medicine could have been withheld."

"Do you think these changes you speak of are a motive for murder?"

"Yes," Sister nodded, no longer sure of herself.

"Sorry, Sister, I don't buy your motives. In all my dealings with crime, not once have sisters been involved. To me," he paused, shaking his head again, "a sister who takes vows and leads the pure life you lead, they would be the least likely to go so far as commit murder. I think you've been reading too many mystery stories. What possible evidence do you have to support your theory, Sister?"

"None. That's why I called you. I needed your advice."

The detective pulled a pencil and pad from inside his coat. "Let's recheck the time.

The deceased had a heart attack Friday. She saw the doctor that day. Was she admitted to the hospital?"

"No, she stayed here, at the Chateau."

"You say she showed improvement Saturday and Sunday, then died Monday. What time was she found dead?"

"About seven thirty in the morning."

"The burial took place yesterday, Tuesday." The detective continued writing then stopped. "Today is Wednesday. It's two days since she died. The scene is cold. I don't want to encourage you to continue this, but if you think of something else, or if you find tangible evidence, a suspicious container, powder that could have been put into her food, or anything that looks irregular, call me. We'd need to talk to the doctor who signed the death certificate."

"That would be Dr. Spence. Would you do that?"

"Oh, no. Not until I feel there's a case." Hank Kummer got up from the chair. "Give your folks my regards, and if you should need me, don't hesitate to call."

*   *   *

Lieutenant Kummer shook her hand and left. The urgent call from Sister Camille wasn't what he expected. He folded his long legs into the blue TR2 and sped out of the circle drive, hoping Sister had pushed a false alarm. The first twenty-four hours were important in solving a crime. If there was a question of homicide, three days had elapsed, a bad break.

With twelve years on the police force, Kummer had seniority and the respect of his chief, Harold Haskell. But this case worried him. The chief was a grand knight in the Knights of Columbus, Stone Hill Council. In the event of an investigation at the Chateau, he knew that Archbishop Millard of the Wisconsin Archdiocese would be on his tail. Kummer's mind leaped from the archbishop to the chief and back again. His Eminence would protect the sisters and denounce anyone working on the case. The end result would be worse than a political scandal. He decided to say nothing.

6

"**O**fficer Henry Kummer came this morning. He said evidence may have been destroyed because Mother Rosaria's been dead three days," Sister Camille said.

Sister Angelica sat beside her friend in the theater. "What was he like?"

"He's tall, at least six feet, nice looking, reminds me of Jimmy Stewart. His voice is soft, not what you'd expect from a policeman. He seems very professional but cautious. And that's good. He said he'd help, though I don't think I convinced him Mother Rosaria was murdered."

"How did you know him?"

"His family lived across the street from mine in Georgetown. He was in high school when I was in second grade. Once he gave me a ride uptown on his motorcycle. After that, I wanted a motorcycle too."

Sister Angelica leaned toward her, "Do you think we can trust him?"

"I'm sure we can. He said we need to look for something that doesn't fit into a regular pattern and soon. Will you help?"

"What do we have to do? Where do we start?"

"I think we need to look for a powder or liquid, anything unusual. I could check the insecticides in the garden shed. And we must search Mother Rosaria's and Sister Eugene's cell. Sister Eugene has a two o'clock appointment with the parent of the new student this afternoon. Would you search her cell? It's next to Sister Bernard's, who takes a nap at that time. Anyway, she's hard of hearing.

"I'll search Mother's cell during the five o'clock meditation. Everyone will be in the chapel. My absence won't be noticed because I'm scheduled for the kitchen, and it's on my way. We can meet at seven fifteen in the courtyard before recreation to share our findings."

Before they separated, Sister Angelica grabbed her friend's sleeve. "Did he say look for a poison? That's hard to pinpoint unless it's labeled."

"Just do the best you can."

"I feel I'm violating Sister Eugene's privacy. And what if someone sees me?"

"I know, but if we want to find out who killed Mother Rosaria, we have to be bold. I don't feel good about searching the superior's cell either."

Later that afternoon after vespers, Sister Camille left the chapel where the sisters were assembled for meditation. She sighed with relief to find Mother Rosaria's cell still intact. Sister knew that before the next superior was elected, the office and cell would be stripped and cleaned and possibly painted. Armed with scotch tape, small bottles, an eyedropper, stamp tongs, several envelopes, and a flower basket to carry everything, Sister Camille worked quickly.

In the washstand drawer were small glass bottles of aspirin and quinidine, which she knew to be heart medicine. The directions read: "320 mg. Take three times a day for ventricular arrhythmia." With scotch tape, she carefully lifted fingerprints from them and then took samples of water from the pitcher and from a glass near the bed. She looked for traces of powder on the bedclothes, and the floor, and then scraped fragments into separate envelopes. Once, she heard footsteps in the hall outside. After they died away, her determination drove her to the neatly arranged desk of the former superior.

Here, Sister found a stack of envelopes, some with handwritten addresses, some with glassine windows. As she searched further, she noticed an isolated postcard in the far left pigeonhole. With her tongs, she snatched it and read:

> Mother Rosaria be careful of the changes you make.
> Hardship and suffering will result for everyone.
> Or you might not be the Mother Superior.

Every muscle and nerve ending in her body froze. Standing like a statue, holding the card with tongs in midair, she read and reread the unsigned card then turned it around. It was postmarked May 29, 1952. She glanced at the calendar on the wall. Graduation had been a week later. Afraid of lingering too long, Sister slipped the card into an envelope, dropped it into the flower basket, and left for the garden shed.

There, she found two bags of insecticide, both labeled "poison," on the shelf. One bag was partly opened with the loose end twisted back. She cut that off and stuffed it into a plastic bag. Two strings unlocked the stitches on the other one. Sister remembered feedbags stitched the same way on her Uncle Ben's farm. He had shown her how to pull the string from each side to free the contents. Glancing down, she saw two strings on the floor. With her tongs, she put them in a bag. After safely depositing samples of powder, she turned to leave the shed when she spied a rubber glove near the door. Sister Camille scooped it into the basket with the other items and went out to the garden.

Although no one was near, she sensed someone watching. To deter anyone, she cut a bunch of marguerites, placed them on top of the basket, and entered the back door to the kitchen.

"Fresh flowers for your table," she announced brightly to Zelda Simmons, who was cutting lettuce for a salad. Sister's hands trembled as she placed the flowers in a vase. She put the basket out of sight in a cupboard then washed her hands.

Sliced cold cuts on platters, tossed green salads, and canned peaches in bowls were already set on the serving cart. Zelda, who stayed later than Miss. Drekel, had the meal under control.

At five thirty, Sister Mercy wheeled the infirmary cart into the kitchen. On the top were two trays, each with place settings, a napkin, and a tiny vase of fresh pansies. The china produced a chimelike rattle as the cart rolled over the floor. The din of empty cups and saucers triggered an idea in Sister Camille's mind. Of course, she thought, the cart. It must be inspected. There could be traces of a substance, although Sister Mercy was particular about cleanliness.

"I have two trays to fix tonight," Sister Mercy said as she looked over the supper menu hanging on the wall to see if any of the courses were suitable for her patients. "I have Sister Bernard, who can eat the regular diet, but Sister Cordelia, poor dear, should have a steak. With all that's been going on, she's been under so much strain these past few days. Would you get one for me, Sister Camille?"

Sister Camille remembered when Sister Cordelia was mother superior. Often special food was served to her table. Mother Rosaria ate the diet served to all the sisters.

She went to the walk-in cooler for the steak. Once inside, she took her first deep breath. She was into this so far and couldn't turn back. With her nerves shooting all directions, even in her eyes, she had to put up a good front, though she felt danger all around her. Sister hurried back with a freezer-wrapped steak for Sister Mercy.

On pretext of assisting Sister Mercy, she lifted the trays out of the cart only to find a shiny, clean chrome on top. The lower level was empty except for a smidgen of colorless powder in one corner. It must have gotten stuck after it was wiped with a wet cloth. Not wanting to arouse suspicion, she planned to dig it out later.

When the evening Angelus rang, Zelda Simmons checked her watch hanging on a chain. As was her custom, she flipped the lid to see if her timepiece coincided with monastery time.

"Just as I thought. Your clocks are off by two minutes."

A picture of Joe, her husband, slid out and fell to the floor. After she picked it up, they dished up the food in silence. As Sister placed the coffee and teapots on the refectory turntable, she scolded herself for thinking uncharitable thoughts about Sister Cordelia's private food.

That evening she and Sister Angelica met. In a secluded corner of the courtyard away from the sisters' cells, where they wouldn't be overheard, Sister Angelica whispered, "I didn't find anything suspicious in Sister Eugene's cell, nothing that looked out of place. Everything looked tidy. Sister's very neat."

Drawing Sister Angelica closer, Sister Camille first looked around her then whispered, "Look what I found in a pigeonhole on Mother Rosaria's desk." She handed the card to her friend. "You can touch it. The fingerprints are safe under the cellophane."

Sister Angelica read it through and then reread it. "This looks suspicious to me. Maybe it will change your friend's mind."

"I'll call him and tell him we have hard evidence now. What do you make of the date, May 29? Can you think of anything that happened that we can link to it?"

"Hmm," Sister Angelica paused. "The long Memorial Day weekend started that Friday."

"Let's give that more thought. What about the grammar? Is the syntax correct?"

"There isn't a comma or colon after 'To Mother Rosaria.' It looks like someone took care in typing it. The *h* is smudgy in the word 'change.' Look, it's the same in 'hardship,' as though the key had some fuzz caught in it. If the person used a typewriter at the Chateau, we can trace it. What else did you find?"

Sister Camille told her about the samples and prints she had collected. To avoid attracting attention, they entered the assembly room separately and sat some distance apart during the uneventful recreation of careful stitching. No telephone calls came through that evening.

After matins and lauds, the sisters retired to their cells. With care, Sister Camille laid each item she collected on the bed and labeled the source and date on each packet. She examined the empty frame on which she stretched scotch tape that had three sets of fingerprints. Careful to avoid damaging any of them, she put the frame into a large envelope. Besides the prints, she had two small bottles of liquid, one labeled "pitcher," the other "drinking glass."

In each small envelope, Sister had tagged scrapings from Mother Rosaria's bed and the floor and lastly the collection from the garden shed. She read the card again, holding it up with stamp tongs to the bare lightbulb hanging on an electrical cord from the ceiling. After fingerprints taken from this card came back from the lab, it would be my most incriminating item of evidence, she thought. It would convince Hank that Mother Rosaria's death wasn't natural. It was her *piece de resistance.*

Putting aside her self-congratulatory emotions, she left her cell to do one more thing. With only five minutes before the ten o'clock lights-out rule, she tiptoed down the hall lit with a forty-watt bulb, past the statues of Saint Joseph and Saint Philomena. Votive lights flickered before each statue, casting wavy shadows against the walls. Sister felt the figure's glass eyes staring at her from all angles. It was so quiet; she could hear the clock tick.

From the corridor light, she could make out the infirmary cart parked in its accustomed place near the door. Using a paring knife she had brought with her, Sister dug out the lump of powder from the corner and deposited it in an envelope.

She tried to tell by feeling with her finger whether she had got it all. Maybe if she turned on the light for just a second. As she reached for it, the floor creaked. Afraid of being caught, she slid around the doorframe and ducked behind Saint Philomena.

Dear God, was someone spying on me? She felt her heart in her throat and had to control the need to cough. Sister Mercy's round figure was recognizable in the shadows. She unlocked the drug cabinet with a dangling set of keys, unscrewed a bottle, returned it, relocked the door, and left.

Sister Camille waited until she heard Sister Mercy's cell door close before returning to her cell.

*   *   *

Lieutenant Kummer picked up the large brown envelope left for him at the front entrance the following morning. The package looked innocent enough, and he hoped he'd have no reason to worry about the contents. He followed through with his promise to send the specimens to the lab.

7

Two days before the election, Sister Diana, the assistant in the community, tacked a list of three qualified candidates on the bulletin board. The council recommended Sister Cordelia, the former superior; Sister Martha, a council member and kitchen supervisor; and Sister Dorothy, a new name.

Sister Dorothy, the procuratrix, or housekeeper, maintained a congenial disposition in spite of her difficult job and constant demands. She answered the phone in the "proc's office" with "praise Jesus" and listened patiently to caller's complaints about a plugged toilet in the academy or a request to have Aloysius fix a desk in the study hall. Sister Dorothy often handled minor jobs by herself, such as removing a sink trap or fixing a lamp that had a short. She filled requests for sundries, tended to summer housecleaning, and accompanied outside workmen when they were called inside the cloister for repairs or installations.

The list of candidates gave the sisters time to think and pray before the election about a choice of superior. To prepare for this solemn occasion, the reading in the refectory warned the sisters to avoid electioneering and urged prayers to the Holy Ghost for guidance. In addition to these guidelines from the order's constitution, the readings focused that day on the life of St. Ephrem the Syrian, deacon, and confessor, whose feast day was designated in the Roman Martyrology. Since Mother Rosaria's death, the superior's stall in the chapel and her place in the refectory remained vacant.

The three days preceding the election added stress to the community. Silence and guarding of the eyes were more visibly practiced, and private conversations avoided. Even the recreations after dinner and supper were subdued. No one wanted to be suspected of talking about a favorite candidate.

Saturday, June 22, election day dawned cloudy with a chance of rain for the Stone Hill area. The temperature reached eighty degrees by noon with high humidity.

The bell rang for the election ceremony. Afternoon sunlight streamed through the large stained glass windows in the chapel. Segments of red, blue, and brownish tinted glass depicted Christ's agony in the garden. The slanting, colorful light from the Lord's red robe refracted toward the two rows of sisters kneeling in oak choir stalls, replicas of the Westminster Abbey stalls. The reek of O'Cedar polish blended with years of incense fumes filled the atmosphere.

Sister Camille entered the chapel. With arms and hands covered in sleeves and eyes cast down, she bowed to the vacant superior's stall then genuflected by her assigned stall in the front of the chapel. Upon kneeling, she automatically kissed the highly polished floor, a reminder of humility. From dust she came, and to dust she would return.

With her head bowed and eyes closed, Sister Camille prayed, struggling with her thoughts. Would Sister Cordelia be elected again? Her hope for Sister Dorothy was a long shot. Grateful that her detective work had started, her mind raced back and forth over the procedures, reviewing her amateur techniques. Had she overlooked anything? She hoped to impress Hank, although that wasn't her purpose. Working side by side with the detective brought an element of excitement.

At the moment, the election claimed her attention. The term of office for the new superior would be three years less three months, the balance of Mother Rosaria's term.

What would happen if there were a murder conviction? Could there be another election soon? Had the community ever experienced two short-term superiors before? How would it be recorded in the annals of the order? She shivered and tried to concentrate on the action at hand and prayed for forgiveness for her judgmental, distracting thoughts. The creaking sounds from the aged birch floor in the chapel quieted indicating everyone was in place. Sister Diana clapped her hands once, the official signal to begin.

> Come Holy Ghost fill our minds
> and hearts. Inspire in us the zeal
> of Thy divine love. Send forth Your
> Spirit as we continue to serve You
> through the inspired leadership
> of your chosen servant. Inspire us
> to accept and obey her direction
> in the practice of our vows, rules
> and constitution and in the
> assignments given to us.

Sister Diana laid down the custom book. "Dear Sisters, we will take up the beans."

At the clap signal, Sister Camille, the lowest in rank, led the community back to the empty superior's stall. Bowing, she reached out her sleeve-covered hand, picked up one black bean and one white bean from the two piles on top of the kneeler. Bowing again, with beans in hand, she returned to her stall. After the sisters had taken their beans, Sister Diana announced, "We will cast our votes for Sister Cordelia." At the sound of the next clap, Sister Camille again led the sisters back to the empty stall. This time a circular box half the size of a Morton saltbox with a little tubular chimney rested on the kneeler. Another similar box sat near it. If a sister wanted Sister Cordelia to be the next superior, she would put a white bean into the first box and the black bean in the other. Sister Camille chose to put a black bean in the first box. It stuck to her sweaty palm as she tried to deposit it. She didn't want anyone nearby to see how she voted.

After everyone voted, Sister Camille heard footsteps in the hall outside the chapel. She knew the council had left the chapel to count the beans. If a majority of white beans wasn't reached, the next name on the list would be voted on, and the whole ceremony would be repeated until they reached a majority.

Footsteps returning to the chapel brought momentary excitement. Sister Camille held her breath and listened for Sister Diana's announcement.

"We have a majority," Sister Diana proclaimed. After a short pause, a heavy figure marched up to the front of the sisters' chapel and knelt a few minutes in silence before reading the formula of acceptance.

Sister Camille recognized Sister Cordelia by her shape and prayed she could knuckle under to the new superior's direction. The majority of the sisters voted for whom they wanted.

Her thoughts were interrupted by a new set of floor creaks as Mother Cordelia retraced her steps back to the vacant superior's stall and mounted the steps to the raised kneeler. It quieted for the final rite of acceptance. At another clap signal, each sister, again led by Sister Camille, processed back to the newly elected superior, bowed and kissed her extended hand. This action represented their obedience and allegiance to the new superior.

With all the ceremony involved, Sister Camille thought she could easily have been at the court of Louis XIV. She counted making eight bows and then remembered their order was established in France in the seventeenth century. Now, these same courtly practices were still practiced in the twentieth century in the United States. Did it make any sense? She hoped the changes from Rome that Mother Rosaria spoke about would come soon but expected the sisters at St. Clotildes would be the last to put them into practice.

After the final clap, the sisters kissed the floor en masse, genuflected to the altar, and once more bowed to the new superior. They processed to the hallway, dipped their fingers in the holy water font, and blessed themselves. It was over. They waited to congratulate their new superior, who came out last.

*   *   *

Later that afternoon, Sister Angelica caught Sister Camille's sleeve. "Look, Sister. Mother Cordelia gave me this book as a memento from Mother Rosaria's personal effects. It's a calendar with a daily meditation for each day of the year."

"I remember seeing Mother Rosaria with this book," said Sister Camille. "It must have been a favorite."

"Nobody else has leafed through it, or they would have found this holy card. Look at it!"

Sister Angelica held the card with care by the sides.

With the picture side up, Sister Camille read, "St. Rose of Lima, 1586-1617. First American Saint." It pictured a female figure dressed in a white robe kneeling before a cross. "It's Mother Rosaria's patron-saint card."

"Turn it around, Sister."

In Mother Rosaria's handwriting, Sister Camille read:

A.M.D.G

In the event that I am not with you when you read this, be aware that
I received a threat typed on an unsigned postcard May 29, 1952

Mother Rosaria June 30, 1952

"Oh my God," Sister Camille exclaimed, her eyes wide enough to startle any onlooker. "I can't believe this. Mother Rosaria wrote this the day after she received the warning on the postcard I found." Dropping her voice to a whisper, she added, "Look, Mother Rosaria placed it inside the calendar on that date too and knew she was in danger. If only Mother had told someone, she might still be alive!"

Sister Angelica continued, "Mother Cordelia surprised me. She called me into her office this afternoon. She had Mother Rosaria's daily missal, her divine office book, a meditation book, and this calendar on her table. She asked me to pick any one I wanted. I just happened to take this."

Sister Camille barely heard her. "Did you find anything else? Let's go through it page by page."

"I did. It's the only holy card. She didn't write any more about the warning in the rest of the book. Has your friend called yet? I guess it's too early to have lab reports on all the stuff you sent him."

"He hasn't called. I hope he doesn't wait too long. Maybe we should alert him to this new evidence. I'd have to call without permission again or wait until he calls. What do you think I should do?"

"Call him right away, Sister."

Sister Camille smiled. Sister Angelica hadn't suggested they pray first.

After vespers, the community gathered for five o'clock meditation. Sister Camille left the chapel for her kitchen duty, having made her meditation earlier. She realized how blessed she was to have the kitchen summer assignment at this time. It gave her more freedom of movement. She never felt the kitchen assignment was a humbling assignment. If it were, she'd turn it into a fulfilling venture for herself and a tasteful experience for the sisters. Sister Camille liked a challenge.

*   *   *

Mrs. Simmons appeared in good humor. She called out as Sister Camille approached, "I have good news. Mother Cordelia hired Joe back this afternoon. Now we don't have to leave our little house down the street. Joe promised to join Alcoholics Anonymous. Isn't that great?"

"What a relief. I'd sure miss you if you left." After reporting in, Sister said, "I'll be right back. I have a short errand." She left the kitchen and continued through the cloister door to the phone on the academy side.

"Hello, Hank?" Sister Camille was relieved to find him at his desk.

"Hello, Sister Camille," Detective Kummer replied.

"How did you know it was me?"

"Well, let's say it's part of my job. I heard your voice a few days ago on the phone and again when I visited you. How can I help you?"

Sister Camille wanted to hear his reaction to the packet she sent. She decided not to ask. "We have new evidence."

"Who are we?"

"Sister Angelica and I. She's Mother Rosaria's niece. The new superior who was elected today gave her a calendar this afternoon from her aunt's effects. Sister Angelica found a holy card with a message written by Mother Rosaria on the back." Sister Camille slowed down. "Mother wrote it in response to the threat on the postcard I gave you. Do you want me to read it to you, or should I send it?"

"Read it."

Sister Camille read the warning message.

Hank said, "Sister, I'm about to leave the station. Put the card inside the calendar as Sister Angelica found it and put it in an envelope. I'll pick it up in a few minutes."

"Good, then I can hand it to you. Don't bother to ring the front doorbell. It will complicate matters. I'll meet you at the gate on the academy side."

She left the phone booth and caught a glimpse of Sister Eugene rounding the corner to the staircase. Sister Camille stiffened, her stomach squeezed her breathless. Had Sister Eugene heard her conversation?

After hurrying back to the kitchen to check on supper preparations, she returned to the gate. She felt as if she was walking in a trance with all her back-and-forth movements.

Hank came. Sister Camille handed the envelope to him through the gate. "I can't talk now." She rushed away.

Hank watched her. "Be careful," he called after her.

*　　*　　*

The festive spirit of the election continued through supper. Mother Cordelia announced after grace, "Dear sisters, you may talk." The reader in the pulpit closed the books and stepped down to take her place with the community. A light patter of voices filled the otherwise-silent refectory.

Later, as Sister Camille ate a bologna sandwich at second table, Sister Eugene walked into the refectory with a covered plate. Another special diet, Sister Camille thought. Why couldn't she just eat what the rest of the community ate? Weren't the meals she planned good enough for her? Then she scolded herself for uncharitable thoughts. She would have to include that in her weekly confession.

The events of the day raced through her mind. So much had happened since the morning Angelus, the election of Mother Cordelia, Sister Angelica finding the holy card in the calendar, calling Hank Kummer, meeting him at the gate. It wasn't a typical day in an enclosed nun's life. Sister chewed her food without tasting it, until she heard the kitchen phone ring.

Moments later the refectorian sister approached her table and whispered, "Mother Cordelia wants to see you in her office."

Sister Camille grimaced and laid down her sandwich. Had Sister Eugene reported her secret phone calls? Better to get this over with as soon as possible.

Leaving her half-eaten sandwich on the plate, she left the refectory. After knocking on the new superior's door, Sister Camille responded "in his name" and entered. She wouldn't sit until the superior invited her to do so.

Mother Cordelia sat at her desk attending to the stack of mail that had accumulated since Mother Rosaria died. Sister Camille recognized the envelopes as the ones she had gone through when she searched the room. What would the new superior think if she knew that?

Finally the superior looked up. Her impersonal glance sent an icy chill down Sister Camille's spine. She remained standing.

Mother Cordelia said, "This past week has been trying for all of us, Sister."

"I agree with you, Mother. What has happened in our monastery has been far from normal."

Mother continued, "Permission is renewed for the use of the phone for your kitchen duties, but only for calling in produce orders. It's been noticed you use the phone at odd hours, and your calls are not to our local markets. What is going on, Sister Camille?"

Sister knelt as instructed by the rule when one was accused. She felt grateful for its further direction to in no way excuse her. She could remain silent with her head down and wait it out.

"Dear Mother, I humbly acknowledge my fault." She hoped the superior would accept that and let her go. According to custom, she kissed the floor and silently prayed, Dear God, how is this interview going to end? It wasn't the penance that bothered her. What if she were talking to the murderer?

Mother Cordelia continued, "Sister Diana informed me that she gave you no permission to use the phone. Sister Camille, you've failed in your vow of obedience. Just because you've been given special permission to call in kitchen orders doesn't give you the right to use the telephone at any other time. Do you realize most of the sisters have never had the privilege of using the phone?" Mother Cordelia's imperious voice bore down on the kneeling figure and ripped through her like a knife.

"Yes, Mother, I do."

"It is a special privilege. And now you've abused that permission. Mother Rosaria counted on you to fulfill your kitchen assignment this summer because Sister Martha needed a rest."

Sister Camille felt her conscience was clear. The accusations of disobedience couldn't hurt her even though each tirade sounded more devious. She couldn't say, "You wouldn't understand; you're an overbearing superior stuck on yourself and your favorites." Sister wondered if Mother Cordelia could even understand her ethics called moral diligence or *epikaya*. How could she explain this philosophy she had studied at Saint Andrews that meant breaking a rule for a greater good. At that time, she never thought she'd have a need for it.

Sister Camille remembered in the novitiate, that her novice mistress wouldn't let her off her knees until there were tears. Did her indifference to the accusations show?

Should she pull a hanky out to sniff into it? No, that was hypocritical. Instead, she again kissed the floor and repeated the formula, "Dear Mother, I acknowledge my fault."

The superior continued, "For your penance, recite ten Our Fathers and ten Hail Marys in the chapel with your arms outstretched and study the chapter in our constitution on the vow of obedience. Please sit down, Sister. What is going on? Who were you calling?"

Sister Camille sat on the edge of a chair. "Mother, I've been worried because Mother Rosaria died so suddenly after she seemed to be getting better. I called a friend of my family, Henry Kummer, a detective." There, she had said it.

"And what does your friend say, Sister?"

"Not much, Mother. Only that I've been reading too many mystery stories." She took deep breaths to control the rapid pulse that pounded in her ears as she tried to sound unconcerned. Sister Camille wouldn't divulge any of the evidence she had collected, particularly the postcard and holy card that was probably written at the very desk where Mother Cordelia sat at that moment. If the superior knew that, there's no telling what would happen next.

"I think so too. I forbid you to read any mysteries for a year."

Sister Camille knelt to receive the superior's blessing.

"Wait, Sister, one more thing." Mother Cordelia adjusted her bifocals as though examining her subject for some minute blemish. "You haven't been looking well. I want you to see Dr. Raymond, a psychologist. You can go with Sister Mildred, who has an appointment Monday. I'll call the doctor and tell him you're coming."

Sister Camille left the room. She passed a window and stood a good minute looking out at a bed of pink lantana. Were they real? Nothing seemed real anymore. She turned and focused her eyes on a crack in the wall. The crack spread and then came together. She repeated the action until the crack stayed the same. Satisfied that she had her head on straight, she returned to the empty refectory.

The refectorian was there filling salt and pepper cellars. Though the rule stipulated that the sisters should leave no uneaten scraps of food on the plate, Sister Camille picked up the unappetizing half-eaten sandwich then set it down. She would never fit into the mold of what superiors preached at the chapter of "Faults." Would their holy foundress who wrote all those rules want her to gag on the sandwich? She put the sandwich in her pocket and disposed of it in the kitchen.

Before recreation, Sister Camille went to the chapel. She walked to the front and knelt on the bare wood floor. The hard calluses on her knees buckled and caused momentary pain as the pressure of kneeling pushed them sideways. She could handle that. All sisters had ripe calluses on their knees. With her arms outstretched patterned by Christ on the cross, she recited her penance. She prayed, Dear God, you know why I used the telephone. I can't be obedient at this time, and I need your help. If you want me to continue the search for the truth, to find out why Mother Rosaria died, you have to help me. I leave it up to you. And please, help me become a proper sister.

After matins and lauds, Sister Camille went to bed, then got up, put on her robe, and went down the hall to the showers. She hoped it would relax her.

Sleep never came.

8

"Dr. Raymond, this is Mother Cordelia from St. Clotildes. I'm calling about our Sister Camille. I'm worried about her. She looks peaked and has strange ideas."

"Why do you say that?"

"Sister Camille thinks Mother Rosaria was murdered."

"Murdered? That's very serious."

"Yes, and she called the police."

"Did she say why?"

"Mother Rosaria's death shocked the community, but it affected her more than the rest of the sisters. I think she's having a nervous breakdown. Could you see her right away? As Shakespeare said, 'Suspicion always haunts the guilty mind; the thief doth fear each bush.'"

The doctor listened to her expertise in literature. He had heard it before. "Yes, of course. Is there any basis for her belief?"

"Certainly not," Mother Cordelia's sharp tone bit back. "I want you to evaluate her. I think she needs a complete rest and should go to a sanitarium for a while."

The superior's evaluation of his patients was no surprise to the doctor either. He had heard her suggested regimens before.

"All right, have her come along with Sister Mildred on Monday, and I'll see her then."

*   *   *

The red and gold taxi arrived at one fifteen to take them to the psychologist's appointment. To an enclosed nun, a trip outside the monastery to a doctor or dentist's office proved an adventure. Sister Mildred paid the driver the thirty-five cents, plus tip she had received that morning from the bursar.

The open-caged elevator made electrical contacts as it lifted the sisters. On each floor, Sister Camille heard the voices of workers greeting one another, high heels echoing down tiled floors, and glass-paneled doors slamming.

The sisters exited on seventh floor and walked side by side down the hall like a pair of penguins. Sister Mildred kept her eyes down and hands in her sleeves. Antiseptic fumes from a physician's clinic faded as they entered Dr. Raymond's office.

The windowless waiting room was furnished with chrome furniture covered in brown and tan leatherette. A dimly lit lamp on a corner table with magazines provided a modest comfort for the waiting patients. Sister Camille took a chair next to the magazines. Sister Mildred would read from a spiritual book or say the rosary. When she went into Dr. Raymond's office, Sister Camille reached for a *Readers Digest* dated February 1952.

Scanning the contents on the cover, she opened it to "Risking Cancer Because of False Modesty," by Collie Small. She thought the author was courageous to use the words "vagina" and "cervix" in the article and held the magazine close in case someone walked in and saw her reading it. When Dr. Raymond emerged through the door with Sister Mildred after her consultation, Sister Camille shoved her magazine under the stack and followed the doctor.

"Good morning, Sister Camille," the doctor said. "Mother Cordelia told me you'd be coming. How can I help you?" He motioned her to a chair. A swarthy man in plastic-rimmed glasses, he walked with an easy manner, tossing his head and swinging his arms like a jumping jack with a slack string.

Sister Camille looked around his office. "Where's the couch?"

"I decided a long time ago to forego the couch. Try this chair; I think you'll be just as comfortable." He sounded amused.

Sister Camille thought he looked friendly enough and sat on the overstuffed leather chair. She sank down and smiled. It had been a while since she enjoyed the comfort of a cushioned chair. The stiff parlor seats at the Chateau were as close as she came to cushions, and she only sat on those when she had company.

"I want you to know Mother Cordelia initiated this visit because I called a friend of my family who is a detective. I don't need a psychologist. I'm wasting your valuable time." Sister Camille remained calm while trying to decide whether to bare her soul about the murder. It might help. "I wonder if I can persuade you it's true."

She caught the doctor's immediate attention. He sat down at a large desk clear of any of the usual supplies. Only a yellow legal pad lay in front of him. He leaned back in his chair and stared at the ceiling. "Tell me about it."

"Mother Rosaria collapsed three days before she died, a week ago." Sister repeated the details leading up to her death. Finished, she looked directly at the doctor who was bent over his writing. "It doesn't seem logical," she said. "How could she be on the road to recovery for two days and die the next?"

Without looking up, Dr. Raymond asked, "What makes you think her death was unnatural?" He spoke as though he was talking about the weather.

Sister Camille sat with her arms on the chair rests, appearing to be a person in command. "Mother Rosaria guided our community in a different way. For many years, some older sisters drifted away from community exercises. Personal practices crept in. A few sisters felt threatened by Mother Rosaria's ideas of building community. She planned to recruit vocations to our order and wanted to build an addition to the monastery to accommodate the new aspirants. Many sisters opposed her ideas," Sister Camille said. The doctor gave her an encouraging nod to continue.

"Last month, Sister Eugene, the directress, wanted Leslie Allen expelled because she was expecting a baby. It was only two weeks until graduation." Sister lowered her voice. She didn't want to sound too excited. "I heard Mother Rosaria recommend over many objections that Leslie should graduate. This caused dissension."

"Is there any proof Mother Rosaria was murdered?" the doctor asked.

"That's the problem. Not yet, but as I told you, I talked to my friend on the Stone Hill police force. Maybe you know him. His name is Lieutenant Henry Kummer."

"And what does he think?"

"He encouraged me to keep my eyes open and look for anything unusual. I collected fingerprints and scraped up fragments from Mother Rosaria's bed before her cell was stripped."

"Who do you suspect would commit this crime?" Dr. Raymond tapped his pencil against his yellow legal pad.

"I don't know. I know who had access to her during those three days. There was Sister Mercy, the infirmarian; Sister Eugene, the academy directress; and Sister Cordelia, the former superior who was reelected mother superior last Saturday."

"It's interesting that you have this suspicion. Was there anything that made you wary before this incident?"

Sister nodded. "I've known instances where responses seemed irrational. One time, Sister Eugene had planned to use the science theater for a parent guild meeting. The home economics teacher, a younger sister, knew it, but when she saw the room was free, she took her class into the theater to see a film. As a result, Sister had received harsh criticism at the chapter of "Faults" and was locked up in a small room for three days. She couldn't mingle or have contact with anyone. The infirmarian brought her meals on a tray. Sister told me those three days almost drove her mad. That shows you the power of Sister Eugene in our community."

"How did this affect you?"

"I knew then that I couldn't count on anyone. I made up my mind to get along with the sisters as best I could. I'd be cordial, keep the rules, and mind my own business."

"And do you still think about it?" Dr. Raymond asked.

"I can't forget it."

"What is your relationship with the sisters in regard to the rules of the monastery?"

"I don't think it's fair the way the rules are bent by some sisters, but I'm trying to look the other way and practice what I believe. I have to remind myself of that often."

"Do the sisters like you?"

"Yes, I think the majority do."

"Have you talked to any sisters about your suspicion of murder?"

"Only Sister Angelica. She's Mother Rosaria's niece. She has the same gut feelings I have."

"You keep these things to yourself. Does that bother you?"

"There's not much else I can do about it."

"Don't you get angry sometimes?"

"I offer it up for the poor souls in purgatory. The saints had to make sacrifices. I can, too."

"How does it feel to keep all this to yourself?"

"I'm getting used to it."

"All right, sometimes sisters will be around. How do you feel when you see something unexpected? How do you react?"

"I'm always polite." The doctor kept his eyes down.

"Do you think they might go after you?"

"No, but they could influence the superior and prevent me from going to summer school at Saint Andrew. I enjoy my classes at the college and associating with the professors. I feel it stretches my mind to be around them."

"You enjoy your studies?"

"Yes, I pray my college education will continue. I'd never talk about my desire, but I'd wait, hoping Mother will call me in each year to tell me the council has decided I should go to summer school. It's the most exciting thing that can happen to me here."

"Who are these sisters? How would they influence your superior?"

"It's a clique."

"It's surprising that they can have so much influence if you are polite. Are you new in the order?"

"I'm the youngest sister with vows," Sister said. "I have trouble sleeping. Could you give me something to help me sleep?"

Dr. Raymond looked up. "You do?"

"I guess because I'm tense." Sister's hands moved to her lap. Her shoulders dropped.

"It seems this is getting to you. What do you do when you can't sleep?"

"I keep busy. As a pianist, I enjoy practicing and learning new compositions. Each composer uses different textures and harmonies that I find inspiring, but there's a problem here too. I have permission to go to the academy to practice, but if a sister is sick and can't do her work, or something else comes along, they always know where I am because everybody can hear me practice."

"Let me ask you this question. Why do you stay in the monastery?"

"Well . . . I've made a commitment. It's like a marriage. If a sister wants to succeed, she has to work at it. I'm afraid of failure."

"Of failure? What are you going to do about it?"

Sister Camille stretched her shoulders and sighed. She felt exhausted by his line of questioning. "Right now, I want to see justice done in the case of Mother Rosaria's untimely death."

Dr. Raymond looked up. "I want you to take a critical look at yourself. I hear you say you're not happy. What should you do about yourself? Also, this lack of trust comes from you. Ask yourself what it is that makes you secretive or suspicious. Are you interested in doing this? I'm willing to help you." He looked up again and made eye contact.

She met his gaze. Until this moment, she felt she had proved all her points. Did Dr. Raymond read more into her answers than what she meant? Did she have the problem he suggested? Anxious to end the meeting, she answered, "I think so."

"If you want to stay in the monastery, you need help. What I'm going to do is talk to Mother Superior. Of course with your permission."

Sister Camille clinched her arms tight, then got up and walked to the window. In the nearby building, she saw a busy office. She wished she were in that room. It looked calm and friendly with ordinary people going about their daily business. "I thought this meeting was confidential."

Undisturbed by his patient's reaction, Dr. Raymond said, "It was Mother Superior who sent you to me and asked for an evaluation. I'm going to recommend one of two plans. I'd like you to take a sabbatical and go to a hospital for several months, or you can see me once a week."

"I'd never go to a hospital."

"Why not?"

"I have a reputation as a teacher at the Chateau and in the community. What would my students and their parents think?"

"A sabbatical shouldn't make anyone suspicious. I would be in close contact with the hospital. However, I'm giving you a choice. Which do you prefer?" The doctor said, "You want to become an effective member of your community, don't you?"

She returned to her seat. "Your recommendations surprise me. I feel I can deal with my problems. Anyway, our sisters don't have such a thing as a sabbatical, and I'm not interested in your choices until after the murder investigation."

"You need to take care of yourself first. The alleged murder is not your problem."

Sister held her breath for a second, stunned at his idea. Her head dropped over her chest. How can he say that? She felt defeated and vulnerable.

She leaned toward the doctor, "What would you think if a judge ordered an autopsy, and the lab found poison in Mother Rosaria's body? What would you think about me then?"

"That's a different situation. If there was a murder, it's not your problem. Why are you so interested in that?"

"For one thing, it would prove I'm right and not imagining it, but most importantly, so justice is served for Mother Rosaria's death."

The doctor ignored her comment. "You need to ask yourself what makes you suspicious. If the case goes to trial, and the court knows you are being treated by a psychologist, are they going to trust your testimony?"

"That would be a good reason to wait. It may not be very long. I expect to hear soon. Surely, I'm not so badly off that I can't wait that long." Sister drew her breath in surprise.

"All right. In the meantime, I'll give my report to Mother Cordelia. Is that all right with you?"

"You don't have to be in any rush." She sat on the edge of her chair.

"All right then, I'll get back to you." Dr. Raymond closed the folder and stood.

Sister Camille joined Sister Mildred in the waiting room. She suggested, "Let's walk back. I need to air out a lot of cobwebs in my mind."

"Oh no, Sister." Sister Mildred's mouth twitched like a scared kitten.

"Think of the money we'd save. We'd practice our vow of poverty." Sister Camille expected a sermon on obedience.

Sister Mildred outranked her. "Mother expects us to return the same way we came."

They took a taxi back to the Chateau.

According to custom, after a trip outside the monastery to a doctor or dentist, the sisters reported to the superior. After Sister Camille found Mother Cordelia absent from her office, she went to the chapel for her meditation before vespers.

She knelt in her assigned stall, holding herself rigid as if expecting a blow. Her heart raced in her ears as well as her chest. She tried to pray but couldn't keep her mind on prayers. She opened *The Imitation of Christ* and read. "My son, always commit thy cause to Me, I will dispose well of it in due time. Wait for my ordering of it, and thou shalt find it will be for thy good."

Though trying hard to concentrate on her reading, Sister Camille found it difficult to believe the terse message. She thumbed to the beginning of the book and read the biographical sketch. The first printed edition appeared in 1471. Doing some quick math, she realized this message was written nearly five hundred years ago. Her mind refused to allow her to meditate on the ancient passage. She closed the book and whispered, "Dear Lord, I'm in shock! What is happening to me and to this monastery? I can't believe I'm in such a bad way that I need psychoanalysis. Imagine if I had to go to a hospital. Who is this Dr. Raymond anyway? I think he's in cahoots with Mother Cordelia . . . And I still have to report to her . . . If only Hank would call . . . He may have already and I wasn't given the message. I should have told him that could happen."

The bell rang for vespers. Camille went through the actions of chanting the Psalms with the other sisters. After that, she reported to the kitchen.

During the evening recreation, Sister listened for the phone. It never rang.

9

Valley temperatures hovered around eighty degrees. The forecast for rain in Stone Hill brought hope that it would clear the atmosphere and lift the humidity.

Detective Henry Kummer tilted his badge toward the receptionist in Dr. Spence's office.

"Doctor's expecting you, Lieutenant. He's with a patient. It'll be a few minutes."

Kummer sat down and thumbed through a dated issue of *Holiday* magazine, when the doctor opened the door.

"Come in, Lieutenant."

After an exchange of perfunctory greetings, the detective said, "I need to talk to you about a deceased patient of yours, the Mother Superior Rosaria, from the Chateau. This may be a false alarm, but to keep my records complete, I need some information."

The balding doctor, who wore a white coat, motioned him to a chair and buzzed for his patient's file. While they waited, the doctor offered the detective a cigarette from his pack of Lucky Strikes. Leaning against a dark oak examining table covered with black leather padding, he scanned his notes on the patient's medical record.

"Let's see, I was called to the Chateau Friday, June thirteenth, about 1:00 PM to attend Mother Rosaria. She suffered an attack of bradycardia." Interrupting his reading, he glanced over his bifocals and explained, "A bradycardia is a slow heartbeat. Many athletes have it."

He flipped the ash from his cigarette into a nearby heart-shaped ashtray filled with butts. "Since the Chateau has nursing care, I felt she could stay right there." The doctor returned to the file in hand. "Saw her the next day, Saturday. Heartbeat improved from fifty to seventy beats, a good sign. Checked her by phone Sunday. Her vital signs were stable."

"How did you react when she was found dead Monday morning?" Kummer asked.

"I was surprised, though hearts are unpredictable. She came from a family with a history of heart disease." He put the file on his desk and appeared satisfied with his assessment.

"When you were called Monday morning to sign the death certificate, how did you find the body? Was there anything unusual? Any sign of stress?"

"She looked natural enough." The doctor rechecked his file. "Body temperature, sixty-seven degrees, rigor mortis well established with signs of abating in the upper extremities. I estimated she died well before midnight, perhaps earlier." He looked up. "Do you think there's suspicion regarding her death?"

"I'm checking every possibility. Your patient received a threat a few days before her heart attack."

"Is that so? Under any other circumstances, there would have been an autopsy, but I had no reason to be suspicious." He said, "Especially in a monastery." Stubbing out his cigarette with a vengeance, he added, "My God, that would be the last place I'd suspect a homicide!"

"My very thoughts," the detective replied. He put out his cigarette and stood. "Thank you for seeing me so soon. We may have a case, but as yet, I can't be sure until we have an autopsy report."

"An autopsy?" The doctor's head bent sidewise.

"I'm going to try." The lieutenant left the office and looked toward a dark cloud as it began to cover the sun. It created shadows on the river shore that made the Iowa side bluffs a deep green.

Returning to the police station, Hank Kummer rapped on the chief's door. Two-inch black letters printed on the frosted pane read, Stone Hill Chief of Police, J. J. Haskell. After a short "come in," Kummer found his chief with his glasses midnose, sleeves rolled up, hunched over the desk reading witness reports. Shaggy eyebrows matched his salt-and-pepper crew cut. In spite of the chief's five-and-a-half-foot height and lean 150-pound frame, the detective knew the chief never felt intimidated by his taller, more muscular subordinates. Jim Haskell was tough, and everyone knew it.

After World War II, the city of Stone Hill had put up a new city hall. The police department relocated in the old city hall on Elm Street. Built in the early twenties, it had a blue and white mosaic-tile floor with high metal ceilings embossed in a geometric pattern. Scratched benches resembling church pews lined the wainscoted walls near the booking desk.

In the squad room, a typewriter sat on an improvised table below the wall telephone. Stained coffee mugs occupied a shelf near a two-burner hot plate where a cold coffeepot perched. A poster of the "ten most wanted" hung below the wall clock, which read ten thirty-two. Filing cabinets, desks, and a portable drinking fountain completed the furnishings.

An officer sat at one of the desks, pecking out a report on a typewriter. Five private offices, including the chief's, had doors opening onto the squad room. Next to the chief's was Lieutenant Kummer's office, and one "interview room." At the rear of the first floor were two detention cells used mostly for weekend inebriates.

The chief raised his eyes, "What's up?" Then he turned back to a stack of forms.

"A situation at the Chateau has come to my attention, Jim."

"The Chateau?" The chief set the papers down and thought for a moment. He knew the sisters rarely needed the police. If they did, it was in the line of civic services. He took off his glasses and laid them aside.

"I know a Sister Camille there. Her family and mine were neighbors back home. Sister Camille called to voice a suspicion that she and another sister had concerning the death of their superior, Mother Rosaria, who died Monday morning. From all appearances, it seemed a natural death caused by a heart attack. The burial took place the next day according to the sisters' custom."

"So? What did the death certificate indicate?" Haskell inquired as he rummaged on his desk for a report.

"That the deceased died of heart disease, signed by Dr. Spence."

"And?"

"The deceased suffered a bradycardia heart attack Friday, June thirteenth, shortly after the Chateau graduation ceremonies. Dr. Spence attended her and prescribed bed rest at the Chateau. He saw her again on Saturday and checked her by phone Sunday. His report showed improvement in her disease. Then the sisters found her dead the following Monday morning. After the burial, Sister Camille called me to express concern. I downplayed her suspicion until she found this." Kummer handed the warning card encased in cellophane to him.

The chief read the unsigned card: "To Mother Rosaria. Be careful of changes you make. Hardship and suffering will be the result for everyone. Or you might not be the Mother Superior." He turned it over. Typed on a three-cent postcard in caps the chief read: "M. ROSARIA, CHATEAU, STONE HILL 15, WISC." The postmark on the unstained card indicated May 29, 1952.

"The typewriter ribbon's been run front to back and back to front," he observed, "and the *h* has a clogged key." He reread it and drew up his lower lip in a so-what attitude. "Where was it found?"

"On the deceased's desk. Since then Mother Rosaria's niece, Sister Angelica, was given a calendar as a memento from her aunt." Kummer handed him the calendar. "In it, she found this card."

Chief Haskell took the book and looked at the picture of St. Rose of Lima pictured in soft pastel colors. He smiled. "This takes me back to elementary school days. I remember the nuns used to give out holy pictures for special occasions, first communion and, oh yes, patron saint name days." He turned it over and read:

"A.M.D.G."

May 31, 1952. In the event that I am not with you when you read this. Be aware that I received a threat through the mail May 29, 1952."

The chief leaned back in his chair. "She thought it was serious. What does AMDG mean?"

"I remember seeing it on a heading from a friend who studied for the priesthood. My Latin's a bit weak, but I think the initials stand for, *Ad Majorem Gloria Dei*, which translates, 'All for the greater glory of God.'"

"What else have you got? You wouldn't come in here just to hear yourself talk. Did you question Dr. Spence?"

"This morning. Said he was surprised to hear of his patient's death but attributed it to natural causes. She came from a family with a history of heart disease."

"Hmm. What do you propose?"

"Request an autopsy."

"That'll be a tough one. With the Catholic Church involved, we can expect repercussions from the archbishop, and it will be awkward for the sisters at the Chateau."

"It was awkward for Mother Rosaria," Hank retorted.

Chief Haskell pondered the situation a few seconds. "I'll see Judge Bryce at lunch and run this by him."

Kummer thanked him and left.

*   *   *

Later the chief popped into his door.

"The judge granted your order for the exhumation. Can you meet me at the Chateau at two thirty?"

"Be there, Chief."

*   *   *

The phone on the superior's desk rang. "This is Mother Cordelia."

"Mother," the sister portress at the front entrance exclaimed, "Police Chief Haskell and Lieutenant Kummer are in the parlor to see you."

Mother Cordelia replaced the receiver with caution as though it might break, holding both her hands on it a few seconds. Her gaze lingered. For only a fraction of a second did she wonder why the police were there. Her thoughts flashed to Sister Camille. Dr. Raymond had called her earlier that morning to report that Sister Camille had a paranoid personality disorder. The report didn't surprise her. She could have told the doctor that. Mother Cordelia had agreed for Sister Camille to begin psychoanalysis immediately, though she would have preferred that Sister be sent to a sanitarium for treatment. Now, at least, that much was started. Sister Camille seemed to have quieted down and looked better, but was it too late?

Chief Haskell and Lieutenant Kummer stood up when Mother Cordelia entered the parlor door. She walked with self-assurance and held her hands in her sleeves. She neither smiled nor met the detective's eyes.

"I'm Mother Cordelia. Would you like some coffee?"

The chief answered, "No thanks, Mother. We don't want to inconvenience you any more than we have to."

They sat on tapestry-covered antique chairs with hand-crocheted antimacassars pinned on the arms and backs. Kummer leaned back with caution to test the chair's strength. A large oil painting of the holy family hung on one wall and smaller decorative paintings ornamented the other walls. A frieze of flowing ivy carved of wood decorated the mantel over a brick fireplace. Above the fireplace, a walnut corpus of Christ hung on a cross.

"A serious matter has come to our attention regarding the death of Mother Rosaria," Chief Haskell began. "I'd like to go over the sequence of events leading up to her death."

The superior pressed her lips together then answered slowly, "I'm only too happy to help in any way I can, but I don't understand your reasons for delving into it. It was obviously a natural death, an act of God."

"Nothing is obvious, but we hope to make everything clear," the chief said. "Was Mother Rosaria ill before she suffered a heart attack? That is," he glanced at his notes, "before June thirteenth?"

"Not that I know of. I can ask Sister Mercy, our infirmarian, if Mother Rosaria asked for any medication."

"We'll check that later." He nodded to Lieutenant Kummer.

Kummer spoke, "I talked to Dr. Spence this morning. He told me Mother Rosaria had a mild attack, and he didn't consider her condition serious enough to admit her to the hospital. It appeared his patient made progress Saturday, June fourteenth, and Sunday, June fifteenth." Kummer said, "Who found her the morning of June sixteenth?"

"Sister Mercy. Why are you asking me these questions? What is wrong?"

"Did you see her Sunday evening, the evening before she died?"

"Yes. I visited her before supper."

"How did she seem?"

"Mother was tired. She'd sat up for the first time that afternoon and visited with a few of the sisters."

"What we're concerned with is the abrupt change in the patient's condition from Sunday evening to Monday morning." Kummer didn't mention any information provided by Sister Camille.

Haskell interrupted, "Did you know the deceased received a warning in the mail?"

"No, I didn't." Mother Cordelia shrugged her shoulders.

"We feel there's sufficient cause to exhume the body, so an autopsy can be performed."

Mother Cordelia stared at the fireplace. A sudden clap of thunder followed by a piercing streak of lightning shot through the room. The superior's eyes snapped to the walls then bounced toward the ceiling.

"Are you all right, Mother?" Lieutenant Kummer walked over and touched her shoulder.

Mother Cordelia's eyes rested on Kummer. When she blinked, he nodded to the chief to continue.

Haskell picked up the questioning. "We realize this comes as a surprise, but I wanted to forewarn you."

The superior whispered, "This is a shock! When is it going to happen?"

Chief Haskell said, "Tomorrow morning. I'll make arrangements with your mortuary and have an officer here. Could you have someone to help?"

"Yes, of course."

Both officers rose, bade respectful farewells, and left.

*   *   *

A series of call bells in the monastery summoned a hasty council meeting. Mother Cordelia didn't lose time consulting her advisers. While the sisters remained standing, Mother coughed, trying to clear her strained voice, then said, "I just came from a meeting with the chief of police and Lieutenant Kummer of the Stone Hill Police

Department." She said, "They came because they think conditions surrounding Mother Rosaria's death are suspicious." She took a deep breath and continued, "The only way to disprove their suspicion is to have her body exhumed and autopsied."

Four sets of eyes, all wearing rimless glasses, focused on their superior. Sister Martha spoke first. "What are you saying, Mother? Why is there suspicion?"

Sister Diana added, "Dr. Spence didn't suspect anything. Has he changed his opinion?"

"You mean," Sister Martha said, "Mother Rosaria's consecrated body is going to be dug up out of the grave and opened up on a marble slab? I don't want to think about it."

"Dear sisters, the decision is not ours," Mother Cordelia answered sadly. "I have no authority in this matter."

"What specific evidence convinced the police to order an autopsy?" Sister Bernard asked.

"A postcard threat that came through the mail." Mother Cordelia dropped her voice. "The police didn't say how it got into their hands, but I can guess Sister Camille had something to do with it."

"Sister Camille?" cried Sister Martha. "How does she enter this picture?"

"Sister Camille found a threatening postcard. The police think it was a warning to Mother Rosaria. Sister considers herself some kind of sleuth. She has a suspicious nature and called Lieutenant Kummer. The poor dear is not well. I've sent her to Dr. Raymond for psychological evaluation."

Sister Bernard spoke up, "I too wondered about the sudden change in Mother Rosaria's condition. I had hoped there would be an autopsy or at least an inquest. As for me, I'll feel better when I hear the autopsy report."

"The body will be exhumed tomorrow. Sister Martha, will you ask Aloysius to help at the gravesite? The sisters should stay away, so the men can do their work. The police will be there, too."

Sister answered, "Yes, Mother, I'll see to it."

Mother Cordelia said, "I'm grateful it's summer vacation, and the students aren't around. It would be awkward to explain why a hearse and the police are out there digging up a grave. There's no need for anyone here or outside the monastery to know."

10

After Sister Camille finished her morning duties in the kitchen, she walked outdoors, circling around behind the chapel to the west academy door. Tuesday promised to be a sunny day with rays of light shafting through low clouds after the rain. As she passed the little theater, Sister Angelica saw her and hurried out to meet her.

"Have you looked out front?" she asked. "Come see." Sister Angelica led her across the hall to the fourth-grade classroom. "The police are in the cemetery."

Sister Camille brought a hand to her lips. "Huh! Oh my God. It's happening. Mother Cordelia didn't say a word about this to the community."

Looking out the windows toward the cemetery, the sisters searched through the trees for the police car.

"Let's go up to our studio. We'll have a better view from the second floor." They hurried up the steps. In a nearby practice room, Natalie Cooper drummed out her scales on the piano while waiting for a lesson with Sister Camille. The sisters entered Sister Camille's studio and searched through foliage to watch the activity.

"There's a police car and Aloysius with a shovel," said Sister Camille.

"I see two policemen sitting in a car, and there's the hearse from Engelman's Mortuary with the back door open."

"It's really happening, Sister. We've gotten our message through to the police. Now, we'll just have to wait to hear the results of the autopsy."

"I wonder how long that will take," Sister Angelica said.

"I wonder what Mother Cordelia is thinking. She must be trying to keep it secret."

"That doesn't surprise me. She's got to be worried about a scandal. I haven't seen Hank Kummer since I gave him the calendar. Do you think he's in the police car? I want to tell him about my visit to the psychologist. None of my family knows about it. I can imagine what my dad will think when he hears. He hasn't much use for 'shrinks.' It's not going to matter anyway. When the psychologist hears about the autopsy reports, he'll change his diagnosis about me." Then, realizing the workmen were digging up Sister Angelica's aunt, Sister Camille asked, "How do you feel, Sister? So much is happening to me that I've forgotten about your feelings. Please forgive me."

"I feel all right, Sister. Thanks for asking. I'm relieved that we'll soon know how Mother Rosaria died. Look, they're bringing the casket up now. Lord, have mercy on her soul." Sister Angelica made the sign of the cross. In a matter of minutes, the door of the hearse slammed shut, and everyone left the scene.

"Now, it remains a step-by-step process to learn the truth," said Sister Camille. She heard her piano student stumbled on a troublesome passage in "Fur Elise." Sister wanted to shout out, play C sharp like her mother used to call musical directions from the kitchen. The sisters left the studio. Sister Camille opened the door to her student. It would be a long lesson. All the drilling on that phrase at Natalie's last lesson didn't help. Once during the lesson, Sister Camille walked to the window and saw Hank's car. Her heart beat faster. By the time the lesson finished, the car was gone.

* * *

Lieutenant Kummer drove to the county morgue on the outskirts of Stone Hill; he felt his usual repugnance about attending autopsies. This one especially. It seemed an invasion into a sacred zone because the sister had made sacred vows, yet he knew the autopsy was essential to open the case. He thought about his favorite fifth-grade teacher, Sister Lucy. It would be difficult to see her in this position. One pathologist he knew from Madison put a towel over the head of the corpse while he worked. He said it made his work more objective. Kummer wished Doc Peterson would do that but knew he wouldn't. He once saw Peterson, with blood up to his elbows, tell a joke about a runaway hearse. The joke went through his head, and he found himself hearing the story again.

"A hearse traveling to the cemetery hit a sharp bump. The back door popped open, and the coffin flew out, slid down an embankment, crashing through the door of a pharmacy. The lid sprang open; the jostled body sat up and asked, 'Have you anything to stop this coffin?'"

Another time Doc quipped about a cadaver of an eighty-four-year-old man. "This guy never went to a doctor. I found colon cancer, hardening of the arteries, and cirrhosis of the liver. It was a blood clot that finally took his life."

Entering the dissection room, which was kept at a temperature of sixty degrees, Kummer nodded to Dr. Peterson who stood by the autopsy table. Peterson was a man in his midforties whose full head of blond curly hair gave him a boyish look with a hint of a roguish smile. Bernice, his assistant, stood next to him. Kummer knew she had undressed the body. The religious habit and veil hung on a hanger. Maybe Bernice felt some reverence too. Usually personal belongings were stuffed in a bag on the floor.

"Thought you'd be coming this morning." Dr. Peterson glanced up.

Hank picked up the police report given to the pathologist and read:

STONE HILL POLICE DEPARTMENT
INVESTIGATION REPORT

MOTHER ROSARIA LEONARD, age 49, of St. Clotildes was found dead by Sister Mercy Brendlin, the infirmarian, the morning of June 16, 1952. The decedent was unresponsive in her bed, eyes open, and showed no external abnormalities. There were no signs of foul play. On June 13 she had suffered a bradycardia attack and was treated at the Chateau by Doctor George Spence. Records at Saint Theresa Hospital show the decedent was never treated for heart disease there. The body was buried the next day, June 17.

The deceased was seen alive as late as seven the night before.

Officer Brian Kelley

The deceased's head was tilted back on a block after the body weight and measurements were taken.

"Looks like you'll be busy with this one," the doctor spoke to the detective. With scalpel in hand, he finished the Y incision from her pearly-skinned shoulders to the chest, continuing down to the pubic area. He pulled the skin flaps back, exposing the rib section. A bitter, yeasty odor, mixed with the pungent scent of embalming fluid, filled the air.

"Have you found any apparent signs?" Kummer asked.

"The eyes show no broken blood vessels, though I syringed out vitreous humor from them." The doctor pulled down an eyelid briefly to show Kummer. "No marks or discoloration on the body except lividity. But we'll soon see." He cut the rib plate and lifted it to the tray. Then he carefully removed the heart and lungs. After incising them, he pointed to the gastro-esophageal juncture. "See this?"

Kummer peered into the bloody cavity.

"You can see a corrosive substance here." From the juncture, the doctor dipped a reddish brown claylike mixture into a vial. "This is sometimes referred to in the trade as 'coffee grounds.' Can you detect the bitter-almond odor, Lieutenant? I'm one of the 40 percent who can smell it."

Kummer shook his head.

"Have you got a penny, Lieutenant?"

Kummer dug into his pocket and dropped a tarnished penny into the pathologist's bloodied glove. Peterson moved it around in the mixture he had called coffee grounds and then rinsed it under the spigot near the feet of his subject.

"Ahha, just as I thought." He held up a bright, minted copper penny. "I can tell you right now, cyanide was ingested."

"I'll send blood and tissue samples of the organs to the lab as a routine," the pathologist continued. After weighing and examining the thymus, the heart chambers, and muscles, he explained, "No sign of heart disease here. A bradycardia heart, which is a slow heartbeat, doesn't necessarily reflect pathology. In fact, I have a bradycardia heartbeat myself."

After bringing out the liver and spleen, which were weighed and sampled for testing, he worked his fingers down to the stomach and bowels. "Cyanide didn't reach this far. It had done its work. I'll take specimens from fecal matter and urine, but I doubt if cyanide will be present."

Kummer knew the pathologist liked his work. The doctor once told him he enjoyed being around cops, which influenced him to become a forensic pathologist. The detective bet the doctor liked his patients in an uncomplaining state.

Dr. Peterson moved to the head of the corpse. Kummer stepped back. He disliked this part of the autopsy the most. Something about the cut from ear to ear over the top of the skull and the removal of the skullcap made his shoulders twitch. He even contemplated returning to Stone Hill, but he needed to wait for the preliminary report with the apparent cause of death. That would provide enough evidence to start an immediate investigation before the toxicology report came back from the lab. With the brain weighed, the autopsy was concluded. Bernice stitched the lower part of the body after replacing the organs, minus the specimen snippets.

"The sisters will be anxious to bury the body, but I think we'll hold it for a while," Kummer said, as he waited for Peterson to wash up.

"I don't know if Bernice would know how to put all those pieces of clothing back on." Peterson directed his voice to her while he toweled. "Would you, Bernice?"

"I think I better let the sisters do it. I'll just pack them up until they're needed."

Kummer returned to Stone Hill, a rural Wisconsin community consisting of eight city blocks of businesses radiating from a town square. Most of the brick and stone buildings were two and three stories in a classical-revival style. A loading platform in front of a feed store provided easy access for transferring hundred-pound feedbags for the farmers. During the summer months, the American Legion Band performed in the grandstand every Wednesday evening from seven to nine. The residents of the thirty-five-thousand-population rural community took pride in their green clipped lawns and tidy flowerbeds. Three patrolmen in the police department enforced the law and kept the peace. Burglaries and accidents filled the dockets, while murder cases were rare. Only in complicated cases were experts called in from Madison.

With the preliminary report in hand, Detective Kummer greeted the desk officer at the police station. "Is the chief in?"

"He was a few minutes ago, probably not far. I'll let him know you're here."

Kummer entered his office and tossed the report on his cluttered desk. He reloaded his pipe, lit it, and, after several puffs, grabbed the sports page from the *Madison Times*. Clips of Joe DiMaggio and Babe Ruth decorated his walls along with family photos. An autographed baseball from Stan Musial rested in an old glove atop the rolltop desk. An upright candlestick phone sat near the edge of the desk by an ashtray filled with ashes.

Kummer had majored in criminal law at the University of Wisconsin, but baseball was his love. He was at his best in left field, catching a high fly or stopping a low ground ball. Quick reaction and speed were the elements that drove the Stone Hillbillies baseball team to the 1951 state championship.

Sergeant Flanagan poked his head in. "Read about the home run Mickey Mantle hit yesterday? Close to five hundred feet."

Kummer answered, "That homer must have been a beauty. The Yankees'll be on television tomorrow night. Now that I've got a set, I'll see it. And besides that, the Stone Hillbillies play Eau Claire Sunday. This weekend should be great."

"What kind did you get?"

"An Admiral," Hank said with relish. He looked up from the paper when the chief entered.

"What ya get?" The chief remained standing.

Hank showed him the report. Flanagan left.

"Cyanide." The chief pronounced it softly. "Corrosive stuff. Death must have come instantly. We'll get on it this afternoon. I'll call the mother superior and tell her we'll begin our investigation at the Chateau. No need to bring the sisters down to the station. I don't want them sitting around waiting to be questioned. It would bring them too much public attention. They'd be more comfortable in their own surroundings. Let's keep a lid on this one. Maybe we can complete it before the archbishop finds out. His Eminence will want to protect the sisters."

Kummer put down his pipe. "Looks like the time sequence is between supper and midnight."

"A good time frame to focus on. Get a search warrant from the DA and take Flanagan with you. I'll call the mother superior. What was her name?"

"Mother Cordelia," Kummer said. "One thing in our favor, the Chateau is a closed community. We may not have to go further afield. On the negative side, the integrity of the crime scene is disturbed. From what Sister Camille told me, it's occupied by the new superior."

After the chief left, Kummer wondered who Mother Rosaria's enemies might be.

11

Sister Eugene sat in Mother Cordelia's office working on the fall term schedule with the superior. She ran her fingers along her side beads, lifting them to her lap. The worn beads of the rosary hung from a belt called a cincture. Hail Marys were said on the groups of ten smaller beads and Our Fathers on the connecting larger ones. Sister asked, "Have you heard anything yet, Mother?"

"No, Sister, it takes at least a week for the final laboratory results." The superior shook her head, her tongue made a sucking sound in disgust when the phone rang.

"Mother Cordelia? This is Chief Haskell. The pathologist finished the autopsy this morning. Dr. Peterson found evidence of cyanide."

"Cyanide?" the superior shouted.

Sister Eugene bolted upright. Her beads clattered to the floor.

The chief continued, "The full toxicology report won't be back from the lab for a week, but Dr. Peterson found enough evidence to start our investigation."

"It must be a mistake. How could that have happened?" Mother Cordelia insisted.

"Mother Cordelia, this is where the law steps in. It's our job to find out. We'll start the interviews this afternoon. We'll come to the Chateau."

"I can't believe we have to go through this, Chief Haskell. Is there any way to keep it out of the newspapers?"

"We can, for a while. That's why I don't want the sisters to come down to the police station. That way, we can keep it quiet. It would be well for you to engage an attorney."

"I'll call Mr. Doyle immediately."

"Lieutenant Kummer is on his way now. If there's anything I can do, or questions I can answer, don't hesitate to call me."

Mother Cordelia replaced the receiver as if in a dream, allowing her hands to linger on it. She stared at the trees in the distance then said, "Toil and trouble, Fire burn and caldron bubble." Her glance swept past the bed in the adjoining cell where Mother Rosaria had died. In a hollow voice, she said, "The police are starting an investigation, here at the Chateau."

"What good will that do? Mother Rosaria's dead! That won't bring her back." Sister Eugene grabbed her beads and missed. They rattled to the floor instead. "It can only bring shame and embarrassment to the sisters and scandal to our academy. Think of the years it's taken to build our reputation. It's only since I've been directress that our enrollment increased." Sister Eugene worked her fingers over the rosary beads she replaced on her lap.

"Yes, you've done so much to build up our academy," Mother Cordelia said, without expression, her eyes locked toward the bed.

Sister Eugene continued, "We've just gotten through that shocking Leslie Allen incident and escaped gossip only because it was near the end of the school year. Mother Rosaria almost ruined everything when she insisted that girl should graduate. How I prayed those two weeks." Sister Eugene's body bobbed back and forth, her eyes closed as in supplication.

The superior said, "That detective, Henry Kummer, will do us no earthly good."

$$* \quad * \quad *$$

Officers Kummer and Flanagan left the police station and drove along the River Road in Kummer's sports car. Flanagan turned on the radio. While waiting for the sports news, he asked, "Did you see Mickey Mantle's line-drive double last night that led to the Yankees' win? That was one hell of a hit."

Kummer's mind was on the investigation, but he quickly responded. "Yeah, and when he bunted in the seventh inning, he ran from home plate to first base in 3.1 seconds."

Flanagan, a devoted family man, enjoyed baseball more than any other pastime. With his wife and three boys, he could be seen every Sunday at the nine fifteen Mass in Saint Edward's Church. Assigned as a marine sentry in World War II at the United States Embassy in Great Britain, Gary Flanagan earned the rank of gunnery sergeant. When he returned to Stone Hill, the experience made it easy for him to transfer into police work. At the age of thirty-six, his round face and black hair combed in a pompadour gave him a youthful air.

The officers approached the Chateau located on a high bluff. The landmark seen for miles around came into view as they drove up the steep drive from the river.

Flanagan whistled and then said, "Geez, there it is. Pretty damn imposing, I'd say."

They entered the drive through an opened iron gate attached to stone pillars and approached the main building which crowned the circle drive. Each addition to the central building showed growth and prosperity. Spacious green lawns on a twelve-acre rustic site were bordered with blooming geranium beds and wisteria-covered trellises. The walnut carved door above the marble steps showed no signs of activity.

Kummer asked, "Haven't you ever been up here?"

"No." Flanagan's eyes continued to look around. "I knew it was here, but until now, nothing brought me up here. Why is it called a monastery? I thought only monks lived in monasteries."

"Beats me. Maybe it's because these nuns are stricter than the Franciscans or the Benedictines. Don't you have a relative in one of those orders?"

"Yeah, but my aunt lives in a convent. So what I want to know is if nuns live in a monastery, do monks live in a convent as well?"

Kummer chuckled, "Guess we'll have to study up on it. Maybe we'll find out while we're here."

Hank parked in the circle. Still seated, he handed Flanagan the postcard with the warning that Sister Camille had found. "You'll need this. We're looking for a typewriter that has the letter *h* smudged. Here's a stack of cards to type samples."

Flanagan tucked them into his inside coat pocket, grabbed the camera, and slid out. Hank ducked his head and automatically reached for the identification kit behind the driver's seat.

"Do you suppose we can smoke here?" Flanagan asked.

"I'll check on it."

"Well, I sure as hell hope so."

"You'll have to watch your language, too."

"Hey, who's on trial?" Flanagan persisted.

Kummer didn't reply. He was used to his partner.

Mother Cordelia appeared as the officers were ushered into the front parlor by the sister portress. Beyond the mosaic-tiled stone entrance they saw a large room with antique furniture. A grand piano covered with a fringed silk scarf sat on a stage. Potted palms and bearskin rugs with glass eyes and lifelike jaws showing yellowed incisors decorated the highly polished floor.

"Good afternoon, Officers." Mother Cordelia stood motionless with her hands in her sleeves, as though some hidden mechanical device had lifted her through the floor.

"Good afternoon, Mother," the officers chorused in unison like students in parochial school. "Mother Cordelia, this is Sergeant Flanagan. He'll be assisting me."

"How do you do, Sergeant?" She didn't offer her hand to either officer. They remained hidden within her long sleeves. Turning to Lieutenant Kummer, she scolded, "I'm shocked at the autopsy report." She held his eyes, accosting him as though he was part of a conspiracy. "I don't know how I can tell the sisters about this investigation you seem so determined to do."

The lieutenant, equal to the situation, responded, "Murder is never a pretty picture, even to the most experienced."

The detective heard the superior gasp, a gasp that sounded more like a snort as she sensed her authority challenged.

"I'll show you to a room where you can work."

They walked behind the superior down the hall in silence. The officers smelled O'Cedar furniture polish and noted that each step squeaks in the polished birch floors.

Once Flanagan lagged behind, teetering on a loose board. "No one can sneak up here."

Mother Cordelia ignored him. She opened a door and showed the detectives into a small parlor. "This is the room we use for interviews and formal visitations by the monsignor." The room had a door to the hall on one side and a large opening that adjoined a larger parlor on the other. Bookcases lined the walls up to high windows. A bronze clock with sculpted angels and a large vase with a garden scene rested on top of the bookcase. An antique pedestal table about the size of a card table sat on an oriental rug in the center of the floor.

Kummer noted a few of the book titles, *The Building of a Cathedral* and *Canterbury Tales*.

Looking around the room, he said, "This is rather small." Across the hall, he saw a larger room with long tables, sturdy library chairs, and more bookcases that looked less parlorlike.

He walked over to the door and looked in.

"Would this room be available, Mother Cordelia? The one exit would make it more private." While waiting for the superior to decide, he added, "Sergeant Flanagan will be with me. We'll need more space."

"Sister Eugene uses that room for parent meetings, but since it's summer vacation, the room is available to you and your staff. The switchboard's down the hall at the main entrance."

"Thank you, Mother Cordelia; we'll have our own line. Wisconsin Telephone will install it this afternoon. Sergeant, would you take care of that and then check the locks on the exterior doors?"

Mother Cordelia interrupted, "One of our sisters will have to accompany Sergeant Flanagan. I'll call Sister Dorothy."

"Before you go, Mother Cordelia, I'd like a list of all the sisters, as well as the lay people who work here, and a copy of your daily schedule. I'll also need an architectural plan of the Chateau and the grounds. Officer Flanagan, go with Mother Cordelia and start checking the locks."

After they left, Kummer pushed one of the large polished tables near the windows. Every piece of furniture in the room gleamed. Even the windows looked freshly washed. He arranged the chairs, so his back would be to the window. He liked to have full light on the faces of the suspects interviewed. It enabled him to read facial expressions and interpret body movements.

The floor squeak from the hall announced Mother Cordelia's return with the requested items. "This is the summer vacation list. You'll see Mother Rosaria's name is still on it."

"I see. Just to give you some idea of what we'll be doing, Mother Cordelia, I want to sit down and go over this list with you. I need to know each sister's assignment."

Mother Cordelia answered, "The sisters' assignments are already on the list."

"Good. When we've finished with that, I'd like a tour of the buildings. I have a search warrant." He handed her a copy and looked at his watch. "Would you have time to go over the list now?"

The superior didn't answer. Instead, she sat down and took up the list. The lieutenant made notes beside names as Mother Cordelia read the list. When she came to Sister Camille, the superior paused then said quickly, "Teaches piano and has summer kitchen assignment."

"I'm sorry to take so much of your time, Mother. I'd like to know one more thing. I see on your schedule there are two seatings for dinner and supper. Which sisters eat at the second seatings?"

"The sisters who have duties during the first table. That would be the portress at the front door, the sister who works in the kitchen, the servers, or whoever needs to be absent from first table."

"I see. May I have their names?" The Lieutenant made more notes on the list.

ST. CLOTILDES MONASTERY JUNE 14, 1952

1. Mother Rosaria—Mother Superior
2. Sister Diana—Assistant Superior

COUNCIL:

3. Sister Martha—Kitchen Supervisor
4. Sister Bernard—Retired
5. Sister Cordelia—Senior English

COMMUNITY:

6. Sister Thaddeus-Latin Teacher
7. Sister Loyola—Wheelchair bound
8. Sister Francis Borgia—Portress
9. Sister Mercy—Infirmarian
10. Sister Eugene—Directress
11. Sister Edward—Retired
12. Sister Charles—Retired
13. Sister Alice—English
14. Sister Delphine—Math
15. Sister Philip—First Grade
16. Sister Hope—Second Grade
17. Sister Mildred—Third Grade
18. Sister Joan—Fourth Grade
19. Sister Ruth—Fifth Grade
20. Sister Rhoda—Sixth Grade
21. Sister Margaret—Seventh Grade
22. Sister Allan—Eighth Grade
23. Sister Laura—Grounds Super/Poor men
24. Sister Michael—History
25. Sister Dorothy—Procuratrix
26. Sister Anne—Home Economics
27. Sister Hillary—Commercial Teacher
28. Sister Angelica—Drama
29. Sister Camille—Piano/Kitchen

NOVICES:

1. Sister Sarah—Kindergarten
2. Sister Alfreda—Refectorian

EMPLOYEES:

1. Miss Alice Drekel—Cook
2. Mrs. Zelda Simmons—Cook
3. Mr. Joe Simmons—Engineer
4. Aloysius Zeis—Janitor

"Thank you, Mother Cordelia. That's all for now. You may go." Mother Cordelia stiffened. Kummer heard her quick breath and sensed disapproval. Being dismissed was a complete reversal of her authority. She rose from the chair and walked heavily out of the room.

After she left, he studied the summer schedule.

SUMMER SCHEDULE 1952

5:00—Angelus
5:30—Meditation
6:30—Mass
7:15—Prime
7:30—Breakfast
8:30—Little Hours
9:30—Assigned Work
12:00—Angelus (Dinner)
12:30—Recreation (Second Table)
1:30—Assigned Work
3:00—Spiritual Reading
3:30—Recreation
4:30—Vespers and Compline
5:00—Meditation
5:30—Free
6:00—Supper
6:30—Second Table
7:30—Recreation
8:30—Matins and Lauds
10:00—Lights Out

12

———————

This room suited Kummer's investigation better than the small museum corner Mother Cordelia offered. Here he didn't have to worry about knocking a valuable vase off a shelf or testing his weight on an antique chair.

After Mother Cordelia left, Kummer spread the blueprint of the second-floor monastery on a nearby table, pulling books from the nearby shelves to anchor it. The windows facing the circle drive gave him his bearings in relation to the campus.

From the hallway, he heard Officer Flanagan's footsteps. From the sound of laughter, Flanagan and his companion seemed to be enjoying a mutual joke. The two detectives worked well together although they were opposite personalities. Flanagan's humor balanced Kummer's reserve. Kummer looked up as his sidekick entered.

"Lieutenant Kummer, this is Sister Dorothy." Flanagan sounded pleased. "Sister comes from Detroit. She used to go to the Tiger games."

"How do you do, Sister Dorothy?" Kummer stood and took her outstretched hand. He repeated her name, glancing down at his list. Looking up, he added, "I see you're," he paused, "the pro-cur-a-trix. Mother Cordelia said you are kind of a general housekeeper."

Sister Dorothy smiled at his pronunciation. "Pleased to meet you, Lieutenant Kummer. I'm called all kinds of things. I call my office, 'the complaint department.'" She nodded good-naturedly.

Kummer liked her friendly humor and thought she'd be a good sister to know. Someone who didn't view them with suspicion as did the mother superior and the sister portress at the front door.

"Mother Cordelia also said you would be my tour escort as well."

"Anytime you're ready, Lieutenant Kummer."

"In a minute, Sister," he answered. "Sergeant, what did you find with the locks?"

"I found the four academy Yale locks in good working order. They comply with state code, opening from the inside when they're locked. I checked each lock with Sister's key. I haven't checked the monastery doors yet."

Kummer asked, "Sister, what time are the doors opened in the morning?"

"At seven thirty. I lock them at five thirty in the evening after meditation."

Kummer made a note and then turned to Sister. He smiled for the first time since he arrived. "Shall we begin the tour? Officer Flanagan, come with us."

"Where do you want to begin?" she asked.

"The kitchen, Sister."

As the trio walked down the hall to the stairs, Sister Dorothy pointed out offices and classrooms in the nearby academy addition. After they turned toward the kitchen from the hallway stairs, Kummer smelled a combination of garlic and grease odors mingled with the scent of a recently served pot roast. He took a moment to view the area and cooks at work. A sister stood at a long table ladling chunks of potatoes and carrots onto plates.

Sister Dorothy explained, "This is Sister Laura. She's in charge of the poor men who come to the back door for work and a handout."

With the kettle in her hand, Sister Laura glanced at the officers over the top of her glasses. "We have nine today."

"How long do they stay on the premises, Sister?" Kummer asked.

Sister Laura straightened up and set the kettle on the table. "They know if they want dinner, they have to show up for work at ten thirty." Sister was in her seventies, tall, with a resigned, compassionate expression, doing what she felt had to be done for these forgotten souls. "I meet and tell them what I want done on the grounds and garden. Sometimes I'll keep one or two for the afternoon if I need them. Otherwise, they leave after they're finished eating."

"Where do they eat, Sister?"

"There're benches in the back."

Placing four plates on a large tray, Sister said, "Come along, I'll show you."

Sister Dorothy picked up two plates. Kummer hesitated then picked up two and nodded to Flanagan for the last one. They followed Sister past a small office, out the west door. Kummer glanced in the open door and saw a typewriter on a desk.

Across the hall was a pantry. Next came a walk-in cooler. Sister Dorothy explained that the small dining room opposite the cooler was for the hired men who worked at the Chateau. They passed through a porch where mops were propped against lattice walls. Refuse barrels sat near them, and a case of empty milk bottles sat ready for pickup.

Outside, the men of the street, referred to as poor men by the sisters, waited in soiled, wrinkled attire, some smoking. If they were hungry, they hid it. Today, they waited in silence for Sister to put the plates on the blue rain-washed table.

Sister Laura intoned, "Bless us O Lord, and these thy gifts . . ." The regulars put out their cigarettes and bowed their heads. Others watched and then sauntered over to check out the plates.

Lieutenant Kummer looked past the men to a garden across the driveway where rows of carrots, lettuce, and radishes grew next to a shed. He walked toward it, and Flanagan followed. Before opening the door, Kummer asked Flanagan for a camera shot then tugged on the door that stuck to the threshold. The rusty hinges gave way. Kummer directed Flanagan to take more pictures. Moving around garden tools and a wheelbarrow tipped against the wall, Kummer peered into open bags of fertilizer and weed killer, sniffing from a safe distance. He read labels and inventoried items on the shelves.

In the corner, he noticed a crumpled brown bag half filled with what looked like peach pits. From the amount of dust, the bag had been there a long time. Kummer made notes then returned to his tour guide, who waited outside.

Following Sister Dorothy back to the kitchen, Lieutenant Kummer noticed Sister Camille by a corner cupboard. She was lifting the wide hem of her skirt and pinning it around the back of her waist. She turned to reach for an apron and came face to face with the detective.

"Lieutenant Kummer, what a surprise. I didn't know you were here." Sister Camille came forward smiling, offering her hand.

The detective held it a few moments.

"You two have met before?" Sister Dorothy said.

"Yes, Sister Camille and I have known each other since we were kids." The detective looked into her face. "How are you, Sister?" He wanted to ask more, but not in this company. Instead, he introduced Sergeant Flanagan and remarked to her, "I'll see you later."

"Lieutenant Kummer, this is Mrs. Simmons." Sister Camille led him over near the steam table where Mrs. Simmons leaned on one elbow surveying the scene. She had eyed the officers when they first entered the kitchen, curious about their presence.

"How do you do, Mrs. Simmons?"

Mrs. Simmons wore a long white denim apron with strings that crossed in the back and tied in front. With the dinner hour over, she seemed pleased to chat with the officers.

"I don't have any relatives or know any policeman on the force." Nodding her head toward Sister Camille, she said, "Sister didn't tell me she knew a lieutenant detective, either. She's a sly one, that Sister Camille."

Kummer estimated she was in her midsixties, approximately five and a half feet tall, 160 pounds. A net held her tinted red hair in place.

He said, "Mr. Simmons is also employed here. Is he your husband?"

"He sure is." Her grin grew wider, showing a false plate of teeth. "We try to get employment where we can both work together. It makes it so much easier, you know. We live in a little house down the street and can walk to work. Ain't that nice?"

Kummer nodded. He sensed this conversation could go on and ended it by shaking her hand. Turning to Sister Dorothy, he asked, "Are there other exterior doors?"

"There're two more. One from the laundry and one at the south entrance. I'll show you." Together they checked the locks, which were older. They could be locked with a key from either side.

"Where would you like to go next, Lieutenant?"

"I'd like to see the room where Mother Rosaria died."

"That's on the next floor."

On the way, they came to a door marked Cloister.

Sounding like a tour guide, Sister Dorothy lowered her voice. "Now we're in the monastery." Opening yet another door, she explained, "This is the refectory."

Walnut benches and trestle tables bare of tablecloths lined the walls of the long narrow room. Three china settings, enclosed in a large linen napkin, sat on each table. Near the ceiling, the quotation "Whether you eat or drink or whatsoever you do, do all for the honor of God" was printed in calligraphy.

A sister, wheeling an empty cart, stopped short. She gave Sister Dorothy the customary greeting, "Praise Jesus," then pulled her aside. "What are these men doing in the refectory?" Her eyes questioned the male intrusion into this secluded space.

"They're police officers, Sister. They're investigating the death of Mother Rosaria. You'll be seeing them around."

The trio left an unconvinced sister and continued down the hall to the elevator. Sister Dorothy explained, "If you're wondering why the sisters are startled by your presence, it's because no one besides the occasional workman or Dr. Spence is permitted in the cloister."

As they walked on, Kummer said, "I can tell a good deal of time has been spent taking care of the buildings. When did the sisters establish this foundation?"

"In 1870, Bishop Davisiae sailed to France and Italy begging for money to establish missions in the Mississippi Valley. He engaged the services of five sisters from the Monastery of Duc de Rohan. With donations, he purchased a house on this tree-lined bluff overlooking the Mississippi River."

"He chose a great view," Hank commented.

Sister Dorothy continued, "The sisters liked the beautiful scenery and the cloister afforded by the natural formation of the bluff. They took in day scholars and boarding students. This prompted the building of the first wing of the Chateau in 1887. Even with the larger building, the sisters often had to give up their beds to paying boarders and sleep on tables and benches until the second, the central building, was erected in 1912. As the order grew and enrollments increased, the original building was converted to a monastery."

"And when was the third addition completed?" Kummer asked.

"The last addition, which is now the academy, was built in 1930. Mr. James Edward Moore, the original architect, died some years before, God rest his soul. One of his associates followed the original plan, updating it to meet modern needs."

The elevator reached the second floor. Sister Dorothy pulled back the grilled doors. Kummer waited for her to step out. He saw seven doors down each side of the hall. Each had a varnished plaque with a saint's name printed on it.

Sister Dorothy knocked gently on Mother Cordelia's office door. The plaque read, Saint Gregory, Bishop and Confessor.

When Sister Dorothy heard "in his name" from within, she responded, "Praise Jesus," and opened the door.

Mother Cordelia sat at her desk in the bay-window area. She rose quickly. "I'm afraid you won't be able to learn much here. I've occupied these rooms since Saturday." She opened the sliding door to show the adjoining cell where Mother Rosaria died. "Since Mother Rosaria died, the rooms have been stripped of her effects and the walls and ceiling painted."

"Painted?"

"That's our custom, Lieutenant, after a new superior takes over this office."

Kummer was struck by the brightness of the room. Everything was white like a room in a hospital. Beside the iron cot stood a washstand with a vitreous china pitcher inside a basin.

A chair beside the bed completed the furnishings. "Is the furniture in the same position as before?"

"It's all the same furniture and in the same place."

Kummer stood quietly. He liked to breathe in the layout of a crime scene, let the secrets get into his skin, so it would be a part of him. Too much time had elapsed. And then, how much personality of the deceased could be seen in a room as austere as this? No curtains hung from the windows; no throw pillows were on the bed; no attractive pictures adorned the walls. Only a sepia print of a nun he believed to be their foundress hung alongside the crucifix. What individual traits could he pick up? The room was designed for sleeping only. Kummer made a few notes and checked the two doors to the hall then stepped to the windows to check the locks and estimate the drop to the ground below. He noticed a nun outdoors in the distance walking with a book. The detective turned back to Mother Cordelia. "Were any of Mother Rosaria's belongings saved?"

"Sister Dorothy has them in the procuratrix's office."

Sister Dorothy spoke up, "I'll get the box for you, Lieutenant. Shall I take it to the library?"

"Can you wait until we return?" Finished with his inspection, he waited for Flanagan to snap pictures before moving on. "Could I see the room next to yours, Mother Cordelia?"

Mother Cordelia corrected him. "Our bedrooms are called cells."

They went into the hall. Mother knocked on a door with a plaque that read, Saint Polycarp, Bishop and Martyr and opened the door.

Kummer viewed a smaller cell, approximately eight by ten feet. A white iron cot, a white spread with a small crucifix on the pillow, a similar white washstand, and a straight back chair were the sole furnishings. The washstand covered with bird's-eye towel fabric held a ceramic pitcher and bowl, and a glass held a toothbrush and paste. A pin cushion hung from a hook, and a bare lightbulb hung on a wire suspended from the ceiling. The only window faced east. He asked, "Who sleeps here?"

Sister Dorothy answered, "Sister Eugene."

"Where are the fire escapes located, Sister?"

The trio walked further down the hall to another cell. After examining the window lock and the ladder escape, Kummer directed Flanagan to check the escape and screens.

13

Next, Sister Dorothy led the officers to the infirmary. The startled Sister Mercy gasped, "How can I help you?" Her saucer-shaped eyes stared disapprovingly at the officers. Few of the sisters, Kummer realized, knew that an investigation had begun concerning Mother Rosaria's death.

"At the moment, I only want to look around, though I'd like to ask you a few questions about Mother Rosaria later." Kummer stood, hands in pockets, his characteristic half grin never quite reaching a full smile. He spoke quietly, trying to ease the speechless, aged sister.

Sister Dorothy said, "Detective Kummer's investigating Mother Rosaria's sudden death."

Sister Mercy drew her hand to her mouth and turned away. Shaking her head, she turned back and looked straight at the detective. "How I wish Mother Rosaria had come to the infirmary to recuperate."

"Why is that, Sister?" Kummer asked.

"I might have had more control over what she ate."

"I see."

Sister Mercy's long black habit dignified her short stout figure. Her shrewd eyes behind steel-rimmed glasses promised truthfulness.

She showed the officers the small infirmary kitchen and a large sunny room with three beds that adjoined another empty sickroom. Kummer noticed she didn't call them cells. "Cells" to him meant jail cells. After Flanagan snapped pictures, the trio left.

Back in the library, Kummer asked Flanagan to call Mother Cordelia. "I'm ready to see her now." Kummer had insisted on a private line. He said the community switchboard was no better than a party line, and his investigation might be hampered unless it was carried out in strict privacy.

Flanagan made the call. "Mother is busy." He said as he hung up the receiver. "She'll be here in fifteen minutes." He spoke out of the side of his mouth. "I think you're supposed to get a message from this."

"I know," Kummer grinned. "She feels under attack and her authority threatened. I'll deal with it."

The officers were bent over the floor plans of St. Clotilde's Monastery, tracing out possible routes for the cyanide transfer to the victim's cell, as Mother Cordelia pushed open the door. Her substantial hips and heavy steps on the hardwood floor drowned out the creaking boards.

Kummer stood, adjusting the top button of his sports jacket. He saw a strained furrow below the white starched headband on the superior's face. "I'm sorry we're taking so much of your time today, Mother Cordelia. Please sit down." He circled around the table and pulled out her chair.

The superior held her head stiff and spoke in a stern voice. "You must realize what this investigation is doing to my sisters." She delivered her concern with authority, not as a suggestion.

Both officers heard her breathy intake of air. "Sergeant Flanagan and I realize that," Kummer responded, nodding toward Flanagan, who took a seat at the table where the plans lay.

Mother Cordelia ignored Sergeant Flanagan and continued, "I called Mr. Doyle, our attorney."

"That's very wise," Kummer said in a quiet tone, trying not to agitate her further.

"Mr. Doyle said you do not have access to our academy files. He assured me it was our duty to keep student information confidential. If you wish to see the monastery files, Mr. Doyle wants to be present."

"I respect his counsel and can easily work within those guidelines." Kummer remembered the game she played at their first meeting and knew it would continue. "Did he advise anything else?"

"Only that you should have a legal warrant from the district attorney's office, which you had."

Kummer nodded and waited.

"You'll find my sisters cooperative. I expect you to treat them with the courtesy that the sisters deserve. I don't want them bullied into saying or agreeing to something just because you're a policeman."

"I wouldn't have it any other way, Mother Cordelia." Kummer leaned back in his chair wondering if the superior used these tactics on her community. She wanted the murderer caught politely. This irritated him. Pausing to see if she had finished pontificating, he continued, "I won't take much of your time, but I have to ask you a few questions."

Looking out the window as if to remove herself from the business at hand, she nodded for him to commence. Through rimless bifocals, her icy blue eyes shifted from the circle drive to Flanagan and back to Kummer. Her hands were folded and outside her sleeves.

The detective asked, "Are the Chateau grounds open at night?"

"We've never secured our grounds, Lieutenant. They're accessible from the main gate which is always open as well as the back service drive. Safety has never been an issue at Saint Clotildes."

"Do you remember if there were late visitors or late deliveries the evening of June fifteenth?" Kummer continued, asking nonthreatening questions.

"What time is 'late'?"

"Anytime after five o'clock."

"I don't remember anyone coming that evening," the superior continued, still holding her head stiffly. "Sister Portress can give you a better account as she keeps a log of all visitors and deliveries. Check with her. She stays at the main entrance until seven thirty. At that time the phone is switched to the monastery."

"When did you last talk to the deceased?"

"I saw her the evening before she died, just before Sister Mercy brought her supper tray."

"Were the windows open?"

"I don't think so." Mother lifted her arm to adjust the fold of her sleeve.

"It was a warm evening." Kummer looked at his notes *The Madison Times* reported the temperature at seventy-eight degrees.

"Lieutenant, I suggest you check with Sister Mercy. She was the last one who talked to Mother Rosaria."

"Just a few more questions, Mother." When he addressed her simply as mother, he felt he was stepping on intimate ground. He decided to use her full name hereafter. "Did the deceased have any enemies, Mother Cordelia?"

"None that I know of." She adjusted the other sleeve.

"Someone hated her enough to want her dead. Tell me anything about her that could provide a motive."

"I don't believe she was murdered, Lieutenant." She raised her voice a decibel. "We've never had a burglary here, let alone a murder." Mother Cordelia shuddered. "I think you should investigate a little further regarding her diet and her medicine. It could be she was poisoned by a combination of these."

Kummer cleared his throat. She wants me to believe Mother Rosaria's death was an accident. He glanced at Flanagan, who rolled his eyes upward as if searching for spiritual help.

"Mother Cordelia, before Mother Rosaria's body was exhumed, I consulted Dr. Spence. I asked him about the medicine he prescribed for her heart disease. He told me he prescribed no medicine. None whatsoever," Kummer emphasized. "He also said the best treatment was bed rest. Now, you speak of the medicine she took. Do you know what that was?"

"Lieutenant Kummer, you'll have to ask Sister Mercy. She knows more about her care. Anyway, I wasn't the superior then."

Kummer noticed that her large pores glistened. "What did you talk about with Mother Rosaria on your last visit?"

He heard her hand rustle beneath her sleeves and looked up from his notebook. Feeling like a third grader about to be scolded, he continued, "I don't want to cause you any distress, Mother Cordelia." He spoke her name softly. "What time did you see Mother Rosaria?"

"It was about five forty-five, before our six o'clock supper bell. She wasn't one to talk about her illness. I thought she'd overdone it that afternoon and shouldn't have stayed up so long."

"And what else?" Kummer urged.

"She asked me to talk to Monsignor Burrows about starting the summer scripture series they planned."

"And did you?"

"No, Lieutenant. When she died, everything changed." Mother Cordelia clipped her words with an air of finality.

"Lieutenant Kummer, when will Mother Rosaria's body be returned? The sisters are asking about it."

"We'd like to hold it until the full toxicology report is completed. That should be in about a week. I assure you, the body is protected in a refrigerated room." He didn't mention the habit hanging on the wall. He knew no one at St. Clotildes wanted to imagine the sister's nude corpse on a cart with a toe tag.

"Mother Cordelia, did you know Mother Rosaria received a warning?" He heard her breathing slow.

"Where did you get that information?"

"Please answer my question."

"If she did, I should think Mother Rosaria would have told someone. Did she?"

"Yes, she managed to do that," Kummer said.

"I suppose Sister Camille had something to do with this. She's a suspicious one with a vivid imagination. As Shakespeare said, 'We are such stuff as dreams are made of.'"

Kummer waited. He felt she wasn't finished.

"If you doubt me," she added, "I can show you Dr. Raymond's report. He diagnosed Sister Camille with a paranoid personality disorder."

"I haven't said I doubted you." Kummer waited. He needed a few seconds to digest this information concerning his friend. Showing no reaction, he continued, "Did you attend vespers on Sunday June 15?"

"No, I was visiting my sister in the parlor."

"What time was that?"

"Helen came at two thirty and left just before five."

"Then where did you go?"

"I went to the chapel for meditation."

As if on cue, the bell in the central tower pealed. Kummer checked his watch then glanced at the summer schedule. "That must be the vespers bell now."

Mother Cordelia nodded.

"Did you eat at the first or second table seating the evening of June fifteenth?"

"I was at first table."

The detective decided to terminate the interview. He rose from his chair saying, "Thank you, Mother Cordelia, you've been helpful. I'd like to talk to you again later. I know this business is a trial to you and the sisters, but you'll have to bear with us for a few days."

Mother Cordelia stood. "You can count on my cooperation." She turned toward the door.

Kummer stepped around and put his hand toward her arm to guide her to the door then decided not to. Behind her back, Flanagan's eye caught Kummer's eye. He smoked on an imaginary cigarette drawing his hand out as he puffed.

"One more thing, Mother Cordelia. Is smoking permitted?"

Mother Cordelia turned back, "You may smoke in here and the academy. Should you be walking around the cloister, the sisters would appreciate it if you refrained." She turned and left.

Flanagan jumped up to open the door for her. After it closed, he whispered, "Damn, you've got kid gloves, Hank. I never saw them before." He whipped out a cigarette and lit it.

Kummer rubbed his brow and dug in his pocket for a pipe. "What else did you catch?"

Flanagan shook the flame out. "Who dusted off Mother Rosaria? I don't know what we have here." He rubbed his thumb over his upper lip, picking off a grain of tobacco. "I used to think there were only two motives for murder: love and money, but I don't think either of those will fly here. If Mother Cordelia is innocent, she's putting herself in a bad position by withholding information. Then, she's in a difficult position to start with. Think of the repercussions she'll face when this story breaks."

"I know." Kummer drew several times on his pipe before he was satisfied with it. "That's why the chief expects us to keep on this case over the weekend until it's solved." Then he added, "Yet Mother Cordelia must have some redeeming qualities if she made vows all her life."

"How much time do you think this will take?"

"At this moment, I'd say at least three to four days. I'm concerned about the medicine Mother Cordelia said the deceased took. I want to check the local pharmacies to see if a prescription was written for her. But if we search that information, there's more of a chance the newspapers will get wind of this grisly affair."

Flanagan said, "There's also the possibility Dr. Spence filled the prescription in his office. He could have withheld that information. I also hear Mother Cordelia censoring Mother Rosaria in so many words. You know what I mean?"

14

Sister Mercy entered the library after a timid knock on the door. She sidled in, sat down, grasping the arms of the chair, testing to see if her feet touched the floor. When they didn't, she decided from long practice to let them dangle. The snug-fitting linen guimpe hid her double chins forcing her cheeks to splay out beyond the fabric. She arranged her habit in pleats over her lap. "Lieutenant, I can't tell you how disturbed I am to hear my patient, Mother Rosaria, was poisoned. It just makes me tremble." She rolled her eyes toward the ceiling and blessed herself. Sister shook her head with a quick movement, and the folds on her lap cascaded down, one upon other. Her figure resembled a shapeless bundle, reminding Kummer of the song "Mr. Five by Five."

Kummer responded, "Indeed, crime is always a tragedy, Sister." He estimated she weighed 190 to 200 pounds subtracting the fullness of her dress, and she was somewhere between seventy and eighty years old. Age was hard to determine with her forehead and throat covered.

Ordinary body-language clues were missing. These disciplined women didn't dig their hands into pockets, and they couldn't brush their hands through their hair but usually kept them covered. He couldn't pick up on a clue like rolling or lighting a cigarette. They didn't dig their heels into the floor, slam objects down, or rub their hands down their sides.

"How long have you been the infirmarian, Sister Mercy?"

An angelic smile beamed below the starched headband. Her eyes widened to full moons that expressed an unaffected look of honesty. "This is my seventh year. I count it a special blessing to tend the sick. I feel I'm ministering to the Lord." As she spoke, her bushy salt-and-pepper eyebrows lifted high.

Kummer nodded with a half smile in agreement. "Mother Cordelia said you would be able to tell us if Mother Rosaria was taking medication of any kind."

"She sometimes took quinidine for her heart condition."

"What time did you take Mother Rosaria's tray to her the evening of June fifteenth?"

Sister Mercy held a fist dotted with age spots over her mouth, half in wonder and half in thought. "It was close to six fifteen that evening. I remember because it was later than usual when I took the cart to the kitchen. I had two for supper, Mother Rosaria and Sister Ruth."

"Try to recall the sequence of time when you first took the cart to the kitchen until you took Mother Rosaria's tray to her."

"As I said, I was late because I looked in on Sister Ruth who complained of stomach cramps. Usually, I take the cart to the kitchen at five thirty, right after meditation."

Kummer glanced at the schedule. Meditation 5:00-5:30.

Sister Mercy said, "It was at least five forty-five before I got to the kitchen that evening. First, I checked the supper menu."

"Do you remember the menu?"

"Yes, very clearly. I've been going over it again and again in my mind since Mother died. It was cold cuts, coleslaw, baked beans, and ice cream. Except for the ice cream, it wasn't a healthy menu for a sick person, although Mother Rosaria's diet wasn't restricted." Sister Mercy beamed, impressed with her medical knowledge. Her eyes blinked and looked larger through her nearsighted lenses.

"Who was in the kitchen, Sister?"

"Mrs. Simmons and Sister Camille."

"What were they doing?"

"I saw Sister Camille mixing the slaw. Mrs. Simmons stood at the stove. I remember the platters with cold cuts were already sitting on the refectory serving cart."

"Tell me the exact order of your actions."

"First, I dished up Mother's plate with the regular diet, filled one teapot and one coffeepot from the urn, and set them back on the stove to keep hot. Then I went to the cooler for two eggs and a dish of Jell-O for Sister Ruth and put them on the cart." Sister Mercy stared out of the window in concentration. "Then I picked up the pots from the stove and put them on the cart and left the kitchen. I got back to the infirmary as the six o'clock supper bell rang."

"On your way upstairs, did you leave the cart for any length of time? Perhaps while you were waiting for the elevator?"

"I remember I did have to wait for the elevator. Sister Loyola had come down in her wheelchair for supper. We greeted 'praise Jesus,' and I assisted her out of the elevator and pushed the cart in."

"Then what did you do, Sister?"

"I went directly to the infirmary kitchen. I set the coffeepot on the pilot light and fixed Mother's tray and carried it to her cell. After I got there, I discovered I forgot her coffee. Mother said not to hurry back with it as she liked coffee later with dessert. So I took Sister Ruth her tray and went directly to the refectory to eat my supper."

"What time did you bring the coffee to Mother Rosaria?"

"About forty to forty-five minutes later." Sister Mercy's pudgy hands moved restlessly inside her sleeves. She pulled out a large linen handkerchief.

Kummer saw it was a man's square. "Let's return to the time you were in the kitchen. Could you estimate the time you spent in the cooler?"

Sister Mercy dabbed at her nose then stared out of the window. She bobbed her head as she counted the steps from the kitchen to the cooler and then stopped. "It couldn't have been more than a minute. I dished up a small bowl of Jell-O and picked up two eggs which were handy."

Kummer added "5:58 to the cooler" to his notes.

"When you returned to Mother Rosaria's cell with the coffeepot, do you remember your conversation with her? How did she seem at that point?"

Sister shook her head disapprovingly. "The doctor advised Mother Rosaria to sit up that afternoon because she felt stronger. Mother had visits from the sisters and was very tired. Before I left, she asked me to put the No Visitors sign on the door, as she wanted to retire early."

"And did you?"

"Yes, of course, Lieutenant. Even if she hadn't suggested it, I would have done it. I knew she needed rest."

"So you were the last to see her Sunday evening?"

"Yes." Sister Mercy nodded her head sadly. "Before I left, I pulled the shades down and drew a pitcher of hot water from the bathroom. Then I took her tray back to the infirmary kitchen."

"Was that the small kitchen I saw earlier?"

"Yes, Lieutenant."

"So you left the ice cream and coffeepot in her cell."

"Yes, Lieutenant. Mother Rosaria was still eating, and it was she who suggested I leave them and pick up the dishes in the morning."

"What did Mother Rosaria eat from her tray?"

"She ate everything, Lieutenant."

"Before you left the kitchen with her coffee, did you test it to see if it was still hot? Did you open the lid?"

"No, I knew it was hot. The heat from the pilot light would keep a small pot like that very hot."

"Did Mother Rosaria pour her coffee while you were there?"

"No, Lieutenant, she didn't."

Kummer took a page from his notebook and handed it to Sister Mercy. "This is your timetable as I see it. Look at it carefully, Sister. Do you agree with the estimated times?"

> 5:30 looked in on Sister Ruth. (3 floor)
> 5:45 took cart to main kitchen. (3-1 floor via ele)
> 5:58 went to cooler. (1 floor)
> 6:00 returned cart to infirmary kitchen(1-3 floor)via elevator.
> 6:10 took tray to M. Rosaria. (3-2 floor)
> 6:15 took tray to Sister Ruth. (3 floor)
> 6:20 entered refectory-supper. (1 floor)
> 7:00 took coffee and ice cream to M. Rosaria. (3-2 floor)
> Placed 'No Visitors' sign on the door.

Sister Mercy bent close, adjusting her glasses. She read and reread the timetable, seeming to have difficulty with the list. "It looks about right. Maybe it was a little later by the time I reached Mother Rosaria's cell. Would a few minutes make a difference, Lieutenant Kummer?"

"We'll see. How well did you get along with Mother Rosaria?"

"I thought she was doing a splendid job, Lieutenant. She put the spiritual needs of the community first."

"What do you mean by that, Sister?"

"Mother Rosaria had a high regard for our holy foundress's rules and customs. She tried to revive them. Our order is supposed to be cloistered. That's why this is called a monastery, but when our order was founded in Wisconsin, dispensations had to be given to open a school until the sisters were financially secure."

"How did you feel about that?"

"I have no problem with it, Lieutenant," Sister Mercy answered.

"How do the other sisters feel about this?"

"Well, you know, Lieutenant, it does take some time to get used to new ways."

"Now, tell me about Monday morning."

Sister Mercy continued, "After Holy Mass, I took the cart as usual down to the main kitchen, stopping on the second floor to check on Mother. She didn't answer my knock; I entered and pulled up the shades. There Mother lay. Dead." Sister Mercy shuddered, placing both hands to her eyes as though blocking out what she saw that morning. Her ruddy cheeks paled.

Kummer asked, "Are you all right, Sister? Do you feel up to a few more questions?"

"I'm fine. I'd rather finish this now."

"Why don't you get up and move around a bit?"

"No, I'm all right. Please continue, Lieutenant."

"Very well, Sister. After you found her Monday morning, did it look to you like someone else entered the room after you left the evening before?"

"I couldn't see that anyone had, Lieutenant."

"Sister, how did you know she was dead?"

"Her eyes were opened and glazed. Her head was twisted toward the door as if pleading for help. It would have been an uncomfortable position for sleeping. I immediately felt her cold hand. She had no pulse."

"Sister, did you notice anything else? Maybe an odor?"

"Not that I can remember. I was too shocked."

"Did Mother Rosaria drink all her coffee?"

"About half remained in her cup, and a half was in the pot. The individual pots hold a cup and a half."

"What did you do with the pot?"

"I dumped the coffee down the sink and washed the pot later with the other dishes in the infirmary."

Kummer scanned his notes and then turned toward Flanagan. "Sergeant, do you have any questions for Sister Mercy?"

Flanagan asked, "Did you detect any bitter odor from Mother Rosaria's body?"

"No, Sergeant."

"Or from the coffee cup or pot as you handled them?"

"Again, I didn't." Sister Mercy looked disappointed that she couldn't be more helpful.

A bell from the tower rang three short peals. Sister Mercy slid down of her chair and announced, "It's the Angelus."

Both officers looked at her, and at each other. Kummer, then Flanagan, stood up with her.

With her eyes closed and head bowed in her clasped hands, Sister Mercy intoned, "The angel of the Lord declared unto Mary . . ." She waited for the officers to respond. When they didn't, she answered their response then continued. "Hail Mary, full of grace . . ."

This time the officers answered, "Holy Mary, mother of God, pray for us sinners, now and at the hour of our death."

Sister Mercy continued the prayer in a singsong voice. After she came to "And the Word was made flesh, and dwelt amongst us," she genuflected. The officers followed her example. Their chairs scraped the waxed hardwood floor, bumping into nearby chairs, while Sister Mercy knelt with poise without making a sound. Oblivious to the commotion, she continued, "Hail Mary, full of grace . . ." At the amen, Sister Mercy resumed her seat. "Isn't that a beautiful prayer?" Her eyes glistened.

Kummer walked around the table and opened the door. "Thank you, Sister. You've been a great help."

Just as she had sat down, Sister eased off her chair with little effort. "I'm glad to help in any way. May the good Lord reward you, Officers." She seemed to glide out the door.

After the door closed, Flanagan snapped his notebook shut and whistled through his teeth. "Cripes, Lieutenant, I haven't prayed the Angelus since fifth grade! I think I just flunked." Then he began to sing, "Who put the poison in Rosaria's coffee?" to the tune, "Who Put the Overalls in Mrs. Murphy's Chowder?"

Kummer nodded. "The coffee is a lead, but what's the motive?"

Flanagan responded, "You got me there. Hell, I thought Mother Rosaria was one of those dames who got to the top by any means possible. Working this case in the monastery is a complete reversal from the last one. There, I had to hang around the riverfront and drink whiskey with the boys, hoping for a lead. I kind of miss that case."

"We're not finished yet. Let's break for supper. I'm coming back afterward to see Sister Camille. You won't have to return. Drop the evidence bags off at the station on your way home, and I'll meet you here at nine o'clock tomorrow. We'll test out all the typewriters before continuing the interviews."

A knock at the door prompted Flanagan to open it.

Sister Dorothy entered. "Would you like to have a supper tray brought here?"

"No thanks, Sister Dorothy, we're going out to eat," Kummer answered.

After she left, Flanagan put his hand over his mouth. "Geez, I'm not eating here."

15

Detective Kummer turned on the Philco radio that sat atop a file in the library. He wanted to catch part of the Cardinal's baseball game, knowing he'd miss hearing the rest of it. Earlier that evening, he had called the chief and given him an account of the day's activity.

"From Sportsman's Park in Saint Louis," Red Barber announced, "Musial at bat—There goes a wicked drive down the right-field line, just fair by a few feet . . . and it bounces into the stands, for a ground rule double. 'Stan the Man' keeps on delivering."

"Marion steps up to the plate . . . He swings and tops the ball over the pitcher's head and into center field. Musial goes to third on the play."

The fans exploded.

A knock at the door interrupted the game action. Kummer opened it to Sister Camille. Smiling, he held out both hands to his old neighbor. It was a full smile that showed his teeth below his trimmed mustache, rather than his half smile that needed coaxing. "Come sit down. I'll turn off the radio."

"No, don't. I don't mind if it's on."

Kummer held up a finger as the announcer sang out, "The inning's over. At the end of the third, Cardinals three, Dodgers zero."

Kummer signaled thumbs-up and switched it off.

"It's been a long time since I've kept up with baseball," said Sister Camille. "We don't listen to the radio or watch television unless it's an educational program like Leonard Bernstein's *The Young People's Concerts* or Bishop Sheen. Do you think the Cards have a chance at the world series?"

"I don't know. It's going to be hard to beat the Yankees. They have a team that won't quit, especially with the new rookie, Mickey Mantle." Kummer looked at his watch. "Much as I'd like to chat about baseball, Sister, I'm afraid we need to talk about this case."

Sister Camille sat down. Her almond-shaped blue eyes focused anxiously on him. "I took a big chance to call you last week. Do you realize how much it means to me that you're here? I still have to pinch myself every time I think about this investigation going on."

"I had you pegged all wrong, Sister, and I apologize for my cavalier attitude."

"I suppose it's too early to find out what you've learned. I still want to help you in the investigation, if I can."

"And you possibly can, Sister. But first, how has it been going for you since the community learned about the murder?"

"After I called you, Hank, I couldn't sleep or eat. My stomach hurt so bad, and I was so scared." Her hand automatically touched her stomach, hidden under the folds of the serge habit. "I thought many times I should have forgotten about my suspicion. Who was I to start an investigation? It would have been so much easier to let it drop. It felt like I was bucking a concrete wall and couldn't go forward or backward, like there was no way out.

"Mother Cordelia, our new superior found out I phoned you without her permission. She called me and ordered me to see Dr. Raymond, a psychologist." Sister Camille ran her finger along the lower edge of her constricting headband, massaging the skin gently.

Kummer noticed the red line on her forehead and waited for her to continue.

"Not all the sisters know about the murder yet," she said. "Mother Cordelia will try to keep it hushed as much as possible. I wouldn't even know you were here if I hadn't seen you in the kitchen after lunch. And when the sisters do find out, they won't even talk about it. It'll be a hush, hush subject." Sister Camille said, "I thank God you're here, Hank. Now I have hope." She heaved a long sigh.

"You've been very brave, Sister. How do you feel about going to Dr. Raymond?"

"I think he's on Mother Cordelia's side. Can you imagine, he wanted to send me to a hospital for treatment? He gave me a choice, either go to a sanitarium or weekly sessions."

"You're still seeing Dr. Raymond then?"

"It's automatic, Hank, once a person starts with him. I'll see him tomorrow and tell him about the autopsy results, that I was right about my suspicion. He may have a different opinion of me then."

The detective didn't want to prod but could imagine how a psychologist dealt with a patient who suspected a murder in a monastery. His compassionate eyes held Sister Camille. He searched her strained expression. Did her family have any idea what was happening? Should he call them? How could he give her more support? He wanted to take her hand, to encourage her. Instead, Kummer got up and moved around the table to a chair next to her.

Sister Camille asked, "Tell me about the samples I collected, Hank. Did they help you or is that classified information?"

"On the contrary, I want to congratulate you on your careful handling of the specimens and especially the postcard. We're able to get some prints from it. Most are smudged, but there's one good partial. It may be significant, but we don't know yet. You did a lot of work. Some of it was negligible." He didn't want to tell her that most of it was. "You're a good detective, Sister." He smiled and then turned serious, tapping the eraser end of his pencil on the table.

Sister Camille rubbed her brow, again trying to ease the irritation from the headband then folded her hands in her lap.

The detective began, "The autopsy revealed that cyanide killed Mother Rosaria. I have reason to believe it was put into the food on her supper tray. You were in the kitchen that evening, and you have above-average insight. Tell me, how do you get along with the cooks? Describe them."

"I enjoy working with them. Miss. Drekel is a spinster, a shy type who's afraid to change anything from the usual way. Sometimes I like to vary Sister Martha's recipe preparation. For instance, last Tuesday the menu was spareribs and sauerkraut. Miss. Drekel wanted to bake the ribs in the oven and cook the sauerkraut and potatoes separately on top of the stove. I wanted her to cook the meal the way my mother made it with the ribs, sauerkraut, and potatoes all in one big kettle on top of the stove."

Kummer said, "That's one of my favorites."

"Well, Miss. Drekel asked, 'But will the sisters like it that way?' I'm sure she talked to Sister Martha about it after I left the kitchen. Aside from that, she wouldn't harm anybody."

"It's easy to get sidetracked just talking about food." He looked at his notes. "How long has Miss. Drekel worked here?"

"She's been here a long time, Hank, before I entered St. Clotildes. I've been here five and a half years."

"Who hires the lay staff?"

"The procuratrix, Sister Dorothy. She interviews applicants, but the superior makes the final choice."

"Which mother superior hired Miss. Drekel?"

"Mother Cordelia."

"And which superior hired Mrs. Simmons?"

"That would also be Mother Cordelia. She's been elected superior three times in the past twenty years."

"How long has Mrs. Simmons been employed?"

"Not as long, Hank. About a year and a half."

"How do you find Mrs. Simmons?"

"Of the two cooks, Mrs. Simmons is the friendliest. She's efficient, and I think she likes to work with me and try new recipes."

The detective continued, "Mr. Simmons is the plant engineer. What does he do in the summer? There isn't a need to stoke the boiler?"

"I've heard Mrs. Simmons say, I call her Zelda, he has so much work to do. He has to break down the boiler and overhaul it for winter."

"Was he hired at the same time as Mrs. Simmons?"

"I think so. But he was let go about a month ago by Mother Rosaria and then rehired the same day Mother Cordelia was elected superior."

"Why was he fired, Sister?"

"Mr. Simmons had a drinking problem."

"How long was he off?"

"Probably two or three weeks. Sister Dorothy would know the exact dates."

Hank made a note to ask Sister Dorothy. "Do you know where the Simmons worked before coming here?"

"Mrs. Simmons often talks about working in a nursing home outside of Chicago. I think Mr. Simmons worked there too."

"Has Mrs. Simmons mentioned the name of the nursing home?"

"She talks about it a lot, calls it Sinai Manor."

Kummer leaned back on his chair. Again, he tapped his pencil. "Now, back to the evening of June fifteenth at the time you were in the kitchen. Do you remember if Sister Mercy or you were out of the kitchen proper at any time that Sunday evening?"

Sister Camille looked at the ceiling. "We were both in the cooler at the same time. I remember she picked up eggs. I went in for mayonnaise."

"And did any other sisters come through the kitchen while you were there?"

"Sister Eugene went to the cooler with some strawberries around five o'clock. Later, she returned to the cooler to get them before she ate at second table."

"Did you see her go any other place in the kitchen those two times? Maybe near the stove or steam table where food was prepared?"

"No, Hank, not unless she did it when I went to the pantry."

"This afternoon Sister Dorothy showed us the small dining room opposite the cooler for the men who work regularly at the Chateau. Do you remember who ate there that night?"

"Mr. Simmons ate there alone that Sunday night as he often does, waiting for Zelda to finish up in the kitchen. The other workmen have weekends off."

"Sister, if you see any unusual behavior, anything out of the ordinary, let me know. Also I want to warn you not to mention to anyone that we've talked tonight. I gather you've kept this quiet from the beginning."

"Oh yes, Hank."

"Let me know if you feel any danger. You have my home phone number." He smiled. "It's unfortunate that it has taken a crime to bring us together."

After the tower bell pealed, Kummer glanced at the monastery schedule then at his watch. "Am I keeping you from anything?"

"I'm excused from matins and lauds if you need me."

"If I keep you too long, just say so." Kummer enjoyed watching her, remembering how skeptical he was at their first meeting. At that time, he dismissed her suspicions, thinking she lived too isolated from the world. Now, he noticed the glow of her creamy complexion, without any makeup, and wondered why she chose the sisterhood. Why hadn't she been snatched by some Casanova? The nuns, where she went to school, must have had a strong influence on their girls to enter the sisterhood. Did she date? Go to a senior prom? He wanted to inquire but respected her position.

Sister Camille said, "You have to understand; it's a huge relief just to talk to you, Hank. I've kept so much pent up. Only Sister Angelica, Mother Rosaria's niece, and I ever discuss what's happened. She was the one who found the holy card of Saint Rose of Lima in the calendar."

Hank nodded. "I haven't asked you yet; who do you think were Mother Rosaria's enemies? Someone here wanted her out of the way. If she continued in her office as the mother superior, it prevented that someone's particular plan, or maybe that person feared damaging information would be publicized. It's the motive that puzzles me."

Sister Camille thought a moment then suggested. "Some of the sisters were dissatisfied with her as a superior. Mother Rosaria always said the religious spirit should be forgiving and noncontrolling. She felt the sisters could use their good sense to make decisions instead of always running to her to be told what to do. All I can think is someone took advantage of Mother Rosaria's ill health at just the right moment."

"If it hadn't been for you, that someone may have pulled off the perfect murder."

"I remember the day she had the heart attack. I worried then, what if her medicine was withheld, or she was given the wrong medicine? And when I heard two sisters whisper outside of Mother Rosaria's cell, 'It only takes a few minutes,' I had to hold myself back from going into Mother's cell to check her. I wish I had, even though the No Visitors sign was on her door."

"Did you recognize the sisters' voices?"

"They were Sister Cordelia and Sister Eugene."

Kummer made further notes. "And what would be their motive?"

"Well, since Mother Rosaria was elected, they weren't getting the privileges they were accustomed to. And they didn't approve of the changes she's made."

"What privileges?"

"Mother Cordelia had been superior so many times; I think she felt she was the only one who could run St. Clotildes and the Chateau. She excused certain sisters, her favorites, from the rules of the monastery. Then there was that incident near graduation. Both Sister Cordelia and Sister Eugene wanted a student expelled because she was pregnant. Mother Rosaria went against their wishes and allowed the student to graduate."

"Could you give me more detail?" Kummer urged.

"This involved Susan Le Clair, a Chateau senior who invited her classmate, Leslie Allen, to her home over the Memorial Day weekend. Leslie got sick there. The doctor examined her. He told Susan's mother, Madge, that Leslie was pregnant. Madge, who was also a Chateau graduate, wanted Leslie expelled immediately. That was two weeks before graduation."

"I see. You think that's a motive for murder?"

"I don't know. Things add up."

Kummer looked at his watch. "Well, if you're supposed to be in bed by ten, I better let you go."

Sister Camille rose from the chair. "I'm so happy to meet you again, Hank. Call me in any time."

Hank escorted her into the hall. He watched her as she walked down the dark hall and disappeared through the cloister door.

Returning to the table, he picked up the box of Mother Rosaria's personal effects that Sister Dorothy had delivered earlier. What would he find from someone who had made the vow of poverty?

From the box, he pulled out a daily missal, the New Testament, a few meditation books, *The Imitation of Christ*, and a biography of St. Rose of Lima.

He flipped through the books, looking at holy pictures, and set them aside. A small metal box contained two wrapped mints. Opening a writing case, he pulled out a black Esterbrook fountain pen, a tablet of stationery with five envelops, two three-cent stamps, and two letters. One was from Cecilia Moorhouse and one from Madge Le Clair.

He opened Madge Le Clair's letter:

674 Euclid Avenue Dubuque, Iowa
June 14, 1952
Dear Mother Rosaria:

Yesterday my daughter Susan graduated from the Chateau. Twenty-one years ago I also graduated. It was an honor to be counted an Alumna because the Chateau was an outstanding school then.

How could you graduate that perverted student, Leslie Allen? I want you to know that I will not be sending my younger daughter, Joan, to the Chateau.

Madge LeClair, '21.

Kummer tucked the letter into his pocket and glanced at the other letter. It was of a friendly nature and not pertinent to the case. He checked his notebook, rolled up the blueprints, and left.

As he walked down the front entrance steps, he heard the rasp of the lock behind him. Someone he hadn't seen was waiting for him to leave. Would that person have listened at the library door during the past hour?

A full moon glimmered through the elms. Branches cast shadows that looked like monstrous hands grabbing then releasing a hold on his car.

He looked back as he drove out of the circle. All was dark except one light that burned in Mother Cordelia's office.

16

H ank Kummer drove into his driveway on Chestnut Street at ten thirty-two. The car lights flashed across the darkened house where his faithful, though impatient, friend, Mops, waited. The eight-year-old mottled gray cat recognized the sound of his car as it rounded the corner. By instinct, it began to stretch on the porch steps. This was the pose that met Kummer as he got out of the car. He bent down to stroke the cat, who trotted toward him leaning against his leg to claim his property. "Poor Mops, you have a hard life. Supper's on the way."

After feeding the cat and opening up his hot, stuffy house, Kummer sat in his favorite chair. He kicked off his shoes in front of the new television with a cold bottle of Schlitz in hand and a Chicken Delite on his lap. The expanding dot on the screen enlarged into the commercial, "Winstons taste good like a cigarette should." Having missed the baseball game he planned to catch the scores in the mornings paper.

The phone rang. His chief's abrupt words crackled in Hank's ear. "I'm calling a halt to the Chateau investigation. His Excellency, Archbishop Millard called me. He asked us to hold off until he can talk to the sisters. Mother Cordelia's outraged. She told him that your interrogations have upset the sisters. His Eminence will be in Stone Hill for confirmation Sunday."

"Sunday!" Kummer shouted. "This is only Tuesday. We'd have this wrapped up by then."

"Sorry, Hank, I've decided to grant His Eminence's request. Put the case on hold until I talk to him. How late did you work tonight?"

"Just got in." Kummer calmed down. He felt helpless, knowing his argument to continue the investigation was like throwing a baseball against a concrete wall. "You don't happen to know who won the Cardinal-Dodgers game?"

"Sorry again, Hank. The Dodgers won. See you in the morning." Click.

* * *

Kummer sat in the chief's office the following morning, his chair tilted against the wall, tie loosened, and straw fedora shoved back on his head. He flipped pages of his notebook and mulled over the equation—cyanide plus coffee equals murder—while waiting for the chief.

Flanagan, with shirtsleeves rolled high, leaned against a file lighting a cigar. A cloud of smoke settled between the two detectives as the chief entered. Chief Haskell snapped papers against his thigh. It was his habit to snap whatever he had in his hand. His subordinates were used to it. If their chief did it to show impatience, it was wasted on them.

"Archbishop Millard was plenty upset with Mother Cordelia's call. What were you doing? Roughing up the sisters?" The chief slammed the door and sat at his desk. "For God's sake, open the window."

"Naw, Chief." Flanagan stepped toward the window, forcing it wide. "Ya' shoulda' seen Kummer. Hell, he was so gentle you'd a thought he was talking to his mother; so polite was he."

Kummer said, "Mother Cordelia felt we were infringing on her territorial rights. She acted like a mother hen protecting her chicks."

"Especially when we went into the monastery side of the buildings," Flanagan added. "Christ, we even prayed with them. There's so many friggin' bells ringing; ya' can't help get the spirit. Hell, the archbishop didn't get a right picture at all."

The chief asked, "What's your make on Mother Cordelia?"

Kummer answered, "She's used to being in charge but plays the game rules against her better judgment."

Flanagan added, "She favors those sisters who put out for her. Seems she thinks for them and makes their decisions."

Kummer tilted his chair down to the floor, ready to state facts. "Maybe we moved in on them too fast, but what we've gotten so far on the poisoning is substantial."

"Okay." Chief Haskell tempered his pitch. "What have you got?"

"We've done the usual investigative route. I believe the cyanide was carried from the kitchen to the deceased on her supper tray. Most likely in the coffee, which was served along with a dish of ice cream about forty minutes after the deceased's supper. The deceased was okay after the main course according to Sister Mercy, the infirmarian, who saw her last."

"Besides Sister Mercy, who had opportunity?" Haskell asked.

"Mother Cordelia," Kummer emphasized. "She didn't attend the four-thirty vespers that afternoon, and she visited the deceased before supper; Sister Eugene, the directress, who walked through the kitchen to put some berries in the cooler; Sister Camille, who assists in the kitchen at meal times; Mrs. Simmons, one of the cooks who worked the ten-to-six shift; and her husband, Joe Simmons, the plant engineer, who ate in the workmen's dining room that evening." Kummer glanced up from his notes. "You remember it was Sister Camille who contacted me last week? She suspected the deceased died from unnatural causes."

"That leaves her out."

Kummer said, "It may be one of the sisters didn't actually put the poison in the coffeepot but may have asked someone to do it for them."

"You say 'them'?" the chief asked.

"It's possible Mother Cordelia was in cahoots with Sister Eugene," Kummer suggested.

"The world is full of religious people who have been known to murder," the chief said with no emotion.

"And I don't discount the Simmons couple. They came to Stone Hill a year and a half ago from Chicago where they worked in a nursing home."

"Did you talk to them yet?"

"Just introduced to Mrs. Simmons. She seemed a chatty sort. I planned to question her next."

"You're finished with the sisters?"

"Not quite. I'd still like to talk to the directress, Sister Eugene."

"I told the archbishop we could keep this out of the newspapers if there were no delays. Now, it's no longer our responsibility. I see no reason why we can't follow up on the Simmons couple. Contact the nursing home and check Cook County court records." The chief continued, "Have you talked to Mother Cordelia yet?"

"Yes."

"What have you got on her?"

"She's cooperative to a point. Any help has been reluctant."

Flanagan jumped in, "Mother Cordelia denies the deceased was murdered. She thinks the death was due to natural causes."

"How does she think the deceased died?" Chief Haskell countered.

"She believes it was a reaction to a combination of her medicine and diet."

"You checked with Dr. Spence?"

"Before the body was exhumed," Kummer explained, "Dr. Spence said he prescribed no medicine at the time of the deceased's heart attack."

Flanagan added, "I know Doc fills prescription in his office. He gave medicine to my wife when she was pregnant with number three."

"We can check local pharmacies for other prescriptions. Maybe, she had a prescription written by another doctor," Kummer suggested.

"Motive?" Chief Haskell spat out, not moving a muscle.

"None so far. I don't buy Sister Camille's theory. She says the deceased played a straight hand. That she treated all the sisters equally. Some were accustomed to the former superior, Mother Cordelia, who had been elected the superior three times before. She favored some of the sisters, excused them from religious practices, and allowed special diets. Hardly a motive for murder."

Kummer said, "But we have to realize these sisters spend their entire lives together. Every moment of their day is prescribed for prayer, work, and whatever they do. They're rubbing elbows until they go to bed. It's an unnatural life. Who knows what could tip one of them off? Flanagan, help me out. What am I trying to say? You have an aunt who is a sister."

"Geez, it sounds like jail time, or maybe the army with a lot of praying and chanting. The only difference is they go into it by choice. From what I heard, the sisters at St. Clotildes never leave the monastery for a vacation or a visit with their families. These celibate nuns are cooped up so long; who knows what could ferment? There's no relief from the tension from all this togetherness. This kind of secluded life could lead an emotional person to lose control."

"It's hard to imagine what goes on behind that peaceful facade. Maybe it was payback time," Chief Haskell retorted. Have either of you thought of suicide?"

"No," Kummer said.

"Me either," Flanagan joined in. "From what I heard, she was upbeat."

The chief said, "The sisters bring a dowry to the community when they join up."

"Oh yeah, I remember my aunt Margaret had to bring a dowry, a thousand bucks. She joined the Benedictines," Flanagan said. "That custom goes back to the old country. A bride has to bring money or property to a marriage."

"Still do in some countries," Kummer added.

The chief said, "Find out who profits from the dowries after a sister dies. Then add the pharmacies and bank records of the Simmons couple to the checklist." Haskell pushed his chair back and left. He called back from the opened door. "We'll keep on this, but stay away from the Chateau!" The glass panel rattled as the door slammed.

Flanagan dumped the ash from his cigarette into a chipped ashtray. "With due respect, His Eminence doesn't know beans."

Kummer started for the door. "Come along to the property room. We'll check the medicines Sister Camille turned in."

From a brown envelope marked Evidence, Kummer pulled out a bottle of quinidine dated February 4, 1950. Dr. Spence had prescribed it for arrhythmia. Foster Drugs dispensed it. The Bayer Aspirin came from Hahn's Drugs.

"Start with these, then contact Sinai Nursing Home. I'll talk to Dr. Spence again to see if he prescribed medicine at another time and call Cook County to see what they have on the Simmons couple."

After lunch, Flanagan entered Kummer's office and flipped his hat into the mail basket on top of the file. It landed "nothing but net."

Kummer hung up the phone. "Bet you can't do that twice." His half smile spurred Flanagan to exit the door and reenter to repeat his basket throw. This time, he missed. It banked off the side and landed on the floor. After he stretched to retrieve it, Flanagan straddled a chair.

"You've had success." Kummer leaned back in his swivel chair, appreciating Flanagan's theatrical prowess as a way of saying he was on to something.

"Yep. Joe Simmons and wife, Zelda Simmons, have brief work histories in their last three jobs. Before coming to the Chateau, they worked fifteen months, from May 16, 1949, to October 2, 1950, at Mount Sinai Manor in Austin, Illinois. Joe was fired for absenteeism, drinking on the job, and suspicion of petty theft. Wife, Zelda, quit after Joe was fired. Personnel at the hospital didn't have anything on her, said she was a good employee."

"What kind of work did she do?"

"Started as nurse's aide then transferred to the kitchen as cook's assistant."

Flanagan said, "Not much in their accounts, nine hundred and forty-three dollars transferred from their Austin account to First National in Stonehill."

"Checked on the sisters' accounts. They made sound blue-chip investments. Then I called my aunt Margaret, the Benedictine in Chicago. She said dowries go into the general account of the community. If a sister leaves the order, the dowry is returned to her with interest. After a sister dies, the dowry goes into the community fund. What'd you get?"

Kummer leaned back in his chair and dug in his pocket for his pipe. "Joe's been busy. Cook County returned my call a few minutes ago. Seems Joe stole a 1950 Merc and spent six months as their guest. Cook County will send a full report." Kummer studied the notes he'd written. "Before that he was hired as a wiper on a freighter that made regular runs from Puerto Rico to Florida, Mobile, and Galveston. Fired for drunkenness on the job. He hired out on another line until word got around, and he couldn't get a job. That was from 1938 to 1942."

"Yeah, he had opportunity, eating in the dining room so close to the kitchen. But what the hell's his motive?"

"If we knew that, the investigation would be over. Could be the deceased stood in the way of something the murderer wanted. Motives are unpredictable." Kummer stared out the window. "But I'm thinking of a way we can keep on this and . . .," he leaned toward Flanagan, "be at the Chateau."

"Whatcha' sayin', Hank? You heard the chief!" Flanagan spat his response.

"I'm not talking about going through the front door of the Chateau, nor questioning any of the sisters."

"You going there against orders? How you plan to do this?"

"In-cog-ni-to, Flanagan," Kummer whispered, keeping a steady eye on his partner. Silence followed like when baseball fans wait for an outfielder to catch a high fly.

Kummer continued, "Anyone dressed as a poor man can go there and for a meal as well. We can nose around and keep an eye on Sister Camille." Kummer looked at his watch. "We're too late for today, but we can be there at ten tomorrow to get work assignments from Sister Laura. Are you game?"

"Cripes, I'm all ears. I'll bring old clothes in the car and meet you here at nine thirty."

"We'll park a distance from the Chateau."

"Or we could use my mud-spattered '45 Chevy," Flanagan suggested. "It won't attract as much attention as that lady catcher of yours."

"Sounds good."

17

"Good morning, Sister Camille. How was your week?" Dr. Raymond said after he opened the door to his waiting room. "You're smiling today."

Sister Camille nodded. "Yes, indeed, Doctor." She followed him into his office and accepted the leather chair as if she'd sat there numerous times before. "Since I saw you, the police started investigating Mother Rosaria's death. They spent all yesterday afternoon at the Chateau and—." She watched him open her file, reading what he'd written before. He didn't look up but kept his eyes focused on her record. Sister waited until she had the psychologist's full attention.

"And," Sister Camille said in a low voice. "Mother Rosaria was poisoned, just as I suspected." Raising her voice. "My suspicion was the reason Mother Cordelia sent me to you." She emphasized her words in a rah-rah, breathless fashion, like I told you so.

Dr. Raymond's dark eyebrows shot up. He gave her his full attention. "How do you know she was poisoned?"

"Her body was exhumed Wednesday. The pathologist who performed the autopsy found cyanide in her tissues."

"Who told you that?" the doctor asked, resuming a professional, dull voice.

"Lieutenant Kummer. Everybody knows it now."

"You sound very pleased with yourself. Are you glad Mother Rosaria died?"

"Of course not," Sister Camille snapped, her expression turning serious. How could he say that? "She was my model, a leader who could turn our community around. Mother Rosaria had a love for God and a love for the sisters. She urged scripture reading instead of writers who preached punishment and hellfire. Mother Rosaria didn't feel the monastery was a haven for the lovelorn and didn't reward tattlers with favors. She once said, 'Humor is like a soft, cleansing wind that sweeps through a room.'" Sister Camille realized she had delivered a wallop of theology and wondered if the doctor could take it all in.

"Tell me, how will you be treated by the sisters now?"

"I faced that before I called Lieutenant Kummer. It won't be easy, but maybe it will be for the good of the community. A petty spirit seethes through our community. A hierarchy of attitudes. No, that's not the right word. It's cliques."

"I'm glad to hear this investigation regarding Mother Rosaria has been ordered. What I'd like to do, if it's all right with you, is talk a bit about your life in the monastery. If I know more about you, it's going to help me understand your attitude toward this issue. Would you like to talk about becoming a sister?"

"It's all right."

"You're a reverend sister now. What made you decide to go into the monastery?"

"I went to school to the sisters who taught in Richfield, Wisconsin. They always seemed happy. I was comfortable around them and liked to visit them at their convent. My girlfriend and I used to look at their clothesline. There were so many odd-shaped pieces hanging on it. We tried to figure out which pieces were underwear."

"How long did you go to the convent school?"

"All the way, from first grade through high school."

"That's interesting. Please continue."

"I also wanted to be a music teacher," Sister Camille added. "I had earned a certificate in piano from the Richfield Academy of Music and wanted to continue my studies. I knew if I entered this order, I'd go to college and get a music degree."

"Did the sisters talk to you about becoming a nun?"

"Not that much. They never tried to grab me. In fact, Sister Justinia said, 'Not you?' I guess she didn't think I was the type."

"How old were you when you entered the order?"

"I was eighteen. I graduated in June and went the following September."

"Did you plan to stay with the sisters after your education?"

"Oh yes. I was determined."

"As a nun, you can't get married. Did you ever think of marriage?"

"No, I never thought I was giving up much by not getting married. I had a younger sister to help take care of. Having children didn't seem that big a deal. I had a lot of work at home. Getting married would be more of that. I went to dances but didn't do any serious dating because the boys my age were off to the war or were 4F. We girls had to dance together."

The doctor started to write.

"One thing I missed was the whole scene after the war, the boys coming back, the new cars, the big bands reuniting and playing for dances. I loved to dance."

Dr. Raymond looked up and continued to write. "How does it make you feel that you can't dance anymore?"

"I knew that. We lived in a farming community where everyone worked very hard. I knew if I were a farmer's wife, I'd be in for a lot of hard work. I wanted to do something different, something noble like giving myself to God."

"You cared for your sister. Didn't you think you'd make a good mother?"

"I wasn't that interested. Besides, my parents never encouraged me to think about marriage and having babies. Up to that time, I never met anyone I cared about. After graduation from high school, I spent the summer volunteering at an interracial center in Chicago. Another volunteer, who was a male nurse, let me know he cared for me. I knew he was interested in marriage, but the sisters at St. Clotildes had already accepted my application. My plans were moving ahead," she said. "I've questioned myself since. Maybe I should have delayed my entrance a year to at least experience a close friendship."

"You didn't want to try that?"

"No. I felt responsible for my decision. Maybe if someone had encouraged me. My family and I were locked into the idea of my entering the monastery. I didn't feel postponing my entrance was the right thing to do."

"So you made up your mind to go there?"

"It seemed like the easiest thing to do. Richfield was a small town with the church as its center of activity. The Franciscan sisters taught us for twelve years. The sisters and the church were the life of the community."

"You thought you could easily make it in religious life?"

"I knew I could. I enjoyed teaching and knew my subject well. I knew I could do a good job."

"Who did you talk to about entering the monastery?"

"I talked to a priest at the interracial center in Chicago who encouraged me."

"Did you tell him why you wanted to go to the monastery?"

"Yes, Father Paulson encouraged me to visit St. Clotildes to see how I liked it. I did and found the sisters busy with their professional assignments and spiritual activities. The spacious grounds and location of the Chateau, that's the academy, looked very inviting, though I did have second thoughts when Mother Cordelia asked me if I wanted to join them."

"Did the visit help you to make up your mind?"

"It did. Also, I admired Father Paulson and realized I'd be living a similar kind of life to his, to teach and do good work like he did."

"What did you tell Mother Cordelia?"

"I told her I'd like to join the sisters at the Chateau but then I was scared."

"Did you tell the superior why you were scared?"

"No."

"Do you think the superior might have held you back from entering if she knew this?"

"It's possible."

"How were you received when you came to the Chateau?"

"The sisters welcomed me as a postulant. They needed younger members and a music teacher on their staff. My novice mistress was a dear. I got along fine with her. She was in her seventies and loved to tell jokes. Sister was different from novice mistresses you hear about who are so stern."

"Tell me something about the process of preparing to be a sister," Dr. Raymond said. "I'm not a Catholic, so I don't have any background. Please continue."

"Well, a girl is first received as a postulant for six months. During this time, the community observes her. The aspirant, that's another term for a postulant, studies the rules and spirit of the order. When the time is completed and the community accepts her, the postulant is invested in the holy habit of the order and the white veil. This is the habit." Sister Camille pulled a fold in her robe forward.

Dr. Raymond nodded as though he knew the vocabulary. "Tell me about your duties when you entered the convent."

"In the beginning, I prepared the refectory, our dining room, for meals. This meant putting bread, butter, milk, water, cream on the tables before mealtimes and cleaning up afterward. I also took piano lessons, and I had a practice time each day."

"How did you feel about working in the refectory?"

"I didn't care for it very much, but I knew it wouldn't last forever."

"Did you tell the superior you didn't like it?"

"No, I offered it up to God."

"You mean you never expressed your feelings about anything?"

"No."

"How did you happen to take piano lessons?"

"I thought my dad left extra money besides the dowry for that. He must have felt I'd need that outlet."

"Did he give you the money?"

"I never saw it. I had no need to."

"So your parents couldn't give you any money in the monastery?"

"No."

"Was all the money used for your lessons? Was there any left?"

"I don't know."

"What else did you do?"

"I attended the spiritual exercises, read spiritual books, and participated in the recitation of the divine office."

"It seems Mother Superior makes all your decisions for you."

"That's right. Some of the early spiritual writers call it surrendering your will to God, a step in achieving a close spiritual union with God."

"Tell me about your vows and your training for them. What was the next step?"

"The canonical year came next. That's when I received the white veil and a new name."

Dr. Raymond interrupted, "Why a new name? Didn't you have a Christian name?"

"My baptismal name was Magdalena, same as my grandma's. A new name is a step in one's dedication to God, like casting off the old life for a new one with a new name."

"Tell me about your vows."

"I never think of the vows as separate categories. To me the vows of poverty, chastity, and obedience are like one package. All our basic needs, clothing, food, and shelter, are provided. The vow of poverty requires us to accept patched clothing used by another sister. Gifts from our family and friends are handed in to the superior to dispose of as she wishes. We never want for anything. Often at evening recreation, a box of Fanny Mae or See's chocolates is passed around that was a gift to a sister."

"What if you went on vacation?"

"We never go on vacation."

"What if you go out shopping, and the superior gives you money?"

"We never go shopping. The order at St. Clotildes is enclosed. That's why it's called a monastery."

"What if someone mails you money?"

"I would hand it over to the mother superior. Besides, she'd know. She opens all the mail and reads it before it's given out to the sisters. We know what time the mail comes and try not to disturb her then, so she can get this done, and we get our mail."

"Interesting," the psychologist mumbled.

Sister Camille explained, "This detaches a sister from the world. It frees her to dedicate her life to God. It sounds harsh, but religious have been doing it for centuries, since the Council of Trent in 1530."

"What if you need shoes?"

"We order them by mail. We pick a style from the catalog, draw an outline of the foot, and send it to the shoe catalogue company." Sister Camille looked down at her oxfords. "These are very comfortable. We only leave the cloister for education and medical needs."

"What does the vow of obedience mean to you?"

"Obedience means following the rules and constitution of our holy foundress and accepting assignments from the superior."

"Can you ask for a preference?"

"I never have. I'm always listed as a piano teacher with some manual duty besides on the fall schedule."

"If your superior asked you to do something that you don't feel good about, what would you do?"

"I'd accept the assignment as the will of God."

"Are you ever asked to do something unreasonable?"

"No."

"Do you want to talk about your vow of chastity?"

"It's not a great temptation. There aren't any men around except our chaplain, Monsignor Burrows, who is in his seventies; the janitor; and the poor men who come for a handout. If you saw them, you'd realize they aren't a temptation." Sister Camille chuckled out loud, picturing them.

"Do you ever talk to them?"

"No. Sister Laura talks to them. She has to direct their work."

The doctor looked up. "You are human. Do you have any sexual feelings?"

"No, not much. One year, I chaperoned day students on the bus. The bus driver was an off-duty policeman. I rode with him every morning picking up students for school and enjoyed his good nature and jokes. The likelihood of a sexual relationship? No, never. When we take our vows, we become brides of Christ. Jesus Christ is our spouse."

"You're human. What do you do if these feelings arouse you?"

"I read, play the piano, and pray. I'm with the sisters who deal with this. I can too."

"Do you ever have a strong feeling toward meeting a nice man?"

"I try to suppress the idea."

"Tell me what a typical day is for you."

"It's different now, during summer vacation."

"What is it now?"

"We rise at five, meditation's from five thirty to six thirty, Mass at six thirty. Immediately after Mass, prime is chanted. However, since I help in the kitchen, I do that later in private. Breakfast follows. At eight fifteen, the rest of the little hours, tierce, sext, and none, are chanted. Assigned work is next. I have three piano students, spaced through the week. They have one-hour lessons. I have a little time left to practice before I return to the kitchen to assist the cooks with the dinner. After dinner, noon recreation begins for an hour. At this time, silence is broken for the first time in the day."

"How do you spend your recreation?"

"The sisters sew, do needle work, darn stockings, or go for a walk. Sometimes I'm finished early in the kitchen and join them."

"How is your afternoon spent?"

"After recreation, I do my spiritual reading for a half hour, and I meditate in private again because of my kitchen assignment. Then I go to the academy to practice for my piano lesson on Saturdays at Saint Albert College. We have another hour of recreation from three thirty to four thirty, and we go out for walks. After that, vespers and meditation, then supper at six, and recreation until eight fifteen. Matins and lauds follow and then to bed, which is about nine. Lights out at ten. That about does it."

"Tell me a little more about your recreation. Besides needlework, what else do you do? Do you play games?"

"Oh no, our holy foundress thought games were unnecessary and forbade them. Recreation is a relaxing time. Since we don't read the newspaper, Mother will sometimes tell us some world news or a joke. It's funny; some of the sisters who are hard of hearing will need repetition. Then that story will continue and continue in the circle."

"I see. Your mother superior sent you to see me. I'm going to leave it up to you to continue. I find you are a person who can make decisions and abide by them. You've been fortunate to be raised by parents who gave you responsibilities at an early age. Now your institution is involved in this murder investigation, which could have an effect on you. If I can help, let me know."

"I'd like to come one more time, Dr. Raymond."

"Good enough. I'll put you down for another appointment."

*   *   *

After Sister Camille returned to the Chateau from her appointment, she met Sister Angelica and went for a walk. "I'm exhausted after my session with Dr. Raymond. Actually he's not a difficult person to talk to, and today he gave me a choice to continue with him or not."

"Did you tell him about the autopsy report?"

"Oh yes. At first I didn't think he even heard me or believed it."

"That news probably made you credible as a patient."

Sister Camille nodded. "He wanted to know about our life and vows. I gave him the straight facts. It seems a lot of nuns see a psychologist because of the life we lead."

"It doesn't surprise me, Sister. I have some bad news. Mother Cordelia announced after dinner that she called the archbishop about the investigation. Mother said His Eminence knew the police chief, and he'd ask him to stop the investigation."

Sister Camille didn't answer but let the information seep in. "How can the archbishop stop a police investigation?"

"I don't know. The archbishop is pretty powerful when it concerns political affairs. I read about it all the time in the weekly diocesan paper."

"I just talked to Hank last night before he left. He seemed so confident how the investigation progressed yesterday. What if the case is closed? I'm scared now; I felt protected with him here," Sister Camille explained. "He gave me his home phone number in case of an emergency." She dug in her pocket and brought out a carefully folded piece of paper. "Here it is." Sister Camille looked at it.

"We can't just sit by, Sister Angelica. I don't think the officers had time to test the typewriters to find out which one had the smudged *h*." Sister looked at her watch. "We have a half hour before vespers. Let's start right now in the academy."

On their way up the steps to the third-floor typing classroom, they heard the phone ring in Sister Eugene's office on second floor. When no one answered it, they entered the directress's office. Sister Angelica handed Sister Camille a clean sheet of typing paper from the secretary's desk. Sister Camille went to Sister Eugene's typewriter, and Sister Angelica tested the secretary's typewriter. After documenting their test, they continued up to the sisters' workroom and the commercial classrooms on third. Sister Camille knew there were a couple of portables in other classrooms. They could wait. In the typing classroom, each took a row. They rushed from one machine with blank keys to the next, pushing chairs in and out, cranking the rollers, typing *h*, oblivious to the noise they created.

The door opened. Sister Eugene stood quietly, surveying the disorderly scene. She waited until she had their attention. "Well, if it isn't the sleuths. Whose side do you think you're helping and to what purpose?" Sister Eugene didn't wait for an answer. She whirled around and disappeared.

"I know Sister Eugene's running to Mother Cordelia to report us right now," Sister Angelica said.

"Let's not stop. We can finish this room before we get orders to quit. Anyway, we aren't breaking any rules."

They finished their project and hurried back to the monastery just in time to fall in formation as the sisters filed into the chapel for vespers.

After vespers, Sister Camille was sure Mother Cordelia remained in the chapel for meditation; she sneaked into Mother Cordelia's office on her way to the kitchen.

She remembered the first time she searched her office after Mother Rosaria died. This time would be a cinch. All she had to do was roll the paper in, strike the *h*, and be off.

Before she finished rolling the paper in, the telephone rang on Mother Cordelia's desk also connected to the third-floor phone. The elevator motor activated, which meant someone was coming. It took a second to punch the *h* key and get out. As she rounded the corner of the elevator shaft, she heard Mother Cordelia enter her office and pick up the phone.

"Hello, Your Excellency."

Another close call, but she got what she wanted. Now, she only needed to test the typewriters in the sisters' study in the monastery and the one in the kitchen office.

Listening to the phone conversation, she heard Mother Cordelia say, "Nine thirty will be fine to meet with you."

At seven fifteen that evening, Sisters Camille and Angelica met in the courtyard. Sister Camille whispered, "Here, you take the paper with the results of our testing. If Mother Cordelia calls me in, I can say I don't have it."

Sister Angelica took her paper. "Did you get Mother Cordelia's typewriter?"

"Yes, but the culprit is the kitchen typewriter as far as I can see. Look, Sister."

"It's too bad we don't have the original to compare. Do you think you should call the detective?"

"Wouldn't I like to?" Sister Camille nodded. "Mother Cordelia gave me strict orders to use the phone only for kitchen business. I don't feel the urgency now. Let's wait a day or two and see what happens here."

Sister Angelica nodded. "Good enough. We might do more good this way."

18

An overcast sky with the humidity hovering near 70 percent settled into the Mississippi River Valley. Shortly after ten o'clock, seven poor men congregated outside the back door of St. Clotildes. They presented themselves as willing to work three hours for a meal. While waiting, two regulars who anticipated Sister Laura's assignments stacked garden tools against the maple tree near the shed. They had come to the Chateau often enough to know what she expected. The others stood around, some smoking.

Soon, Sister Laura came. "Gentlemen, I need one man to weed and hoe the flowerbeds by the Sacred Heart Shrine." She looked over the group.

A man with a weathered face and a growth of stubble spit a wad of tobacco into the bushes. He reached for a hoe, grabbed a tarp pieced together from burlap bags, and left the group. He was accustomed to Sister's directions.

"Then I need someone to help Joe in the boiler room. He'll tell you what he wants done."

Another man stepped forward. A wobbly gait that made his head jerk with each step indicated painful arthritic joints.

"Steve," Sister called to another regular, "take two men down to the tennis courts. Show them how to trim the bushes and clean the area. You, two gentlemen, follow me. We have a cleanup job by the garbage cans on the porch." One of the men in a coat with threads hanging out of it chewed on a matchstick.

To the other poor man, Sister scolded, "Please, no drinking. Put that bottle in the shed. You can pick it up when you leave the campus." This produced a ripple of laughter from the regulars who knew Sister's expectations.

"Damn." He shook his head, muttering. Turning away, he wiped his mouth with the back of his sleeve then fell in with the match-chewing volunteer. They entered the trellised porch near the kitchen. He glanced back at his friend, who was walking toward the heating plant. Their eyes met for a second. Each knew their mission. Amid dumping barrels of rubbish and swabbing the concrete floor, Flanagan was assigned to keep an eye out for Sister Camille.

He and Kummer worked together as a team on cases of murder, fraud, and burglary. Flanagan respected Kummer for his impassive, systematic approach. He thought Kummer's German heritage made him methodical, but in this case, Flanagan wondered if his "leut" was getting soft on his informant, Sister Camille.

Flanagan saw her once after he emptied a barrel of tin cans. She had walked through the porch, her eyes cast down, with her skirts hiked up and enveloped in an apron. A little later, he saw her typing in the office, near the kitchen, probably a menu. He could report to Kummer that Sister Camille looked cheerful and busy. He was tempted to introduce himself and ask to check her typewriter. He didn't.

*   *   *

Joe Simmons met his helper in the boiler room. Joe wore a faded plaid shirt and an engineer's cap. A carpenter's pencil stuck out of the center pocket of his worn Oshkosh overalls that fit snugly over his rotund body. He had just carried a ladder to an area below a network of heating pipes that stretched around the high ceiling. The exertion of moving the ladder made his chest expand like bellows.

The poor man offered his hand. "Name's Pete. You need 'elp?" Pete wore an uneven short beard with burrs of blanket fluff stuck in it. His hands were as soiled as his face and the greasy shirt stuck to his skin. He looked and smelled as though he hadn't bathed for months.

Joe refused the offered hand and avoided looking at his disheveled helper. "Grab a broom from the corner," he pointed toward the area, "and sweep down the place. I have to finish insulating these new pipes I replaced yesterday." He lumbered up the ladder with care, keeping an eye on his helper.

Pete found the broom and swept with wide lethargic strokes, often missing a pile of dirt. He glanced up at Joe, noting details of the room as he worked.

"Hand me that small wrench from the workbench," Joe yelled. Pete abandoned his broom, allowing it to fall to the concrete floor with a snap, and searched the bench area. A half-open bag of peach pits caught his eye. Finding the wrench, he handed it to Joe.

"You new? Don't believe I've seen you around," Joe said.

"Worked at a lumberyard in Madison. Stacked lumber. Got laid off."

"Not much work around here either."

Pete didn't answer but continued circling the room with the broom.

"You plan to stay in the area?" Joe asked.

"Don't know. Depends on what I can git."

"I've had all kinds of jobs," Joe boasted. "The other day I counted up nine since I left the merchant marines. I wouldn't want to go back to any of them. Always had a smart-ass boss who had it in for me. I'm an engineer. Certified!"

Pushing and twisting the asbestos material into place, he gave a satisfied grunt. "This is the best place I ever worked, but some of the sisters are awful hard to please. They want everything just so." The next section slipped around the pipe with a snap.

"That last mother was sure quick to fire me when I was sick. Too bad she died, but I was sure glad the other one came back. She rehired me the same day she was made the mother. My wife's the head cook for the sisters."

Pete didn't respond. He finished his sweep and asked, "You got somethin' else fer me to do?"

"You can haul those old pipes over by the wall out of here. Put them on the north side of the boiler room then come back."

Pete stared up at Joe for a few seconds. "I can do what you're doing. Was a snipe in the navy."

"Oh yeah?" Joe said. "Where were you stationed?"

"Cuba. Did my basic at Great Lakes."

"I been to Cuba. I was a merchant marine. I used to see a lot of you, navy boys, there. When were you there?"

Pete said, "Nineteen forty-five." He picked up a load of pipes and made several trips to the north side of the boiler room. From that angle, he could view the back of the chapel and the academy.

"Got anything else to do?"

Still high on the ladder, Joe continued, "I always had a high respect for you, navy boys. I guess you never saw action if you stayed in Cuba."

"Nope. If that's all you want, I'll go now."

Joe answered, "Come back tomorrow. I'll have this job finished. There'll be more cleanup then."

Pete left.

At one o'clock, the work crew gathered by the garden shed waiting for Sister Laura to bring out their dinner. Soon, she appeared with plates heaped with pork stew and homemade bread. One man ate listlessly, chewing every morsel. Kummer recognized him as a regular who was often picked up for inebriation. Another bolted down his stew, making slurping sounds with each mouthful. The officers followed his example, mopping up the gravy with bread.

Moving out of earshot, Kummer said, "We're going to Madison after we clean up. I want to visit the police lab."

*   *   *

Back at the police station, Kummer called the lab.

"Dane County Criminalist Lab, Captain Bruce Chadwick here."

"Hello, Bruce. This is Hank Kummer, Stone Hill Police."

"Hank, good to hear from you. It's been a long time. Things in Stone Hill must be quiet."

"We like to keep it that way. How's Joan?"

"Great. We just had our fourth, two weeks ago, a girl this time. Named her Sandra."

"You were lucky to find Joan. I'm still looking."

"You got time, Hank. So what are you working on?"

"The mother superior at the Chateau Monastery was poisoned with cyanide."

"Huh? Don't believe I ever heard of a nun poisoned. Is this a joke?"

"No joke, Bruce." Before Kummer could continue, his friend broke in.

"That reminds me of the story about the man who worked as a day laborer."

Kummer would have been surprised if his classmate didn't have a story. He answered, "What did the day laborer do?"

"Well, whenever this guy, we'll call Welch, had ten dollars in his pocket, he felt like a millionaire and went to the neighborhood saloon to celebrate.

"One day a friend told him, 'You ought to put a little money aside.'

"'What for?' Welch asked.

"So when you die there'd be some money to bury you.

"Welch thought a moment, hiccupped, and said, 'Well, they never left anyone lay on top of the ground yet.'"

Kummer laughed. "But this is no joke, Bruce." He outlined the case briefly. "I've pinpointed the time and have suspects with opportunity, but none with a motive for murder."

"Sounds classic. How can I help?"

"I need to know all you got on cyanide."

"Sure. Come over later this afternoon. I have some work I need to finish, then we'll see what we can dig up."

"Thanks, Bruce. See you then."

*   *   *

Later that afternoon, as the officers drove through Stone Hill's town square, Flanagan remarked, "Sure wish we'd have gotten the typewriters tested yesterday before the archbishop interfered. We could have taken it along to the lab and been that much farther ahead."

They passed two retired farmers sitting on a bench in the square. One wore a green and yellow DeKalb Seed Corn cap, the other a straw hat that had seen many a threshing party. Kummer recognized them and waved.

Stone Hill was a town where everyone knew each other and knew their business as well. Residents sat on their front porch gliders and waved to passersby. If a person didn't wave, it was interpreted as a slight. They drove past the A & P, busy with shoppers, and the bank. A bicycle-shop owner stood in front of his store with a long pole, adjusting his awnings. Hank drove on out the east end of town along the river.

With the morning's overcast worn off, the hot sun bore down on them. It was after five o'clock when they reached the lab adjacent to the Dane County morgue.

The officers found Captain Chadwick in the drug and alcohol lab. The acidic odors reminded Kummer of chemistry class. Stacks of brown evidence envelopes sat in a carton on the floor waiting for analysis. Tables were cluttered with vials in slotted holders. Control substances used for color testing sat in ovenlike enclosures with a row of centrifuges on top of a counter. Because of the late hour, Chadwick worked alone.

"Look what the cat drug in." With a nod, the chemist glanced up from his microscope and then continued writing in a notebook.

"Wise guy," Kummer retorted.

His head still bent over the microscope, the chemist said, "See where your man, Hook, got a life sentence."

Kummer responded, "Yeah, I'm against capital punishment, but that guy deserved a death sentence if Wisconsin had one."

"Nasty case." Chadwick looked up. "How's the baseball? Still at it?"

"Win some, lose some." Kummer walked over to his friend and waited for him to complete his notes. "We appreciate your staying late for us."

Chadwick stood up and shook hands with Flanagan and Kummer, slapping his friend on the back. "You, fellows, get into some incredible situations. Now, let's see what we can do with your latest. What do you want to know?" He picked up a package of Camels, lit a cigarette, and tossed the package on the table toward the officers. Flanagan reached for it and lit up.

"How do you make cyanide?" Kummer dug for his pipe.

"What makes you think we make poisons here?" Bruce's organ-toned voice rang out. "We test and isolate substances pertaining to drugs and alcohol," he said. "Cyanide does come under drugs." He searched through a bookcase and pulled a large volume from a shelf.

Hank said, "I've read cyanide crystals can be made from apricot pits."

After running his finger down a page of fine print, Bruce replied, "It says here from apricot, peach, and cherry pits and apple seeds, too. But what we need to find out is if it's the skin or the kernel that has the most concentration of cyanide. Then the seed would have to be ground and soaked in a basic solution. After that it'd take a little time to evaporate. Cyanide is very unstable. Your perpetrator would have to make it shortly before administering it."

Searching another tome, the chemist flipped through a couple of pages then stopped. "Here is a process that's being tested. This is with apricot pits." He read aloud, "Kernels are defatted with ether, boiled in alcohol, filtered, and cooled. The result is a white crystalline substance."

"Hum, could this be done in a kitchen?" Kummer asked.

"Don't see why not. It's not a complicated procedure. But again, the crystals are very unstable."

"How soon would they lose their potency?"

"My guess is a day or two. Don't try boiling the pits in hydrochloric acid. That's what's used in the gas chamber." Bruce removed his white lab coat and hung it up. "Will this information help you?"

"It might."

19

After ten-thirty Mass at Saint Edwards, Henry Kummer changed into his Stone Hillbilly baseball suit and drove out to the municipal park at the edge of town. He had missed Saturday's practice to catch up on paperwork and wanted to limber up by running the bases before the other players showed.

Starting slowly, he loped to first base, his back straight and long limbs speeding gradually. With the fluid ease of an athlete, he rounded second. His movements weren't flashy, but commanding as his fit, lean body continued around to home base.

The detective's thoughts switched from the upcoming game with the Holy Cross team from across the river, to Sister Camille. He thought about her family. How much they knew of her situation. Most of all, he deplored the unnecessary delay in the Chateau case at the archbishop's orders. He could imagine the outrage in Mother Cordelia's voice as she explained to His Eminence. Having the police in the monastery without her request compounded the insult to her authority.

Kummer felt that Sister Camille might be in danger and wondered what role Dr. Raymond played. Mother Cordelia and the doctor held a lot of power. Maybe he ought to talk to Dr. Raymond, though he knew how psychologists coveted their doctor-patient confidentiality.

Changes needed to be made to ensure Sister Camille's safety even though Flanagan had reported that she was okay. The superior would have to influence the sisters to respect Sister Camille for her courage. If that condition wasn't met, Sister Camille might have to make other plans. What plans? Leave the cloister? Then what? How could she remain there for the rest of her life after instigating the investigation?

She kept coming up at the strangest moments, like back at his office and even now. How would she look in a dress, with her hair flying in the wind. He wasn't concerned about solving the crime. That would come. Instead, he pictured the intense expression on Sister Camille's face, the sound of her voice. Hank found himself enjoying these reflections. Was this the reason he felt so irritated when the chief postponed the case? He missed being near the Chateau, being near Sister Camille. And what did she think? What did she feel?

Kummer had run the bases a third time when Ed Kelly, Al Blaine, and Joe Lindsey showed up for batting practice. The rain forecast held off, and the game went a full nine innings with the final score, the Hillbillies eleven and Holy Cross ten. In the eighth inning, they were up with two outs. Ed Kelly dug his cleats into the loose dirt at home plate ready for the pitch. He smashed the ball over the fence for a two-run

MAGDALENA'S CONFLICT   111

homer. This put the Hillbillies one run ahead. Next up, Tom Sullivan struck out. During the last inning and a half, the Hillbillies held on to their one-run lead. They won the game. Kummer caught a high fly in left field for the last out.

At six o'clock, Kummer slumped into his Naugahyde Barcalounger, feet up, in front of his television. His baseball sat in a still-warm glove on the nearby table. The New York Yankees were about to play the Chicago White Sox at Comiskey Park.

Still in his Hillbillies uniform, he slaked his thirst with a bottle of Schlitz, watching his new nineteen-inch television. John Cameron Swayzee filled the television screen, holding up a Timex watch he pulled from a tank of water and saying, "It takes a licking, and it's still ticking." The reception came in clear on his new toy. It was worth the money to have the supplier install the expensive antenna on top of his house, though it was times like today, he wished he had someone to share it.

Two years ago on July 4, Beth's car slid over an embankment. She had been on her way to meet him from her aunt Lena's farm near Eau Claire. Beth was pronounced DOA at the hospital. They had planned to meet in the police-station parking lot and go from there to a dance in Guttenberg, Iowa. Tiny Hill's orchestra played there every Fourth of July. He remembered the color of her dress, the scent of her hair that morning before she left. His eyes looked toward a bookcase where her three-by-five framed photo sat.

Henry Kummer had gone into mourning. Since then, he had made his job a full-time commitment and became a stubborn-headed loner. He knew his strange hours would make marriage difficult. Besides, he hadn't found anyone he wanted to spend the rest of his life with yet.

The morning newspaper announced that Bishop Millard would be in Stone Hill for confirmations that day. Tonight, he waited for the chief's call. If the case resumed tomorrow, it would give him three days to complete it before the Fourth of July ball game. Tonight, he'd enjoy watching Mickey Mantle, the new switch hitter from Commerce, Oklahoma.

Hank closed his eyes during the commercial. The last thing he heard was the ball rolling out of his glove to the floor.

20

S trains of the Brahms's E-flat Minor Intermezzo flowed through the open windows vibrating the walls of the music department. Sister Camille poured her heart into her music, tempering the dynamics to capture the composer's inspiration. She sensed the thick, textural phrases dissolve as the ascending melodies rose and fell, diminishing into a pianissimo resolution. Sister Camille lost herself in the welter of harmonies, which offered a temporary escape. Often she arrived at the end of the composition with reluctance.

To her, music provided more spiritual insight than did prayer and meditation. She wondered, is this blasphemy? If praying blocks out worldly distractions, why didn't playing a glorious masterpiece do the same? It opened her mind to the beauty of God's creation that words couldn't express. If she told this to any of the sisters, she'd be judged as a nonconformist in a community where conformity was the norm. None of the spiritual writers ever taught or even hinted at such an idea. Most of them, as well as Mother Cordelia, considered music and art to be self-fulfillment. This being the case, Sister Camille hid her feelings. Maybe it was the high she experienced after her practice that showed. The superior seemed to sense it when Sister Camille's expression didn't reflect the norm. Sister Camille took a deep breath and closed her eyes. She opened them to a blank expression. Now, she was prepared for the evening recreation.

In the monastic world of silence, reading facial expressions worked both ways. Since Lieutenant Kummer hadn't been to the Chateau in the past three days, Sister Camille read a smug satisfaction on Mother Cordelia's face. A look that said she had everything under control.

Sister Camille's pocket watch showed seven twenty-one. She needed to wash up and collect her sewing basket for recreation. If she came late, she'd have to kneel by Mother Cordelia's chair to give her excuse. That wasn't difficult, but it would make her singular. Sister wanted to meld into the group. Besides, she had no reason to be late, except she never had enough practice time to prepare for her piano lesson and often would steal a few extra minutes. Sister left a page of her music open with a difficult phrase. She'd have it handy to practice between her student's lessons the next day. As Sister walked toward the door, she noticed a three-by-five card shoved under it. Picking it up, she read:

> Sister Camille, Meet me by the costume closet
> before you leave the academy.
>
> S. A.

Sister Camille mentally thanked Sister Angelica's thoughtfulness in leaving the note instead of interrupting her practice then left to meet her.

In the shadows on the first floor, Sister Camille saw a figure in a clown costume. It hurried toward her, wearing a mask with a fixed smile. Dressed in a black baggy suit covered with large white dots, the figure looked larger than Sister Angelica. Costumes tended to do that especially if they were worn on top of the habit. Sister Camille remembered the time they had dressed in costumes when they were novices. She smiled. "You didn't say you'd be in costume. I've always wanted to play a clown again."

The obliging clown opened the closet door in silence. In graceful pantomime, she made a low bow and, with one hand outstretched, bade Sister Camille to enter. Playing along, Sister Camille performed a half curtsey, giggled, and poked her head inside the dark room, reaching for the light cord. The next moment, a violent shove sent her headlong into the tiny windowless closet.

"What are—" Her words died as she fell down the concrete steps.

*   *   *

After the last prayer of the day, matins and lauds, Sister Angelica tapped on Sister Camille's cell door. No one answered. She opened the door a crack. The light from the hall flashed across Sister Camille's made bed. Sister Angelica reasoned there must be a good explanation for Sister Camille's absence from matins.

Monday morning dawned sunny and warm. After prime, Sister Angelica went to breakfast. Again noting Sister Camille's absence, as well as Mother Cordelia's, she rechecked her friend's cell. The bed hadn't been slept in. The washcloth covering the top of her water pitcher was dry as well as the basin. Sister Angelica sensed danger and wished Lieutenant Kummer was still at the Chateau. Heading toward the infirmary, Sister Mercy met her. "Is Sister Camille sick?" asked Sister Angelica.

"No, she's not on my list, today. Let me know if I can help. I noticed she was absent for Mass."

Sister Diana stepped out of Mother Cordelia's office. Sister Angelica asked her, "Have you seen Sister Camille?"

"No, I was wondering why she wasn't at Mass," Sister Diana answered. "Mother Cordelia is with her council preparing for a meeting with the archbishop this morning, so don't bother her yet. Did you talk to Sister Mercy?"

Sister Angelica related her information and headed toward the kitchen. A large kettle with a soup bone simmered on the stove. Miss. Drekel, who was cutting up carrots and celery, looked up and asked, "Where is Sister Camille?"

Sister Angelica gave her a brief explanation and left. She remembered the time a young novice left the Chateau in the middle of the night. The white-veiled sister dressed in clothes set aside for the poor men planned to hop a train to Chicago. The severe cold temperatures that January night caught her by surprise. To survive, she went to the police station for warmth. Of course, they escorted her back to the Chateau. She left the next day in more comfortable circumstances. What could have happened to Sister Camille?

* * *

The council sisters' bells rang announcing the archbishop's arrival. As they entered the bishop's parlor, each knelt and kissed the archbishop's ring according to rank. The sisters sat in a circle, hands covered by their long sleeves. Except for their faces and sizes, each replicated the other. His Eminence hitched up his trousers and sat in the large cushioned chair offered to him. A cigar in his amethyst-ringed hand created a pleasant odor in a room that rarely held smoke. In a deep voice that sounded like Walter Huston, he said, "I don't know how we can keep this affair quiet any longer. After talking to Chief Haskell this morning, I've come to the conclusion the police have solid reasons to continue the investigation. They now have the complete pathology report from the lab. There's no longer any doubt. Mother Rosaria was poisoned by cyanide." The archbishop paused to clear his voice. "Chief Haskell said Mother Rosaria's blood sample registered point six milligrams of cyanide. That, my dear sisters, is lethal. Now, let me hear your side of the story."

No one spoke. The sisters looked toward Mother Cordelia. Her head slumped. Slowly, Mother shook it from side and spoke in a soft voice. "Yes, we have a serious problem, Your Excellency. The police are under the false impression that this is a homicide. It's an impossible, unbelievable premise held by none of the sisters except one, Sister Camille. Do we look like murderers? We are sisters consecrated to God. Surely, you don't think one of us did it?"

Her protest acknowledged fear. She moved her hand from beneath her sleeves to her throat trying to swallow. "How?" Mother Cordelia coughed and then coughed again while everyone waited. Recovering, she continued, "How can we carry on our teaching? How can we maintain the respect of our alumni and the Stone Hill community if this investigation continues? If the newspapers print the story, our apostolic work in the school and our monastery is finished." She'd spoken her piece and waited for the next response.

"No one likes a scandal, especially the Catholic Church," the archbishop said.

Sister Martha bit her lips tightly before speaking. "I think Sister Camille should be put away. She's been nothing but trouble since she entered the Chateau. She lacks a deep religious spirit, the foundation for a true vocation. She's indifferent to those around her to the point she's 'singular.'" Sister Martha emphasized "singular," in a derisive tone as though it was a quality akin to disobedience. "Saint Augustine refers to singularity as not conforming to the little ways of our rules. Of course, she's obedient, but again, her compliance is insufferably indifferent. I can give you an example. Sister Camille makes her dishes to suit her individuality. I hardly recognize the meals that come to the refectory table. That's not our way and unnecessary. Our meals should provide sustenance, not a gourmet display."

The archbishop put his hand to his face to hide a grin. He chose to wait for the council to finish before making recommendations. "Sister Diana, how do you feel?" His hand slid from his chin to finger the gold chain that crisscrossed inside his black suit coat.

Nodding, Sister Diana related, "Yes, we have a problem here that needs resolving one way or another. If the police are prevented from investigating, there will always be a pall of suspicion over our community. I can't see it any other way. I hesitate to mention this now, but it's as good a time as ever. Sister Camille has been missing since last night. She was last heard practicing the piano in the academy. Her bed wasn't slept in."

"Has there been a search?" the archbishop was quick to respond and stood.

The council stood with him. He was the highest-ranking person in the room. If he stood, the sisters stood. If he sat, the sisters sat. And so it continued.

Mother Cordelia said, "Surely, we can finish our meeting." She looked around at the sisters for reinforcement. "I can only deal with one crisis at a time. I'm sure Sister Camille is all right. Your Excellency, please sit down."

Sister Diana intervened, "Sister Angelica has been searching for her all morning."

The archbishop's tall stately figure stepped toward the door leading to the switchboard. "Call Sister Angelica."

The archbishop and the sisters waited, listening to Sister Angelica's bell repeat until she received the message. After a timid knock, she opened the door. Never before had Sister Angelica been called to appear before the archbishop and the council, the highest of all meetings at St. Clotildes. She knelt on one knee and kissed his amethyst ring.

Before she could rise, he asked, "Have you found Sister Camille?"

"No, Your Excellency. I've searched everywhere. There's no sign of her."

"Call the police." He stood up again.

"Wait," Mother Cordelia pleaded, her pores glistening, "we'll all search after our meeting." She again made a gesture for all to sit.

The archbishop waved her aside. "I talked to the police this morning. Chief Haskell said Sister Camille could be in danger. If you don't call the police, I will." He strode toward the door.

Mother Cordelia, sufficiently chastised, left the parlor. Returning a few minutes later, Mother Cordelia said, "While we wait for the police, I'd like, Your Excellency, to hear the other sister's opinions."

"There won't be time. I hear the siren."

21

"Stone Hill Police. Flanagan here."

"Archbishop Millard. Let me speak to the chief!"

"One moment, Your Excellency." Flanagan pressed the lever to the chief's line and hung up. He caught Kummer's eye passing nearby. "Psst. His Eminence." He pointed with his cigarette to the phone.

Chief Haskell stomped out of his office. "Go to the Chateau right now. Sister Camille's missing! When you find her, continue the investigation. The archbishop wants answers fast!" The officers rushed out to the parking lot. Flanagan took the wheel of a police car. He yelled over the blaring siren, "Now His Eminence wants answers. This is all his damn fault."

Kummer remained silent. He wished he'd continued his charade, dressed as a poor man looking for a handout, another day. It was his only possible contact with Sister Camille.

They careened to a stop at the front entrance. Mother Cordelia and the archbishop met them at the door. Kummer dismissed a formal greeting due a prelate and a mother superior. Instead, he asked, "Who saw Sister Camille last?"

"Sister was heard practicing in her studio last night around seven," Mother Cordelia said.

The archbishop intervened, "She never returned to her cell. Her bed wasn't slept in."

Kummer scowled. Why weren't the police called sooner? Arguing that point served no purpose. Turning to Flanagan, he ordered, "Sergeant, begin on the top floor in the academy. Check every room and closet, even if they are locked. Mother Cordelia, the keys please?"

Mother Cordelia said, "I'll call Sister Dorothy. She can meet Sergeant Flanagan with the keys on the fourth floor." Sister Angelica and Flanagan left to meet her.

To Mother Cordelia, Kummer said, "I want to search Sister Camille's cell." Without asking her permission, he led the way down the hall toward the door marked Cloister No Admittance. Mother Cordelia followed. The archbishop's long legs kept up, eager to assist.

They found Sister Camille's bed made, her night veil neatly folded under the pillow. Kummer lifted the thin mattress. The polished birch floor could be seen through the spaces in the chain-link spring. Two spiritual reading books sat on the wooden chair. Kummer opened them, read the backs of the holy cards, and then handed them to the archbishop who held out his hand. An empty enamel pitcher covered with a washcloth sat in the porcelain basin on the commode. The washcloth had dried in the shape of the pitcher's mouth, indicating Sister hadn't used it that morning. A single towel hung from a bracket on the side of the commode. The top of the washstand appeared without the usual array of cremes and cosmetics. Only a small framed picture of Saint Camillus sat next to a glass that held a partially used tube of toothpaste and a toothbrush. He felt the side of the toothbrush for dampness.

Kummer heard Mother Cordelia's quick breath as he worked through Sister Camille's private things. Only a murder investigation superseded cloister privacy imposed by constitution directives. The usual delicate lace-trimmed slips, panties, and bras were absent. Instead, Kummer found bulky folded cotton pieces that he guessed were a change of underclothes. The only garments he recognized were two pairs of rolled-up black stockings and a stack of man-size handkerchiefs. In the bottom drawer, he found the space filled with folded muslin napkins. Again, he heard Mother Cordelia gasp. Neither the archbishop nor Kummer asked their use. Hank put his hand through them to see if anything was hidden underneath and closed the drawer. Kummer looked around the cell for a closet. Only a hook on the back of the door provided storage for Sister's robe.

Kummer asked to see her prayer books in the chapel. There he found nothing irregular. They returned to the first floor where Mother Cordelia pointed out Sister Camille's cubbyhole. Mother Cordelia opened the door and brought out a pair of black gloves marked with her number +41 in India ink. Another book, *The Confessions of Saint Augustine*, and a spool of black darning cotton completed its contents.

As they moved toward the academy, the archbishop kept pace, following Mother Cordelia and Kummer up three flights of stairs to the fourth floor in the academy wing. Pausing to catch their breaths, the archbishop in particular, they met Flanagan, Sister Dorothy, and Sister Angelica coming from the attic. Now, the six-member party split to search opposite ends of the boarders' vacant twenty-five private rooms. They went through closets and bathrooms, jerking doors open and rattling drawers that stuck due to the summer humidity in the river valley. Amid the cacophony of sounds, a toilet flushed. Kummer straightened and went toward the source. He ran head to head into the archbishop who was smoothing his higher-than-usual belt.

"Have you found anything yet?" the bishop asked.

Hank shook his head and muttered, "No, Your Eminence," returning to the search. After they finished the fourth floor, a brief meeting of the search crew revealed no Sister Camille and no clues. They combed the third floor of classrooms then descended to the second floor, which consisted of more classrooms and the music department.

In Sister Camille's piano studio, Kummer paid special attention to the contents of desk drawers, music shelves, and bulletin boards. He crawled under the grand piano and reached into crevices of the rarely viewed underbelly of the instrument.

Descending to the ground level of the academy, the crew continued working opposite ends of the hall.

Flanagan's group started at the west end. They searched the showers and locker rooms, the gym office. Next, they came to the locked costume closet located midway down the hall. Flanagan stumbled over a bundle on the steps. Sister Dorothy suggested she'd go first to find the light string.

Kummer's crew began in the theater and gym. They pulled curtains to reveal a garden scene painted on the backstage wall. Kummer asked Sister Angelica to raise the backdrops. Together, they climbed to a catwalk above the stage where a range of spotlights and pulleys controlled the theatrical effects. From there, they viewed the entire stage floor, front, back, sides, and apron, separated by the curtains.

Shouts further down the hall brought them to the stage floor. Sister Dorothy met them. "Come quick; we found Sister Camille! She's hurt. I'll call Sister Mercy."

In the closet doorway, Kummer found Flanagan kneeling on the concrete steps. Sister Camille's motionless figure faced downward. She moaned as Flanagan lifted her and turned her around. In the dim light, they saw a crusted flow of blood from a gash near her right eye. It stained her white linen guimpe and wimple. The swelling extended to the left side of her head, leaving her with two huge black eyes. The veil and headband were shoved to one side giving her a whimsical, cockeyed appearance. Kummer edged up the three steps to take Flanagan's place.

Sister Mercy arrived with her medical kit. She took Sister's pulse and nodded that it was satisfactory then snapped open a capsule of smelling salts and applied it to Sister's nose. This brought a slight movement and tears to her swollen eyes.

Sister Mercy said, "She's coming around."

"What happened?" Sister Camille whispered, looking to see who massaged her shoulder.

"That's what we'd like to know," Kummer answered, easing her up into a sitting position.

Sister Camille, still dazed, opened her eyes a slit. She tried to focus on the group around her.

"Let's get her out of here," Kummer commanded. He gathered her up and carried her down the steps across the hall where Sister Dorothy unlocked the door to the gym office. There, he eased her onto the cot. At the door, the archbishop had stepped forward trying to assist. After Sister Mercy swabbed Sister's head cut, Kummer asked, "Who has the keys to the costume closet?"

Before Sister Dorothy could answer, Sister Angelica answered, "Oh my God, I have a key."

The archbishop and Mother Cordelia looked sharply at her. Neither spoke, leaving the questions to the detective.

"Sister Angelica?" Sister Camille whispered then closed her eyes. She wanted to continue, but she couldn't form the words and fell silent.

"How about a shot of bourbon?" Flanagan offered.

"Not yet," Kummer answered. "Sister Angelica, do you have the key with you?"

Sister Angelica reached deep into a pocket inside her habit and pulled out a set of keys. "This is the one."

Sister Mercy snapped another capsule and pressed it to Sister Camille's nose. She groaned and opened her eyes again. Her eyes looked around the group then rested on Sister Angelica. Becoming more focused, Sister Camille tried to speak. Kummer leaned closer attempting to understand her mumbled syllables. She stared at Sister Angelica and asked, "Did you put a note under the door?" Rummaging around in her pocket, she found a card.

Kummer took it from her, holding it by the edges. He read it then held it out to Sister Angelica, but didn't let her touch it, then slipped it into an envelope from his pocket.

"No, Sister," Sister Angelica answered. "I wasn't in the academy last night."

"I thought it came from you, but you always put AMDG at the heading," Sister Camille spoke in a weak but resigned voice then put her hand to her headband, trying to right its position.

"These initials were on Mother Rosaria's holy card."

"Yes, I see." Hank recognized it as a religious practice. To Sister Angelica, he said,

"We'll talk later."

Sister Mercy took Mother Cordelia aside. "Sister Camille received a powerful blow. She may have a concussion. I think she ought to go to the hospital for an X-ray."

"She seems all right to me," Mother Cordelia said. "Just knocked out. She'll come out of it."

"What time is it?" Sister Camille asked.

The archbishop answered, "Eighteen past eleven."

"What day is it?"

"It's Monday, June twenty-ninth," Kummer said.

"That means I've been out since last night! It happened so fast." She put her hand up to her sore eyes, touching the puffy lids, and winced. "After I finished practicing, I found the card under the door. I thought Sister Angelica left it."

Lieutenant Kummer asked, "Do you remember what time you went to the music studio last night, Sister?"

"About ten minutes to seven."

"And what time did you leave?"

"I left at seven twenty."

"Whoever had that key roamed the dark halls at that time. Not much light comes into a hall between classrooms," the detective explained to Flanagan.

Sister Dorothy interrupted, "The only person who has a key to that closet other than the master is Miss. Palmer, the gym teacher. She's on vacation. Sister Eugene has her address."

"Thank you, Sister. I'll talk to Sister Eugene. What time did you lock the exterior doors last night, Sister?"

"Between five thirty and five forty. I always lock them after five-thirty meditation."

Sister Camille continued, "When I came down the stairs to the first floor, I saw someone in the distance dressed as a clown. I thought it was Sister Angelica dressed in the costume. In fact, I joked with her about it. The clown heard me; she came quickly toward me. She was in that black-and-white polka-dot clown suit with the smiling mask. Then before I knew it, the clown opened the door and pushed me inside. I lost my balance and fell down the steps. I never had a chance to be scared." Sister Camille sipped on the hot broth Sister Mercy set before her on the desk. She glanced at Mother Cordelia, realizing she was eating in front of the lieutenant and the archbishop. According to their rule, the sisters never ate in the company of guests or lay persons.

"Did the clown touch you anyplace else?"

"No, just a forceful push on the stairs. It seemed more like a flash because it came so fast."

"Was the clown costume taken from this closet?" Kummer asked Sister Angelica.

She went back to the closet to check. "It's been hanging on the rod for years. Now it's gone," Sister said.

"Sister Camille, how tall was the clown?"

"About the same height, but heavier than Sister Angelica." Turning toward Sister Angelica, she apologized. "Sorry, Sister, for comparing the clown to you. That was my first impression. I figured wearing the costume over the habit put extra pounds on you."

Kummer asked, "How tall are you, Sister Angelica?"

"I'm five feet seven, Lieutenant."

"Sister Camille, can you estimate how much the clown weighed?"

"That's harder to guess because the clown suit was baggy."

"Flanagan, how much do you weigh?"

"In my birthday suit? Whoops!" He put his hand to his mouth, realizing the sister's presence. He glanced at the archbishop, who pretended not to hear, then continued in a dignified voice. "I weigh 190 pounds."

"Sister Camille, would you say the clown was about Sergeant Flanagan's size?"

Sister Camille smiled at Flanagan and shook her head. "I'd have to see him dressed in that clown suit."

"That's a good point, Sister. Sergeant, check around the kitchen, back porch, garden shed, the grounds, and boiler room. See if we can find it."

The group started to break up. The archbishop leaned over, shook Kummer's hand, and thanked him for his prompt action. "If I can be of any assistance, call me."

Mother Cordelia spoke, "Please continue with your investigation, Lieutenant. Don't keep Sister Camille too long. She needs to rest."

Kummer thought he only received orders from the chief, who had already given them. He walked a short way with the archbishop and Mother Cordelia. "Sister Camille's had a sharp blow and seems all right, but to be on the safe side, she should have an X-ray."

Mother Cordelia started to resist Kummer's order. Instead she said, "I'll call a cab."

"No, I'll take her." He was thinking not only of Sister Camille's health, but also of keeping her in a safe place until he made an arrest.

Mother Cordelia responded, "I'll call Dr. Spence. Sister Mercy will accompany Sister Camille to the hospital. I'll tell her." She left with the archbishop.

Sister Camille braced her head with both hands. Kummer returned to the gym office.

He said, "You've been very brave, Sister. I think you're too tired to answer more questions now. I'm taking you to the hospital for a checkup. We'll talk tomorrow."

To Sergeant Flanagan, he directed, "After you find the costume, get the portress's sign-in log for June fifteenth and yesterday. If time permits, test out the typewriters. Sister Dorothy, would you take him into the monastery, so he can do that?"

"No problem, Lieutenant Kummer. Ring when you're ready, Sergeant."

Sister Camille staggered as she got up from the couch and would have fallen if it hadn't been for Kummer's quick support. He held her for a moment and suggested, "You'd better sit down, Sister."

"No." Sister Camille righted herself and stood motionless until the room stopped spinning.

Sister Mercy went with her to gather the few necessities a nun would need for the hospital. Kummer waited at the front entrance. He put his arm around her shoulders and led her down the steps to the police car. He refrained from bringing her too close. Her odd-shaped headpiece prevented it. "This investigation will soon be finished," he whispered in her ear.

Sister Camille reached for his hand and squeezed it.

22

Kummer stayed at Saint Francis Hospital until Sister Camille was checked into a room. Then he phoned for a police officer to guard Sister's door. Returning to his car, he saw Dr. Spence swerve into the Doctors Only parking spaces.

"What happened at the Chateau?" The doctor yelled as he slammed the car door shut. "Not another . . ." He didn't finish his sentence.

"Don't know yet." The detective walked toward him. "I brought Sister Camille in ten minutes ago." He flicked his head toward the hospital complex. "Someone pushed her with considerable force. It appears she hit her head on concrete steps."

"Is she conscious?"

"Now she is, not when we found her. Call me at this number after you've examined her. It's our PD number at the Chateau." Kummer wrote the number on a slip of paper and handed it to him. "Just as a precaution, would you admit her to the hospital? I've requested security outside her room."

"Glad to cooperate, Lieutenant. I'll call as soon as I get the X-rays, in about a half hour."

"Good." Kummer left and returned to the Chateau.

He found the tables in the library moved back to their original position. After he rearranged them to his liking, he looked for the phone. It took a few minutes to find it. Someone had placed it in a low cabinet with just a few inches of wire exposed near the floor.

Flanagan walked in with the typewritten cards. "Just as I thought, Hank. It's the typewriter in the kitchen office." Flanagan handed the card to his partner. Kummer sat down and placed it on the table. From inside his coat pocket, he pulled a jeweler's loupe. Adjusting it to his eye, he studied the card in silence.

"Take it to the lab, but before you go, come with me." They left the library and went to the head of the steps near the directress's office. "I want to hear the exterior door close. Go down and let it close naturally. Then hold the door open and swing it closed."

After Flanagan complied to Kummer's satisfaction, the detective stepped into the directress's office. He poked his head in the open door. "Is this a good time to ask you a few questions, Sister?"

Sister Eugene's practiced arched eyebrows gave a look of surprise that lifted her headband and veil. Could she wiggle her ears at the same time?

"I've been expecting you. If you wait a moment, I'll cancel an appointment." Instead of using the telephone on her desk, Sister Eugene swept into the adjoining secretary's office. Her veil trailed in the breeze, as did the rosary beads that hung from her belt. In tandem, they reversed direction when she returned to sit down. Sister sat, feet together, straight and rigid, a practiced posture. Her eyes avoided the detective's gaze.

Kummer caught a flicker of irritation in her voice. To him, her expression was neither anxious nor distressed, just indifferent. He walked toward the bay window, with hands in his back pockets. Potted plants of African violets, begonias, coleus, and vines filled the windowsills.

Sister Eugene adjusted the angle of her head. "Wouldn't this be part of the elimination process, Lieutenant Kummer?"

Hank ignored her question, allowing a few seconds of silence. Instead of answering, he commented, "Your plants thrive in this location with all the light." He appeared to enjoy himself walking from plant to plant, taking his time. "From this window, you can see in three directions." He stood a moment longer then took a chair and pulled out his notebook.

Sister Eugene pulled her rosary into her lap, fingering the black beads. Hank noticed her poised hands. He remembered his teachers in grade school. It didn't matter if they wrote on the board, held a pencil, or handed out papers. The sisters' hands were immaculate, almost angelic, especially folded in prayer.

He asked, "On Sunday, June 15, did you attend vespers?"

"No, Lieutenant." Sister's cultured voice was barely audible. "I'm excused from reciting the Office with the community by Mother Cordelia because of the pressures of my position as the directress of the academy. I say the Office in private, but I make every effort to attend with the community on feast days."

Kummer noted her comfort level and countenance at the mentioned Mother Cordelia. Individual differences of each sister did come out despite their uniformed dress. Some characteristics could never be hidden, even behind the folds of the religious habit. Why does she say the Office with the community on feast days? He decided to ignore that statement. Maybe later it would be relevant.

"Did you eat at first or second table that evening?"

"I ate at second table."

He looked at the schedule. "That's six thirty. What did you do between four thirty and six thirty?"

"I had a parent that afternoon who enrolled her daughter. We toured the academy, which took over an hour."

"At what time was that?"

"They left after four thirty. I remember I heard the vesper bell. They were still here in the office."

"What was the name of the parent?"

"Elizabeth Kielhold."

"Then what did you do?"

"I had vespers and compline to say, and I was behind in my spiritual reading."

"Where did you do your reading, Sister?" Kummer pursued.

"I said vespers and compline here in the office." Sister's beads rattled to the floor.

Kummer noted her impatience but decided to continue. "How long does that take?"

"About ten minutes." She leaned down and brought the beads back to her lap. "Then what did you do?"

"I went to the chapel for meditation at five. After that, I went to our cell for spiritual reading."

"How long did you read?" The detective noted a gasp in her throat.

"Thirty minutes. That's our rule, Lieutenant," She choked back a catch and swallowed.

Kummer continued, "Sister, did you go to the kitchen at any time en route to the academy or monastery?"

Sister rubbed the bridge of her aquiline nose in thought. "Yes I did, Lieutenant. Elizabeth brought me a small basket of strawberries. I took them to the cooler before meditation and returned for them just before I ate supper."

Her righteous tone and attitude puzzled Kummer. He spent a minute writing then took the sheet out of the binder and handed it to Sister Eugene. In an uncompromising tone, he asked, "Would you say this schedule is correct?"

        3:30-4:30 Student enrollment (Academy)
        4:35-4:50 Vespers (Academy)
        4:50-5:00 Took berries to cooler (Kitchen)
        5:00-5:30 Meditation (Chapel)
        5:30-6:00 Spiritual Reading (Monastery)
        6:30-6:35 Returned to Cooler for berries (Kitchen)
        6:35-7:00 Second Table Supper (Monastery)

Sister Eugene studied the paper. Kummer thought he had never seen a face that expressed so little emotion. She barely moved in her chair.

Handing the schedule back to him, Sister nodded. "That's correct, Lieutenant." He returned the schedule to her. "Please, Sister, take your time. Notice there's a half hour unaccounted for between your spiritual reading and going to the cooler. Could you tell me what you did then?" The detective watched her movements like a camera and thought he heard her sudden intake of breath.

Sister's eyebrows pinched together. She put her hand up under her stiff wimple.

Kummer thought there must be a hidden pocket under it. Maybe for a watch or handkerchief. Sister withdrew her hand, regaining her poise. Her face darkened, and her mouth parted to answer then closed. She shifted her position. "Well, of course I had to wash my hands."

She wouldn't mention the indelicacy of going to the toilet or the bathroom. He felt she stopped herself from saying too much. "Let's say that took ten minutes. You still have twenty minutes left."

"I remember now. I went back to the academy to water the camellia plant."

Kummer noted a sense of triumph in her voice. "Is that the name of that flower?" He pointed to the tall potted plant with red blossoms on the file case.

"Yes, it was a gift from my uncle in Florida."

"It's beautiful." The detective was silent a few seconds.

"Sister Eugene, your cell is next to Mother Rosaria's, facing east. While you were reading, did you hear or notice anyone entering the circle drive?"

"I didn't hear anyone, Lieutenant, and I was sitting in the chair by the window."

"And at six thirty, you left your cell to go to second table. Did you meet anyone in the hall?"

"Only Sister Mercy who brought a tray with a dish of ice cream and a pot of coffee for Mother Rosaria." Sister Eugene sat up straight, almost defiantly, and added. "Surely, you can't believe any of the sisters were involved in Sister Rosaria's death." She raised her voice in protest.

Kummer noticed that she omitted the words "poison" and "murder."

"And surely, you realize I am investigating an actual crime with a victim who experienced actual pain," he answered, unmoved.

Sister Eugene's head bent forward.

"Did you stop to talk to Sister Mercy on your way to supper?"

"No, Lieutenant."

Kummer said. "Up to now, we only had the pathologist's preliminary report. Now the full toxicology report confirms cyanide poisoning as the cause of death." He let this information sink in. "How well did you get along with the deceased?"

"She wasn't my choice for superior."

"Why was that?"

"She was inexperienced, Lieutenant. I know what it takes to run a school. Sister Rosaria was knowledgeable in library science and was our first qualified librarian, but she lacked the qualifications to be a superior. Sister Rosaria made changes in customs that had become tradition."

Kummer noticed that she referred to the deceased as sister rather than mother as the other sisters had. "Who do you think were Mother Rosaria's enemies?"

"She may have made some enemies." Her voice dropped to a lower register. "I doubt any of them are murderers."

"Who would they be?" Kummer continued.

"Madge Le Clair, an alumna. Madge discovered one of our seniors, Leslie Allen, who visited them, was pregnant. I as well as Madge wanted Leslie expelled. I felt Leslie wasn't fit to be a Chateau graduate."

Kummer remembered the letter from a parent to Mother Rosaria in the deceased's box of belongings. In it, the parent stated her younger daughter wouldn't attend the Chateau. "Could you tell me about that incident?"

"Lieutenant Kummer, I put that awful incident behind me, but if you insist."

"I insist."

Sister Eugene retold the event as though she predicted the end of the world. She faulted Sister Rosaria for interceding on Leslie Allen's behalf. "Susan Le Clair was hurt the most. In my mind, Sister Rosaria failed as an administrator. And because of her, Madge Le Clair has refused to send her younger daughter to the Chateau," she said. "And now, Leslie Allen's picture hangs on the wall with all our Chateau graduates."

Kummer turned toward the newly framed picture on the wall behind him. "Is this the picture?"

"Yes, Lieutenant." Sister nodded.

"I see. Now, let's move on. Had you visited Mother Rosaria anytime the evening of June 15?"

"I stopped a few minutes after I had supper."

"How did you find her?"

"She was very agitated about a postcard she received in the mail. She said it was a warning."

"Did you see it?"

"No."

"What did you make of it?"

"I offered her one of my Miltown pills. She seemed glad to take it."

"I see. How late did you work in your office last night?"

"I was here until seven forty."

"Do you have a key to the costume closet?"

"I have a master key in the safe."

"May I see it?"

From the top drawer, she picked up a key and unlocked a cabinet door that matched the rest of the maple cupboard doors. It was opened to reveal a safe secured in the wall. She twisted the dial and removed a set of keys. After reading the tags, she handed one to Kummer. "This is the master to the academy classrooms, and it also opens the costume closet."

"May I borrow it?"

"Surely, Lieutenant."

He slipped it into his pocket. "While you were working last evening, did you hear an exterior door open or close?"

"No, Lieutenant."

"Did anyone stop in your office from six thirty until the time you left?"

"No one did, Lieutenant."

"And after you left your office, did you notice anyone in the halls? You must have been the last to leave the academy wing."

"I didn't meet anyone, and surely not a clown, Lieutenant." Sister Eugene dropped her voice as if this was an outlandish possibility.

"How tall is the gym teacher, Miss. Palmer?"

"She's a large woman, quite tall."

"Do you know where Miss. Palmer is spending her vacation?"

"She's visiting her parents who have a cabin on Lake Mendota."

"Do you have her telephone number?"

"I'll have to look it up, Lieutenant."

"If you don't mind, Sister."

The interview was interrupted by a tap on the door.

Sister Dorothy popped her head in. "Your phone's ringing in the library, Lieutenant."

Kummer left the directress' office.

*   *   *

"Lieutenant Kummer, this is Dr. Spence."

"Yes, Doctor. How's Sister Camille?"

"The X-rays show a slight concussion. Her other injuries are superficial. I put a couple of stitches in the laceration. I've given her a sedative, and I'll keep her here. She'll be all right after she's rested."

"I'm glad Sister's there. I'd like to see her this evening. Would that be all right?"

"Don't stay long. I've never seen two shiners like she got. Call you tomorrow."

23

Kummer nodded to the nurse at the desk and walked down the hall to room 217 in Saint Francis Hospital. The guard, new to the force, sat outside Sister Camille's room reading a newspaper. He saw the detective coming, closed the paper, and stood.

A story had circulated about this rookie who had been assigned to the graveyard shift and had pursued a car on Route 31 for a speeding violation. The suspect careened off a timber road, jumped from his car, and disappeared into the woods with the cop in chase. After the officer's gun fell out of the holster while he was climbing over the fence, the chase ended. A cop without his gun out in the field was like a minnow out of water. His fellow officers had waited to hear if he found his gun.

Hank pressed him back into the chair. "Any visitors?"

"One, Lieutenant. A lady who said she was from the hospital staff. She walked by me as though I wasn't here, ready to barge into Sister's room. I stopped her."

"Have her description?"

"Said her name was Hope Jackson. She had short reddish gray hair, gray eyes, about five foot six. Wore a blue-and-white-striped smock, black oxfords, and carried a clipboard. I didn't let her in. She left in a huff." The officer tore the report from a pad and handed it to the detective.

"Good. I'll check on her. Anybody else?"

"Only that cute blond nurse." He rolled his eyes toward the chart desk. "I wouldn't mind if she worked over me."

Kummer shook his head. These young cops. "When does your shift end?"

"Seven o'clock. O'Brien will take over then."

"Good. I'll see him before I leave." Kummer tapped on the door and entered Sister's room. At first, he saw only two black eyes, like two pieces of coal, staring at him from the pillow. Sister Camille's white head covering and white bed linens blocked out the rest of her. He thought she must weigh less than a hundred pounds, so few ridges showed under the covers. The veil partially hid a dressing on the right side of her head.

Sister smiled and braced her arm to sit up. "How are you, Hank?"

"I'm fine, but I believe you're supposed to lie flat. You've had a concussion." He eased her back onto the pillow.

"I guess you're right." Sister smiled, enjoying his instructions.

"Did Sister Mercy leave?" Kummer walked to the open window to check the screen closure. He estimated the drop to the ground to be about thirty-five feet. A fire escape was about the same footage to the north.

"After I got settled in the room, there wasn't any reason for her to stay. I didn't need any special attention."

"How do you feel?" He pulled a chair close to the bed.

"I still have a headache." She fingered the edge of the dressing over the stitches and then rubbed her forehead. "I'm scared, Hank. It's finally hitting me what happened last night. I'm afraid here, and I'm afraid to go back to the Chateau. I don't know what I'm going to do." Tears welled in her eyes and ran down her face. She reached for the hospital tissue on the side table. Hank got it first, and then, as gently as he could, dabbed her darkened eyes. The moisture made them glisten like wet coal.

"That's understandable, Sister. You've been through an ordeal."

"I keep running last night's scene through my head like a broken record. I was sure one of the sisters put the poison in Mother Rosaria's drink. Now, I'm not so sure. I keep asking myself who would want Mother Rosaria dead. I can only come up with one or two sisters who disagreed with some of her new policies. That isn't enough to commit murder. Besides, a sister is dedicated to God, becomes a bride of Christ, and strives to lead the best life she can.

"But who'd want to hurt me? Maybe he or she thought I wouldn't be injured, only wanted to scare me because I was on the track of finding him or her."

She said, "I was so sure it was Sister Angelica at the costume closet door. It was dark, and I thought she was in costume. Even if I hadn't hit my head on the concrete steps and passed out, I'd never be able to let anybody know I was there. If I banged on the door and yelled, nobody would ever have heard me that time of the evening."

The detective nodded, allowing her to think it through.

"Hank, have you ever had a case like this? Are you closer to finding the murderer? I've wanted to help you more."

Hank squeezed her hand gently. "You've been very brave, Sister. Did you know you have a police officer outside your door? You can relax now and rest. I plan to keep him here until it's safe for you to return. Do you mind talking about yesterday's events?"

"No, not at all."

He pulled out his notebook. "Did you notice a change in anyone around you yesterday, Sister? Start early in the morning and take your time."

"Do you want me to go through the whole day?"

"That would be a good idea."

"We rise at five and don't break 'great silence' until after seven o'clock Mass. Up to this time, we're at prayer. I didn't notice anything. Then I went to the kitchen, made toast, dished up hot cereal, and filled the coffeepots from the urn. I ate cold cereal, canned apricots, toast, and coffee in the kitchen alcove. I was alone until Miss Drekle came in at eight o'clock. We went over the dinner and supper menus, then I went to chapel to chant the little hours with the sisters.

"Miss Drekle seemed her usual self. She's a typical spinster, always wears her hair the same, pulled back in a roll. She brings a fresh apron every day.

"After little hours, I went to the academy to give Natalie Cooper her piano lesson."

"Did you meet anyone on your way to the academy wing?"

Sister Camille shook her head. "No, I walked outside, around the back of the chapel to the west door of the academy and up the back steps. I like to feel the morning air and avoid any activity around the directress' office by taking this route. Also, it's handy to our studio, which is at the top of the steps. I didn't meet anyone going or returning. It's still silence time, so I wouldn't plan to meet Sister Angelica unless it was necessary."

"The piano lesson was at what time?"

"Nine thirty to ten thirty. I had forty-five minutes left after the lesson to practice before returning to the kitchen."

"Was Mrs. Simmons there at that time?"

"Yes, she comes in at ten."

"How did Mrs. Simmons appear to you when you came to the kitchen?"

"Well, come to think of it; she was quiet. I thought she had some family problems bothering her. She often does because of Joe's drinking. Sometimes she's very talkative and sometimes not. After I checked on the dinner, I helped her dish up the bread-pudding dessert. At this time, we aren't very talkative. It's a busy time just before dinner. We're anxious to get the food on the table hot, and everything is clockwork. At the first stroke of the Angelus, we're all in action."

"How about the sisters? Did you meet any?"

"No, Hank, only Sister Laura came to the kitchen to take care of the poor men about twelve thirty."

"And Mother Cordelia?" Hank asked.

"What do you mean? I didn't see her all morning."

"Did you notice any reaction in her since the investigation stopped?"

"Oh yes. She's acted like the investigation was finished, and that she stopped it. She ignored me, but that's nothing new. I respect her as my superior, and that's that. I had heard she called the archbishop and that he stopped your investigation. However, this was never discussed in the community. I learned about it bit by bit."

"You must have felt defeated after what you went through to get the investigation started," Hank said.

"You're right there, Hank, but I still had your phone number. Sister Angelica and I were determined to see this through. We didn't get you here for nothing. Also we heard His Eminence was coming Monday."

Sister Camille continued, "Since you were only here one day, Sister Angelica and I figured you didn't get the typewriters tested, so we did it."

"What did you discover?"

"We found the typewriter in the kitchen had the fuzzy *h*. But I wasn't sure without comparing it to the card I gave you."

"Good work, Sister. That corroborates our findings."

"I almost got caught when I tested the typewriter in Mother Cordelia's office. She was called to the phone during meditation. I don't think she saw me leave."

"But you were treated okay after the investigation was interrupted?"

"Yes. I was anxious, though."

"Okay, so you ate dinner at second table. Was that in the kitchen alcove or in the refectory?"

"The refectory. The only reason I eat in the alcove in the morning is because Miss. Drekle hasn't come yet, and someone is needed there to take care of refills. We never eat in front of lay persons."

"Then what did you do?"

"I continued with my regular routine. After recreation, I went to chapel to do my spiritual reading and afternoon meditation. I make my meditation early because I go to the kitchen when the community makes theirs."

"That's at five o'clock?"

"Yes. After meditation, I met Sister Angelica. We went for a walk and circled around the monastery grounds to the cemetery even though Mother Rosaria's body isn't there."

"Continue, Sister," Kummer urged.

"At four thirty, we went to chapel to chant vespers, and at five, I left the chapel and went to the kitchen."

"Did you notice anything out of the ordinary with Mrs. Simmons?"

"No. We had a tossed green salad and spaghetti for supper. I buttered the garlic bread and put canned peaches in bowls."

"And after supper?"

"Mrs. Simmon's shift is finished, and she's gone home by the time I eat. I had a little time before the seven-thirty evening recreation."

"What do you do then, Sister?"

"Not much. Sometimes I go to our cell and take the spread off the bed. Maybe draw fresh water in our pitcher for later, or read. But last night, we finished by six forty-five. I went to the academy to practice."

"Did you mention to anybody that you were going to practice?"

"No, I don't think I did."

Hank looked at his watch and put his notebook away. "I've taxed you too long." He rose to go. "You need to rest now."

"I'm not a bit sleepy." Sister held out both hands to him.

"I know." He smiled and held her hand for a few seconds. "I'll see you tomorrow. It won't be long now. Sergeant Flanagan and I will be finished in a few days."

"I'm so glad you're back." She remembered saying this before.

Lieutenant Kummer left and greeted the relief officer outside Sister's room. He warned him about visitors from the hospital staff who weren't nurses and told him to check the list of nurses on duty that evening. Then he went to the nurses' station. He recognized the blond nurse the guard had spoken about. "Sister Camille is feeling tense. Did Dr. Spence leave directions for another sedative tonight?"

The nurse pulled up Sister's chart. "Yes, Lieutenant. Dr. Spence ordered a sedative if she asks for one. I'm going to see her in a few minutes."

"Good, I think I kept her too long. Do you have a Hope Jackson on your hospital staff?"

"Hope Jackson?" The nurse shook her head slowly. "I don't know of her. I'll check with administration tomorrow. Is there a problem?"

"The officer on guard intercepted a Hope Jackson who tried to enter Sister Camille's room this afternoon. Claimed she was on the hospital staff. Do you have the phone number of your administrator?"

24

Sister Dorothy entered the library a few minutes after Kummer rang for her. "I was nearby with the house cleaners in the academy when I got your message, Lieutenant." She tucked her folded apron under her arm, at the same time unpinned her rolled-up sleeves. It wasn't customary for a sister to appear before visitors in an apron and with bare arms showing.

"You have house cleaners working? Tell me, Sister, how long have they been here?" Kummer asked.

"We started in the academy Thursday, Lieutenant. The Roberts are a husband-and-wife cleaning team. They've helped us the past three summers." Sister finished unfolding her sleeves and slid her hands inside them.

"Where are they working today?"

"We're in the seventh-grade classroom."

"And where were they yesterday? I didn't see them when we searched for Sister Camille."

"They weren't cleaning yesterday. They asked for the day off to go to a funeral."

"I see." Kummer stalled for a moment. "I want to ask you about Joe Simmons' work history. When did Mrs. Simmons and Joe begin work at the Chateau?"

"They started in October year before last. Do you want the specific date? I can check my records."

"No, that won't be necessary. Has Joe been laid off at any time since you hired him?"

"Yes, Lieutenant, he was." Sister Dorothy's face grew serious. "Mother Rosaria fired Joe a few weeks ago, just before graduation. It was early in the week of the Memorial Day holiday. Then Mother Cordelia rehired him the day of her election. That was June twenty-first."

"Why was he let go?"

"Joe claimed he was sick. After the weather turned warm, Joe didn't show up for work. We asked one of our school bus drivers, an off-duty policeman, to check on him." As an afterthought, she added, "He didn't go as a policeman. He found Joe drunk, his garbage pail full of whiskey bottles."

"And what about Mrs. Simmons? Did she report to work every day?"

"Yes, Lieutenant. She came in every day right on schedule and reported Joe sick. I could tell she was worried because Mother Rosaria had warned her Joe would be fired if he didn't come to work the following Monday."

"And?"

"He skipped again. Mother Rosaria fired him that same day."

"What was that date?"

"On a Monday, I remember." Sister Dorothy went to a calendar on the wall, flipped the page back to May, and fingered the weeks. "Monday, May twenty-sixth, Lieutenant."

"So Mother Rosaria fired Joe Simmons May twenty-sixth, and Mother Cordelia rehired him June twentieth. Thank you, Sister, for your help."

Eyeing the newspaper on the table, Sister Dorothy asked, "Before I go, could you tell me what's happening to the Detroit Tigers? How do the box scores read?"

Kummer smiled, always happy to find someone who shared his interest in baseball. He opened the sports section to the American League stats. "Here." He closed the paper and handed it to her. "Take it with you. I'm finished with that section."

Sister Dorothy put her hand to her lips as though she had talked out of turn. "No thanks, Lieutenant. We don't read newspapers."

"You don't?" The detective raised his eyebrows, searching Sister's face. He shaped his lips to protest but noticed she was embarrassed. Opening the sport pages, he read, "The Tigers rank second. Yesterday, they played Boston and won. They had three runs, ten hits, no errors, and one of the runs was a homer."

"I bet that was Al Kaline. My brother wrote to me about him."

"You're right, Sister. He's good, a complete ball player. Anything else? Another team?"

"No thanks, Lieutenant. I need to get back to my workers."

Kummer folded the newspaper and laid it on the table. "Then I'm going to take a walk to the boiler room."

They left the library and walked partway down the hall together. Sister Dorothy returned to the house cleaners. Kummer went down the stairs. The eighty-five-degree temperature that second day of July, at 68-percent humidity, hit him as he opened the north door. The sun burnt off the early-morning overcast, and the day promised to be muggy. Now that the officers knew their way around, they didn't need an escort, though Mother Cordelia still demanded it in the monastery. He walked down a gravel path, past bridal wreath and rose bushes, to a detached red brick building about eighty yards away. The roses were not as manicured as those in front of the Chateau, though the sweet scent remained. He stooped to smell them then continued. After repeated knocks on the boiler room door, Kummer unlatched it and looked in.

He saw Joe Simmons walking toward him. Joe's hair stuck out as if he had just gotten out of bed. Besides his surly appearance, he wore the same faded plaid shirt with a yellowed ring of sweat around the collar. A carpenter's pencil poked out of the middle pocket of his Oshkosh overalls. On his left arm, a tattooed pair of shapely legs danced below a rolled sleeve.

Kummer extended his hand and held up his badge. "Detective Kummer. Just tying up some loose ends, Joe. Can I take a few minutes of your time?"

"Sure, come into my office." Joe blew a breath of eighty-proof whiskey into the detective's face. "How's it going? Heard you were back." He ran his hands through his oily hair and led the detective through the furnace room past the workbench into a tiny adjoining room.

A cot was crowded into it along with a large rolltop desk and a swivel chair. The oak desk, stained from oily hands, rags, and coffee, hugged the wall just inside the door. A once white ceramic mug, now blackened from coffee stains, sat next to the phone. From the radio atop the desk, Perry Como sang, "Don't let the stars get in your eyes; don't let the moon . . ."

Joe snapped off the radio, picked up his engineer's cap, and put it over his unruly hair. Except for the long hairs extending out of his ears, the cap gave Joe a perky engineer's appearance. He swung the swivel chair around and motioned the detective to sit. When Kummer sat on it, the spring squawked like a mule.

Joe leaned over the side of the cot and held up a bottle of Vat 69. "Want a shot?"

"Not now, Joe, thanks."

Joe started to unscrew the cap then decided against it. He returned the bottle to its resting place and sat back on the thin mattress. His barrel-shaped belly sank between his knees.

Without preamble, Kummer asked, "When were you fired from the Chateau, Joe?"

"Fired? Who told you that?"

"I have my sources."

"I wasn't really fired, Lieutenant. I was sick."

"What were the dates, please?"

Joe stood up and reached to the wall for the greased, stained calendar featuring Vargas nudes. Fumbling through the month of "Miss. May," he pointed to a Monday, mumbling, "May twenty-sixth."

"Who released you from your job?"

"Mother Rosaria."

"And when were you rehired? The date?"

"Well, if you want to call it that. I don't." He got up again, puffing from the exertion. He flipped the calendar pages again. "Mother Cordelia called me June twenty-sixth." He sat back on the mattress and laced his fingers across his protruding stomach. His large boxerlike knuckles rose and fell with each heaving breath. "I just needed the rest." He shifted his hands to his suspenders and hooked his thumbs in them.

"Where were you the afternoon of June fifteenth? That was a Sunday."

"Most Sundays, you'll find me home watching the ball games. I put in a long week and need to rest. Had supper at five o'clock, then me and the wife walked home."

"Thanks, Joe, that's all I wanted to know." Kummer left the boiler room and left the Chateau for lunch.

25

Kummer and Flanagan sat in the chief's smoke-filled office waiting for him to finish his phone conversation. Hank picked up the morning newspaper and read from the *Madison Times* to his partner. "The jury reached a decision on the Hook case. Our man Hook got a life sentence."

Flanagan looked over his shoulder to see the news item about a case they'd partnered on more than a year ago. It involved a farmhand who claimed he fell asleep beside a creek. He said his five-year-old nephew had fallen into the creek and drowned. The attending physician called the sheriff after he found an absence of water in the boy's lungs and abrasions on the body.

"We were lucky that Doc sure clinched it," Flanagan said. "If it wasn't for his testimony, I doubt the jury would have returned a guilty verdict."

"But bringing the defendant to the morgue without his attorney nearly blew it."

Chief Haskell hung up the phone. "That was His Eminence. What have you got?"

"There's a hell of a lot of opportunity all over the Chateau," Flanagan said. "Mother Cordelia was the last to see the deceased. Sister Mercy brought the coffee laced with cyanide. Sister Laura spends time in the kitchen at mealtimes feeding the poor men. And then there's Sister Eugene, the directress, who's free to wander all over the joint while the rest of the sisters are at prayers and meals. They all have alibis."

"Lame alibis, Flanagan," the chief was quick to reply. "Any witnesses?"

"None," Kummer answered. Homicide by poison was the most difficult of all murders to solve because it often resembled suicide, especially in an older person.

"Where do you think the sisters got the cyanide?"

Kummer said, "Could be rat poison or silver polish. Anyone could have a supply of these commercial products. The chemist at the police lab knew of a process developed from peach and apricot pits."

"Motive?"

Kummer said, "Both Mother Cordelia and Sister Eugene worried about the reputation of the academy after an alumna discovered a Chateau senior was pregnant. The parent and Sister Eugene wanted the girl expelled. This occurred only two weeks before the June graduation. The deceased overrode their decision and allowed her to graduate. This caused a rift."

"Mother Cordelia had most to gain," Kummer said. "After Mother Rosaria was poisoned, she was reelected mother superior again.

"As for Sister Eugene, she seems pissed off about the deceased's management ways. No special treatment for the older gals. Seems like the perfect crime."

"Seems?" The chief glared at Flanagan then asked, "The infirmarian, what's her name?"

"Sister Mercy," Kummer answered. "She's clean. Happened to be in the right place at the wrong time."

"That's it? Terrific. Are you telling me what we got so far is worthless?" The chief got up from his desk, banging a brown envelope against his leg. "The archbishop will be glad to hear that!"

"We'll begin with Mrs. Simmons, one of the cooks, today. She worked only a half day yesterday. She and Mr. Simmons left the city in the afternoon," Kummer said, unshaken by the chief's abrupt manner.

"Check the typewriters?"

"Found the culprit in the kitchen office. Sent the typewriter to the lab for verification."

"Any latent prints?"

"Sent them in too," Flanagan added.

"*Tempus fugit*, gentlemen. Find out who the hell is passing the poison before we have another corpse on our hands." Chief Haskell opened the door. He tagged Kummer's sleeve. "How's your friend, Sister Camille?"

"She has a slight concussion and is still in the hospital."

"Good. Keep her there. Nasty shock."

The officers left the police station and arrived at the Chateau at nine thirty. Before leaving the car, Kummer said, "We'll start with Mrs. Simmons. Call for a pitcher of water and three glasses. Set them at the end of the table."

"Sure thing. I'll call Sister Dorothy for that."

Sister Portress opened the front door, smiling for the first time. "Good morning, Officers." She dipped her finger into a holy water font hanging on the wall and made the sign of the cross.

The officers greeted her. "Good morning, Sister." They followed her example and dipped their fingers into the font. Flanagan held his up, ready to flick the water at Hank, but reined in his impulse when Sister glanced back. They continued unescorted down the hall to the library. The morning sun slanted through the spotless windows as they settled in.

Flanagan called Mrs. Simmons. She appeared wearing a long white apron appropriately spattered with tomatoes and other stains more difficult to define. She stood at the door with her head bowed, as though she didn't want to trouble anyone.

"Good morning, Mrs. Simmons." Kummer beckoned her to a chair. "Glad you could spare the time to see us. Please sit down."

They watched her tilt her head in a coy way and wink as if she had something in common with them. With one hand braced on the table, she bent over to aim her ample bottom at the seat. "I guess you know we goin' to be shorthanded in the kitchen if I'm here."

"Sergeant, call Mother Cordelia and tell her Mrs. Simmons is with us." Turning back to her, he said, "As you know, Officer Flanagan and I are here to investigate the death of Mother Rosaria."

"Ain't that an awful way to go?"

"It must have been very painful," Kummer agreed. "Now then, tell us about yourself. What is your full name?"

"Zelda Simmons, sir." She said it proudly, twisting an elastic band on her wrist. "Call me Zelda."

"How long have you worked for the sisters?"

Moving her head from one side to the other, she added up the months. "Me and Joe been here since February '51. We come here from Sinai Manor, a nursing home near Chicago. Ain't it awful what happened to Sister Camille?" She stretched her legs out and lolled to one side of the chair.

"It certainly was," Kummer agreed. "Sister Camille speaks highly of you. Says she enjoys working with you."

"And I like her." Zelda allowed her smile to remain a few seconds. "She's an interesting person, and genuine too. Ain't all the sisters as real as her."

"What do you mean by that?" Kummer decided to let her go on. He was used to listening, however boring the talk.

"I see what goes on." Mrs. Simmons tossed her head in the direction of the monastery.

Kummer sensed she was going to put every nuance into her performance and waited.

"Sister Camille's her own person. She don't brownnose nobody and don't care what others think. And she don't wear her religion on her sleeve." Mrs. Simmons tilted her head at Kummer. "But she's cheeky. I think she made a big mistake about the death of Mother Rosaria. Poor Mother Cordelia has her troubles now." Mrs. Simmons shook her head. "Whew."

"Did Sister Camille talk to you about Mother Rosaria's death?" Kummer asked.

"Call me Zelda, Lieutenant."

"Zelda, did Sister Camille tell you anything after Mother Rosaria died?"

"No, she'd been unusually quiet, used to be fun to be around, so I asked Sister Laura about her. It was Sister Laura who told me the body was dug up, and Sister Camille started the whole mess."

"What else?"

"Well, I knowed something was wrong on the other side of the wall," Mrs. Simmons said. "That's the monastery." She jutted her chin in that direction then leaned closer to Kummer and whispered, "Who knows what goes on there? It's so secretive. You get that feeling when you work on this side, know what I mean, Lieutenant?"

"Have you and Joe worked continuously at the Chateau since February 1951?"

Mrs. Simmons leaned back in her chair, twisting the elastic on her wrist. "Yes, we have, Lieutenant."

She was telling him too much, a nervous habit displayed by both the guilty and innocent, though the innocent usually calmed down after a bit.

"I suppose you're going to ask me what I was doing that Sunday, June fifteenth?"

"I had that in mind," Kummer responded with a half smile.

"Well, Sister Cee and I was working together. That's what I call Sister Camille for short. I got nicknames for all of them. Well, we was making supper together. She stared at the wall as if the menu was printed on it. It was cold cuts, baked beans, and coleslaw, with ice cream for dessert. Everything seemed okay to me."

"I see. Did you leave the kitchen area for any length of time that afternoon? Maybe you got tired and took a little nap?"

"No," she said. "I'd never leave for a reason like that." She spoke slowly, shaking her head.

"For what reasons would you leave the kitchen?"

"If Joe needed something, I might leave for a few minutes." She winked.

"Did he need you, or did you need him that afternoon?" Kummer coaxed, joining in with her playful suggestion.

"No, I didn't leave the kitchen for nothing."

"Did you notice anything unusual with the coming and going of the sisters?"

"No. Just Sister Mercy come in around five thirty with her cart, and oh yes, Sister Eugene come through to the cooler. She often does."

"What is 'often'? Once a day or more than once a day?"

"Almost every day around mealtime. She eats early and helps herself at the stove to the choicest cuts or sometimes comes in late to second table."

"Zelda, where did you attend school?" Kummer leaned his chin in his hand.

"I went to a country school near Moberly, Missouri."

"Did you ever take a typing class?"

"No, I only went to eighth grade. They didn't have no typewriter machines there."

"Have you ever tried to type? A lot of us do what we call 'hunt and peck.'" Kummer turned toward Flanagan. "Isn't that what you do, Sergeant?"

Flanagan nodded. "Only way I know."

"Mrs. Simmons, have you done any 'hunt and peck' typing in the kitchen office?"

"On the typewriter in the kitchen?"

Kummer noticed that she made statements into questions. "Yes," he repeated. "On the typewriter in the kitchen."

"I might have, once. Why?"

"We have a postcard in the evidence file at the police station that Mother Rosaria received in the mail a few weeks before she died. It was a threat. We also have fingerprints taken from it. Did you type the message on that postcard?"

"What you talking about? I told you I don't know how to type, and not your 'hunt and peck' style either." Her fists balled.

Fingerprints tell the truth better than words. Kummer poured water into a glass and pushed it toward her. "It's warm today; perhaps, you're thirsty." Then he poured a glass for himself.

"Thank you, sir." She smiled, took the glass, and drank it. "Thoughtful of you to think of it." Zelda reached for her watch hanging around her neck to check the time.

Her movement caught Kummer's eye. "That's an attractive watch."

"Yes." She caressed it. "Joe give it to me on our anniversary." She pressed the stem button to see the time and then snapped it closed. She pressed again to reveal a picture of Joe on the reverse side. The photo, cut from a snapshot, fell to the floor. "I can't seem to make Joe stay in there," she said, laughing, and bent down to pick up the photo.

Kummer watched as she reinserted the picture and snapped it closed. "May I see your watch, Mrs. Simmons?"

The once-playful Mrs. Simmons gave him a cold stare as though she hadn't heard him. Kummer repeated his request. She sat motionless then slowly raised the chain from the back of her neck, dragging it over her hair that was kept in place by a hair net. She laid it on the table as though it was a newborn infant.

Kummer took it and pressed the stem downward. As it opened, the photo of Joe fell out onto the table.

"Does this snapshot always fall out?" he asked. He studied Mrs. Simmons' expression intently, waiting for her answer.

"It stayed until." She stopped then added, "I need to glue it in, I guess."

Kummer noticed her hesitation and continued examining the cavity without touching the cavity then snapped it closed. "I'd like to borrow your locket for today. I promise you'll get it back. Will that be all right with you?"

"No, sir. Me and that watch don't separate. I plan to shorten and solder the chain, so it can't come off." She reached out for it. "It's genuine eighteen-carat gold!"

The detective handed it to Flanagan who played with it like a new toy, snapping the front and back.

"Mrs. Simmons, Officer Flanagan will write you a receipt for the locket, and I promise we'll return it to you tonight or at least by tomorrow." He added, "I'm sorry to have to take it from you. I'll call you after we're finished with it. I suggest you stay in Stone Hill in case I need to reach you." He got up from his chair indicating the end of the interview.

Near tears, Mrs. Simmons got up and waddled out of the room. Kummer closed the door after her.

He turned to Flanagan. "What do you think?"

"She paints one hell of a smoke screen, if you ask me." Flanagan pulled an evidence bag from his pocket and held it open.

Kummer tented a handkerchief over Zelda's drinking glass and placed it in the bag, the locket in another. "Mark it 'urgent' and take it to the lab. I'll call Bruce to see if he can test it while you're there. The rest of the reports should be ready too. Check on them."

After Flanagan left, he called the crime lab. Bruce Chadwick came on the line. "How do I get rid of you, Hank?"

"This is important, Bruce. Sergeant Flanagan is on his way over with a locket. How long would it take you to test it for cyanide residue?"

"If you know for sure what you're testing for, maybe an hour."

"Good. Could you get right on it?"

"I'll do my best, Hank. What I'll do is send a summary with Flanagan and a full report in the mail. Will that do?"

"That's all I need. I'm much obliged, Bruce."

Kummer spotted a hearse by the cemetery gate. He walked toward the small group of nuns gathered for the reinternment of Mother Rosaria. Mother Cordelia was there as well as Sisters Diana, Dorothy, and Angelica. Monsignor Burrows read a brief prayer by the grave as the coffin was lowered into the hole. Aloysius stood near ready to heap dirt on the pine box.

Kummer waited until the ceremony was finished then joined the sisters. He greeted Mother Cordelia. "You must be relieved to have this part of the investigation completed. It hasn't been easy. I hope to have my part finished soon."

Mother Cordelia's eyes settled into a deep scowl. "Lieutenant Kummer, it will be a long time before our community recovers from your investigation." She then added as though it churned in her mind, "'Heat not a furnace for your foe so hot, that it do singe yourself.'" Without waiting for his response, she turned away dismissing him.

Kummer thought quoting Shakespeare was her way to ensure the final word in a conversation. Did the sisters find it entertaining, or were they hiding their amusement in her presence? On his part, he was beginning to enjoy her salient quotations delivered with an Ethel Barrymore touch. He followed a distance behind the sisters as they walked toward the monastery entrance.

Settling back in the library, he went over his notes. He placed the schedule of each person he had interviewed on the table. His work compelled him to go over the schedules until they made sense, and now they did. As he reviewed them, Flanagan phoned from the police lab. Flanagan's message brought a smile to his face. He hung up, called Dr. Spence, then Mother Cordelia, and drove to the hospital.

26

Lieutenant Kummer called Zelda Simmons back.

She asked, "What did you find out?"

Kummer noticed a distinct change in her expression, her attitude, and her walk. "We haven't determined anything yet, but we're ready to push forward." He stood, waiting for her to sit.

"I told you all I knowed," Zelda Simmons said.

"But I have more questions. Did you or Joe have any disagreements with Mother Rosaria, Mrs. Simmons?"

"Zelda," she insisted. "Call me Zelda."

"Zelda, how did you and Joe get along with Mother Rosaria?"

"I thought she was a saint." Zelda smiled.

"How many men ate in the dining room that Sunday evening, June fifteenth?"

"Just Joe. It was Sunday. Aloysius and the handyman don't never work Sundays."

"And you worked until six o'clock?"

"Yes, Lieutenant. I gotta go now. We're short in the kitchen with Sister Camille in the hospital."

Kummer studied her dreary expression. Sister Camille had returned to the Chateau the evening before, but he didn't give Zelda that information. Earlier that morning, he directed Flanagan to stay at the police station. In final interrogations, he wanted to gain the suspects' trust and felt this could be effected if he acted alone. A perpetrator was more inclined to confess if he or she had privacy with no witnesses. He had also worn a gun holster under his coat.

"I told you all I knowed," she repeated.

"I haven't given you all the questions yet, Zelda. I have reason to believe that cyanide crystals were put into the deceased's coffeepot." Kummer watched her eyes. "We've carried out extensive lab tests, and I believe you were involved."

Mrs. Simmons sat immobile. "I told you I don't know nothing about that."

"You don't?" He knew she was scared, and he expected her to deny the accusation. Suspects lied to protect their self-esteem, a typical pattern during interrogation. "I had your watch tested. The Dane County Drug and Alcohol Laboratory found traces of cyanide in the cavity of it."

"That's impossible. I wasn't never near that poison."

"That poison?"

"Yeah, that poison." Zelda sat straight with her arms folded against her breasts.

"Then what poison were you near?"

"No poison. None, never." Her arms jerked tighter together.

Kummer watched her intently.

"I was not near no poison, Lieutenant." Her voice rose.

"I believe cyanide crystals were carried in the picture side of your watch and dumped into the coffeepot Sister Mercy put on the kitchen stove. You knew the coffeepot was for Mother Rosaria's tray."

"That's not so." Mrs. Simmons sat very straight and stiff. She didn't move. Her eyes darted back and forth wildly to an invisible object behind him. They finally rested, though unfocused, on the picture of Raphael's *Madonna and Child*.

As though there had been no interruption, Kummer continued, "Did you put the poison in Mother Rosaria's coffeepot?"

"No."

"I'm warning you, Zelda. You lied to me before when I asked you about Joe's work history at the Chateau. You're in an awkward situation when you lie in a murder investigation. I can make it very difficult for you. You can refrain from answering my questions, and I'll record that. Now, you have to convince me what you say is the truth."

"Ain't you never been scared?" Her fingers clamped the arms of her chair. She stared at Kummer like a frightened kitten ready to pounce. "I thought you was a nice person."

Kummer said, "In a murder case, niceness is not my first priority."

"I ain't listening to no more of this. Don't I get to have a lawyer here?"

"You have that right, Zelda. We can go downtown to continue the questioning with your attorney present, or we can stay here." Kummer spoke softly. "I haven't arrested you yet or violated your rights. Right now, I want the truth. Would you prefer the police station, Mrs. Simmons?"

He stood up abruptly. His chair shrieked as it scraped the floor. He reached back to unclip handcuffs under his coat. In that motion, his coat fell open, revealing a holstered Smith & Wesson .38 Special. He resumed his seat. Ominous handcuffs clattered on the smooth table surface.

"Zelda." Kummer leaned across the table, maintaining eye contact.

Mrs. Simmons recoiled as he drew closer.

"Zelda, you've been a good worker and a dedicated wife. You must have had a difficult life, moving from job to job when Joe got fired. Your records from Sinai Manor and other places report exemplary work. Mother Cordelia and Sister Camille both speak highly of your cooking skills and your ability to get along with other employees at the Chateau. You're a decent, reliable, hard-working lady. You've had a rough time looking for employment and looking for places to live for how long, Zelda?"

Her eyes widened, shocked that he knew so much about her. Kummer waited a few seconds. "Anyone else in your situation might have done the same thing." He appeared to be in no hurry. Nor did he wish to browbeat her. That would come later if he didn't get a full confession. Now, he wanted to bring in a tidy package, a signed, recorded confession that would leave no doubt to a jury.

Zelda pulled a tissue from her pocket and blew her nose.

He continued, "Many others have committed far worse, more shameful crimes than you, Zelda, and just possibly, you didn't mean to kill Mother Rosaria. Maybe you only wanted to put her out of commission for a while. Or maybe you didn't realize the cyanide dose was fatal." He provided her with a face-saving excuse.

"I ain't done it, Lieutenant," Zelda said weakly.

Using technique straight out of the interrogation manual 101, he leaned over the table and spoke in a sympathetic voice. "I never met Mother Rosaria, but from what I've heard, she was a woman who wanted to make drastic changes in the community. Some of the sisters resisted her ideas just as you did." He let that sink in a moment. "Maybe, it wasn't entirely your fault."

"When do I get my watch back?" Mrs. Simmons demanded.

"In good time, Zelda," he said. "So you made one mistake in your fifty-five years. If you confess now, you can learn by this one mistake and avoid other crimes later."

A first offender often could see the rationale of this suggestion. Kummer watched her head and shoulders slump forward. Her chest folded within itself; her arms closed tightly over her middle.

He continued, "There's no point in denying your involvement, Zelda. We have enough evidence to convict you even if you don't confess." He chose his words carefully. "What I want now is that you have a chance to tell your own story."

Zelda couldn't hold back the tears. Hank reached into his coat pocket and handed her a folded handkerchief. Then he flipped the knob of the tape recorder and picked up his pencil.

"I had so much trouble in my life," Zelda sobbed. "Nobody," she blew her nose, "nobody knowed how much I been through. You don't know how it felt being shoved from one job to another.

"Joe drank too much. I knowed that." She wiped her eyes. "Everything woulda been okay if she didn't fire him." Zelda emphasized "she" in a resentful tone. "But she said she had other information. She said the law was after Joe for a murder he done years ago, thirty years ago in Alabama. Where she got that information I don't know. I thought, I can't never move again. I liked working for the sisters.

"Joe got me that nice house, and it all seemed like it was working for us. Then, she come as the new superior." She dabbed her tears.

"What exactly happened the afternoon of June fifteenth?"

Zelda laid the handkerchief in her lap. "Joe knowed how to make rat poison from apricot pits when he was in the merchant marines. So I says we got rats in the kitchen and make me a fresh batch. Before I went to work, I took out Joe's picture from my watch and put the crystals in it. Then I dumped the crystals in the coffeepot I knowed would go on Mother Rosaria's tray. I couldn't never make Joe's picture stay in after that."

"You say before you went to work? What time was that, Zelda?"

"Must of been between nine and nine thirty. I can't remember the exact time."

"Did you send the postcard to Mother Rosaria?"

"Just wanted to scare her. I hoped she'd leave things be." Zelda buried her eyes in his handkerchief and shook her head. "It almost worked. To almost everyone, her death looked natural except Sister Cee. Then I found out she called you; that's when I dressed as a clown and locked her up. Aloysius give me the master key, and I typed the note and put it under her door. That was easy cause there was no sisters in the school at night. I knowed Sister Cee often practiced her piano after she left the kitchen. I only wanted to scare her. I didn't mean to hurt her. It was an accident." Mrs. Simmons wiped her nose. "I heard the bishop was coming and knowed he'd stir up trouble again."

Still writing, his head down, Kummer heard a big sigh that seemed to come from Zelda's toes.

He looked up from his notes and saw relief on her face. "Did Joe know why you wanted the rat poison?"

"No, he ain't had nothing to do with my plan, and that's no lie. What will happen to Joe? He needs me."

The detective laid his pencil on the table. "You'll see Joe, Zelda. I salute you for your clear confession. I hope the judge will take your circumstances into consideration."

He turned off the tape recorder and called headquarters to request transit. Then he went over the confession with her in detail. Mrs. Simmons listened to the tape, occasionally welling up in tears.

"Do you have any questions? Or do you want to add anything?"

Zelda read Kummer's notes, nodding her head sadly. "It's all there."

"Please sign this and date it, Zelda."

She took his pen and signed. Her hand shook as she wrote her name.

Two police officers appeared at the library door. At Kummer's nod, they handcuffed Mrs. Simmons and led her out to the waiting black and white.

Then Lieutenant Kummer made one last call to Mother Cordelia.

The superior entered the room and sat down. "Did I just see Mrs. Simmons go off in the police car, Lieutenant?"

Kummer observed a friendlier attitude. "Yes, Mother Cordelia. It's all over. You can rest easy. Mrs. Simmons confessed to putting cyanide crystals into Mother Rosaria's coffeepot. The police officers have taken her into custody. Sergeant Flanagan and I are finished. I'll call the phone company to disconnect the line." He said this while packing his briefcase and tape recorder.

Mother Cordelia watched him a few seconds. "'The web of our life is a mingled yarn, good and ill together.'"

Lieutenant Kummer shook her outstretched hand. He couldn't resist showing off his limited knowledge. "And all's well that ends well."

A small smile started to develop then grew on Mother Cordelia's face.

They both broke into relieved laughter.

"Thank you, Lieutenant. You managed to carry on even though I put obstacles in your way." She turned and left.

Off in the distance, Hank Kummer heard a piano. He looked at his watch. It was a few minutes before eleven. Stretching his limbs, he walked out the door and down the hall toward the music department. Although he didn't keep up the trumpet he had played in high school, he appreciated a well-executed piece. The music he heard now sounded unfamiliar. Kummer waited outside Sister Camille's studio door until he heard the chord repetition at the end of the piece then knocked. Sister Camille opened the door.

"What a nice surprise. How are you, Hank? Come in." She beckoned him to a chair and sat on the piano bench facing him.

"I can't stay. I just wanted to see how you are today. You're looking better." He didn't want to tell her the black eyes were fading into a greenish yellow. "How do you feel otherwise?"

"More like myself. It's the first time I felt like practicing."

"You play very well. That piece you just played was beautiful. What is the name of it?"

"It was the Liszt B Minor Sonata."

"That's a powerful piece of music. Play something else. I can spare a few minutes."

"Would you prefer Bach or Brahms?"

"I'll pick Brahms."

Sister Camille sat at the grand piano and started the slow opening of the intermezzo. She played as though there wasn't any one else in the room. Her fingers moved gracefully, receiving commands from her mind that had fully digested the themes and thick textures created by the composer.

Kummer sat back watching her hands, and arms in coordination. Then he closed his eyes, giving himself entirely to the sounds. He pictured a forest landscape with rivers and flowers waving in a gentle breeze. Sister Camille played the final cadence. Kummer remained quiet at a different level of awareness. Maybe Sister needed time to recover from the glorious sounds she produced. He thought he would like to take her for a ride in the country or maybe a picnic by a quiet stream, any place away from the monastery. He hadn't indulged in such thoughts for years. Today, he wanted to do something for her.

"That was beautiful, Sister." Hank could see she shrugged off his compliment. No doubt their holy foundress taught that a nun shouldn't take pleasure in flattering words and must guard against the sin of pride.

Hank stood up and took both her hands in his. He pretended to examine them, turning them this way and that in a detective-like way. "I see you keep your fingernails clipped. Does that help your touch?"

With their hands joined, Sister Camille smiled, ignoring his question, "I'm so glad you're here."

Kummer refrained from leaning his head closer to her hands. He just wanted to touch them with his eyes, not his lips. Would that be so awful? He didn't do either. Instead, he released them.

"I'll be leaving. We arrested Zelda Simmons this morning for poisoning Mother Rosaria and for aggravated assault."

"Really, Hank? It's all over? I don't feel a bit like rejoicing. I thought I'd be so happy after this was completed that I'd want to sing Handel's "Alleluia Chorus." But what about the voices I heard? Was that my imagination?"

"Sister Eugene had given Mother Rosaria a pill to relax."

"Was that it?"

"You sound disappointed. You know, if ever you need me, just call. You've got my number." Kummer wrapped his arms around her loosely and then left.

Sister Camille closed the door after him and leaned her head against it. What was this sudden invasion into her life supposed to mean? She was honest with herself when she said she was glad he had come, and she enjoyed playing the piano for him. Was that it, or was there more to Hank's visit to her studio?

Sister pulled out the pocket watch and checked the time. It was time for her to return to the kitchen. Miss. Drekel would be alone. She opened the door and walked down the back steps. Through a window, she stopped to watch Hank getting into his car.

Through the influence of the archbishop and the chief of police, a short, discreet news item appeared on the back page of the Stone Hill *Agrarian Gazette*.

CHATEAU COOK ARRESTED

Yesterday Stone Hill police arrested Mrs. Zelda Simmons on suspicion of poisoning Mother Rosaria, at the Chateau. The suspect was a cook at the monastery for almost two years. A reliable source reported that Mrs. Simmons was taken without resistance for further questioning.

27

Once the investigation ended, life in the monastery became the usual day-to-day bell-scheduled routine, with one big distraction for Sister Camille. Thoughts of Hank Kummer wandered into her prayer time. Sister's heartbeat quickened when the phone rang during the evening recreation. Though the investigation had distressed Mother Cordelia and the sisters, they recovered. Now, they looked toward Sister Camille with new respect.

Sisters Camille and Angelica sat on a bench near Mother Rosaria's grave that bore a simple white painted wooden cross. It identified the grave by name and dates.

"I feel so empty, Sister Angelica. After all we went through, I thought I'd feel relief to have the truth known about Mother Rosaria's death. It's like the letdown I sometimes feel after a recital. My students and I invested so much effort to make it a success. Do you ever feel that way after the senior play?"

"Yes, Sister, I've had that feeling, but I try to rise above it. Now that Mrs. Simmons has confessed to putting poison in the coffeepot, we should feel confident the police arrested the right person."

"I didn't have a clue. Maybe that's why I feel this way."

"The sisters don't have to worry about the reputation of our academy either. I heard parents and alumnae have been calling in to express their sympathy and support for the sisters. That's good."

"If only our efforts had brought Mother Rosaria back to us."

"Oh, Sister, please." Sister Angelica shook her head. "We know that can't be."

"Let's pray, Sister." Sister Camille surprised herself. Usually it was Sister Angelica who initiated prayer.

She didn't want to discuss her feelings toward Hank with Sister Angelica. Instead, she suggested, "Please, Sister, pray for a special intention."

*   *   *

Sister Camille waited for Dr. Raymond to speak. Since her last week's appointment with the psychologist, a clown had stalked her and locked her in the closet. She spent a day and a half in the hospital; Mrs. Simmons confessed, and Lieutenant Kummer had finished the investigation that she caused to be opened.

Today, Sister didn't care if she talked about it or not. Her black eyes had faded. She didn't think Dr. Raymond would even notice. Most of all, she was grateful to have this chance to discuss her future with him. What would he think? Could she trust him? She knew of a psychologist who called the superior after each consultation. Sister Camille didn't think Dr. Raymond would do that.

It gave her an uncomfortable feeling to verbalize even in her mind the thought of leaving the monastery. She preferred to think of it as "future plans" because that sounded more vague.

Sister liked talking to Dr. Raymond rather than to the father confessor who came to the monastery weekly to hear the sisters' confessions. Speaking to the priest seemed impersonal in the dark, curtained confessional. The priest didn't even know her. And if she said all that was on her mind, the sisters might wonder what took her so long.

If she talked to Sister Angelica or any one else, they would try to influence her, especially if word got around that she was considering a change. Sister Camille knew she had to make up her mind alone.

Looking over his patient's record, Dr. Raymond glanced at her and said, "Making decisions is difficult for you, Sister, because this is done for you in the monastery, for how many years?"

Sister Camille answered, "I entered the novitiate seven years ago this September."

"The death of Mother Superior and the experiences that came with it has affected you." He spoke kindly, not impersonally as in their initial meetings. "Have there been any developments concerning the investigation?"

"Lieutenant Kummer arrested Mrs. Simmons Wednesday." She paused. "Mrs. Simmons and I worked together in the kitchen this summer. I'll miss her."

"How did that make you feel?"

"I was shocked, Doctor, but she confessed to poisoning Mother Rosaria."

"Continue, Sister."

"Lieutenant Kummer left that day. I haven't seen him to find out what evidence led to her arrest. Nobody talks about it, and we don't read the newspapers, so I may never know. I hope to see him again. I wish I could call him. Mother Cordelia has prohibited my use of the telephone. Maybe I could call him from your office."

"Yes, but first, why were you surprised that Mrs. Simmons was arrested? Did you think one of the sisters did it?"

"I did. I was so tormented over Mother Rosaria's death that I was ready to blame anyone. The conversation I heard the night before she died pinpointed one thing in my mind. I found out Sister Eugene had given Mother a Miltown."

Dr. Raymond asked, "What steps are required if you decide to leave the monastery?"

She looked down, rubbing her eyebrows with her thumb where the tight headband rested on her forehead. The rubbing released loose skin above her eyes, more than what ought to show by custom. With a little movement of her eyebrows and fingers, she worked the headband back to its original position. She looked up. "It means I have to first tell my superior." She hesitated. "Then I have to write for a dispensation of my solemn vows from the Office of the Sacred Congregation in Rome."

"Is this the first time you've said that out loud?"

Sister Camille's hand returned to her eyebrows but didn't rub. She would offer up the uncomfortable itch to the honor and glory of God. "Yes it is."

"How does it make you feel?"

Her eyes opened wide. "Very scared."

"From what you told me about your life in the monastery, you're obliged to give up your preferences, your friends, and your ability to make decisions. Is this true?"

"That's right, Doctor. The early fathers of the church wrote and taught that if a sister is to reach a spiritual union with Christ, she must submit her will in what we eat, dress to formal prayers, penances, and assigned work."

"Do you realize this theology defies humanity?" The doctor referred to his notes. "We discussed this last week when we talked about your vows. You speak about these restraints that make each member of the community the same, a clone so to speak. Does it occur to you that you're prevented from developing into a mature adult? The monastery is nothing like the real world."

"I think about that, but I chose it and accepted these restraints."

"Do you wish to remain this way for the rest of your life, having someone else direct all your actions?"

"I'm not sure."

"You're affected when others make your decisions. You should be able to develop your skills, make mature choices, and still arrive at a full spiritual life. When you use your talents, you are relying on the resources and gifts God has given you to grow. God works through you."

Sister Camille's eyes blinked several times, stunned at the doctor's theology. She looked at him, scarcely able to believe what he was saying. It seemed true, yet she never had it explained to her in this way. He seemed a different psychologist as he sat across from her.

He continued, "I'm not a Catholic, but I read Catholic writers. It helps me to understand my patients who are nuns."

"You make it sound so simple." She repeated the doctor's sentence. "'God gave us our humanity, our talents, to show us it could be done.' That makes sense."

"One other factor I want to discuss with you today is, if you do leave the monastery and get into a relationship with a man, you're going to have to trust. You've mistrusted the mother superior and the sisters. This can carry over to people you meet."

"I think my mistrust was valid. I had grounds for mistrust."

"You must work it out."

"How do I do that?"

"Do you trust yourself in terms of making decisions? Will you be able to take charge after you've been taught to suppress your feelings and regulate them for the past years? You've no practice at making choices because every activity, even thoughts, are planned around the rule or the superior's requests. If you leave monastic life, you'll smell exotic fragrances, feel warm hugs and kisses."

"You're right, Doctor. It's always 'Yes, Mother,' or 'Whatever you think, Mother.' Making decisions will be difficult. I hadn't thought of that. My greatest fear is, if I do leave, I won't be a success."

"Yes, you've lived within safe boundaries, never feared for a job, for food on the table, or had to plan for the future. You took a vow of poverty, but do you know how it feels for a struggling family to make it?"

Sister nodded thoughtfully.

Dr. Raymond continued, "You can do it, Sister. One step at a time."

"I'd like to go back to school and get a master's degree. I think the university would be a good place to start over. But I won't have any money, just a small dowry my dad gave the Chateau."

"There are ways, scholarships and grants. You can borrow money," the doctor suggested. "You need to work on trusting people."

"I make some decisions in my work. I plan the materials I teach."

"You need to build your self-esteem. If you don't, you'll be less able to deal with people who are critical. By building self-esteem, you can learn to be assertive, to speak up."

"That will be hard."

"Step by step, you can. Would you care to role play, to learn how to take charge of your life?"

"That's a good idea, but I'm not in any rush."

PART II

Remaking Magdalena

28

Mother Cordelia and the four members of the council surrounded Sister Camille. They stood with grim faces, hands covered in their sleeves. Although she made an effort to keep calm and controlled, Mother Cordelia's breath raced, as though a disaster worse than death was impending.

"Sister Camille, your papal dispensation came in the morning's mail." The superior handed the sheet of parchment to Sister Camille. She knelt and kissed the superior's hand to receive it, a monastic custom practiced for receiving anything from the mother superior.

Having some familiarity with Latin, Sister Camille translated the word, *dispensatione*, on the cover page and date, May 1957. Satisfied it was the document from Rome that released her from the vows of poverty, obedience, and chastity, she reached into her pocket for a pen.

"Before you sign," the superior stepped toward her, "consider the gravity of your action. I can hold this dispensation for you while you pray for guidance."

"Mother Cordelia, I'm ready to sign it now." For a moment, Sister Camille wondered if the superior would hold it back.

Sister Martha spoke up, "This is a drastic decision. Please reconsider what you're doing."

"You don't realize what a sinful life is out in the world. Terrible things are happening all the time." Sister Mercy's double chins vibrated. Because of her asthma, she too struggled for breath.

None of their exhortations deterred her for a second. Sister Camille said, "For five years, I've prayed. I've gone through the anguish of making this decision. I don't want to wait any longer." She signed the document as though it were a grocery receipt. It was hard to keep excitement from showing. Mother Cordelia and the council couldn't comprehend her desire to reenter a world they thought was so full of evil.

"Then call your parents." Mother Cordelia shoved the phone toward her. "Tell them to be here between twelve and twelve thirty when the sisters are at dinner."

Sister Camille realized Mother Cordelia didn't want her exodus witnessed by the community. She reached for the phone.

Her parents anticipated their daughter's release from the vows after her dad's earlier visit. At that time, Dr. Brenner encouraged Sister Camille to come home that day with him without waiting for the Vatican dispensation. Sister Camille decided to request secularization required by canon law, even though she had to wait the undetermined time for her release. This meant writing for a dispensation to the Sacred Congregation in Rome.

"Give me your ring and cross," the superior said, void of all emotion when Maggie hung up the phone.

Maggie slipped the silver band engraved with a crown of thorns off her finger then reached for the crucifix that hung on a cord around her neck. Both had been symbols of her final vows of poverty, obedience, and chastity. She handed them to Mother Cordelia.

"Take your things to the bishop's suite," Mother Cordelia said. "You can change your clothes there. Leave your holy habit and veil on the bed." Mother Cordelia turned away shaking her head, realizing she could do nothing to change Sister's radical decision.

Sister Camille turned to leave. None of the sisters said goodbye, shook her hand, or wished her well. It seemed awkward for her to say goodbye. She walked out the door down the squeaky hardwood floor to her cell for the last time, thinking I'm no longer Sister Camille, a cloistered nun, and it only took my signature. She was surprised how little sadness or remorse she felt. Instead, exhilaration urged her on to the next step of a new life.

At St. Clotildes, a nun must have a docile spirit, and an unquestioning mind to fit the mold. Sister Camille tried to play this role but didn't fit into the seventeenth-century rules and customs still practiced. Smiling, she pronounced her baptismal name aloud, "Magdalena Brenner, Maggie Brenner." It had been her grandmother's name. She had been born on her grandmother's birthday.

Looking around her cell, she wondered what to take. Would anything here be of value? Not the black robe that hung on the back of the door, nor the black stockings in the top drawer of the washstand, the one piece of furniture besides a cot and a low chair. She pulled the toothbrush out of the glass next to the ceramic pitcher and basin. Opening the top drawer, she stuffed a vial of capsules and a man-size handkerchief into a paper bag. One side drawer held a week's allotment of convent sewn underwear and white guimpes. The other held cloth sanitary napkins. She'd be glad to go back to a commercial brand. A door on the side opened to a space that once held a chamber pot used only decades ago. Now, her night slippers and Sunday shoes were there. Her excitement grew as she collected the box under the bed, her mom had sent earlier in preparation for this day, and left the cell. Without as much as a glance back, she walked down the long hall, through the double door marked Cloister, No Admittance.

Finding the bishop's suite, Maggie removed her veil and habit following the monastic custom of kissing each in turn and reciting the prescribed prayers for the last time. From the box her mother had sent, she laid out each piece of clothing on the bed. She removed her underclothes all home made in the same style as the sisters had worn in the seventeenth century. A chill struck her bare skin. Aware of Saint Augustine's admonishment that a nun should not behold her bare body, she whispered, "I'm too cold to look at my body. What do I put on first?" She stepped into the rayon panties edged in lace and put on the bra. This piece would have mystified Saint Clotilde, who founded the French order in the 1600s. The peach satiny slip made her feel so feminine, so modern. Standing before the mirror, she smiled and couldn't resist running her hands over the smooth finish. Glamorous is what it was supposed to be, but how could she feel that way when goose pimples covered her arms?

A blue-print two-piece dress consisting of a skirt and button-down overblouse came next. Rubbing her bare arms unaccustomed to the light cotton weight, she decided to add the white blouse from the box and wear the printed top over it like a jacket. Even with this addition, the new clothes felt light and airy, like tissue paper compared to the long-sleeved serge habit. She had to look down to the hem to see if the skirt hung straight.

On the bed lay the seamless, sheer stockings. Maggie held one up toward the window to see if she could see through it then slipped it up her arm as far as it would go, careful not to snag it on her calloused hands. She smiled feeling the smoothness against her cheek. After slipping them on, with the elastics from the black stockings discarded on the floor, Maggie stood in front of a floor-length mirror staring at her reflection. Oh my God. Who was that short pudgy figure in the short skirt? Had her five feet seven inches shrunk? The long black habit had made her look taller. She stood on her tiptoes to get the effect of high heels she hoped to get. Aside from feeling she hadn't anything on, something else was wrong. The rolled stockings at her knees poked out from under her skirt. If she walked out like this, people would think that she had come from some kind of institution.

Rummaging through the box, she found a garter belt hidden under the wrapping. Maggie held it up and wondered should it go over her underclothes or next to the skin. "How could I have forgotten?" Maggie whispered into the mirror. Wearing worldly clothes was more complicated than she thought. Of course, the garter belt must be next to her skin. She had to undress and start over.

Finished, Maggie walked across the room and sat down to wait. With the sisters assembled at dinner, there would be no farewells. It would have been difficult to say goodbye to Sister Angelica and Sister Dorothy and the other sisters she'd known the past twelve years. She didn't want to see the shock in their eyes when Mother Cordelia announced the news of her departure after dinner. Maybe someday, she'd have a chance to explain. Would they understand why she chose to leave? Maggie hadn't discussed her decision with anyone. It had to be made by her and her alone.

Memories raced by, the time Mother Cordelia had sent her to Dr. Raymond. The superior had ordered her to the psychologist because of her suspicion when Mother Rosaria died of unnatural causes. Maggie had resisted going to the psychologist, but it turned out to be a blessing. Dr. Raymond's sessions helped her realize that her decision to join a nunnery was based on the wrong reasons. Her fourth-grade teacher, Sister Mary Basil, had said a family that had a vocation to the priesthood or sisterhood received a special blessing. She had wanted her family to have that blessing, and she also had wanted to please her mother. Both were unreliable motives.

She had never suspected Zelda, the cook, had put the cyanide crystals in the coffeepot of Mother Rosaria. She thought it was one of the sisters whose voices she overheard through the transom of her cell. The judge at the trial sentenced Zelda to thirty years in prison.

It was time to forgive, time to forget. Her hand brushed across her brow to rub an itch where the tight headband of the habit had rested. She felt empty space instead, and a distinct crease in her forehead. Would it look like a wrinkle? Maggie didn't get up to look.

When her mother and sister drove into the circle, Maggie ran down the steps before the car came to a complete stop. In her hand, she clutched a brown paper bag containing her sole possessions: a toothbrush, a partial prescription of tranquilizers, a thick business-size envelope with two hundred and fifty dollars in cash, and the dispensation document. Maggie didn't look back at the carved walnut doors where minutes ago her name had been Sister Camille.

The passenger door of the car swung wide. "I'm out; I'm out!" she shouted to her mom and younger sister Kate, who slid to the middle of the seat to make room for her.

Neither Kate nor her mother made a move to kiss, hug, or even greet her. Their necks stretched long as their eyes strained to take in every inch of her. Their expressions at seeing Maggie out of the religious habit resembled the intense concentration of suspicious chickens when they hear a noise.

Maggie ignored their lack of welcome. They just needed time to get used to seeing her without the veil and long black habit that had enveloped her for so many years. How they rationalized her decision to leave the monastery, she didn't know and couldn't deal with now. She hadn't the opportunity to discuss it with them, nor did she want to. It had to be her decision. It wasn't frivolous.

In silence, Mrs. Brenner disengaged the gear, stepped on the gas, and sped out of the drive. Kate fidgeted with the radio. She announced, "This is Elvis Presley. He's very popular now."

"Who is he?" Maggie listened a few seconds. "His voice sounds nasal, not like Frank Sinatra or Bing Crosby."

"This is rock and roll. Elvis is the hottest singer around. You'll hear a lot of him."

Mrs. Brenner said, "First we'll stop for shoes in Richfield on the way home. I think you should get a coat, too. It's been cool for June. Then you'll look all right to go to church Sunday. There'll be so much gossip when you appear."

"Do I have a choice?" Maggie tilted her head and grinned with teasing eyes.

"Well, of all things," Mrs. Brenner's head jerked toward Maggie then refocused on the traffic ahead.

Her mother had bragged about having a daughter as a nun. To have this daughter leave the cloister was tantamount to failure, as bad as a divorce. If she didn't go to church, there'd be more scandal. Maggie had faced her homecoming before making the final decision to leave. Other concerns, like earning a living and learning to live alone, worried her more.

Her mother maneuvered the car into lanes to make the correct turns. "This is a beautiful car, and you have a radio too. I haven't been in a car since I went to a doctor about my ear. That was five years ago." Looking out the window, Maggie said, "I don't remember seeing these turning lanes before. It looks like a new highway. Didn't it used to be a two-lane road?"

"Now it's an interstate highway," Kate said.

"Someday I'll own a car and drive on freeways like this. I wonder how long it will take."

"My, you're talking big," Mrs. Brenner said. "Don't you think there are other basic things you need first?"

"Of course, Mom. I know I need everything. Just dreaming about it makes me feel free." Maggie smiled.

"Better to be practical. You want to go too fast, Magdalena."

Maggie remained silent. She expected her mom's reaction and knew this freedom had to wait. Soon they were on No. 94 speeding homeward past fields where the corn stood about a foot high.

"That blue dress is all wrong on you, Magdalena," Mrs. Brenner said, her face long without a hint of a smile. "I didn't know what to send."

Her mother's comment sounded like an admonishment, as though it was Maggie's fault. Maggie remembered those sly rebukes and wasn't surprised that her mother had yet to smile. Her family couldn't be as excited as she. Her mother expected her to be toned down like a nun.

Maggie glanced at her mother, who could have been a model. Mrs. Brenner wore a black linen skirt. A black-and-white-printed sleeveless overblouse with a matching jacket. "This dress is lovely. I liked the idea that the top could be worn as a jacket or a blouse. I'll get a lot of wear out of it." Maggie adjusted the skirt over her knees where it had slid up when she entered the car. It had reached its limit. "Thanks for all the work you put into it."

"It was all the pieces of underwear that gave me the most trouble. I wondered how to hold up these sheer stockings." She leaned down to finger the smoothness of the nylons, so transparent compared to the black cotton stockings she left behind. She tugged the hem of the skirt down again, adjusting the back. When the hem wouldn't go any further, she took a deep breath accepting the skirt's short length.

Mrs. Brenner asked, "Was the bra the right size?" She glanced over at her daughter.

Maggie looked down. "It didn't look quite right. I stuck out too much, so I sewed a tuck in each cup to hold me in tighter. I was used to the lining of our habits that laced up like a bodice. Sometimes it put the curves in the wrong place." Maggie giggled, knowing neither Mom nor Kate could understand her description. Neither reacted.

"When did you get the box?" her mother asked.

"It came three weeks ago. I had a dress rehearsal one night after matins and lauds. I had to stand on our cot to see my reflection in the window. Whoops, I shouldn't say 'our' any more." Maggie laughed at herself. "The sisters always referred to articles they use as 'ours' instead of 'mine,' because the vow of poverty forbade personal possessions. Well," she continued, "that night, I sat down in my new outfit crossing my knees like people in the world do. I thought, soon I'll walk out the front door. Who will I meet besides my family, and what will I talk about?" Maggie considered how hard it would be. So far, she wasn't doing too well. Every word she uttered reflected her former life. This had to change, she decided.

Kate shook her head, glancing at her mother to catch her reaction. Mrs. Brenner kept her eyes on the road. Maggie could tell they had a hard time understanding her.

Opening her purse, Kate brought out a tube of lipstick. "I think you should start with this shade. It's Tangee natural." She dabbed it on Maggie's lips as they drove along the River Road. Maggie looked into the compact mirror her sister held. Working her lips to even the color, she shook her head. "It's nice, but I'd like to try a redder shade. Do you have a tissue?"

Mrs. Brenner cautioned, "You should go slow with makeup, Magdalena. You're not used to wearing cosmetics. What will the neighbors say? You don't want to look like a hussy."

Maggie stiffened, stunned by her mother's words. She tried to picture how her mother wanted her to appear at church with no makeup, low-heeled shoes, and a coat to cover her. "Well, I want to look like everyone else. I don't want to look like I just came from the old country, like the Lentz girls who wore long dark dresses and never wore makeup. Wearing red lipstick can't be that hard to get used to. It's my hair that concerns me. And from now on, I want to be known as Maggie, not Magdalena."

Kate lifted the scarf off Maggie's head. She cried, "It's so short, too short for a perm. What are we going to do with it?"

Mrs. Brenner glanced over, "Betty Lou can give her some suggestions. I talked to her about you coming home last week, when I had my appointment."

Her hair taken care of, Maggie took a deep breath. "Now about shoes, I had a pair of high-heel patent leather shoes in high school. Are they still in style?"

"There again," her mother answered. "You're moving too fast. You should get a sensible pump with a moderate heel." Glancing at Maggie, she continued, "You've changed, Magdalena. Hank Kummer told me about you when he was assigned to the case of the superior's sudden death. He said it was you who caused the case to be opened."

Maggie felt her tone was accusatory again rather than complimentary. "Lieutenant Kummer." Maggie smiled, remembering the pleasure she had working with him. It was a novel experience for a nun in a cloister to work with a detective. At first, Mother Cordelia had resented her for it. She feared for the reputation of their school at the Chateau.

"What else did he say about me?"

"He wondered why you became a nun."

Maggie let that remark sink in. Nodding her head, she said, "I did change after that, but it wasn't because of Hank. It was Dr. Raymond who made me realize I didn't belong in a cloister."

Mrs. Brenner didn't comment. She set her mouth in a straight line.

Kate suggested, "How about a pair of stacked heels? They'd be perfect."

Maggie heard their words of caution. "If it was all right for me to wear patent leather when I was seventeen, why isn't it at the age of thirty-one? Anyway, stacked heels? What do they look like? They sound like old-lady shoes." Maggie wondered whether this would be the first of many phrases that sounded strange. She wanted to look her age, thirty-one. She eyed her mother's pumps with heels of the same color, black.

"No," Kate said, "they aren't like Mom's. It's a medium-size heel made of stacked pieces of leather shaped into a heel."

"Hmm, that's hard to picture. I'll look around the shoe store first." Maggie pulled out the envelope from her bag, waving it in the air like a trophy. "Mother Cordelia gave me two hundred and fifty dollars to get started. This should buy a complete outfit."

"Oh no, it won't," Mrs. Brenner warned. "You'll be surprised how little that will buy. You've got a lot to learn."

Her mom was holding up well for their first meeting. Before she entered the novitiate at St. Clotildes, Mrs. Brenner had said, "Just because you get homesick, that's no reason to leave. Don't even think about coming home." To Maggie, it sounded like her mother meant forever.

Her dad had said, "I had two cousins who joined the sisters in St. Louis. They decided the sisterhood wasn't for them. Both girls had returned home, married, and had families."

When Maggie decided to leave the cloister, it was her dad she chose to tell, letting him relay the news to her mother. Also, Maggie wanted him there when she told Mother Cordelia. She worried how her mother would take the news. Now, Maggie could see her mom took an interest in being a part of her new beginning, the task of remaking Magdalena.

They stopped in a parking garage in Richfield, Wisconsin, and entered Walkers Shoe Store, where the Brenners' feet had been fitted for decades. Maggie didn't remember parking structures when she was younger and thought how convenient it was to park there. As they entered, the clerk recognized Mrs. Brenner and Kate, greeting them by name. He ignored their ill-dressed companion wearing black nun oxfords. Mrs. Brenner didn't introduce her. Maggie wondered if her mother felt a shoe clerk wasn't important enough to rate an introduction or if she didn't measure up to the standard.

Mrs. Brenner nodded toward Maggie, directing the clerk's attention toward her daughter. "She needs shoes."

Do I ever? Maggie thought. Not just one pair, but at least two or three. She sat down, took off her shoes, and kicked them under the seat to hide them.

After the clerk adjusted the levers to measure her foot, he reached down for one of her shoes under the seat. Holding it high, he turned toward Mrs. Brenner. "She's wearing the wrong size. This shoe is 6AA. She measures 7AAA."

Maggie felt heat rise from her shoulders to her face. Why doesn't he speak to me? Am I some kind of freak because I'm wearing the wrong-size shoe? Do I look like I've just been released from a prison or an asylum and can't communicate or, worse yet, a nunnery? Not wanting to make a scene, Maggie took a deep breath, reminding herself, who cares? What would the clerk and her mother think if she told them the sisters drew an outline of their feet and sent it to a mail-order house? It was best to keep silent.

In a quiet voice, her mother said to the clerk, "Magdalena takes after my side of the family. We have long lasts."

Maggie said, "I'd like to try on the patent leathers displayed on the table near the window." No warning sounds came from Mom or Kate as the clerk fit the shoes on Maggie's feet. They felt smooth and snug like a pair of gloves. She turned her foot to one side, admiring the high gloss, and touched its smoothness. Yes, these were what she wanted. They were like the shoes she wore at her high-school graduation. When Maggie stood up, her ankles wobbled unaccustomed to the four-inch heels. She managed to walk to a floor mirror that reflected her exposed legs in sheer nylons all the way to her knees. Wow, they still had a good shape. Her head inched upward. What would the sisters say if they saw me in these sophisticated heels? They'd have plenty to say. Maggie turned sideways, appreciating that the reflection in the mirror didn't show her hair.

After trying on more styles, she examined the black stacked-heel Florsheims. "These are classy too and more practical. I'll buy them." Maggie heard a sigh of relief from Mom as she gathered up her purse. To herself, she promised to come back for the patent leathers later.

Reaching for the paper bag squashed down in the seat behind her, Maggie pulled out the envelope of bills. She counted out the specified amount and held the money out to the clerk. The clerk ignored her outstretched hand. He walked toward a curtain and disappeared. All of her two hundred and fifty dollars in cash spilled onto the floor.

Kate leaned down to help gather the bills. She whispered, "You don't pay the clerk. Pay the cashier at the desk."

Mrs. Brenner said, "She's not used to handling money."

Maggie paid for her first purchase. She wanted to wear the new shoes, but her mother cautioned her to wait and try them out at home on a rug. They left the store.

Down the street, they walked past store windows with attractive, colorful displays of women's clothes. Stopping in front of one shop, Maggie said, "I need everything in that window." Pointing to a multicolored dress, she asked, "Wouldn't that dress with the ruffle look good on me?"

Mrs. Brenner said, "Why not wait? I have some fabrics at home we can sew on, and I can refit a few of my dresses if you like them."

Maggie remembered her mother had sewed beautiful dresses for her daughters when they were children. Each spring, three to four new outfits were finished for them to wear. Once, when her mother didn't have time to sew, Maggie had to settle for a store-bought dress, which she still remembered wasn't as nice.

"I need a purse," Maggie said. She wasn't going to wait for direction on what to buy next.

The counter near the entrance of Clinton's Department Store displayed perfumes and cosmetics. The pleasant aromas of lilacs and carnations, the sparkling glass bottles reflected in mirrors, and pastel posters decorating the counter displays dazzled Maggie. She stopped and closed her eyes. Was this wonderland? Looking up, she was jarred back to reality. Thirty feet ahead, her mother and Kate stood at a table looking at purses.

Mrs. Brenner came toward Maggie and stopped to greet someone.

"Why hello, Sam Mercken. I didn't see you before."

The clerk behind the perfume counter was wrapping a bottle of Channel No. 5. Finished with the transaction, she handed a small bag to Sam. "I hope your wife will be happy with your fine choice of fragrance."

Sam grabbed the package and deposited it in his pocket as though he was caught stealing a lollipop in a candy shop then turned toward Mrs. Brenner.

He greeted her with a smile and nodded toward Maggie with interest. "Who's this?"

"Sam this is my daughter, Magdalena. She's come home from St. Clotildes. Magdalena, this is Sam Mercken, our neighbor, from Orchard Lake."

The elderly man with a handlebar mustache said, "Oh, the one who was in the cloister." He shook her hand. "Such a waste. A pretty thing like you locked away in a cloister."

Mrs. Brenner bit her lip.

Maggie smiled. She didn't want to elaborate on her motives but decided she liked him already.

Sam turned back to Mrs. Brenner, "When are you coming to the lake?"

"Next week. Tell Amelia to get ready for some hands of bridge. I remember the last time we beat you, men."

"She'll be glad to hear that. Since we left Milwaukee, all she complains about is not finding people to play bridge at Orchard Lake. Good luck, young lady." He walked away from them.

"He seems like a nice man. Did you see that large stone on his hand?" Maggie said after Sam walked away.

"Sam is a retired jeweler from Milwaukee. His cabin is just across the road from ours. I wonder if Amelia will ever get to smell that fragrance. You should hear him yell at her when we play bridge. He puts on a good show."

Catching up to Kate at the purse counter, Maggie picked up a red bag. It had four compartments. "What will I put in all these spaces?"

"I have a French purse for you at home," Mrs. Brenner said. "I brought it back from Europe. It's like a billfold with a change purse on the side. It will fit into this space. And Magdalena, since your shoes are black, it's a good idea to pick a matching purse."

"A billfold? Like men use?"

Kate opened her purse. "See? I have a billfold. Everyone uses billfolds."

Maggie accepted this advice, thinking about many changes since she had left home in 1945. She loved the bright-colored purses. Buying everything black didn't please her, but she had to agree it was a good idea to keep her beginning wardrobe coordinated. "Haven't I worn enough black the past years? My new coat won't be black, I promise you."

Instead, she bought a gray double-breasted denim coat lined with a farmer's red handkerchief print. Remembering the display windows earlier, Maggie suggested, "Let's go back to the Roxie Shop. I saw a blouse there in the same print. It would match this coat lining."

Mrs. Brenner said, "I'm tired. Let's go home. Dad will be waiting."

Accustomed to obeying the slightest rule, Maggie said nothing even though she might not get back to the Roxie for several days and then find that the blouse was sold.

After her purchases, Maggie counted one hundred and twenty dollars left. Next time, I'll go shopping by myself. I don't need someone to tell me what to buy.

29

Maggie's dad, a practicing dentist in the rural town of Georgetown, Wisconsin, stood at the screen door waiting when the car drove into the driveway. He checked his daughter from head to toe as she stepped out of the car. It was his habit if he hadn't seen someone for a while. Her new appearance in street clothes held his attention longer. When he opened his arms, Maggie blinked back tears. "I'm home, Dad." She had forgotten the feel of his warm, protective arms around her and didn't want to let go. He, more than anyone, would understand her decision to leave Saint Clotildes as an accomplishment.

"How lovely the house looks," Maggie said, trying to divert her dad's attention, still conscious of her nun shoes and her short unstylish hair. What was he thinking? Would she ever get over caring how she looked to others?

"You've made so many changes in the house since I left," Maggie said.

They entered the house and walked through the rooms on the first floor. Mrs. Brenner spoke with pride, "We added the sunroom six years ago." An antique oval table held family photographs and a bowl of fragrant pink roses from the doctor's garden. "Collecting antique furniture is my hobby. I got this table from an estate sale of my friend, Mabel. Mabel was Henry Kummer's mother."

Maggie smiled. "Hank Kummer? How old do you think he is?"

"He's been a bachelor for years, must be close to forty years old; don't you think, Matt?"

Her husband nodded. "Isn't he in one of those pictures?"

Mrs. Brenner leaned over and picked out a family group. "Here he is, in his army uniform. This was taken before he shipped overseas."

Maggie picked him out of the group. "He looks so young, like the picture was taken right after he graduated from high school."

"Is he still a police detective?"

Mrs. Brenner said, "I think so. Now, take your new things upstairs. You can sleep in the guest room. Kate, go with her and show her where to find towels, toothbrush, and anything else she needs. Then come down and join us for a drink."

Turning around, Maggie half expected Blondie, a Boston terrier, to come running into the house to greet her. Leaving him behind had been hard when she entered Saint Clotildes. She felt maybe she could pick up where she left off twelve years ago if Blondie were here.

With the packages under her arm, Maggie lingered by the grand piano near the stairway. Sliding her hand around the sleek curve of the dark mahogany, she remembered the recital pieces she had practiced on it. One year it was "Minuet in G" by Beethoven, the next year, "Minuet in G" by Paderewski. Then came MacDowell, Tchaikovsky, and Mendelssohn. If asked, she could even name the compositions and composers her mother used to play when she grew up. Maggie's mother liked to brag about her teacher, Madam Kline, who had been a student of the famous Clara Schumann in Germany. Mrs. Brenner was brought up in a cultured family; her father was a doctor, her mother an opera singer. It had always been her hope Magdalena would be a concert pianist.

Kate's room had been hers before Maggie left. Glancing around, Maggie noticed the walls were still pastel blue, a choice she had made as a teenager. Chintz drapes replaced dotted Swiss curtains. Instead of her doll collection, the two-tiered shelf held her mother's antique toothpick holders in many shapes and colors. What had happened to the dolls, her Shirley Temple doll?

Maggie asked Kate, "Would you mind if I slept here in the empty twin bed instead of the guest room? It would seem like old times." Maggie sat on the bed and ran her hand over the tufted chenille bedspread, different from the one she remembered.

"Well, I have a date tonight. I might come in late. If that doesn't bother you, it's okay." Kate took a yellow-print dress from her closet and laid it on her bed.

"What a beautiful dress, Kate." Maggie picked it up and held it against her in front of the mirror. When she took a step with it, the full skirt moved with her. "Who's your date? Do I know him?"

"He's Grant Page, the brother of Germaine Page."

"You mean he's still around? I'd have thought he'd be married by now."

"No, after Grant served in the Korean War, he came back and went to college. He just graduated last week from Wisconsin."

Maggie thought back, figuring 1941-1945, World War II. It was the Korean War dates that eluded her. She couldn't let on that she was unaware of this terrible conflict that had affected so many lives. Only the superior and the history teachers were given permission to read newspapers in the cloister.

Without further comment, Maggie turned the dress around to see the back. Kate would soon leave home. It would be helpful to spend the summer with her. Similar in size, Maggie hoped to try on her sister's clothes, although Kate made no offer. She enjoyed watching the ease her sister took in getting dressed. It was so natural for Kate to lean over in front of the mirror to brush her hair and touch up her makeup. Maggie tried to feel this was an ordinary experience.

After Kate left, Maggie opened her packages. The smell of new shoe leather lifted toward her from the box. Slipping the medium-size heels on, Maggie held one leg out. She stood with her back to the mirror, twisting sidewise to get the rear effect of her legs in the sheer hose and shoes. The stockings were seamless, another change. She remembered only stocking with seams up the back. During the war, when nylons were scarce, the girls drew a line up their bare legs. Finished, she walked down the stairs carrying the new purse and coat over her arm. Her free hand reached down automatically for the hem of a long garment, a gesture the sisters practiced so the blessed habit wouldn't mop the steps. Instead of wool serge folds, Maggie grabbed nothing but air. She laughed and straightened up, holding her head high. Yes, this was the way ordinary people looked and walked. It felt so free.

"Want to try a cocktail?" Dr. Brenner asked when she walked into the sunroom.

"Let me taste yours." Maggie sat down and crossed her knees, glancing down at her legs again, and an unseemly posture for a sister. She sipped her dad's drink, "Ooh, that's good. It tastes sweet and syrupy. I'll take one just like yours. What's it called?"

"Just a highball made with whiskey and 7Up. I'll put less whiskey in yours. You're not used to it."

Returning with the drink, he asked, "What did you buy today?"

Maggie got up and modeled her new possessions, explaining each choice. She transferred the remaining cash into the French purse her mother handed her and put it into her new bag. Swinging it by the handle, she said, "I'm on my way now, but I still have empty compartments. I could put in a hanky, but I only have this." She waved a man-size square in the air. Handing it to her dad, she said, "You can have it."

"Help yourself to a handkerchief in my dressing table," Mrs. Brenner said.

Her dad took the hanky from her. "I don't think you'll need the tranquilizers I sent. Let me have what's left."

"That's easy. It's one of the few things I brought with me." Maggie pulled the plastic container with green and white capsules from her pocket and handed it to him. "It sure helped to relax me, so I could sleep while I waited for the dispensation. I'm glad that's all over. Thanks, Dad, for sending them."

He took the prescription bottle. "You've had a lot to deal with these past months. Have you some ideas on what you want to do now?"

"I want to get a master's degree at the university then get a teaching position. I could still sign up for some summer courses."

Mrs. Brenner said, "With your talent, Maggie, you could be a concert pianist. It's not too late, if you put your mind to it."

Her dad massaged an old X-ray burn on his hand. "We plan to go to the lake next week. I'm taking two weeks' vacation. Why don't you come with us?"

"That sounds like heaven." Maggie sighed. "There's nothing I'd like better than to relax near the water. I could get some sewing done while we're there, but then I wouldn't be able to take any classes this summer."

"You'll have plenty of time later."

"How long have you had the cabin?" Maggie asked, taking another sip from her drink.

"We've had it seven years, furnished it with some of our old furniture you might recognize. We don't have a telephone or a television, but we're comfortable with the radio. The cabins are spread out around Orchard Lake. It gives us privacy."

"How far is the cabin from the lake?"

"Just about seventy feet from our back door. We have our own dock, good fishing too." Her dad frowned. "They've had some trouble there. The sheriff was called last week when our neighbor, Sam Mercken, reported a break-in. His cabin is across the road from ours, hidden in an overgrowth of brush and trees. We don't know the details. I'm anxious to check our cabin. It's been vacant all winter."

Conversation continued through dinner over a casserole of steaming chicken and rice, accompanied by a fresh salad that Maggie made with greens from the garden. Mrs. Brenner said, "Orchard Lake has always been a refuge for us. I hate to think it's become a haven for criminals. We met Sam Mercken today. He didn't say anything about his break-in."

While Maggie washed dishes, Dr. Brenner watched the news on television. Once he called to Maggie, "President Eisenhower's going to give a speech on *Face the Nation* in a half hour. Come, see this advertisement. You might need it."

Maggie watched the screen, admiring a glamorous female as she brushed polish on long fingernails filed to a point.

She laughed, shaking her head, "Dad, painting my fingernails is the farthest thing from my mind. I need more important things. I'll be glad to hear the president speak. I'm so behind in current affairs."

Mrs. Brenner tightened her lips. "Magdalena doesn't need nail polish. As a pianist, she shouldn't let her nails get that long." Her scolding voice sounded as though Maggie had bought a bottle of nail polish that afternoon, another situation where her mom worried her daughter was going too fast.

Maggie said, "You can never tell. I might like to try it someday." Her dad's eyes met hers. They kept silent.

Later, the family watched the president's speech. The nation's leader clinched his hands until the veins showed as he spoke about aid to countries bordering Communist nations. His face filled the whole television screen. "These free countries would suffer a slow strangulation as fateful as sudden aggression. The cost of peace is high. Yet the price of war is higher and is paid with the lives of our youth. The road to disaster could easily be paved with good intentions of those blindly striving to save money that must be spent as the price of peace."

Her dad picked up a *Time* magazine. "This is his second speech. Ike's had a hard time convincing Congress of his plan."

Maggie said, "It's amazing to see this interaction on television. Some of the senators clap and some don't. What about Russia? Is the United States so afraid of their influence?"

"Khrushchev has promised to keep out of the affairs of the neighboring countries, but he could renege like his predecessor, Molotov. We don't trust him," Mrs. Brenner said.

"I wonder if I'll ever catch up or understand the world problems. I'll be asking a lot of questions that may seem dumb to you. Bear with me until I get a hold of what's happening."

"Don't expect to understand it in a week's time, Magdalena. When you graduated from high school in 1944, winning the war was our main concern. We understood that. After you entered the monastery, our economy prospered. Your dad bought a new Plymouth after driving that '39 Chevy during the war years."

Maggie remembered the old car that took her and her girlfriends to wedding dances. They danced with one another because all the boys were in the service. If she had delayed entering the cloister one year, would she be married? When the boys returned from the service, life changed for everybody. She had missed that.

"I left just a few weeks after the atom bomb was dropped in '45. Whatever happened to those poor people in Japan?"

Mrs. Brenner reached under a stack of magazines for the current issue of *Time*: June 3, 1957. "There's a good article in here about the A-bomb and its repercussions." She handed it to Maggie.

After the president's message, they watched *What's My Line?*, *Gun Smoke*, and *Jack Paar*.

"These programs made me forget where I was, especially when Jack Paar interviewed Jonathan Winters. What a funny man!" Maggie said.

"We go to bed after the news," Mrs. Brenner said. "I put a pair of pajamas on your bed. Is there anything else you need?"

"No, I can't think of anything. It's eleven o'clock. I'm not a bit tired after this unusual day."

"Stay up as long as you like." Her dad got up from his chair.

Expecting him to say it was bedtime for her too, Maggie smiled at her new freedom. There'd be no lights out anymore. She stayed up watching a late movie, *The Corn is Green*, and went to bed well after midnight.

Through the open bedroom doors, Maggie heard her dad snoring and an owl hooting in the distance. It had a chilling effect, though she knew it shouldn't. She drifted to sleep about four, long after Kate came in.

Instead of the five o'clock Angelus rising bell, Maggie woke to a welcoming sun shining through the south window. The aroma of coffee and sounds of cupboard doors closing downstairs brought back childhood memories. She turned over, burying her head in the soft pillow. It smelled like lilies of the valley. Stretching, she flexed her muscles on the comfortable innerspring mattress. It would be easy to forget woven metal springs and easy to forget promptitude to the sound of the rising bell.

Her thoughts drifted back to the cloister. By this time, the sisters would have discussed and rediscussed her departure in censorious tones. Her close friends, Sisters Angelica and Dorothy, would have been questioned. They had no answers. She didn't want to be influenced nor did she want to influence them.

Maggie threw back the covers and moved to the dressing table. The three-sectioned mirror reflected her in pink pajamas topped by a meager growth of short wheat-colored hair. No matter how long she looked at herself, the reflection amazed her. Not because she wasn't dressed in a long black habit and veil, it was something else. The habit and veil were external. What she wanted to know was, who is Maggie Brenner? How much time would it take to find out? She wanted to be independent, to shed all the care and help her parents showered on her. As if obsessed with her image, Maggie adjusted the side mirrors. She picked up Kate's comb and ran it through the sleek short ends. When she brushed them up from her forehead, the stubborn strands flipped back. Tomorrow Betty Lou would fix her hair. Her new wristwatch read 9:38.

She moved away from the mirror and looked through Kate's closet full of colorful skirts, crinolines, and blouses. One skirt had a felt poodle stitched on it. Maggie grinned. The tufted coat on the poodle was cute. How long would it take to accumulate that many clothes?

Before going downstairs, she straightened the bathroom and made the beds. In her parents' room, a framed picture hung on the wall. It was a picture of herself as a nun taken the day she received the habit and white veil as a novice. Stunned and unable to breathe, she whispered, "Why did she leave that picture up?"

All of yesterday's excitement deserted her, leaving an uneasy feeling. What was wrong? Everything was wrong. She felt cold. Was it withdrawal from the tranquilizers she had taken? Maggie wanted to reach for the little white and green capsules that would make everything right. Not finding them in her parents' bedroom or the bathroom, she ran down the steps to find her dad. She caught him leaving the house. "Dad, I need the capsules back."

"No more tranquilizers, Maggie," Dr. Brenner said. Coming back into the doorway, he said, "It won't be easy, but you can do it."

She saw concern in his face, but it didn't match her feeling. Her stomach churned. "Just one? I'll taper off them."

He said, "Kate's gone to an early class; Mother's going to her bridge club, and I'll be at the office. How would you like to mow the grass this morning? I'll start the mower for you, but you'll need to change your shoes. Maybe Kate has an old pair."

Maggie's head jerked upward, her eyes spun, unable to focus. Was this a goal for her second day at home? Did her dad think she was addicted? He was from the school of "cold turkey." If the pills weren't in his pocket, she'd find them after he left.

She wanted to blame her need for a tranquilizer on the picture she saw in her parents' bedroom. What was the matter with her? Why did she feel so desperate? She was where she wanted to be. Being alone this morning shouldn't bother her, she reasoned. Life has to go on with my family. Of course, they had their routines.

Searching through Kate's closet, she didn't know which shoes to pick. She had high-heel strap sandals, a new pair of loafers, and others in pastel colors that were too nice to wear mowing grass. Finally, Maggie chose white thongs from the closet floor. They looked like outdoor footwear but felt uncomfortable.

What I want is to go shopping, she thought. That would lift my mood. While Mom played bridge, I could go back to the Roxie Shop for the red blouse that matched the lining of my coat. I could look at all the beautiful clothes and not be rushed instead of being towed around like a ten-year-old.

But Maggie was accustomed to being compliant. In the cloister, it was better to have a full-blown case of acne or boils than to voice an opinion.

The lesson on how to run the mower seemed simple enough. After cutting a few swathes across the lawn, Maggie stopped, out of breath even though it was a power mower. A neighbor across the street came to greet her. Soon, another neighbor joined them. At first, Maggie thought they came through curiosity. She wanted to disappear. But they stayed, recounting memories of earlier years when she had baby-sat their children, relating what they were doing now, and wishing her success. Unused to being singled out and receiving attention, Maggie struggled to keep from crying.

When her dad came home for lunch, he fixed a couple of hotdogs with sauerkraut and suggested Maggie to have a beer with her lunch. Something was wrong with this picture, Maggie thought. The grass wasn't mowed. Dad, who had worked all morning, made lunch. Kate's uncomfortable thongs made blisters between her toes. The tongs had grass stains all over them. Would she be upset? Maggie could have taken out her old nun shoes from the wastebasket. That idea was repulsive. She never wanted to see them again. Her new environment puzzled her.

30

"I'm ready for a vacation, away from the sewing machine." Maggie packed two unfinished dresses, one a striped green pattern and the other a soft white twill. "I'll finish the handwork on these at the lake."

"All we can do is handwork. There's no sewing machine at the cabin." Mrs. Brenner handed Maggie a pattern and a piece of rose-colored wool fabric. "You can cut out this suit at the lake. Add these buttons and fasteners with them."

"Would Kate mind if I borrowed one of her bathing suits? I don't have one yet."

"She's got several. Better try one on," Mrs. Brenner said as she sorted out matching spool of threads.

Facing the mirror in the room she shared with her sister, Maggie modeled a one-piece flowered bathing suit. Kate also had a two-piece suit in the drawer, but Maggie didn't have the nerve to try that one. It would show too much bare skin.

"It looks good on you, Magdalena, but you look like an albino. Your skin's so white. It hasn't seen the light of day."

"I'll look better when I get a tan," Maggie assured herself, nodding. "Then I won't look like I just came out of a grave."

"If you stood straighter, you'd look better and younger, too." Her mother threw her shoulders back to show her daughter. "Are you afraid to show your figure?"

There's nothing wrong with my figure, Maggie thought as she mimicked her mother's posture. When would her mother let her be? She felt like a child. Maybe it would be better if her parents went to the cabin without her. Glancing at her side-view reflection, she walked away from the mirror, pirouetting like a model would walk. "When I get a tan," she repeated, "I'll look like everyone else. That's my project for the next two weeks."

She didn't tell her mother that she'd use a few cuss words and even tell a shady joke, anything to throw off someone who suspected her past.

"What are those dark spots on your knees?" Mrs. Brenner asked. "One looks red. It's bleeding."

Maggie stooped to massage her callused knees that sometimes got infected when the hardened area separated from the soft flesh. "Oh these," she tried to sound casual, "they come from kneeling. All nuns get them; they'll heal now." She laughed, "Saint Jerome referred to nuns' knees as 'holy knees hardened like a camel.'"

"Put some Vaseline on to soften them."

*   *   *

The Brenners left the next day for the sixty-mile trip to the lake. Her sister Kate didn't come. She had summer classes plus her social life in which Maggie had no part.

They followed the River Road with lush greenery on the Wisconsin side of the Mississippi.

"Looks like a good year for corn," Dr. Brenner commented. "'It'll be 'knee-high by the Fourth of July.' But we need more rain."

Maggie remembered crops were important to the farmers. It was a daily topic of conversation. Often it was not enough rain, or too much rain for cutting grain or for planting.

They drove past farmers cutting alfalfa. Maggie recalled spending weeks on her aunt's farm when they made hay. Farmers wanted dry weather, so the hay wouldn't get moldy in the barn. These memories were better than reading or hearing about the purgative life of a sister's spiritual journey.

After another hour on the road, they arrived at the south end of Orchard Lake, one of the few lakes in Wisconsin that didn't have an Indian name. When they rounded the bend near the Green Apple Deli and Bar, they caught sight of Sam Mercken's house. Mrs. Brenner stiffened. She made the sign of the cross. "I hope the Merckens are all right. The break-in must have happened right after we met Sam last week in Richfield."

"Maybe they aren't there now." Dr. Brenner turned into the drive of their brown shingled cabin. "You, girls, wait in the car. I'll check the cabin to see if anything is disturbed."

"I'm coming with you, Dad."

"Wait, Magdalena, do as your father says," her mother demanded.

Maggie followed him out of the car. She wanted to tell her mother, I'm thirty-one, not nine years old. Instead, she said, "I might be lacking in worldly wisdom, but I'm strong and can put up a struggle as well as anyone if there's trouble."

Together she and her dad went around the house checking the windows. With her hands shading her eyes to block out the sun, Maggie peered into the rooms. When her dad flashed a light through the glass, she saw furniture covered with sheets. One window at the back of the cabin where the ground sloped down to the lake was too high to reach.

Satisfied, her dad unlocked the door and entered.

"It smells damp," Maggie said. She opened a window and signaled to her mom that all's well.

The cabin consisted of a kitchen, a living room, two small bedrooms, and a bath plus a screened-in porch in the back facing the lake. Helping to remove the sheets from the furniture, Maggie said, "I remember this old brown davenport." She sat down on it, patting the pillow. "I used to lie here with a hot water bottle when I had an earache." Looking up, she recognized some of the pictures on the wall: The End of the Trail and The Bluebird. Maggie took a second look at the trail picture. "As a kid I used to wonder about that hopeless rider. It still looks like he can't go forward or backward."

A brass floor lamp with a pull chain stood by a floor-model Gruno radio with a circular dial of station call letters. As if by habit, Maggie stuck her finger into the dial and spun it to a station. In the chilled silence, Bing Crosby crooned, "Gonna take a sentimental journey . . ."

Maggie smiled. "He's still popular."

While they dusted and vacuumed, Maggie found a magazine rack filled with back issues of *Good Housekeeping* and *McCall*. The yellowed pages cracked at the corners as she leafed through one. "These will help me catch up on some of the styles and events I've missed," she told her dad.

When they finished opening the cabin, he suggested, "How about a swim?"

"Give me two minutes, and I'll join you." She left to change.

At the pier, Maggie took in the calm grayish blue water, reveling in the natural beauty of the scene. Orchard Lake was larger than she expected. Individual docks like theirs connected to cabins in both directions. Beyond a raft, a skier skimmed over the water towed by a motorboat leaving a ripple-design wake. A lazy smile formed on Maggie's lips. She felt past burdens of decision making lift. "I am blest," she whispered.

Jumping in, she started to swim, as though she had been swimming the past twelve years. As her body buoyed and splashed about, the warm water aroused a sensual feeling. She closed her eyes, enjoying the weightless sensation and the caress of the warm sun on her shoulders.

"Race you to the raft, Maggie," her dad challenged.

"Not yet, I need more exercise if I'm to be any kind of competitor. Anyway, I want to get a tan." She stepped out of the water.

"Don't stay too long. Fifteen to twenty minutes will be enough today. Put this on." He tossed a bottle of lotion to her. "See you later."

Maggie found a grassy spot for her blanket and watched him swim to the raft. It looked to be about 150 yards or more from the pier. Tomorrow, she'd try it.

That evening, after they played three-handed euchre, Maggie went to bed early. The exertion of swimming and the sun had left her exhausted. She never heard gunshots.

*   *   *

The next morning, Maggie saw her dad talking to police across the road at Mercken's house. Two Dane County Sheriff's cars plus an unmarked car were parked across the road. "What's going on?" she asked her mother.

"I don't know. Here comes your dad now."

"It's bad news," Matt Brenner said. He sank down on the davenport. "You better sit down too."

"What happened?" Mrs. Brenner's eyes went from her husband's to across the road where a policeman was digging up Amelia's flowerbed.

"Sam Mercken's body was found this morning. He was shot to death. I just don't understand it."

Mrs. Brenner struck her breast. "*Mon Dieu*! Eternal rest grant unto him, O Lord. What's going to happen next? First, the break-in, now this. Is Amelia there? Is she all right? This is terrible."

"One of the deputies said Amelia's nephew Gilbert came down this morning. He took her to his home in Milwaukee. I talked to Jim Mooreside. He heard the gunshots around one and called the sheriff."

"Gunshots? I didn't hear anything. Did you?"

"I didn't hear a thing."

"Who on earth would do such a thing? Sam wouldn't hurt anyone."

"Henry Kummer is there. He must have left the Stone Hill precinct."

"He is?" Mrs. Brenner said, "Orchard Lake may be in the Stone Hill jurisdiction. It's about forty miles from here."

Maggie sat by the window most of the morning, measuring and basting a hem. Though she had met Sam Mercken only once, the murder of a neighbor so close to home unnerved her. Fear gripped her bringing back the memories of terror she felt when Mother Rosaria was murdered at Saint Clotildes.

I have to remain calm, she said to herself, laying her hands in her lap to quell the tremors. There's a murderer out there that has to be caught. She remembered Hank's help in solving Mother Rosaria's murder and hoped to catch a glimpse of him from the window. So far, all she could see were the uniformed deputies in and out of the house and digging in the cordoned-off yard.

Mrs. Brenner said, "Sam and Amelia retired here a few months before we bought this cabin. We often played bridge with them."

After lunch, Maggie answered a knock at the door. Their Hank stood, tall and handsome as ever, his trim pencil mustache still in place. She remembered describing him to Sister Angelica, "He looks like Jimmy Stewart with a voice like Cary Grant."

"Is Dr. Brenner in?" He flashed a badge. "I'm Lieutenant Kummer. I'd like to ask him a few questions. You must be Kate."

Maggie's heart sank. Hank didn't recognize her. How could he? Here she was, dressed in shorts at a lake resort instead of covered in yards of long black serge and tucked away in a cloister. She ran her hand through her short curly hair and didn't correct him. It was too awkward to explain.

"Please come in, Lieutenant; I'll call him. He's fishing down at the cove."

"No need to call him. I'll go down there."

Maggie reacted to his thin smile, debating whether she should identify herself.

"Is your mother here?" he asked.

As if waiting for him to ask, Mrs. Brenner walked in and greeted him. "How are you, Hank, and how's your mom?"

"I'm fine. Mother's doing great since she moved to an apartment. She often asks about you."

"I miss her. Mabel and I were more like sisters when we were youngsters. We lived across the street from each other, you know. But, Hank, what's happening to our peaceful Orchard Lake?"

Hank shook his head. "You never can tell where crime will strike. Since the war, we're seeing an upswing of violence. Training soldiers makes them more knowledgeable about guns, and more guns are available."

"It's so sad when a person like Sam Mercken, who worked so hard his whole life, has a tragic end. I feel for Amelia. We were friends, and we were both piano students of Madam Kline in our younger days."

"Yes, murder is always a tragedy," Hank said. "I didn't expect to see you here. Mother will be glad when I tell her I saw you."

"Please give her my greetings."

"I'll find my way to the cove."

Maggie wanted to follow, but she felt awkward. How would she explain her presence to him? After an agonizing few minutes, she questioned, why am I sitting here sewing? I don't need permission. Maggie left and sauntered down the path after him. She didn't want to appear too excited about seeing him, just casual.

Seeing Maggie approach, her dad asked, "Have you met my daughter, Lieutenant?"

Hank Kummer turned back toward her. "Yes, at the door."

Maggie smiled and held out her hand. His smile and firm handshake gave her confidence. "You don't remember me, Lieutenant Kummer. We met five years ago at the Chateau in Stone Hill. I phoned you when Sister Angelica and I suspected Mother Rosaria was poisoned."

Maggie watched various expressions chase across his face. First, there was a look of denial, then puzzlement. An awkward silence filled the moment. Then his eyes registered a possible memory. Soon, his eyes sparkled, and his lips broke into a full smile. He was a detective. He had all the clues.

"How are you, Sister?" He extended his hand again, a much firmer handshake than before. "I had no idea it was you at the door."

"How could you have known that I left Saint Clotildes last week? You'd have to be some kind of magician to recognize me. Anyway, it's been sometime since we last met. My name is Maggie now."

He stared into her eyes for what seemed a long minute then smiled. "It's a pleasure to meet you again."

Turning toward Dr. Brenner, he said, "When Sister—" He stopped himself. "I mean, when Maggie was at the Chateau, she was a tremendous help in solving the murder of the mother superior. Without her, it never would have been investigated nor have gone to trial."

"I heard about that. Now she's made this courageous change from the cloistered life. We've been having some good times since she came home."

"And some hot euchre games." Maggie chuckled. "How is your investigation going?"

"As I told Dr. Brenner, you and your parents are in a good location to observe the goings and comings at Mercken's house. I just asked your dad to call me if he sees any cars stop or any strangers in that area."

"Do you have any inkling who did this to poor Mr. Mercken? Maybe I should major in criminology instead of music at the university this fall term."

"Don't change your major yet. The deceased had a break-in a few weeks ago, but that appears to be unrelated at this time."

"What happened?" Maggie's dad asked.

"When Sam heard the glass of his front door shatter, he and his wife locked themselves in their bedroom and called the sheriff. The deputy found a fellow named Fritz Shipman passed out on the living room rug. Unfamiliar with the area and stone drunk, he had made his way to the Mercken cabin thinking it was his host's. We couldn't charge him with criminal intent."

"Mr. Mercken wasn't so lucky last night," Maggie said.

"No, and we haven't much to go on. The autopsy report will tell us more. The victim was shot twice in the head. One .32 caliber shell was found in the house. They're searching the grounds for the other one. Here's my telephone number." He handed his card to Maggie and repeated, "If you see any cars stopping, anybody loitering, or anything that looks unusual, don't hesitate to call me."

Maggie and her dad agreed to keep a lookout and inform him of anything out of the ordinary.

"How is Officer Flanagan?" Maggie asked.

"Sergeant Flanagan is still on the Stone Hill force. I see him from time to time."

"And you? Did you leave Stone Hill?" Maggie continued.

"I transferred to the Dane County Sheriff Department two years ago. About the only thing I miss is my old ball team, the Stone Hillbillies."

Her dad asked, "Do you think the Cubs have a chance at the world series?"

Hank laughed. "What they need is a player like Mickey Mantel or Lou Gerhrig. But the Cubs have loyal fans."

"If you have any off time while you're in the area, why don't you join me for some fishing?" Dr. Brenner said.

"Thanks, I'd like to if I have time. I have to go now, but I'll see you again."

Maggie watched him walk back to the cabin alone.

*   *   *

During her afternoon swim, Maggie ventured out to the raft, swimming with a slow, comfortable stroke that wouldn't win a race. She saw motorboats cruise by on the far side of the raft, some pulling water-skiers. No sooner had she reached the raft than another swimmer swam to the edge. He looked to be in his late twenties, used to being outdoors, if his deep tan was any clue. His relaxed, winning smile made her think he was a summer vacationer.

He climbed up, dripping water close to Maggie. "Hi there. When did you come?" He spoke like someone who knew all the summer people.

"We came yesterday. Isn't this a glorious spot for a vacation? I'm lucky my parents have a cabin here."

"Would that be Dr. Brenner?"

"Yes it is. Why do you ask?"

"It's just that I've never seen you here before." He emphasized "you" in such a way she knew it was going to be difficult to explain.

"I've been busy doing other things."

"Name's Rudy. What's yours?"

"Maggie." She didn't want to encourage conversation and made a move to go. Rudy spoiled her plans to sunbathe on the raft. She'd feel uncomfortable with him there.

"I have to go back now. Nice to meet you." She slid into the water.

Back at the pier, Maggie spread a blanket on their dock and watched Rudy dive off the raft. He repeated his dives at least seven or eight times. Was he searching for something?

31

The next morning, Maggie watched her mother cut out a pattern on the dusty rose fabric. Holding a scrap in front of her, she looked in the mirror. "This is a great color. I'd like to have my picture taken in the suit when it's finished." She didn't tell her mom she'd like to have her picture taken in all her new clothes, even the refitted dresses from her mother's closet.

"My, aren't you getting vain? Didn't your novice mistress teach you about vanity? Or are you renouncing humility as well as your vows?"

"Mom, I know you're disappointed that I left the cloister. My entering St. Clotildes was not a mistake, and my leaving it wasn't either. Having my pictures would give me a sense of history, my new beginning. Everybody has photo albums. I don't have one yet."

"You can go through our old albums back home and pick out some. If you want a sense of history, start with some when you were a child. There's the one of you sitting on the hood of our old Reo, when we used to cross the Mississippi on the ferry at the Macgregor, Iowa, crossing."

Maggie smiled. "I remember that one. Thanks for the suggestion."

Later when Maggie returned from a swim, her dad met her with the camera at the pier. "How about a picture?"

Had he heard the discussion with her mother earlier? "Do you realize this is my first picture since I'm back?" Maggie bent over to finish toweling her wet hair. Loosening the short curls, she heard a click.

Her dad laughed. "There's a candid shot. Now just smile and act natural, Maggie." He focused the lens on her.

"I don't want to look too sexy."

"Don't worry, you won't."

She shifted her weight to one leg, standing with her hand on her hip like a magazine picture she'd seen.

He snapped the shutter.

"I wonder what the sisters would say if they saw this picture."

"That won't happen. Let's go for a walk."

After Maggie changed her clothes, they walked toward the Green Apple Deli and Bar with a list of groceries Mrs. Brenner sent along. Mailboxes dotted the road in front of each cabin. Cars were parked at angles, some on front yards. License plates suggested vacationers came from as far away as Mississippi. A few dogs lazed near doorways trusting passersby to ignore them. Further on, the lakefront stretched away from the road. A large growth of elms and maples stretched to the water's edge, providing shade from the hot sun.

When her dad opened a pack of cigarettes, Maggie asked, "Let me have a puff."

He shook one loose from the pack. "Here, try one yourself."

Maggie pulled one out and held it between her fingers. With her arm posed at an angle, she liked her sophisticated look. After her dad lit it, she puffed on it and started to cough. "Oh." Bent over, she tried to get her breath. "I need to go slower."

Turning downwind, she tried to inhale again, but her coughing persisted.

Dr. Brenner patted her back and took the cigarette out of her hand. "Don't rush to get this bad habit. It's hard on your lungs and expensive, too."

Maggie nodded in agreement after regaining her voice. They walked on.

She asked, "Who is Rudy? Do you know him? He seems to know everyone. He's curious why I never came to the lake before. I wasn't ready to explain."

"Oh? You're going to have to deal with that, Maggie. Don't you want anyone to know you were a sister? They're missing half the fun."

"What do you mean?"

"You can't expect to come back after spending twelve years in a nunnery and act like it didn't happen."

"But if I tell, it could spoil every relationship. I wouldn't even have a chance to know a man, if he knew I was a nun. What would he think? That I was too goody to be around."

"Well, that's up to you. Now, what about Rudy?"

"Do you know him?"

"I've seen him around. Rudy comes to visit his uncle, Al Steger, a bachelor. Never knew much about him. Where did you meet him?"

"On the raft, yesterday."

"And?"

"I was surprised. That's all. Nobody was around when suddenly his head popped out of the water by the side of the raft. I hope he won't be there this afternoon. I want to get some sun."

When they reached the Green Apple Deli and Bar, four men sat around a table playing whist. The bar was a place where patrons could sit and read newspapers, play cards, or pick up staples from the deli. The game stopped when Maggie and her dad appeared.

One man with a prominent Adam's apple called out, "Hey, look who's here. Welcome back, Doc." After introductions all around, he stood up. "Want to take my place? I have to go."

"No thanks, Al, can't stay now; count me in later," Dr. Brenner said as Al left.

"Glad to see you back," someone called as he came from behind the divider between the deli and the bar. "Terrible about Sam Mercken. How's everything at your cabin?"

"Sure is, Butch. We don't expect anything like that to happen at Orchard Lake." They shook hands. "We feel safe with the deputies and police all around us. This is my daughter, Maggie."

"Merdoc's my name. Butch Merdoc." He offered Maggie his moist hand. "Call me Butch." A grape-stain birthmark covered his left eye and part of his cheek. His bulging belly hung over a soiled white apron.

To Maggie, his hand felt like a chunk of meat. She noticed a tattoo of a nude female on his right biceps. It was hard to avoid, though she found it interesting, especially when the figure bounced around when he turned his arm.

Butch continued, "I bet whoever shot Sam is three states away by now." He rapped his knuckles on the bar to emphasize his statement. "I sure hope they catch him."

Maggie's mind was ready to pick up clues.

A short man with a double chin carried a glass of beer over to a table, taking Al's chair. "Catch who? Just got here this morning," Ted Bryson asked.

Jim Mooreside raised his heavy eyebrows that met across his nose, "You remember Sam Mercken?" He flipped his pompadour back, patting it with soft strokes. "The old man who always wore a suit."

"Yeah, yeah, the jeweler. You don't mean he's dead?"

"Stone dead. Shot twice."

"Oh my God!" Ted said. "I've known him for years, back when we both lived in Milwaukee. He suggested I buy my place here."

Ted continued, "He sold me a beautiful bracelet for my wife. Gave me a good price too. Where is Sam's wife? Is she at the house?"

"Amelia went to visit her nephew yesterday; the detective told me," Jim answered.

Maggie listened, hoping to hear some detail that wouldn't be included in Hank's routine questions. She asked Butch, "What time does the Green Apple close?"

Merdoc glanced at her dad as if to ask, what's she getting at? Maggie could tell by his expression she better leave the questioning to Hank.

Turning his back on her, Butch rearranged packs of Lucky Strikes on a stand. His laugh sounded more like a cackle. "We're out of here by one or two o'clock. Ain't we, Elaine?" he yelled over to the deli section.

Elaine came around the partition snapping bubble gum. She popped a six-inch bubble like an expert. "Jeez, boss, if I'm any later, my old man will let me know." The fresh, fruity gum flavor trailed her.

The men at the table cheered. "That's telling it, Elaine."

She glanced at the new arrivals, hoisting her bra into place then patted the back of her bouffant hairdo. Like her boss, Elaine carried surplus poundage around her middle.

Elaine could take down anyone with sarcasm, if she had a mind to, Maggie thought.

Ted Bryson scraped his chair to get attention. He lowered his voice as if he were about to relay confidential information. "I remember once there was talk of a partnership between Sam and Al." Ted's cherub face turned solemn. "It was Al Steger who told me about it. I never did hear how that turned out."

"Well, Al used to be Sam's accountant," said Jim.

Maggie took note. Did Ted think Al had something to do with the murder? Al had left in a hurry when she and her dad arrived.

Ted continued, "When Sam and Amelia lived in Wawatosa, they had a thriving jewelry business and worked long hours. It's unbelievable that this could happen to him, and here at Orchard Lake."

Jim said, "Sam purchased his vacation home back in '33. When he sold his business in 1950, he and Amelia moved here to stay."

"Always kept up his business appearance," Butch chimed in. "Wore a suit, white shirt with gold cuff links, even when he walked on the shore."

Jim added, "Poor Sam. I wonder who'd want to kill him."

Maggie and her dad picked up their groceries, paid Elaine, and left.

"What did you think about the group? I can see you're forming some ideas."

"An interesting place, and interesting comments."

That afternoon, Maggie swam to the raft, bent on getting a tan. Satisfied she was alone after searching every direction, she pulled herself up and got comfortable on the artificial green turf. The sun warmed her chilled skin. Her thoughts returned to the Chateau and the different kind of life she now led. How would Mother Cordelia look in a bathing suit, or Sister Mercy? Would God punish her for such frivolous thoughts? Her expression turned sober when she felt a splash on her legs. The raft heaved to one side as Rudy pulled himself up on the platform.

"You're getting a nice tan." He stood near her, still dripping. The raft rocked back and forth from the force of his jump out of the water.

Maggie rolled over and sat up, careful to keep her knees together. "Hi yourself. Are you enjoying the lake?"

"Can't be beat." He sat down on the edge of the raft, his feet splashing in the water. "Where do you live when you're not here?"

She felt trapped like a captive on the raft. "Well," she paused, "this summer, I'm visiting my parents in Georgetown. I'm a schoolteacher." Did this sound too composed? She must put slang into her vocabulary.

"No kidding. Where'd you teach?"

"At a private school in Stone Hill."

"Stone Hill?" He leaned back on his hands, looking up at the clear sky. "I once knew a girl who went to that school. She wanted to be a nun."

Maggie caught her breath and held it, bracing herself for details she didn't want to hear.

"So what do you do for fun here?" he asked. "There's a dance pavilion at the north end of the lake. Want to go with me tomorrow night?"

Maggie jerked her head toward him. "I'll be busy then." Her clipped words had a ring of finality, maybe too quick. The lake might be a good place to have a practice date. If she made a bad impression, it wouldn't follow her back to Georgetown or the university. She didn't want people to remember a girl so proper and acts like an old maid or a wallflower sitting with her hands in her lap? Did it matter if she felt no attraction for Rudy? He seemed presentable in a swimsuit. He had a tanned, beautiful body.

"Nobody's that busy at the lake," he said. "You sound like you have a class and have to study for a test."

"Okay." Maggie drew out the syllables, pleased with her slang. "You're right. Sounds like fun."

Rudy stood up, making the raft rock. "Good. I'll pick you up at eight thirty."

Better find out more about him, Maggie thought. "Are you practicing your diving skills? I see you out here diving off the raft."

"I've been diving for treasures in this lake for years. There's an old tale been circulating in these parts about a treasure buried in the lake. I want to find it." He opened a safety pin from a pocket in his jungle-print trunks and pulled out a knife. "I find all sorts of things. Look what I found today." He turned an eight-inch blade around, admiring it. The sun reflected off its tarnished surface. Pointing to a rock about one hundred feet away, he said, "I found it under a log over there."

Maggie flinched, not enjoying his treasure. Her eyes followed his direction. "Where do you live when you're not visiting your uncle?"

"In Madison."

"Did you attend the university?"

"Yeah, I did for a while then dropped out. I could think of better ways to make money than going to college."

"Will you be staying here all summer?"

"Naw, just a few days."

"Then what?"

"Back to Madison. Got to go now." He put the knife back into the pocket and jumped into the water. Looking back, he yelled, "See ya at eight thirty tomorrow night." He disappeared.

Maggie watched him swim back to shore. Was her snap decision to go with him to the dance made too fast? What repercussions would his intrusion into her life have? Would she be comfortable with him? Maggie rolled over on her stomach. Down through the clear water, the sun picked up a reflection of a shiny object on the lakebed, something Rudy missed. She'd investigate later rather than disturb her time in the sun. Maggie laughed to herself; she'd tell Rudy he has another treasure. That sounded so junior high.

Maggie was flattered to look the part of a datable girl. Did young people still dance the jitterbug? She could still dance that, also the fox-trot. In her mind, she mimicked the foot patterns, making dance gestures with her toes. How would it feel to dance close to Rudy?

Looking down again through the water, she detected the outline and glided into the water. The slight movement of the water shifted the object from her grasp. Maggie had decided to abandon it when her toe scraped something hard. Feeling down her leg to her foot, she grasped a cold metal object. It had the shape of—it felt like—a gun! An alarm clanged in her head. Terror claimed her consciousness, as well as a need for air. Is this it? Is this the murder weapon?

As she rose to the surface, Maggie bumped her head against the bottom of the raft. With her find in one hand, she edged out toward lighter water for what seemed an eternity. With care, she laid her trophy on the raft, as though it were made of glass. Seeing the gun at eye level made her body shiver, causing goose bumps to form on her arms. After she got her breath, Maggie looked around in every direction to see if Rudy or anybody else witnessed her actions. With care, she tucked the gun inside her suit next to her heart. Using slow strokes back to shore, she tried to keep it steady, so it wouldn't fall out. Nor did she want to admit the gun might be loaded. Were the fingerprints disturbed? All that mattered now was to get back and call Hank.

Not waiting to dry herself on the pier, she slipped a twig through the trigger guard of the gun and carried it to the picnic table near the cabin.

"Dad, see what I found in the lake," Maggie called.

Dr. Brenner, hearing the urgency in her voice, swung out of the hammock where he was reading a dental journal. Together, they stared at the gun in silence. Mrs. Brenner joined them.

Still out of breathe, Maggie explained, "It was at the bottom of the lake."

"How did it get there?" her mom asked. "Do you suppose someone threw it in to hide it?"

"Can you tell if it's been there a long time?" Maggie asked her dad. Her nerves felt raw with shock.

He shook his head. "Hank said the shell was from a .32 automatic pistol. I don't know what this is. I'll call him." He placed a towel over the gun to prevent anyone else from seeing it.

On the way to the phone booth outside the Green Apple, he warned his daughter, "Don't tell anybody about finding the gun."

He didn't have to tell her.

32

F ew cars occupied the parking area at the Green Apple Deli when Maggie
and her dad drove in to use the pay phone. The late-afternoon crowd hadn't
gathered for spirits or card games. It gave them more privacy.

"Keep a look out, Maggie. I don't want anyone to overhear this call," her dad said
as he closed the booth door.

Maggie had wanted to call Hank herself but stepped aside for her dad. She
hoped Hank would let her be part of the investigation. Now, she had more freedom
than at the Chateau, and she had found the gun. If this wasn't the murder weapon,
it might be a link to something else. Through the glass panels, she followed the
gist of her dad's conversation, watching him nod his head, point his hand down,
then hang up.

"I got straight through to Hank. He's coming right over," her dad said when he
stepped out of the phone booth. "He also said to leave the gun on the table and not
touch it, which of course we knew."

"Not so loud." Maggie said as a car pulled up and parked next to them. She
recognized Al Steger, one of the card players she had met at the Green Apple that
morning. He yelled out the open window. "Have you seen Rudy?"

Maggie explained she saw him at the raft earlier. They left.

Hank arrived twenty minutes later at the Brenners' cabin. Maggie and her parents
watched him examine the gun with practiced eyes, waiting to hear his expertise. He
wrote down the serial and model number then inserted a pencil into the trigger loop
and sniffed the end of the barrel. Water dripped from its inner workings. Hank explained,
"It's a .32 automatic Remington." With gloved hands, he opened the cartridge. "Two
shots fired." He emptied the bullets from it and wrote down the brand. Then he tested
the trigger pull and the safety catch.

"Do you mean it was still loaded when I brought it back?" Maggie said and
coughed as if she had swallowed too much water.

"Yes." Hank searched Maggie's face. "Did anyone see you bring it up to the raft?
Were there any boaters or skiers around?"

"I don't think so. Rudy had been in the area. I saw him swim back to shore at least
thirty minutes earlier. He showed me a knife he found in the lake this afternoon."

Hank didn't respond.

"Could the gun have accidentally fired when I swam back from the raft?" Maggie
gasped a quick breath.

"How did you carry it?"

She pointed to her stomach. "Right here, inside my suit." Maggie snapped the elastic fabric across her middle, though the gun had fallen lower.

They heard Mrs. Brenner's quick breath. "She could have been shot."

"Not likely," Hank said as though he was asked the time of day, "even with the safety clip off." He looked down the barrel. "It's clean with some pitting." Finished with his examination, Hank inserted the gun into a plastic bag. "We'll have to wait for the ballistic test to find out if this is the murder weapon. How did you happen to find it, Maggie?"

"I was lying on the edge of the raft looking down into the water. Something shiny caught my eye. At first I thought I'd leave it for Rudy. He collects treasures from the lake. Then I felt uneasy about it and went down to get it. Can you get fingerprints from a gun that's been in the water?"

"If the gun is well maintained and oiled, the prints could be protected." He took the loaded bag out to his car.

Maggie followed along, curious to see what Hank carried in the trunk. From a box in the trunk, she read, Footwear Evidence. "How do you use that?"

"That's for taking impressions of shoe prints. The casts we take can be used as evidence. We also make accurate reproductions of tool or jimmy marks and tire prints in snow, mud, sand, and dirt."

"Did you make any casts at Sam Mercken's house?"

"Uhhuh, we got a partial print of a size-10D shoe impression and, of course, fingerprints. The absence of tire marks leads me to believe the suspect arrived on foot," Hank said.

"What kind of shoe print would that be? A tennis shoe, work shoe, or dress shoe? I could be looking for that kind when Dad and I walk around here."

Hank looked pleased at her interest. "It looks like a work shoe. The lab is checking it now. When we get the report, we'll be able to determine the brand name and possibly the shoe store that sold it."

"That's a lot of information. I haven't a clue what a man's size 10D looks like. Wonder what my dad wears."

Hank put his foot up on the rear bumper. "Mine are eleven."

"Hmm." Maggie put her shoe next to his to compare her shoe for length and width. "I just wanted to get an idea. Does the shoe have treads?"

Hank nodded. "Maggie, would you mind swimming out to the raft with me? I'd like to check the area where you found the gun." He pulled out what looked like a dusty plaid rag from under the spare tire before closing the trunk.

"Sure, Hank. Now is as good a time as any." She no longer felt tired.

After Hank changed to his swimming trunks in the cabin, he explained to the Brenners. "I'd like to draw the least amount of attention to this. It'd be better if you waited indoors in case someone's watching. The suspect who threw it may be watching with binoculars."

Maggie and Hank walked to the pier. His bathing suit she thought was a rag looked good on him. He wasn't as tan as Rudy, but he looked lean and strong. She had to keep from staring at his whole body. They set out. Maggie preferred the sidestroke, so she could look around. It took less breath than the breaststroke Hank swam. He reached the raft first and jumped up, offering her a hand.

Maggie walked over to the spot where she had lain. "Right here." She tapped her foot. "I looked down and saw a shiny object on the lakebed about here." Kneeling down, she dipped her finger into the water. "It wasn't until I decided to return to shore that I went down to investigate."

Hank remained silent.

Maggie continued, "At first, the water movement shifted the gun under the raft. I thought it wasn't worth the struggle to find it in the dark water, but then my toe happened to snag it."

Hank nodded. "That doesn't necessarily mean it was dropped from the raft. If it's been in the lake since Sunday, it could have been dropped or tossed from any place. I'll check the currents at the coast guard station." He peered through the clear water. "Must be ten to fifteen feet deep at this point. I'll go down and look around." He let himself over the edge and disappeared through the bubbles.

Maggie wondered if he was searching for something else. A few minutes later, he surfaced empty-handed and climbed onto the raft.

After he got his breath, he sat next to her. "I didn't find anything." He looked around the perimeter of the lake with a half smile she remembered so well. "This is a beautiful spot. Are you enjoying your vacation?"

Maggie realized all this dramatic activity was part of a day's work to him. "Yes, it's a great place for me to start a new life. My parents have been so helpful since I came home, but too protective. How has it been for you since you moved?" She turned to look at him.

"Pretty much the same as Stone Hill PD. Now that you made this big change in your life, what are your plans?"

Making designs in the water with her feet, Maggie said, "I had planned to take a few classes this summer at the university, but my folks urged me to come here. I'll register for the fall term and start working toward a master's degree. After that, it's looking for a teaching job to make some money."

Hank nodded. Listening was part of his job.

"I'll rent a room in Madison this fall, then I won't need a car."

"What else are you doing here besides swimming?" he asked.

"Well," Maggie delayed, wondering if she should mention her date. "Do you know Rudy?"

"Rudy, Rudy Davidson? The lad who visits his uncle? Where did you meet him?"

"Right here on the raft. He's an excellent swimmer and dives for treasures he claims are buried in the lake."

"That old tale?" Hank snorted, shaking his head. "I doubt anyone but him believes that."

"I'm going with him tomorrow night to a dance at the north end of the lake."

"You are?" His head jerked up. He looked Maggie straight in the eye.

She looked down to avoid his look and cringed to think what he thought. Would he understand it was a practice date? Rudy wasn't her type; she'd be the first to admit. Hank must think she left the cloister to meet men, that she was "boy crazy," or whatever they call it these days. Now, she'd have to accept whatever he thought.

"Just a warning, Magdalena. Don't tell him or anyone else you found the gun or that we came to the raft together."

"I wouldn't." She had better sense than that.

"Better still," Hank paused lost in thought, "tell Rudy you found the gun and threw it back in the lake."

"You mean I should lie?" Maggie raised her voice.

Hank stared at her, shaking his head. "Yes, Magdalena, if you're going to help me, you'll need to know when to tell the truth, and when to lie to set up a scene."

"Oh, that's the right-to-know ethic." She nodded. "I remember that when I studied ethics. Hank, why don't you call me Maggie?"

He smiled. "Maggie, shall we swim back to shore?" He led the way.

After Hank changed his trunks, Dr. Brenner asked, "Do you think there's something else in the lake?"

"There may be another weapon. The deceased had a contusion on his left temple. We haven't found the instrument that hit him. But thanks to Maggie; we're making progress." Hank smiled at her.

"I'm glad I can help," said Maggie.

"Just keep doing what you did. Look out for anything unusual or different. I'll be on my way now. Have a good time at the dance, Maggie." He was off.

Dr. Brenner returned to his reading.

Mrs. Brenner suggested, "Maggie, let's get the buttonholes done on your blouse. If I were home, I could put them in with the sewing machine."

"I'll do them by hand. We did a lot of fancy embroidery work on pieces that were gifts for doctors and benefactors." Maggie sat down to thread her needle.

"All you think about is getting a tan." Mrs. Brenner watched her daughter sew buttonhole stitches so each one would be even. "I hope you aren't thinking of playing detective again, are you?"

"I'd like to work with Hank. It'd be so much easier here." Now that she had found the gun, she felt she had a chance. "Why do you ask?"

"Because that's when you started to question your vocation."

Maggie pushed the fabric aside. "Mom, I never had a vocation! I entered the cloister for all the wrong reasons."

"You did have a vocation! And you changed when you got involved in Mother Rosaria's murder. Everything about you changed. I could see it each time we visited you."

It was useless to argue with her. Maggie wanted to tell her that it was her life and not her mother's to live. No amount of explanation would change her mother anyway. "Mom, I can be just as good a person serving God here, living on the outside as in the cloister." Maggie refused to believe that the murder of Mother Rosaria had anything to do with her decision. Seeing Dr. Raymond did help her come to terms with her motives for becoming a nun. One reason was to please her mother, to get away from her. This made her smile.

"Why are you grinning? Are you laughing at me? Let me tell you, young lady, it's no laughing matter to give up your vocation. It's, it's like a divorce!"

Maggie could either yawn or scream. Instead, she drew her lips back, shaking her head. In a calm voice, she said, "Please, Mom. You talk funny." She couldn't say her mother acted stupid. Maggie had to be polite. Her mother probably thought she was going to hell.

For the first time, Maggie wondered whether her mother had ever wanted to be anything other than a doctor's wife or maybe a nun.

The next day Mrs. Brenner told Maggie not to dress up for the dance. Everyone dressed casually in the lake area. Of the four dresses in her wardrobe, she chose the dress her mother sent to the Chateau for her departure and a pair of tennis shoes with smiling faces printed on them. The skirt with a matching overblouse buttoned up like a jacket. It was a bad choice; she found out later. A one-piece dress would have been better, also a long-line girdle.

At eight thirty, Maggie sat on the porch waiting for her practice date. For the first time since coming to the lake, she applied eye makeup. It took time to make a clean line without smudges. After adding rouge and lipstick, she looked in the mirror. Did she look cheap? Was the lipstick color too bright? She wiped it off and applied Tangee natural her sister had given her and looked in the mirror again. It seemed foolish to spend so much time getting ready for a practice date.

Eight thirty came and went, followed by nine o'clock. Maggie hadn't felt comfortable about going with Rudy, and when the clock stroke nine thirty, she congratulated herself for getting out of a decision made on impulse. Just then Rudy pulled up in a truck. When he honked the horn, she called to her folks, "See you later."

"Wait, Magdalena!" Mrs. Brenner called, rushing to the door. "Tell him to come in. It's not proper for him to sit there tooting a horn." She turned toward her husband, who sat listening to the Cubs' ball game on the radio. "I've seen that truck before. Come take a look."

Dr. Brenner went to the window. "Didn't it used to be red? Now it's gray, a very shiny gray, like it's been repainted."

Maggie went out to his truck. "Hi, Rudy. Please come in and meet my folks."

Rudy frowned and looked down at her from his high seat. "Jesus, do I have to?"

It was clear he too had second thoughts about the date. His eyes looked bloodshot and heavy. Rudy just sat there. He made no movement to get out of the truck. With deliberate motions, he pulled the hand brake, jerking it repeatedly, then switched off the engine. Crushing out his cigarette in the ashtray as if still deciding, he opened the door and stepped down. Wearing tight jeans, a sullen-looking Rudy followed Maggie into the house. He tossed his head to one side when he acknowledged her parents' greeting, as if to say big deal.

"What was all that about?" Rudy said when they returned to the truck. "Did I have to pass their approval? You're not sixteen, or are you?" His voice trailed off as he turned the key in the ignition.

"It's just their way." Maggie wasn't going to tell him her folks were concerned about the date as if she were indeed sixteen. She didn't comment on his lateness either, which was okay with her. Now they'd have less time together. So far, dating was hard work. Maggie wished the evening were over. What would tomorrow's story be?

Her foot kicked something hard on the floor. She looked down. It was a rifle. Trying to make conversation, she asked, "Do you hunt animals as well as treasures?"

"Naw, I don't know how it got there. Belongs to my uncle." He banged it under the seat with the heel of his foot.

Maggie caught her breath, wondering if it was loaded. Could it take this rough treatment? It didn't go off. She sat back on the seat. After a five-minute drive, they approached an area of bright lights outlining the roofs of three buildings.

Rudy pointed, "That's the arcade; next to it is a theater and the dance hall." His bored expression became alive.

"Seems like a large crowd," Maggie said.

"They come from all over. Not that many people around Orchard Lake."

Rudy parked near the theater. The marquee on the theater announced, "Invasion of the Body Snatchers." He steered her into the nearby arcade. "I know a lucky pinball machine in the back. Come on." He grabbed her hand and pulled her through rows of machines and noise. From his pocket, he dug out some coins and pushed them into the slot of a machine he thought was the lucky one.

Maggie heard the band playing "I Don't Want to Set the World on Fire," a song she remembered from the forties. Rudy whacked the sides of the machine and swore, encouraging the little metal balls to fall into the openings. She took a quarter from her purse and played the machine next to him. When quarters rolled out, Rudy growled, "Beginner's luck." He grabbed her arm. "I hear one of Elvis's songs. Let's go and dance."

He guided her toward the dance pavilion and pulled her out onto the floor. Maggie thought this wasn't jitterbug or a fox-trot. Everyone danced apart from their partners, not close like she remembered. Soon, she swung around, managing to copy his head and shoulder movements. It was easy, no one to hold on to or follow. One guy did a funny gyration with his hips that Rudy imitated, making a show of himself. Maggie had to hold herself back from laughing in his face. He looked like he was in pain.

After a few more dances, Rudy said, "Let's get a drink." Maggie stood with him at the bar and ordered a beer. She remembered her mom's stern reminder that it was a cheap girl who stood at a bar and drank with the men. Well, she was doing just that, and it didn't feel bad at all. Other girls stood there as well. They left when they finished their drinks. Playing pinballs and dancing to music called rock and roll wasn't her style. Maggie wondered if she'd ever learn to like it and felt relieved to leave the dance. So far, her practice date wasn't much fun.

Rudy took a different route back to the south end of the lake. Feeling uneasy, Maggie wondered where he was taking her. As they drove along, a full moon reflected a zigzag design on the calm water surface, stretching its radiance to its full width. Frogs and crickets poured out their evening harmonies. It would have been an enchanting evening with anyone other than Rudy.

He pulled off the road and shut off the engine. Maggie thought she heard a frog plop into the water, when Rudy grabbed her shoulders and pulled her to him. "I want to kiss you, Maggie, not just on your lips, but over your whole body."

Maggie let out a noisy breath that sounded more like a shriek. The scintillating idea sent goose bumps through her. Did people really talk like this? Did they do such things on a first date, let alone a practice date? Before she had a chance to answer, he kissed her hard. Soon his hands were under her blouse. They felt warm, awakening dormant feelings. When he unfastened her bra, Maggie reached back and brought his hands down. "Stop that, Rudy! What do you think you're doing?" In that action, he managed to brush his hands across the nipples of her unhaltered breasts.

He jerked away from her, beating his fists on the steering wheel. "Damn it, Maggie. What's the matter with you? Don't you want to?"

The moonlight outlined his tight jaw line. Maggie didn't want to make him angrier. In a firm voice, she tried to reason. "No! I hardly know you, Rudy. Please take me home now."

"Aw, Maggie, you don't have to know a guy to have fun."

"Maybe for you, but not for me. Let's go." Her cool mind refused to become emotional. If she showed fear, she would lose control.

He slammed his body back in the driver's seat and remained silent. Finally, he stepped on the starter and drove along the lake for about a mile and then stopped again. His voice softened, "Let's take a walk, Maggie. It's a warm night."

"No thanks, Rudy. Take me home."

"Damn it, Maggie." He banged on the wheel again. "Here I thought you'd be fun."

33

They rode back to the Brenner cabin in silence. Do I thank him for the date? The sisters always thanked everyone for the slightest act of kindness, even if they were asked to shine someone's shoes or assigned a penance by the superior. It became second nature. For a practice date, she learned a lot and became worldly-wise in just a few hours. Whole novels were written about dates like hers and its repercussions.

As soon as Rudy braked, Maggie opened the door and stepped to the ground before he had any ideas of a good-night kiss. "Good night, Rudy. Good luck." She heard his fists slam on the steering wheel, as he grumbled an expletive. Did he say "some broad" or "damned broad"? Her first impulse was to tighten her shoulders and cringe. Instead, she walked away, head high, shoulders square, congratulating herself. She felt his eyes following her to the door, waiting as though she might change her mind. Perhaps, this was his first failed conquest. Poor boy, she giggled.

Her parents hadn't waited up, though they might have entertained the notion. She slipped in without a sound. The picture of a thirty-one-year-old daughter thrust upon middle-aged parents without any preparation struck her. For the past twelve years, they had the comfort and joy of knowing their daughter was settled in a nunnery for life. Half awake, Maggie decided to move out and get a job in Madison as soon as she returned to Georgetown.

*   *   *

Maggie heard Hank Kummer talking to her parents when she wakened. She wished she hadn't told him about going to the dance. Would he be concerned about her date as well? Was that the reason he was here? There'd be no news of the ballistic test yet.

The pinball machines were so adolescent, along with the crazy dancing, and the ride home with one idea in Rudy's mind. The gun never once entered her mind. She hadn't relayed Hank's message.

When she entered the kitchen, Maggie ignored the break in their conversation and poured a cup of coffee. Her mother and Hank sat at attention as though waiting for a report. "Good morning." She turned to face them.

"Maggie, how do you want your eggs, over easy?" Her dad cracked eggs into the frying pan.

"It doesn't matter. I'm used to getting eggs any way."

"How was the dance?" her dad said after he slipped the eggs on her plate.

"They sure have new ways of dancing these days. This rock and roll had me puzzled for a while, but then I joined in like the rest. It was crazy. No one to hold on to or follow, just sort of twist around." She laughed. "You should have seen Rudy gyrating."

"Like the rock star, Elvis the Pelvis?" Hank quipped in an amused tone. Both the Brenners echoed his humor between sips of coffee.

"No!" Maggie shouted in disbelief. "Is that what he's called? It was too funny to describe." She got up from the table and mocked the steps, twisting her hips and shoulders. They laughed, relieving the tension.

Hank said, "I was telling your parents we did a background check on a few people here, including Rudy. He's been in and out of our records. Be careful when you're with him."

"Don't worry about that! I won't be going out with him again. It was just a practice date." Maggie smiled. Cups scraped saucers as her parents settled back relieved.

Hank passed the toast to her. "Sam Mercken's body has been released for burial. The funeral will be tomorrow in Milwaukee. Do you want to come with me?"

"I'd like to." Maggie noticed obvious approval in her parents' faces and concluded Hank had discussed the trip with them earlier.

"Good." He carried his cup and saucer to the sink. "The funeral's at eleven o'clock. I want to see Sam Mercken's lawyer in Milwaukee before that. I'll stop for you at nine. Thanks, Esther, for the coffee. I'll be off."

"Wear the new flowered dress you just hemmed," Mrs. Brenner said. "And my pearl earrings if you like."

"Oh dear. So many details to think about, what dress to wear, what jewelry to put on, my hair, makeup, and money." Also my virginity, she added to herself, which could have gone as fast as the eggs over easy. She went through the sewing pile to find the dress to iron. "Females have to fuss so much more than men. To please the men, or is it just expected? All men have to do is shave."

"Yes, it was simpler in the cloister. There you never had to bother with money. The same style fits all your needs. You should have thought about that before you left," Mrs. Brenner said as she cleared the dishes off the table.

Wouldn't she like that? Her mom could put an unfavorable spin on anything she thought was good for her.

The next morning, Hank arrived in a red-with-white-trimmed 1956 Crown Victoria. He went around and opened the passenger door.

"This is a nice car," Maggie said, feeling the leather seat covers. "Is it a convertible?"

He nodded. "If the sun comes out, I'll put the top down. Right now, it looks like rain." He surveyed the sky as he closed her door. "I started to get an unmarked car from the lot, but I thought you might like my car better."

"Have you any more information on the gun I found in the lake?" Maggie asked as he got in next to her.

"The ballistic test identified it as the murder weapon," he said it as though he were talking about the weather.

Her hand went to her stomach and shivered, thinking of the close contact she had with it. "But you're still looking for something else like a heavy object?"

"Always looking, Maggie. Also for a missing cat."

"A cat? What kind of cat?"

"It's a black and white, short haired, with a black spot on his chin. He's called Smudge."

"I hope we find him. He sounds cute."

Hank shifted into high. "I'll be at the Mercken house tomorrow to interview some of the Orchard Lake residents."

"If you let me come, I won't disturb you. I'll sit in another room." Maggie looked sidewise at him.

"Let me think about it. Sometimes it's better if I'm alone."

In Milwaukee, Hank parked at the corner of Twenty-third and Wells. "It'll be about twenty minutes. Will you be okay in the car?"

"Don't worry about me. I like to sit in the car and watch people. Anyway, I see a dress shop over there. Maybe I'll pop in and look around," she said, pleased to be making a decision on her own that didn't have to be run by her mother.

Maggie watched him cross Twenty-third Street to the district attorney's office. He looked trim and professional in a navy blue business suit. She remembered the tweed sport coat with leather-patched elbows he wore in Stone Hill.

Next to the dress shop, a window displayed lingerie. She still had that problem bra that her mother had sent, as well as sizes with other clothing. Maggie often got a size too large or too small and wondered how others found their correct sizes. Now was a good time to find out her correct bra size. No one would know her in Milwaukee, which gave her courage.

Inside the shop entrance, a table displayed a bra on a model. Next to it, bras were spread out in all sizes. One bra looked like armor with hard, sharp points. Maggie examined the inside and then laid it aside, settling on a softer model.

"May I help you?" a friendly clerk asked as Maggie examined the size tags. "What size are you looking for?"

Maggie kept her voice low even though nobody else was around. "I'm not sure. Would you measure me?"

The saleslady pulled a tape from around her neck. "Put your arms up, ma'am." She tightened the tape around Maggie's breasts then lowered it to measure her rib cage. "You measure a 34B." The clerk picked one up from the table. "Here is your size. Would you like to try it on?"

"Yes, if it won't take too much time."

"Step over here to the fitting room." The clerk opened the door. "Call me if you want help. I'm a certified corsetiere."

Her framed certificate hung in the dressing room. Maggie undressed in a hurry. She didn't want Hank to return and have to explain what she did. It would have been easier if she went into the dress shop. After the try-on, she still found the same gaps in the bra.

"Do you have the correct size, ma'am?" The clerk said near the dressing room door.

"I'm not sure if I do," she hesitated. "Would you come in, please?" It was embarrassing, but she had to get her sizing settled once and for all.

The corsetiere adjusted the straps, snapped the back in place. "Now, my dear, lean over."

Maggie obeyed. The clerk repeated her check on the bra. "It fits you much better now; don't you think?"

She looked in the mirror then down at her filled-out cups. "Thanks so much. I'll take two." What a relief, she thought and looked at her watch. It took ten minutes, and all I had to do was to lean over. The old bra had been the right size after all. Did the clerk think she'd just come from the backwoods or some asylum?

Back in the car, Maggie tucked her new purchases under the seat and sat back with an air of calm and assurance. The question of sizes still gnawed at her as she watched people walking by. They were so important with the fitted styles. Everyone knew their size of pants, shoes, dresses, etc. Maggie could hear what her mother would say if she mentioned that. She'd say the sisters wore one size that fit everyone, which was almost true.

Heavy trucks rumbled by, causing the car to vibrate. A police car with a blaring siren passed in the line of traffic. When would she drive in heavy traffic like this? Maybe her dad would let her practice at the lake. That would be her next project. Driving the new-styled automatic shift should be easier than the stick shift she learned before leaving home. Her eyes followed the imposing outline of the tall buildings. On top of one, a neon sign read, Miller High Life. She could almost taste the satisfying, bitter lager on her throat. Her dad always made sure there was ample supply in their frig.

A newsstand at the corner displayed Milwaukee's *Daily Sentinel.* The bold headline read: "Cuba Factions at War." Maggie slipped out of the car and bought a paper. Opening it, she read about a jewelry heist in Lansing, a town located on the Iowa side of the Mississippi River. Maggie wondered if there might be a connection to the murder of Sam Mercken, who was also a jeweler.

Mist covered the windshield when Hank returned. "Did you find what you were looking for?" he asked.

"It was a nice shop." She didn't tell him she bought two bras and didn't know her size.

He explained, "I met with Sam Mercken's lawyer. He'll be reading the will this afternoon at one o'clock. I'll be there. You can come along."

"Sounds interesting. I imagine you learn a good deal about a family at a time like that."

Hank nodded. "If the weather clears up, I'm hoping we'll have time for a ball game. How does that sound? Will it fit into your plans?"

"I'd love to see a game. Who's playing?"

"The Milwaukee Braves and the New York Giants."

"I heard my dad talk about the Braves and Hank Aaron. Is he on that team?"

"Yep, he sure is. Milwaukee has a good chance for the national league pennant this year."

"Here we are." They arrived at Old Saint Mary's Church on the corner of Broadway and Kilbourn Street in the downtown section. Hank found a parking space nearby.

A small group sat in the front pews near the flocked, covered casket. Hank and Maggie, both Catholic, sat in back observing the rituals of kneeling and standing during the requiem Mass.

At the gravesite, the mist changed to a light rain. From under Hank's umbrella, Maggie spotted Elaine, from the Green Apple Deli. She checked to see if the waitress chewed bubble gum. Not at a funeral, though it was hard to imagine her without snapping it. She wasn't. The widow and nephew of Sam Mercken were identified under the canopy near the grave along with their neighbors she had met before, Jim Mooreside and his wife. Maggie also recognized Mr. Bryson, whose thin hair was parted in the middle of his bowed head.

Apart from them, a lone woman shielded herself from the rain under a tree. She wore a tight black skirt and white blouse with a plunging neckline. Large dangling diamond earrings flashed under her red hair. Maggie glanced at Hank to see if he noticed her. Had Hank ever seen her before? Maybe it was the size of the diamonds that sparkled even on a rainy day. What was her story? What was her connection to Sam Mercken? Were the earrings a gift from him? What about the perfume he bought in Richfield?

As the priest sprinkled holy water on the grave, Maggie was reminded of Mother Rosaria's funeral at the Chateau. A full investigation had begun by Hank after the cyanide was found in her body. The sisters said Maggie's prayers had brought about the discovery, but she could never see how prayers could accomplish the myriad petitions of the sisters. She once asked Sister Angelica, "Does God help only those who are prayed for? What about the souls who never get any prayers? Are they doomed?"

Why was she going over this old stuff anyway? She felt Hank's strong arm next to hers. When Maggie glanced toward the tree again, the girl was gone.

*   *   *

Assembled in the lawyer's office were the widow, Amelia Mercken; Gilbert Paradyze, her nephew; Albert Steger; Jim Mooreside; and the redheaded girl from the cemetery, who Maggie soon learned was Virgie Pinski. I wonder what role she plays in this drama.

Three large glass-front bookcases filled with law books lined one wall of the walnut-paneled office. Harold Stalling, Sam's attorney, expressed his sympathy to the widow and greeted the group. "All documents have been filed appropriate to the laws of the state of Wisconsin. I've called this meeting to read the will of Samuel Mercken, who died the fifteenth day of June, 1957.

"I will now read the last will and testament of Samuel Mercken, which I prepared for him June 6, 1949." He removed a blue-covered sheaf of papers from the folder and read the multipage document from beginning to end. Then he addressed the assembled group.

"In plain English, the will provides that all of Samuel Mercken's property, real and personal, is left to Amelia Mercken for her sole use and control so long as she lives. At Amelia's death, the remaining estate will be divided among Al Steger, and Virgie Pinski."

Amelia let out a little scream. The lawyer looked up and walked over to her. He whispered something to her. When Amelia nodded, he continued, "The will appoints Al Steger as executor, to serve without bond. I have filed this will with the court and the first hearing, to admit this will to probate and to confirm Al as the executor, will be held on July 10. Are there any questions?

"We hereby certify that this and the foregoing pages contain a true and complete abstract of all entries of record in the state of Wisconsin.

"Are there any questions?"

Albert Steger jumped up. His face reddened as he shouted, "Sam told me I was to get my inheritance when he died, not when Amelia died." He remained standing, tapping his foot as if he could change his employer's last will and testament. "There's got to be another will some place. I'm going to find it." He looked back and forth from Amelia to the attorney.

Amelia, a petite lady shrouded in a black dress, with a veil that hung over her shoulders, sat in silence.

The attorney said, "Albert, see me later." He went over to Amelia and shook her hand.

Amelia rose from her chair and walked with the aid of a cane toward the detective. "Have you found my cat, Lieutenant?" she spoke enunciating each word.

"We're still looking, Mrs. Mercken. I have a helper who will keep an eye out for Smudge. Meet Maggie Brenner, who's visiting her parents at the lake. She's promised to look for him."

"How do you do, Maggie?"

Maggie shook her hand. Amelia's eyes had a vacant, unfocused look; maybe it was the veil that clouded them. "I'm just across the road from your house, Mrs. Mercken. I'll be watching for Smudge."

Hank and Maggie left the lawyer's office. When the sun came out, Hank's face lit up. Glancing at his watch, he said, "We'll be a late for the game, but it'll be worth it to see these two teams play."

As they drove to county stadium, Maggie asked, "What do you think of the will?"

Hank shook his head. "Wills can either bring family and friends together or have the opposite effect."

"Does Amelia realize that she could be the next target?"

"Well, for one thing, I don't think we'll see her back in Orchard Lake."

"Who is Virgie?"

"The department is questioning her. She was in Milwaukee the night of the murder."

They pulled up to the stadium. Hank led Maggie through the stands just as the crowd stood and cheered a ball player who slid into third base. It was the third inning.

Maggie said, "That must have been the famous Hank Aaron."

Hank nodded. "He came to the Braves three years ago hitting twenty-seven homers his first year with a batting average of .314. I hope he hits a home run today." After the inning ended, Hank opened his baseball program. "Warren Spahn's going to pitch. He's a lefty. There used to be a saying 'Spahn and Sain, and pray for rain.'"

Maggie looked at Hank with raised eyebrows. "And that means?"

"If Spahn and Sain are pitching, the Braves never lose. Only rain would postpone the game. The fans are betting on the Braves to win the world series, and the Giants have a good team too."

"Are you playing on a baseball team? I remember you did in Stone Hill."

"Just a pickup team in the sheriff's department. We play the police department and the highway patrol on special occasions. I'd like to get on a regular team."

The fans cheered as the New York Yankees came up to bat.

"Here's another Golden Glove prospect." Mickey Mantle picked up the bat. "The Giants are also contenders for the pennant race. They're moving to San Francisco next season. New Yorkers don't like that. Even I have a hard time imagining them called the San Francisco Giants."

Maggie listened to Hank's sports talk. Hank could come from an event such as the reading of the will and thoroughly engross himself in a baseball game. She'd have liked to discuss the two prominent figures, Amelia and Al Steger. "It'll be interesting to see the sports write-up in the newspaper tomorrow," Hank said.

She remembered it was the section her dad read first.

The Braves won three to two. It was five o'clock before they started back to Orchard Lake.

34

When Hank arrived the next morning, Maggie walked across the road with him to the Mercken house. The faded gray one-story clapboard sat back two hundred feet from the main road. A gravel path separated the house from a garage that was built in the same bungalow style. An overgrown vine hung on an arbor near the side entrance. To the right, an untended garden patch yielded tall stringy cosmos among weeds. Roses struggling to bloom pushed through a thicket of bushes.

Maggie thought no one would ever think this serene scene was the setting of a murder. After going with Hank to Milwaukee and watching the baseball game, Maggie felt awake to every detail of life. She lifted her head to smell the pines and noticed the steam from the sun-warmed ground. From the trees, birds sang their morning tunes. They were so free. So was she.

"Why are you conducting your investigation in the murder house?"

"The investigating team has relinquished the crime scene," said Hank.

Maggie asked, "Did you have to get a warrant to search the house?"

"In triplicate." Hank smiled and continued, "The crime scene has reverted back to the owner, so you can come in. Amelia's allowed me to use it, mostly for convenience. It'll save the residents an eighty-mile round-trip to Madison. I'm hoping to jar a memory or jog someone's senses to build a body of evidence. Some of them have already given their statements to the police. All we have so far is coincidence. What we're lacking is probable cause. We have no substantial evidence linking Sam's murder to a suspect."

Hank hesitated at the roped-off area. "This won't be pleasant. You don't have to come."

"Don't worry about me. I've been around death scenes before. Once I stayed up with Sister Alexis. The night Sister died, she clasped me with both arms and pressed me to her. She took her last breath, still holding me. I wasn't frightened. It was, 'peaceful.'" She stooped under the rope still in place. Hank inserted a key into the Yale lock and opened the door.

An eerie coldness greeted them as they entered the closed house. Maggie felt goose pimples rise on her arms. They walked to the chalked outline traced on the brownish red flowered carpet. A swivel desk chair still remained off center where it had careened away from the desk.

Near the head and shoulders of the outline, pools of dried blood showed scrape marks of evidence taken earlier. Maggie watched Hank kneel on one knee to examine it further. He took tweezers from his pocket and snagged at something she couldn't see. He stood, holding it up to the light like a trophy.

"We've had a visitor."

"What is it?"

"Cat hair. Smudge, Amelia's cat, has been in here, sniffing around." Hank put the cat hair into a plastic bag.

"Amelia will be happy to hear that. I wonder where he's getting food."

"Don't worry; a cat can take care of itself. I wonder how he's getting in." Hank stepped away to survey a wider angle of the death scene. "Judging from the report, the coroner wasn't sure if the contusion, which was not lethal, or the gunshot wound, was delivered by a right-or left-hander. The victim could have been wounded before he was shot."

"Where were the gunshot wounds?" Maggie asked.

"The bullet entered the right temporal area above the ear and exited on the left side. The trajectory was in an upward direction fifteen to twenty degrees. Brain damage was the cause of death. It was quick."

Maggie saw a trail of blood. She wondered why the murderer bothered to hit him if he was already shot. "Could Mr. Mercken have been hit with the barrel of the gun?"

"Possibly, but there's always the danger of the gun discharging in the wrong direction."

"How long did he lie here before the police came?" Maggie asked and turned around to see if she could find some clue to support the left-handed theory.

"The sheriff's deputies responded to the call in fifteen minutes."

"I used to be a lefty. The sisters at school struggled to retrain me to use my right hand. Sister Mary Adelaide, my first-grade teacher, made me feel I'd go straight to hell if I made the sign of the cross with the left hand. My parents promised me a 'real watch that ran' if I changed. But when I earned a Palmer Method Writing Certificate using my right hand, they gave me a play watch with a promise of a real one when I was older. Maybe the suspect could switch hands like me, a retrained lefty."

"Or like Leonardo da Vinci," Hank said. "Many of his notes were written from the right side of the page to the left."

"And how about Mickey Mantle, a switch-hitter?" Maggie smiled at the sports information she had learned from him. "Or it sounds to me like there could have been another person visiting Sam Mercken. Maybe that's why the coroner couldn't be sure."

"Everything's possible. That's an interesting angle."

Maggie said, "I read an article about right-and left-handers. Eighty-five percent of people are right-handed. Of the 15 percent lefties, half have mixed brain dominance. I think that means they can switch hands, like a retrained lefty."

Hank opened two windows to let the warm summer breezes from the lake into the house.

When Maggie took the vase of limp tulips and lilacs from a drop-leaf table to the kitchen, it left a round dustless circle on the varnished surface. Together, they moved the table near the window. Hank placed a chair with its back to the window.

Maggie continued her exploration. An upright piano stood in a dark corner covered with photos, some formal, some informal snapshots on a scarf embroidered with red and yellow roses. Moving closer, Maggie recognized the wedding picture of Amelia and Samuel Mercken. She studied the picture of a much younger Amelia with brown hair and a full face. It had little resemblance to the black-clothed Amelia she saw at the funeral. Samuel Mercken looked like a stern businessman. He held his head high. In a group picture, Jim Mooreside, their neighbor, stood out tall and handsome.

Lifting the dusty lid over the keyboard, she played a few chords. "It's a Chickering, and in pretty good tune. I wonder who played it." She opened the piano bench. A copy of "There's An Old Spinning Wheel in the Parlor" topped a pile of music. Maggie lifted the torn sheets onto the music rack and began to play.

Hank, already at work reading reports, leaned back in his chair. He hummed along, then got up, and came to the piano, singing some of the words. "My mother used to play that piece."

"You have a nice voice, Hank."

"Well, I did sing in the glee club at Campion Academy," he said.

"Campion? That's a Jesuit academy in Prairie du Chien." Hank nodded.

Together they sifted through the pile of music and found a few more pieces Hank wanted her to play. He looked at his watch. "We could continue this all day, couldn't we?"

"Let's make a date to do that," Maggie suggested.

"Fine with me. How about next Sunday? Maybe we could do something else, too."

Maggie smiled and closed the piano. "I'm beginning to feel like I know Amelia. Tell me what happened that night. Did she discover her husband here on the floor? Was she up when the sheriff deputy came?"

Hank looked up from his papers. "Amelia had gone to bed. She wakened when she heard gunshots and found Sam on the living room floor. When the ambulance came, she wanted the driver to take Sam to the hospital. He went to the morgue instead."

"How awful." Maggie shivered; her head and shoulders shook. She avoided looking down at the scene just inches away and moved to the desk. It had already been examined for clues, but she wanted to see it. The water and electric bills for the month of May and a roll of lilac-colored four-cent stamps bearing a portrait of Lincoln lay on it. A sheet of stationery imprinted J and M Gems with the Milwaukee address bore a handwritten date, June 14, 1957, the day before the murder. It looked as though Samuel Mercken, a right-hander, had planned to write a note. Did someone he knew interrupt him?

Maggie pulled out the center drawer and found a stack of Christmas cards held together with a rubber band. "Look, Hank, here are last year's Christmas cards. They include notes and letters. Should I go through them?"

"Just scan them, Maggie. We can come back to them if need be."

Maggie moved toward the bookcase. Her eyes fell on the Bible. When she pulled it down, the leaves fell open to a pressed rosebud and ferns. A handwritten title, "A Complete Record of Amelia Paradyze Mercken" appeared on what had once been a blank page. Maggie ran her finger down the list of names and found Phillip Mooreside among Amelia's ancestors. Hmmm, she thought, I wonder if their neighbor, Jim

Mooreside, was related to Phillip. After the entry of Amelia and Samuel Mercken's marriage, no children were listed, but looking closer, Maggie saw a smudge from an erasure. She opened her writing tablet and made a note.

Looking around, Maggie noticed games were neatly stacked at the end of the library table. Games of scrabble, checkers, and decks of cards filled one side. The other side held a set of Britannica encyclopedias. She reminded herself this was the house of Sam Mercken, the man she met at the perfume counter in the department store. He had seemed like a nice person, interested in people.

Finished with her examination, she said, "Maybe this isn't done at your regular interviews, but I could make a pot of coffee. You could offer your interviewees a cup."

Hank smiled. "Uhhum. If a suspect smells fresh-perked coffee, it might make him more relaxed. That's okay with me."

"Good, I don't think Amelia would mind if I use her kitchen. I bet there'll be some cat food there, too."

"While you're doing that, I'm going outside to check on something. Show Albert Steger in when he comes. He's due in about ten minutes."

Albert arrived at ten o'clock after the coffee began to perk. Maggie estimated him to be in his sixties with balding hair, sallow complexion, and a prominent Adam's apple.

"Hmmm, that coffee smells good," he said, taking a chair.

"Mr. Steger, would you like a cup? It's almost ready." Maggie left and returned with a mug of steaming coffee.

"Thanks. I like it black." Al took the hot mug, cradling it in both hands.

Maggie noticed he reached for it with his right hand. She checked his shoes before returning to the kitchen, where she picked up a skirt ready to hem.

Through a little hall passage that also served as a pantry, she could hear the conversation and not be seen. Hank had said he liked to be alone during the interviews. Maggie congratulated herself. She would have missed this adventure if she'd stayed in Georgetown. Maybe Hank thought she was a busybody.

Hank returned through the front door. "Good morning, Albert. I see Maggie's made you comfortable." He seated himself. "You had given your statement regarding Samuel Mercken's death earlier in Madison. I might be asking some of the same questions you already answered at the sheriff's office. How long have you been coming to Orchard Lake?"

"Had my cabin over twenty years ago; never been sorry. Real estate prices were dirt-cheap. Got it for a bargain. What do I call you? Lieutenant? Detective? Or deputy?"

"Any of them," Hank answered. "As you know, I'm investigating the murder of Samuel Mercken. To the best of your knowledge, I want the truth. At this time, you're being interviewed as a witness, not a suspect, but you can be prosecuted for any false statements. You also have the right to be silent. If you claim that right, I'll record that."

Hank had struck a nerve. Al's Adam's apple bobbed up and down as he eased his long neck to a more comfortable position. He patted his breast pocket and pulled out a pack of cigarettes. Hank declined his offer and reached for a pipe in his coat instead.

Striking a match on his shoe, Al lit his cigarette.

"What is your address and telephone number?"

202 FRANCES BRIES WOJNAR

Al laid his cigarette down in the ashtray. "I live on Elderberry Road near the lake. Right now my phone's disconnected."

"You were one of the last persons to see Samuel Mercken alive. Tell me about your conversation with him on Sunday, June 15." Hank continued to write in his book. When Al didn't answer, Hank looked up, allowing the silence to linger.

"Well, uh . . . I want to help all I can, Lieutenant," Al began. "Don't get me wrong." He drew on the cigarette and blew out a cloud of smoke. It made his eyelids contract, giving him a masklike expression. Ashes spilled on the floor. Ignoring them, he said, "Sam phoned me to come over; I didn't ask why. It was the way Sam always called me." This time he deposited the ashes into an ashtray. Then he brushed the tabletop as though some ashes landed on it. "Little did I know what would happen. Sam was my friend. He gave me my job and could always count on me." Al took off his glasses and pulled out a gray wrinkled handkerchief to dab his eyes. His eyes flitted to the chalked outline and back.

"I thought you said your phone was disconnected." Hank lifted one eyebrow as if he was puzzled.

"Sam knew how to reach me, often called the Green Apple and left a message."

"Is that where he called you that day?"

Al nodded.

"Okay, let's start there," Hank said. "When did Samuel Mercken hire you?"

"Must have been twenty years ago, before he moved here to Orchard Lake. I was the one who told him about this place."

"Did you live here in Orchard Lake then?"

Al nodded. "Been here off and on most of my life."

"When did you meet Samuel Mercken?"

"I was at Marquette University. He hired me when I was a student to do the accounting for his jewelry store in Milwaukee."

"Is that where you studied accounting?"

"Yep." Al cleared his throat.

"Was that steady employment?"

"Once a month, I did Sam's books and at tax time." Al's voice grew hoarse. He coughed to clear his throat again.

"So you had access to his business books? Were there any irregularities? Any time Sam went in the red?"

"Sam and Amelia were always careful to have their inventory covered, and they were careful about hiring extra help to save expenses. Often he and Amelia worked late at night to avoid paying another salary. You might say they ran a frugal, costly gem business." Al laughed without humor at his joke.

Hank drew on his pipe until the flame had taken hold, inhaled once more, and then laid the pipe in the ashtray. "Why did Sam want you to come that day?"

"He wanted to advise me about his will. Sam wanted to write a codicil to it."

"What did he tell you?"

"That I was to get half of his assets when he died."

"It's odd that he called to talk about his assets on the day he was murdered. What time did you arrive?"

Al rubbed his arms as if they were cold. "About four thirty that afternoon."

"What time did you leave?"

"Amelia invited me for dinner, which was around five thirty. They always ate early. I left a little after six thirty."

"Did anyone see you leave? It's still light then."

"I don't know, Detective. I did notice the Brenners had arrived at their cabin for their vacation. Don't think they saw me." He shot a questioning look toward the pantry to see if he could see Maggie.

"Where did you go?"

"To the Green Apple."

Maggie saw Al turn his mug around as if asking for time or more coffee. She noticed he did this with his left hand. She made another note in her book.

"Tell me, how did you find Sam? What was his mood?"

"When I came up to the door I heard words, loud, angry shouts. Sam and Amelia were having a god-awful fight. I used to hear them arguing at the store, but never like that afternoon."

"Did you know why they were fighting?"

"I thought it had to do with property, the codicil Sam wanted to add to his will. I couldn't get the gist of it. Then I heard a loud crash and broken glass."

"How long did you wait until you knocked?"

Al rubbed his temples and massaged his neck. "A few minutes, Lieutenant. Amelia was sweeping up the glass. She seemed to have recovered from the argument. Sam sat at his desk. Neither one explained to me what had happened. That was the way they always were after a fight. I was never privy to their arguments. I just had to guess."

"What did you guess, Al?"

"This time I couldn't. I figured I'd have to wait and see."

Maggie sat quiet. She had a creepy feeling Al knew but wasn't going to tell. Then she heard Hank ask, "Have you ever bought a piece of jewelry from Sam?"

"I bought this ring." He raised his right fist to show a large square ruby set in a gold band on his third finger.

"When did you buy it?"

"When I did Sam's accounting. Must have been back in the forties," Al said. "Now I remember; it was when Truman was elected, 1947."

"Where did you go after you left Sam's house?"

"I went to the Green Apple for a drink. Elaine and Butch can vouch for me there." He spread his hands out on top of the table and stared down at them.

"What time was that?"

"Seven o'clock."

"And when did you go home?"

"Around eleven o'clock."

"Had you been drinking before you went to see Sam?"

"Not much, maybe a couple of beers." Al tapped his shoe on the floor.

Maggie thought he sounded impatient, or was Hank getting too close?

"Al, have you ever had blackouts?"

"Well, I've been drunk, if that's what you mean. Had to sleep it off."

"Blackouts are when you can't account for your actions. Has that ever happened to you?"

"No, not that I remember." Al sat straighter and crossed his legs.

"Tell me about your nephew, Rudy. Was he home when you returned at midnight?"

"Don't think so. He has his life, and I have mine. We don't interfere and don't check on each other."

"When did Rudy come to live with you?"

"Rudy was nine when my sister Rosie, that would be his mother, died. She had divorced Frank earlier. I took Rudy in and tried to bring him up. Good kid."

"What were his parents' full names?"

"His mother was Rose Steger and his father, Frank Davidson."

"Where does Rudy live when he's not at Orchard Lake?"

"In Madison."

"Do you have his address?"

"3848 Center Road."

"And his telephone?"

"Don't think he has one right now." Al straightened his back.

"Al, do you own a gun?"

"Sure do, Lieutenant. It's a .32 Smith & Wesson."

"When did you last use it?"

"About a year ago. Had a damn rat in the cellar."

"That's a violent method to get rid of a rat, Al; don't you think?"

"That rat knew how to evade every trap I set. So I went down and shot it." Al clenched his knuckles until they showed white.

"Does Rudy own a gun?"

"You'd have to ask him. I haven't seen any."

"So you didn't see Rudy from the time you left Sam's house that evening until when?"

"The next morning."

"Who do you think killed Samuel Mercken?"

Al scratched his neck. "Jesus, I mean Holy Moses, I don't have the damnedest, Lieutenant, but I'd sure like to get my hands on that son of a bitch. Sam was my friend."

"Albert, have you ever been arrested?"

"Once." He scratched his neck again.

"For what?"

"I was involved in an investment deal that didn't pan out. And I was blamed by a bunch of high and mighty investors from New York." Al waved his head around as if this had to be the most outrageous thing to happen to him.

"Were you incarcerated?"

"For sixteen months." His eyes darted from Hank to the kitchen door when he heard a chair scrape the floor.

"We haven't arrested anyone yet. You can go for now, but don't leave the area. I may need to see you."

Al stood up. "Like I said earlier, I want to help you all I can." He left.

When the door closed, Maggie rushed in. "Hank, I dumped a bucket of water on the ground just below the front steps. Al just stepped on it. It might match the treads of the size-10 shoe print you got earlier."

Without a word, Hank opened the door and looked at it. "We can try to make a cast. Good work, Maggie." He patted her shoulder.

Shy to accept praise, Maggie avoided looking into his eyes. "Thank you, Hank."

35

H ank brought his casting kit from his car and mixed the plaster in the kitchen. "How did you happen to think of this?"

"Men's shoes have been on my mind; I remembered you said you had a cast of a man's size 10, so I went out and poured water on the ground where I knew Al would step."

When the plaster was mixed to Hank's satisfaction, they went outside. He outlined the print with a flexible frame from his kit.

Maggie said, "Let me pour it."

"Dip it in slowly. Sometimes the weight of the plaster can push the tread design out of shape."

Dressed in her sister's T-shirt and shorts, Maggie got down on her knees and spread the plaster inside the frame with small dainty motions.

Hank smiled as he watched her movements and caught her arm in midair.

She searched his eyes for explanation.

He said, "It's fun to see you react to new ideas and new experiences. I continue to find out new things about you every time I see you."

They turned their attention back to their project.

Touched by his comments, she enjoyed his closeness and wanted to tell him. Instead she said, "Thanks, Hank," as though he had complimented her on a new pair of shoes.

"You learn fast, Maggie. How long has it been since you came home anyway?"

She slowed her trowel to a stop, to look up at him again. "It's been almost two weeks. When it's a month, I'll have a history, if history can be counted by the weeks." She troweled the plaster into the toe of the print. "It's hard to imagine where I'll be next year or the next. The routine at Saint Clotildes seems to have stunted my imagination."

Hank hadn't referred to her return home before. Did he think she deserted a sinking ship? Or that she broke her vows, like a divorce? She didn't break any vows as some might think. Rome released her from the vows of poverty, chastity, and obedience. Maybe he thinks I'm too inexperienced to be romantic. How long will it be before we have a real date? He may be worried what my parents will think if he shows me affection. Mom would think I went too fast for sure. Maybe she's told him that already.

"Everything must seem new to you after spending years in the monastery," he said.

Maggie nodded. "It's like a second life." She sat back on her feet, pleased with her handiwork. "Don't get me wrong. I'm not bitter, even though it was a time of life when most girls were having fun, getting married, and having babies. We worked and prayed together many hours of the day and were silent except at recreation, which was twice a day. In spite of this, there was a closeness I didn't think I'd miss."

"You had too much life in you to stay at Saint Clotildes. I saw this when I first met you there.

"You've covered that enough. You can quit now." Hank took the trowel from her and rinsed it under the hydrant. "After the mold dries, I'll drop it by the lab on my way home."

"Drop?" Maggie raised her eyebrows. She glanced at her finished work.

"No, I won't drop it. Just a figure of speech we often use." He found a cloth to dry the trowel. "Do you miss playing the piano?"

Maggie nodded. "It seems strange to be away from it." She glanced toward Amelia's piano when they returned to the parlor. "I was thinking I'd come back when you're finished today and practice. But I wonder if I'd be brave enough to come into this house by myself."

"I think you're brave enough, but I don't recommend it. I've scheduled more interviews today. After I'm finished this afternoon, I'll still be here for a while to do paperwork. I'd like to hear you play," Hank said.

Out the front window, they saw Jim Mooreside, Sam Mercken's neighbor, walk toward the door. Hank opened the screen door and directed him to come through the kitchen entrance because of the cast. He met him there and shook hands.

"You've met Maggie?" Hank motioned him to a chair at the table.

"Yes, couple days ago at the Green Apple." Jim looked frightened. His eyes avoided the taped outline.

Maggie noticed that Jim hesitated to touch the back of the chair. He pulled his hand away from it and then used his foot to position the chair before he sat down. Was he afraid to leave a fingerprint? I wonder which hand he would have used. I'll find out.

"Would you like a cup of coffee, Jim?" Hank asked.

"Sure, ah, with sugar please," he said.

"Maggie, would you bring coffee for Jim?" Maggie appeared with the coffee.

After Jim sat down, he glanced at the chalked outline on the rug. His head and body jerked upright

Maggie assumed he hadn't seen it before. Hank ignored Jim's reaction.

Hank said, "You're being interviewed as a witness, not as a suspect. I expect the truth." He said, "I've talked to you before. Now I want to ask you a few more questions. You had a terrible shock Sunday night when you heard the gunshots and found your neighbor, Sam Mercken, on the floor. Perhaps now you've had a chance to recall more details."

"You don't think I s—shot Sam, do you?" Jim's eyes bulged, a network of red veins stood out. This time, he kept his eyes confined to the perimeter of the table. "I had nothing to gain by killing Sam. Just saying his name makes me shiver." He hugged his arms; his head twitched as if he'd seen a ghost. "We were friends." His voice shook.

"I repeat," Hank said, "you're interviewed as a witness, not a suspect." He reached for his pipe and a package of Amphora from an inside pocket. He tapped the ashes into the wastebasket. "It would help me if you could remember as many details as possible about that evening."

Jim sat still as though any movement would indicate guilt.

Hank said, "How long have you known Sam?" He lit his pipe and studied Jim through the flame and smoke as he drew on it.

Jim took a slow breath. Color eased back into his face as he concentrated on the simple question. "I met Sam when he and Amelia came to the lake for summer vacations. That was before they moved here to stay."

"I'm one of the old-timers, lived here almost thirty-five years now." Jim moved his head to one side as his confidence grew.

Hank remained silent.

"We've never had any crime here, Lieutenant." He bent his head closer. "Not even a burglary. I never lock my doors at night. Nobody does. But since that night, I do now."

"Did Sam lock his doors?"

"Always. City people who move here lock their doors. They're used to it." Jim's head reached higher with a sense of self-righteousness.

"When was the last time you saw Sam alive?"

"I saw him from my front window that same Sunday morning. Sam was out for his 'daily constipation' as he called it." More at ease, Jim laughed at Sam's earthy description. "He walked every morning unless it rained."

"And when did you last talk to him?"

"Not that day. It was," Jim scratched the nape of his neck, "two or three days before. We talked about going fishing next Friday." Jim shook his head in sadness.

Maggie knocked at the open door. She carried a steaming mug of coffee and set it in front of Jim, along with a sugar bowl. "Would you like a cup, Hank?"

"Thanks, Maggie; I would."

Maggie turned to go, but not before she observed Jim stir the spoon with his right hand.

Hank asked, "Were you awake before you heard the gunshots?" He opened his book to write.

"I go to bed after the ten o'clock news and get up once. It must have been close to that time."

"Did anyone else in your house hear the shots? Mrs. Mooreside?"

"Molly was asleep. I had to wake her. The shots came from the direction of Sam's house. It was a calm night with no wind rustling the leaves. A dim light still burned in Sam's front room. We couldn't see or hear any action after the shots." My wife thought I had a nightmare, but I knew it wasn't a nightmare or a dream. They were gunshots. I told her, I'm going to call the sheriff, and I did."

"Did you hear any other sounds outside, like the sound of an engine or footsteps, a door slam?"

"No, not a sound. I went out to check around my house. All I heard were the crickets and frogs near the lake."

"Any sign that Amelia was still up?"

"No, Lieutenant. And I was afraid to go over to see. That's why I called the sheriff. When the deputy came, I went over. Thought maybe I could help. At that point, I didn't know who was shot, Sam or Amelia. Amelia came running from the house. When she saw me, she screamed, 'Help, Sam's been shot.'

"The officer said she could stay at our cottage until they questioned her. Poor Amelia, she rattled on and on. She was in shock. We tried to comfort her. Molly made up a bed for her, though I knew there wouldn't be any sleep for anybody that night. Her nephew, Gilbert, arrived later to take her to his home in Milwaukee, but the police wouldn't let her go yet. So we had Gilbert and Amelia for the rest of the night."

"You did the right thing." Hank drew on his pipe. "Did you hear any loud voices earlier that afternoon or evening at the Mercken house?"

"Can't say I remember that. I knew Sam and Amelia had their differences, just like anybody else. I've heard them scrap, but not that Saturday."

"Have you ever purchased a piece of jewelry from Sam's business?"

"Oh yeah. I bought my wife a lavaliere set with three diamonds."

"When was that?"

Jim sat back in his chair and closed his eyes. He nodded his head as though counting off years. "It was nine years ago on our silver wedding anniversary, December 16, 1948."

"How did you pay for it? Cash or check?"

"I paid cash. Sam wanted it that way."

Maggie caught the inference. Hmmm. Sam must have wanted cash, so there'd be no record.

Hank continued, "Okay, now back to the night of the murder. Do you know anyone in Orchard Lake who disliked Sam?"

"No, Lieutenant. Sam never mixed with the Green Apple crowd, except when he shopped for groceries. He stuck closer to us neighbors."

"Did you drink that night?"

"I played cards at the Green Apple and had a few beers."

"What time was that?

"About seven."

"Who played with you?"

"Ted Bryson, Butch, and Al."

"Was Al Steger there when you arrived?"

"Yeah, he was there. No, he came in after me. I remember now. I rolled dice with Butch for a drink before Al came about fifteen minutes later."

"What time did you break up?"

"We stopped at ten."

"How well do you know Amelia's nephew, Gilbert Paradyze? What do you know about him?"

"He's a hotshot engineer with Klusner, Brown, and Holt firm in Milwaukee. But he's the kind that stays to himself and has some funny ideas." Jim frowned as if he wasn't sure he should mention that. "Sam hated him, wouldn't let him into his house, even to see Amelia."

"How do you mean?"

"Sam never told me. I never asked. I figured it wasn't my business. But when Gilbert came to the lake, he never came near Sam. He'd meet Amelia someplace at the north end, not sure where. I heard he was raised in an orphanage."

"Go on," Hank urged.

"Once Gil went hunting with Butch and me. We took our decoys along and planted them in a slough, bagged quite a few. Gil was inexperienced, didn't have much luck. When he shot one. You could see it was dead, but he kept filling it with lead. No one wanted to bring that duck back. I thought that was strange."

"Did Gilbert serve in the military?"

"Yeah. Maybe if I had his war experiences, I'd act strange too. Gilbert was one tough marine. Amelia told me Gilbert was a marine guard at the United States Embassy in Peking. When the Japanese attacked Pearl Harbor, all the Americans were taken prisoners and sent to a Japanese prison camp."

Maggie listened to the history lesson. She knew so little about that time.

Jim continued, "Must have been a god-awful place; all the prisoners were cramped together in a small room. Every morning, they had to line up to be counted. If the number was less than the day before, it meant one had escaped. One of them would be taken out and shot. The guard would yell out, 'one, two, four, five.' The prisoners never knew if he didn't know how to count, or if the guard was inciting fear.

"Gil told us he had to haul large rocks in a wheelbarrow up a long hill, dump them, and repeat the heavy labor until it was so dark they couldn't see. He figured the Japs wanted to find out how much work the prisoners could do and still survive on decreased rice portions. He made notches on the wall for every load of stone he took up in a day. Toward the end, he could count the rice kernels in his bowl. Gil had become so interested in the Japanese experiment; he felt his energy stimulated. He thought that's why he survived. When the Japs surrendered, Gilbert was sent back to the States."

"And he never married?"

"Not that I know of."

Hank closed his book and stood. He held out his hand to Jim, thanked him, and walked him back through the kitchen door.

He found Maggie in the kitchen with a needle and thread.

"I finished the hem on this skirt." She folded the dress away.

"We have about thirty minutes before the next person comes. Would you like to play the piano?"

"Thanks, Hank; I would." She went to Amelia's piano. "While I waited for the dispensation to come from Rome, one thing that calmed my nerves was to memorize pieces. I'll see if I can still play the Beethoven sonata. Unlike other sonatas, he composed this in two movements, omitting the traditional slow second section." She didn't mention the opus number or key because it wouldn't make any difference to Hank.

The slow, adagio four-bar introduction of the first movement gave her the chance to enter an aesthetic world, a world of beauty, a foreign language to most. To her, music was a secret world where she could see and feel God's inspiration better than in any prayers.

Hank sat on the sofa with his eyes closed. When she came to the final cadence, Hank sat still, in the same position. While the music was still in her, the echoes of the notes settled around him. He opened his eyes. "That was beautiful, Maggie. I need more music in my life."

36

When Hank carried the empty coffee mugs to the kitchen, he found Maggie on her hands and knees, her ear to the floor. "What are you doing, Maggie? Did you lose your needle?"

"I need a flashlight," she said, "I hear a cat."

"It must be Amelia's cat. What's his name?"

"Smudge. Sometimes I hear him on this side of the room and sometimes there." She pointed over to the stove. "He must be under the floor. He can't find his way out."

Hank sat on his heels listening. Maggie's eyes darted from the stove to the oven, but Smudge chose not to cooperate.

"I'm afraid he'll starve if he hasn't had food since Amelia left," she said.

"Don't worry; cat's are resourceful." Hank stood, offering his hand to her. "We knew he'd been in the house. Now he's being cautious, hearing strange voices." Hank opened a cupboard. "Does Amelia have any cat food? We could put some out for him." "There're several cans in the pantry. I'll get one."

"How about joining me for lunch at the Green Apple?"

"Sounds good. I'll take this skirt back to the cabin when we return. Do you have any more interviews today?"

"One more at two o'clock. Would you make another pot of coffee?"

"Sure would." Who was coming? Maggie decided to mind her business. "I think Smudge is under the house. I've been checking. There's a partial basement under the kitchen; maybe there's a crawl space under the rest of the house."

"You're right. There's a crawl space opening on the other side of the house. Let's check it when we get back." Hank thrummed his fingers on the worktable. When he saw disappointment in Maggie's eyes, he said, "Or we can check it on our way out."

Maggie noticed Hank getting impatient. They found a crawl space opening at the side of the house. Through spiderwebs, a rusty Blatz beer can lay half buried at an angle in the ground. Inside the concrete opening, the flashlight beam spotted a head of a rubber doll, and a broken Kerr jar. Sections of galvanized sheeting that looked like part of a heating system lay abandoned on the dirt floor.

"Here kitty, kitty, kitty," Maggie called into the opening. "Here, Smudge." Maggie and Hank listened, but Smudge was neither seen nor heard.

"I'll get somebody from the department to check this," Hank said.

"I'll go in." Maggie volunteered. "I'm smaller than a man."

"Thanks. I'd rather have a deputy from the evidence department go over it. They may have overlooked something else. He can do it this afternoon with stronger lights than ours. Come on, Maggie, my stomach's making hunger sounds." They left for lunch after Hank made a phone call.

At the Green Apple, Hank asked Butch, "When's the best time for you to come for an interview?"

Butch said, "Two to three are slow times at the bar."

With the interview arranged, Maggie and Hank ordered lunch.

Maggie stopped at her parents' cottage to pick up a blouse that needed buttons. Across the road, she saw a panel truck marked Dade County Sheriff Department parked in the Merckens' driveway. She entered the kitchen door and made a pot of coffee. None of the cat food had been eaten. When she heard a gentle meow below the floor, Maggie ran outside around the back of the house to the crawl space to see what the deputy had found.

A man in oilskin coveralls crawled out of the opening. Beside his flares, he carried a plastic bag covering a dark object about fourteen inches long and four to five inches round. He handed it to Hank.

"Did you find Smudge?" Maggie asked.

"Didn't find a cat. Went all over the whole area," the deputy replied.

"I just heard him again in the kitchen wall," Maggie said.

"Must be inside the walls," the deputy said. "Sometimes there's a space behind kitchen cupboards, maybe an opening in a corner. I'll check."

Hank opened the plastic bag, examining the object through the opening. Closing it, he said, "I'd rather you take this to the lab as soon as possible. We can deal with the cat."

"Get right on it, Lieutenant." Hank handed the object back to him.

To Maggie, it looked like a ceramic lamp base or a vase. She wanted to ask and hoped Hank would tell her, so she didn't appear too nosy. Probably he'd want a lab report before making a positive identification anyway.

Back in the kitchen, Hank pried out the kickboards around the base of the cabinets. With the tools from his kit, he pulled out the stove.

"Do you often have to take appliances apart when you're on a case, Hank?"

"Once in a while. I had a case once where I took apart a wall heater because of a rotten odor. A squirrel had gotten caught in it."

"Here's something." Hank found an opening in the corner next to the refrigerator. His hand disappeared in a hollow space above the kickboard location. "Looks like Smudge has a secret passageway that runs from this side, back around the sink to the stove."

He flashed his light through the opening. Two shiny eyes of a frightened cat peered back. "He's here all right. Take a look."

Maggie looked in. "Here, Smudge, we won't hurt you." She brought the dish of cat food closer to the opening, hoping the odor would entice him out.

"Let's leave the cat alone. He'll come out when he's ready," Hank suggested.

They left the kitchen and watched through the doorway. Soon Smudge's head appeared through the opening. He sniffed and looked around. A black-and-white short-haired feline emerged. He swished his tail up and tiptoed to the food. Feeling secure when no one rushed at him, he sniffed the bowl. In a matter of seconds, he gobbled down the cat food as though he was starved and moved to the bowl of water Maggie had added. Finished with his meal, Smudge stretched his neck and back full length and began licking his paws, seeming to accept the presence of Maggie and Hank in the doorway.

"He's got white paws with black pads. He's so cute. Have you ever had a cat, Hank?"

"I had a gray tabby a few years back. Faithful to me even though his feeding was often at odd times. After Tabby died, I decided it wasn't fair to have a cat and give it so little attention. With my schedule . . ." Hank left the sentence unfinished.

Smudge interrupted his grooming to listen. He hiked his tail and walked past them into the living room. After sniffing at the chalk outline, he turned toward Hank and meowed as if to say, "If only I could tell you." He settled down beside the chalk line to nap.

Maggie crept over to pet him. "His coat is so soft, and he's friendly too. You can tell he was a pet in this house."

Without a word, Hank joined her and started to pet Smudge. The cat began to purr, expressing his gratitude.

"Time to get back to work." After Hank reconnected the stove, Maggie went in search of rags to stuff up the opening. Just as she prepared to shove in the packing so Smudge couldn't disappear again, Maggie discovered something else. "Look, Hank, what Smudge brought us. It's a matchbook." Her first impulse was to pick it up. Instead, she read, "Eastside Loan Office Pawnbrokers, Largest Pawnshop Jewelry Inventory in Madison."

Hank looked over from where he was replacing the floorboards. For a second, Maggie thought he looked bored with the cat affair until he spotted the matchbook. In silence, he took a fork from the drawer and scooped the book of matches into a plastic bag. "I wonder, which way this case would have turned if you hadn't insisted on finding the cat. Smudge may have helped us find valuable evidence, the blunt object that may have been used to strike the victim's head and this." He held the bag up to read the advertisement. "Interesting, it's a Madison address."

They walked back into the living room together to check on the cat and found him dreaming cat dreams. His hind legs jerked as if he were running. Was the cat seeing something else? Maggie wondered.

Hank settled himself at the table, put on his glasses, and opened a manila envelope the deputy brought along. He checked the autopsy report first.

DADE COUNTY, WISCONSIN
SHERIFF-CORONER DEPARTMENT
CRIMINALISTICS LABORATORY DIVISION

Name of Deceased: Samuel George Mercken   Age: 76   Sex: Male

Coroner's Case Number: 3456312

Requesting Deputy: Lieutenant Henry Kummer

Delivered by: Frank J. Bruce, M.D.   Date: June 15, 1957

Apparent Cause of Death: Homicide. Death resulted from a ventricular tear from a bullet wound that led to massive bleeding into the pericardial sac.

Other Findings: Contusion on left side of skull caused a concussion that led to an intracerebral bleed. Not lethal.

Type of Specimen: Date Collected: June 19, 1957

    Blood: Type O.

    Urine: 1.0 mg/DL

Examination Request:

    Alcohol Analysis: negative

    Drugs of Abuse: negative

    Basic Drug Screen: negative

    Acid/Neutral Drug Screen: negative

Victim showed no evidence of cuts, bruises or broken nails to indicate a struggle.

Signed ...... *Thomas Smith* ....
Date .... *June 17, 1957* ....

Hank looked at the profile fact sheet of the suspect. The murderer was described as a male, someone who knew the victim, who was familiar with the house. Age, fifty to sixty.

Next he reviewed the ballistic report that showed striation marks from the gun Maggie found in the lake.

"How fortunate you're such a good swimmer, Maggie," he called into the kitchen.

She came and looked over his shoulder, trying to translate the report. Hank pulled out eight-by-ten black-and-white glossies of the death scene. He slapped them to his chest. "These pictures are ghoulish; maybe you shouldn't look at them." He looked up at her. "How about a cup of coffee?"

She said, "After being here in this room next to the bloody death scene, I think I can take it. You don't believe me, do you? I would have been scared to come here alone, but with you, with your businesslike attitude toward the murder scene, it made it easier."

Hank searched her eyes and then laid the photos on the table.

Despite her heroic speech, she shut her eyes when she saw the close-up of Sam Mercken's head and stepped back to hide a gasp. Turning to look at Smudge, who slept a few feet away, Maggie knelt down and caressed his silky fur. He stretched his paws to their full length then fell back to sleep.

Hank put the pictures back into the envelope without comment.

Maggie asked, "Do you have any inkling who did it yet?"

He nodded. "I want to finish up the interviews before I go back to Madison. That should be a couple days. Right now, I have to sift between truth and lies." He looked up at her and smiled. "Do you think you can hang on a little longer?"

"Sure thing." Was that it? Will this case be over in two days? Hank had spoken with no bravado, no sense of completion. But to her, it would mean the end of the partnership she shared with him. Next week, she and her parents would be packing up to leave Orchard Lake. It would be hard to stay another week here without Hank. She was grateful her dad suggested that she come to the lake with them. It was a great start to a new life, even though it involved a murder. Hadn't she dated that crummy Rudy, gone to a dance, and worked on her needed wardrobe? Best of all, she was reunited with Hank and felt useful.

A knock on the door brought both heads up. Butch didn't wait to be admitted. He opened the screen door and walked in. "Right on time," he said, shifting the toothpick from one side of his mouth to the other. Before sitting down, he walked to the edge of the chalked outline. He removed his Cubs baseball cap and bowed his head in reverence. "So this is where it happened."

Hank stood with him, not rushing him into the interview.

"Do you have any leads to finding the son of a bitch yet?"

"Not yet," Hank answered. "Thanks for coming. Guess the Green Apple can get along without you for an hour." They both sat.

"Elaine's covering for me. She usually goes home at noon and comes back at four o'clock." When he sat, his protruding stomach minus the stained apron seemed to pour off the chair.

Hank opened his book. "What is your address?"

"I live in a cottage on the north end of the lake. It's on Sinsinawa Pond Road, no number."

"How long have you worked at the Green Apple?"

"Since the war. When I came back from Korea, I came up here to try to forget bad memories and relax. I liked it so much I stayed. Ed Warner gave me a job at the Apple, and I've been there ever since."

"Does Ed Warner still own it?"

"Yep. He lives in Milwaukee."

"How often do you see him?"

"Haven't seen him since Christmas. He lets me run the Apple lock, stock, and barrel."

"What time did the Green Apple close on Saturday night, June 15?"

"It's always two, unless we're empty. Then I close earlier."

"What did you do on the night of the murder?"

Butch's heavy shock of hair swung backward. "Is it important?"

"I won't know until you tell me. Any details about that night are important to me," Hank replied.

"We played euchre. Al Steger, Jim Mooreside, and Ted Bryson came in seven and left at ten."

"Who came in first?"

"I think it was Jim, then Ted. Al came in about fifteen minutes later." Butch took out a pack of Camels from his pocket and lit one. His eyes blurred under a cloud of smoke.

"Was there anyone else in the bar?"

"Dick Doyle was there and so was Jim Lindsey. Both locals. They left around eleven."

"Did you close after they left?"

"I stayed 'til around eleven thirty cleaning up." He clasped his thick hands together. "No one came in after them, so I closed early. The Saturday night activities on the north side attract our usual clientele. There's the theater, the dance pavilion, and the arcades."

Maggie entered with coffee. She saw Butch's hands clasped, right thumb over the left one and made a mental notation of left-brain dominance.

"What did you do then?"

"I stopped at Elaine's house. She left prescription medicine by the cash register and called to ask me to bring it by."

"What time did she call you?"

"After she got home, about ten o'clock."

"Is that her usual time?"

"Yep."

"Who won the game?"

"Al and I won. We were partners."

"How did Al seem that night?"

"Well, his mind seemed far away when we started. I had to point out that the jack of clubs was a high trump in the spade suit. Have you ever played the game, Lieutenant?"

"Don't believe I have. How is it played?"

"Euchre's played with a partial deck, nines through aces. The jacks rank highest. Then come the ace, king, and so on. It's a fast game, five cards dealt to each player."

"What time did you leave Elaine's place?"

"Well, I don't know if I can tell you the exact time, Lieutenant. I stayed about an hour."

"What is your relationship to Elaine?"

"We spend time together if that's what you mean. It's personal business."

The detective nodded. "Where did you go when you left Elaine?"

"Straight home."

"Have you ever bought any jewelry from Sam Mercken?"

"Just about everyone around here has. Sam gave us good deals on pieces he had left after he retired and closed his store in Milwaukee."

"What good deal did Sam work for you?"

"I bought a pair of pearl earrings for Elaine. She wears them all the time. If I don't see her wearing them, I know I'm in the doghouse."

"When did you buy the earrings?"

"Hmm, sometime ago. I think it was in November 1950."

"Do you still owe Sam Mercken any money?"

"None." Butch shook his head.

Hank closed his book and took off his glasses. "Thanks, Butch, for your time."

37

Hank surprised Maggie after he interviewed Butch. "Tomorrow, we're going sailing."

"You mean you're going to take a day off without a criminal to pursue or somebody to question?"

He nodded. "And I'll bring a picnic lunch."

"A day off from sewing won't be bad. Mom and I have almost completed our sewing plans for this vacation." She'd wear the new blue slacks and a white knit shirt she had purchased in Richfield, when she went shopping alone.

*   *   *

"I guess he wants to relax from the stress of finding the murderer," Maggie told her mother. "After listening to his interviews, I sense tension."

"When does he plan to make an arrest?" Mrs. Brenner asked.

"Hank doesn't discuss his theories with me. I have my own, but they aren't important to him. I've made a list of clues like who's right-handed and who's a lefty. That's about it.

"What will we talk about all afternoon? Think I'll take a book along."

"If it's a sailboat, you'll be kept busy helping to navigate it," her mother said.

That evening while Maggie showered she wondered what Hank had in mind when he had caught her arm and held it. It seemed like a friendly gesture. Up to now, he seemed attentive, allowing her to get involved in his case by making coffee for his interview clients and inviting her to go with him to the funeral in Milwaukee.

If I'm any assistance, it isn't that important. Is Hank humoring me, or does he find me attractive? She closed her eyes and smiled enjoying the thought. Her smile faded when she faced her fragile future. She felt so vulnerable. Maggie had to get her degree, be debt free, and independent before thinking of a serious relationship. Marriage and a family would come later, a sensible way of thinking. Deep down, she wanted more. A sexual relationship had been surrendered the past years. That didn't mean she planned to remain a virgin.

What I have is an adolescent crush on Hank at the old age of thirty-one. The humbling truth made her aware of her human frailty. It didn't end her fantasy. She wanted to model all her new clothes for him, especially the refitted beige dress of her mother's. The soft fabric fell over her breasts and accented her small waist. The dress needed a smoother bra like the satin one she saw in the lingerie shop in Milwaukee.

Wrapping a towel around her, she stepped out of the stall and stood in front of the mirror. Lowering the towel inch by inch from her shoulders, she asked herself, are my breasts too large, too small? Beads of moisture dripped between them. I don't want to look voluptuous like Jane Mansfield in, *The Girl Can't Help It*, a late-night movie she'd seen. Taking a step back to see her profile, Maggie remembered a friend once said she could have been a model. She straightened her shoulders and held her head high. Posture had never been a problem. Even as a nun, she'd worn the religious habit in a dignified, almost-aristocratic stance.

The towel slipped to the floor in a heap. Maggie stared at her reflection, resisting the urge to recover the towel. What would Hank think if he saw her? Why is the female body so attractive to the opposite sex? She picked up the towel and stretched it catty-corner behind her, striking a coy movie-star pose, then held it peekaboo style in front. To other girls, this was normal. But not to her who had read the rule of Saint Augustine every week. The former discipline was hard to ignore. Aloud she murmured, "What's to behold anyway? God made it."

The next morning, her dad called, "Are you ready, Maggie? Hank is backing his car out from the Mercken house. He'll be here in a few minutes. Are you ready, Maggie?"

"Not much to get ready," she said.

Mrs. Brenner looked her over. "Don't forget to comb your hair."

When Maggie left to check her hair, she heard her mother say, "She's been so used to wearing the same clothes every day; she forgets about makeup, or to take a purse."

Maggie had also heard them earlier discussing Hank. "They make a nice twosome. Don't you think?" her father asked.

"What about his age? He has to be at least nine or ten years older than Maggie."

"That has its pluses and minuses. Right now, I think they're just friends," her dad said.

"She's going too fast, trying to make up for lost time."

"Don't worry, that'll even out." He opened the screen door when Hank walked up to the house. "Maggie's ready. Do you want to take my fishing poles?"

"A good idea. We might use them. I'll pick up bait at the marina."

Her dad brought two rods from the shed and helped attach them to the passenger side of his Crown Victoria convertible. Hank held the door for Maggie to enter from the driver's side. With the top down, he drove, one hand on the wheel, his elbow resting on the open window. His smile gave him a carefree spirit so different from what Maggie had seen the past days. He turned and eyed Maggie's clothes. "Did you bring a bathing suit?"

"I've got it on, under this." She pulled out a strap from inside her collar.

He looked at her feet. "Good, you have tennis shoes. First, we'll stop at the Green Apple to pick up sandwiches and drinks. I also ordered a bottle of wine. We'll go to the marina to get our boat. Have you ever sailed?"

She shook her head and laughed. "It would have had to be in my dreams."

"If you live in Madison with all the surrounding lakes, you'll have to get used to sailing."

"That sounds like a prerequisite I can live with. Maybe I should take sailing lessons."

"You'll do fine. I'll show you what to do."

Hank stopped at the deli for the lunches. The smile on his face never changed as he packed the basket in the trunk. "Now we're off."

At the marina, he suggested, "You stay here while I talk to Floyd. See that boat at the end of the slip? That's ours for today."

"That blue and white boat with the name *Blue Sky?*" Maggie asked.

"It's a thirty-foot Coronado." He left the car and returned a few minutes later with bait. "She's all set. Let's get aboard." He untied the fish poles and reached for the basket.

"Let me carry something," Maggie called. She grabbed the blanket from the backseat and the poles, almost losing her footing when she stepped aboard. Hank held her arm steady until Maggie was inside the cabin. When she glanced up, Hank showed only protective concern, nothing else. After being tucked away from the male population for so long, she had to check overreaction. She'd do her best to think of Hank as a big brother. The slightest attention from anyone made her feel special. Even when he asked her if she had any suntan lotion, she had to remind herself this was being practical. Maggie didn't need Mother Cordelia or even her novice mistress to warn her about the temptation to concupiscence, a stylish name for lust that had been a favorite term in one of her spiritual reading books. She felt tied into a knot from all those years in the cloister, and now that knot wanted to be loosened. Those years spent in the monastery was a time when she was never touched by a human being.

When they stripped down to their suits, Maggie noticed Hank's firm back and legs. For a forty-year-old, he looked much younger. Hank helped her into a life jacket, tying the strings for her.

"It's too tight. Do I have to wear this?" Maggie squirmed. "I can swim."

"Hold still." Hank crisscrossed the straps around her back, fastening the ends on her tummy. "The law requires everyone to wear a life jacket."

Maggie smiled and leaned into his hands, slowing down his action. She enjoyed the feel of his hands. "And what happens to a detective if he breaks the law?"

"You're teasing me, Maggie." He gave the finished knot a pat. "Now you're legal."

After he explained the tiller, the boom, and the lines, he named her duties as second mate. These included tying a line on a cleat in a figure-eight design and taking a turn at the tiller.

Hank started the engine. "Ready to cast off the bow line," he called, tossing it on the dock. "*Blue Sky's* made for a day like this." The craft crept out to the main channel, where he cut the motor and hoisted the sails. "From now on, it's the water, the wind, and us." Maggie held the tiller until he took over.

A west wind came up that allowed Hank to tack several hundred feet. *Blue Sky* cut through the water with the ease of a racehorse. The sound of the wake made a smooth swishing vibration, sending Maggie's short curls flying straight up in the air. The wind changed, causing a loud clatter in the sail. "We're in chains. Duck your head, Maggie," Hank yelled. "We're coming about."

Maggie crunched lower, watching the boom swing over her head.

"You take the tiller now." Hank sat back.

Another gale blew up causing the craft to heave low on one side, tossing Maggie into Hank's arms. He had to push her away to grab the tiller.

"We're tipping over," Maggie cried, losing her balance, sliding down into the cockpit. The railing on the low side of the boat was water level. She scrambled to the high side that extended out of the water by eight feet.

"Coming about, Maggie, duck." The boat stabilized.

"Whee!" Maggie cried. "Do you call this a pleasure craft? We almost lost our lunch."

"It's exciting, isn't it?" After tacking for five minutes, the wind slowed to a stop. "We're in chains."

"Good, I like chains. It's gentler. Here, I thought I could read a book on board."

"We'll drop anchor on the other side of the lake and have our picnic on shore. Maybe try our luck at fishing."

Anchored in a cove, they carried their gear up on the bank. Maggie helped Hank spread the blanket on the grass. Hank brought out a bottle of Chablis and two plastic cups. "I think this is cause for celebration." He pulled the cork and poured. "By the time you start classes at the university, you'll be a seasoned sailor."

"Are you celebrating anything else," Maggie asked, "like solving the murder of Sam Mercken?"

"We're not going to talk about the case today." He sipped again and smiled. "I can't help thinking back to the time I took you to the hospital in Stone Hill. But first," he pulled a bottle of Coppertone from a bag, "we better protect ourselves from the sun. With your fair skin, you'll burn. Turn around; I'll put some on your back. We can take off the life jackets now."

Maggie sat in front of him. Hank applied the lotion to her shoulders. "You were a tragic sight with those two black eyes when Flanagan and I found you locked in the closet and so frightened. Now you're free. How does it feel?"

"Feel? In what way? Sometimes I feel like a ghost, as if this is a passing experience, and I'll have to go back. Maybe, I haven't landed. I need to sink some roots.

"As for Mother Rosaria's murder, the only redeeming feature that came out of that horrible time was meeting you. Do you remember? You didn't believe me when I suspected foul play. Both you and Dr. Raymond, the psychologist, thought I had some kind of suspicion complex. He helped me realize I hadn't a vocation."

Hank nodded. "I didn't believe you when you called me. I couldn't believe a mother superior could be murdered.

"For a person who spent, was it ten years in a cloister? You present yourself as . . . so normal even in a bathing suit."

Maggie didn't correct him. It was twelve years. Instead, Maggie shut her eyes a moment to enjoy his description of what was normal. "I'm glad to hear you use that word. I'm trying to accept everything as normal whether I'm used to it or not."

"Whatever made you decide to join a cloister? You were so young."

"That answer is more complicated. Someday, I'll tell you. Now, I want to block out the last twelve years as though they never happened. I wish I could be less self-conscious and more open. All I want is to be part of a normal group. That's a comfortable feeling."

"That sounds drastic. You'll be surprised how open your teachers and fellow students will be toward you."

"That may be, but I want to be treated like everyone else. Can you imagine? One of our neighbors in Georgetown thought she shouldn't serve cocktails when we visited her, because I was along. Who knows what other strange ideas people will have?"

"When you're at the university next term, my office is close by. Maybe we can meet sometime for coffee." Hank got up and stepped into the shallow water, wading in up to his neck. Maggie set her wineglass down and slipped into the water. She saw Hank do a complete somersault and thought, Show-off. Coming up from the deep, he swam toward her with open arms. Maggie turned and splashed water at him. When Hank splashed back, they ended in a free-for-all water fight with squeals of laughter.

"That was fun," Maggie said as they came out of the water.

Hank pulled a towel from his basket and threw it to her.

After Maggie finished drying herself, she folded the towel, placed it on the grass to use as a pillow. "Hank, if it's not too personal, tell me; why are you still single?"

"That's a fair-enough question. I was engaged to be married once." He looked toward the far side of the lake then reached for ham sandwiches, handing her one. "Virginia was in an accident and was killed," Hank continued. "It was on the Fourth of July. We had planned to meet in the station parking lot in Stone Hill after she returned from visiting her aunt in Eau Claire." Hank reached for his shoes. "She never showed up. Her car had slid down an embankment."

"I'm so sorry, Hank. I had no idea. That must have been very difficult for you." Maggie wanted to put her arm around him but stayed in her place.

He continued, "I became a loner, making my job a full commitment. I decided my strange hours would make marriage difficult." Hank raised the bottle of wine to pour into Maggie's glass.

By the time they returned to the marina, Maggie had become a seasoned sailor. She learned to tack with the wind. When a gale wind came up, Hank reefed the sail until they came closer to her parents' cabin.

Maggie spied someone diving off the raft. "There's Rudy again, diving for his treasures."

Hank studied the situation, without comment.

38

Hank continued his interviews in the Mercken home the next morning while Maggie sewed buttons on a blouse in the kitchen. Smudge, Amelia Mercken's cat, ate from the dish as though he hadn't been fed for a week. Together, they waited for the coffee to perk.

Ted Bryson stood inside the front door dressed in a gray sharkskin suit with a blue and yellow chevron tie. Maggie recognized him from the Green Apple. He stood so quiet, clutching his hat with both hands, no sound or movement.

"Come on in." Hank walked toward him. He offered his hand. "You're right on time. Have a seat."

Ted sat on a chair next to the door, as if he might want a quick getaway if a chance came his way. He shifted his strawhat from one hand to the other.

"This interview will go easier if you sit here at the table." Hank indicated the chair by the table.

Ted took baby steps toward it. First, he inspected the chair as though he expected to see a bug or a wet spot. He brushed off the seat of his pants and sat on the edge. "I don't know why you called me here, Lieutenant," he said in a voice that Maggie had to cradle her ear to hear. He laid his hat on his closed knees and looked up at the detective.

To put him at ease, Hank told him he wasn't being interviewed as a suspect. "I hope to get information that will shed light on this terrible tragedy."

This did little to relax Ted, who ran his hand over his slicked-down hair, his finger hesitating on the center part. "'Twas awful what happened to Sam." This time, he spoke up.

"Crime is always a tragedy," Hank said and sat at the table. "Mr. Bryson, have you ever purchased any jewelry from Sam Mercken?"

"Have I ever purchased any jewelry from Sam Mercken?" Ted repeated, his eyes concentrating through thick lenses on Hank.

Hank nodded and waited.

"Well, a," Ted stopped, "I bought a diamond bracelet from Sam after he retired. Sam gave me a good price. It was the proud possession of my wife, Lucy. Lord have mercy on her soul." He made a hasty sign of the cross. His voice shook when he mentioned her name.

"I'm sorry to hear of your loss. When did your wife die?"

"Lucy died in 1950, before I retired. She never had a chance to enjoy our retirement."

"What kind of work did you do, Mr. Bryson?"

"I was an accountant at Washington Savings and Loan in Milwaukee."

"And when did you retire?"

"I retired in 1952."

"Did your wife work?"

"Yes, she was a secretary for one of the big shots at the Gavison meat-packing plant."

"What happened to the bracelet after Lucy died?" Hank asked.

"It's still in a locked box at the bank." Ted held his breath as if he expected a scolding.

"A diamond bracelet costs a lot of money. More than an accountant's salary. How did you manage that?"

Ted took a big breath. "It took a long time. I made time payments over ten years. Sam said his father had purchased pieces for his special customers who couldn't afford them after the crash. Also Sam used to buy vintage pieces from people who needed money during the Depression."

Back in the kitchen, Smudge stretched out his hind legs, sniffed Maggie's sandaled foot, and settled on his haunches to lick her dangling foot. Maggie giggled and reached down to pet him. She slid him to her lap appreciating his gentle purr when Ted said,

"That was before the robbery. When Sam retired, he brought a few of those special items of jewelry with him to Orchard Lake."

"You say robbery? When was the jewelry store robbed?"

Ted looked up to the ceiling. Squinting through his thick lenses, he said, "It was sometime after the crash, 1930 or 1931."

"And you knew Sam Mercken then?"

"No, not then, but I've known Sam a long time, Lieutenant, way back to the late thirties." Slowly, Ted released the clasped hands that held his hat and placed it on the table in front of him.

"Can you be more specific?"

"We go back to when Sam and Amelia lived in Milwaukee. I met him in 1937. We belonged to the same church, Saint Anthony's. He and I used to work the bingo games at the church bazaar on Labor Day. When Sam retired to Orchard Lake, he suggested I come to the lake for a visit. I did and bought my small cottage down the road."

"What is your address?"

"It's just four houses down on the other side of the road, a brown shingled house. It doesn't have a number."

"What's your shoe size, Ted?"

Ted brought his foot out to the side. Both the detective and he stared at a well-polished russet-colored wingtip shoe.

"Size 9, sometimes 9 1/2."

The detective wrote in his book. "You played cards with Jim, Al, and Butch on June 15."

Maggie made a note in her notebook. She heard Hank ask, "What time did you leave the Green Apple?"

"We always split up around ten o'clock."

"Where did you go?"

"I went home to catch the news."

"Do you remember what was on the news that night?"

"I remember Hank Aaron hit a home run for the St. Louis Cards."

Maggie knocked on the open door and entered with two mugs of coffee on a tray. After Hank introduced her, she asked, "Would you like sugar or cream, Mr. Bryson?"

"Just a little sugar, please."

Maggie returned with it. Back in the kitchen, she added another note to her little book and picked up her sewing.

When Mr. Bryson left, she joined Hank. Did he have any inkling of who killed Sam Mercken at this point? She wanted to ask him that and more questions but felt reluctant. Hank sat reading over his notes. Not wanting to disturb his concentration, she looked over his shoulder and saw four pages spread in front of him.

"Can I look, Hank?"

"Go right ahead."

Al Steger	Address: Elderberry Rd., Orchard Lake, phone disconnected.
	Pt. time accountant to Sam in Milwaukee 1929-1950
	Bought ruby ring from Sam M. Nov. 1948
	Left Sam Mercken's house, 6/15, 6:30 PM.
	Played cards at Green Apple 6/15, 7:15-10:00 PM.
	Left Green Apple 11:30 Shoe size, 10.
	Didn't attend funeral.
Jim Mooreside	Address: Highway #245, across the road from Sam Mercken. Ph. 161
	Purchased lavaliere with 3 diamonds-Dec. 1948
	Heard gun shot at 2 AM 6/16, called sheriff
	Last talked to Sam Thursday, 6/13.
	Met Sam at Orchard Lake summer of 1948.
	Played cards at Green Apple. 6/15, 7:00-10:00P
	Went home watched ten o'clock news-to bed.
	Attended funeral
George Carter (Butch)	Address: Sinsinawa Rd. ph. 298, 12 years
	Purchased pearl earrings Nov. 1948
	Employed and played cards at G.Apple 6/15 to 7:00-10:00PM
	Closed Green Apple at 11:00, stopped at Elaine's.
	Claims Al came to Green Apple @ 7:15.
	Shoe size, 13.
	Didn't attend funeral.

Ted Bryson   Address: Hy # 69, 4 cottages down on left. Ph.325
                    Knew Sam Mercken in Milwaukee in 1937
                    moved to Orchard Lake in '52
                    Purchased diamond bracelet Nov. 1948.
                    Reported a robbery at J & M Jewelry business.
                    Played cards at Green Apple 6/15, 7:00-10:00 PM
                    Went home for evening news. Remembered
                    Hank Aaron's home run.
                    9 1/2 shoe size.
                    Nervous/well dressed.
                    Attended funeral.

Hank asked, "Do you see anything unique here?"

"Well, I see that Al Steger came to the Green Apple later than the others for the card game."

"Uhhum. Anything else?"

Maggie bent over Hank's shoulder studying the papers closer. "Isn't it interesting they all bought jewelry from Sam Mercken about the same time? I wonder if there might be a connection to the robbery Ted mentioned."

"It might be relevant." Hank started to put the sheets back into the notebook.

"You said you didn't have much evidence the other day. What exactly do you have?"

Hank scratched his chin and looked at Maggie. "Okay, Sherlock Brenner, are you ready for Evidence 101?"

Maggie smiled. "Try me."

"First, there is what we call direct evidence. That's when a witness can identify the suspect or can repeat what he's heard. It can be direct words of the victim or the perpetrator. In this case, we have none. Amelia would be our best witness but was sound asleep in another room."

"What bad luck."

"Then there's indirect evidence, which is circumstantial, like fingerprints, the partial footprint we found on the carpet, or the mud print outside. None of these prove a thing. They require further investigation. One of the reasons I wanted to use Sam Mercken's house for questioning was to observe reactions. Body language is valuable in solving a crime, even changes in speaking tone."

Maggie remembered some mannerisms.

"There's what's called proof of fact. That's when a controlled substance is found in a person that reaches illegal levels. That's not relative to this case."

"I see," Maggie said. "We either have to get a confession or get Amelia to remember something."

"Uhhum."

"What about the fingerprints on the gun I found in the lake?"

"Not direct proof. It could lead us to direct proof, at best contribute to a body of evidence. What we're lacking is probable cause. We have no substantial evidence linking Sam's murder to a suspect."

"If you're interested, I've made a list too."

Hank looked up at her. "I hope you'll share that list."

"I have it in my sewing box." Maggie left and returned. She laid it on the table in front of him.

Clues by an Amateur Sleuth:

> Sam Mercken wrote with right hand.
> Albert Steger reached for coffee with left hand. Lefty.
> From family Bible, Al Steger possibly related to Amelia through ancestor,
> > Philip Steger.
> Albert Steger's shoe size?
> Jim Mooreside held his cigarette in his left hand. Lefty.
> Butch—right handed.
> Ted.—first to speak of a robbery. May be a link.

Hank flipped the page over and saw her rough drawings.

Their heads close together, Hank said, "This is interesting, Maggie." He glanced at her with a big smile. "You've been a first-rate detective right from the beginning."

"Thanks." She placed a quick kiss on his forehead and then drew back. Maggie slapped her hands over her mouth. "I'm so sorry. I shouldn't have done that."

Hank smiled, making no effort to disguise his pleasure. "I liked it."

Still scolding herself, Maggie knew she had been too forward. Did it happen because of her inexperience? I'm going to have to watch myself.

"Come on, Maggie, let's break for lunch." Over a hamburger at the Green Apple, he explained, "I have to go to Milwaukee for a couple of days."

Maggie's brow turned to a frown.

"Today is Sunday; I should be back by Tuesday, maybe earlier. I need to see Amelia and to check her insurance policies."

Maggie folded her arms and tilted her head in a ho-hum attitude. "Well, I guess I can go back to sewing and swimming." She stretched her arms out in front for inspection. "After this sunburn fades, I should have a nice tan."

"When are your parents returning to Georgetown?" Hank asked.

"This Friday. I plan to find a place to live in Madison right away and get a job before the fall semester."

"That's four days from now. Good. I'll see you before you leave Orchard Lake," he said.

"When you see Amelia, tell her we found Smudge. Ask her if she still wants to keep him. If she doesn't, I'd like to adopt him."

"I'll tell her you and Smudge have become good friends."

After lunch, they locked up Sam Mercken's house and stopped at the Brenners' cabin. Hank left the key with Matt and Esther and made arrangements to feed the cat. "I know Maggie feels comfortable in Mercken's house after spending the last couple of days there, but I recommend that she doesn't go alone to feed the cat."

Dr. Brenner suggested, "We'll go together. Is it all right if she practices on Amelia's piano? I hear her saying she needs to practice to get ready for her audition. I can stay with her."

Maggie chimed in, "Great idea, Dad."

Hank nodded. "If anyone questions why you're there, tell them I okayed it."

This arrangement agreed on, Maggie walked with Hank to his car, still parked across the road.

"Take care. I'll miss you." Hank got into his car.

After Hank left, Maggie decided to go swimming. She swam out to the raft enjoying the cool water on her sunburnt skin. No longer would her life be empty and lonely. Being around men was so interesting.

As she reached the raft, a familiar voice called, "Hi, Maggie. Want to dive for treasures?"

Maggie recognized a hard edge in Rudy's voice. She wanted to ignore him, hoping he'd go away, so she could return to her daydreams.

"I know you found the gun, Maggie. What did you do with it?"

Not deterred by his threatening voice, Maggie raised her head. "That old gun? I threw it back. Who'd want that rusty piece of metal?" Pleased with her acting ability, she sat up and saw his face tighten in anger. She was suspicious of anything Rudy initiated and wanted to leave. Pushing off the raft, she started to swim toward shore when he intercepted her.

He grabbed her arm and pulled it back, her legs thrashing in the water. "You know what I'm talking about. I know you found the gun. What did you do with it?" he yelled over the splashing water. Before she could take a breath, he pushed her underwater. For a few moments, Maggie floundered then broke away from him. When she surfaced, Rudy anticipated her move and jumped from the raft on top of her. They went down struggling. Maggie managed to kick him in the groin to break his grasp and rose to the surface for air where a solid force stunned her. She had come up under the raft. Was it his intention to keep her trapped, or was he just trying to scare her?

Adrenaline rushed through her veins. Maggie told herself not to panic. I will get away. She put her hand to the underside of the raft to edge out toward lighter water. Knowing Rudy would be ready to push her down again, she grabbed a deep breath and returned under the raft breathing through a crack in the boards.

She couldn't hear any movement from Rudy, only her exhausted breathing which she tried to mask by taking shorter, quieter breaths. Why is he doing this? Is Rudy the murderer, or is he doing this for his uncle? Maggie waited to get control before considering a start for shore. Easing her head out again, she saw him swimming away from the raft.

"He's not going to scare me," she said aloud. "He'll be watching for me." She searched both directions for a boat or water-skiers. If only somebody else would pass this direction. Farther up the shoreline, two children played, jumping off a dock into inner tubes.

I've never learned to swim underwater, but now is the time. Waiting to control her breathing, she dove deep in their direction from her underwater prison and swam as long as she could, holding her breath. When she surfaced, the children were within a hundred feet. Maggie reached them swimming on the surface.

When the boys saw her approach, they splashed water toward her. "Hey, get off," one yelled. He hit her hands when she grabbed hold of their inner tubes.

Maggie couldn't speak but hung on gasping for breath, grateful to be shielded from Rudy's view.

"Leave her alone," the second one cried. "She's hurt. Are you all right?"

Coughing, Maggie kept her eyes and head down, letting the water drain out of her throat and head. She lifted her head, trying to keep calm. "Thanks for helping me out, guys. What are your names?"

"I'm Ron, and he's Jim."

"I need your help." She didn't want to tell them someone tried to drown her at the raft and feared Rudy watched her every move. "Would you come with me to Brenners' cabin with your inner tubes? It's just around the cove," she pointed, "about three docks down."

"Sure," Ron, the spokesman, who looked to be about ten years old, answered.

"What's your name?" he asked.

"Maggie Brenner. I'm staying with my parents there."

They set off. The boys swam in their inner tubes toward the dock with Maggie between them. Still shaking, she tried to make light conversation, asking them what grades they were in school, where they went, and so on. All the time, she kept searching the area to see where Rudy could be hiding. Looking back, she saw the empty raft. When they reached her dock, Maggie said, "Would you like to come and have some lemonade?"

39

M aggie put her fingers to her lips to quiet any comments from her mother when she entered the cabin with the boys.

"What have you gotten into now?" Mrs. Brenner ignored her signal.

"I'll talk to you later. This is Ron and Jim," Maggie pointed to each as she pulled out chairs from the table. "They were kind enough to help me."

The boys nodded to Mrs. Brenner and sat down.

"Where do you go to school?" Maggie asked, reaching for the cookie jar to fill a plate. She poured glasses of lemonade, trying to cover up her frightened feelings.

Jim answered, "I go to Tennyson in Milwaukee. Ron lives here."

"I go to Bryant," Ron answered with a mouth full of cookies.

Maggie motioned her dad quiet, when he walked in.

"Well, hello. We have visitors."

After introductions, Ron stood up. "We have to go now. Thanks for the drinks and cookies. I've never been this far from our cabin. My mom will be worried."

After they left, her dad looked to his wife for an explanation. She shrugged her shoulders, shaking her head. "She's playing detective again. When will you learn to leave that to professionals?"

Dr. Brenner walked over to his daughter, still in her bathing suit. "What happened to you? Have you looked into a mirror?"

"I feel better now." Maggie got up and looked into the mirror over the sink. Her eyes widened. "Whew." She blew her breath between her teeth, touching her swollen eye, and slumped in a nearby chair holding her head between her hands.

Dr. Brenner asked, "Let me see your eye."

Maggie lifted her head up for him to examine her bruises. She spoke in a low, tired voice. "Rudy swam out to the raft." The words caught in her throat. She took a sip of lemonade. "He knew I found the gun. I didn't tell him the police had it. Hank had said to tell him I threw it back in the lake. So I did." She was hesitant to continue. Taking a deep breath, she forced herself to go on. "I'm not sure if he was trying to scare me or drown me." Her voice cracked; her body shook as if she were cold. Maggie closed her eyes, trying to numb her experience. What was the use of getting emotional? It wouldn't undo her fear.

Her dad said, "You look pale. Better get dressed. I'll call Hank."

"He's in Milwaukee by now. It won't do any good to call him," she said.

"I'll call his Madison office." He pulled the card Hank had given him from his billfold. "Someone there will know how to reach him."

When Dr. Brenner returned from making the call near the Green Apple, he said, "Hank hadn't left for Milwaukee yet. He said to keep you indoors. You'd be worried about the cat, but don't go over to the Mercken house. He's coming back here tonight."

That evening, the Brenners sat around the kitchen table with Hank. Mrs. Brenner put on a full pot of coffee.

"Tell me everything that happened, Maggie." Hank studied her with concern. "You were with Rudy alone on the raft. Did he touch you any place on your body?"

She frowned between sun-bleached eyebrows. "Not the way you're thinking. After I told him I threw the rusty old gun back in the lake, he didn't believe me. I wanted to get away from him and started to leave when he intercepted me. We struggled in the water. That's when he must have hit me here. She pointed to her temple, fingering the sore spot. Then he pushed me down in the water."

Hank and her parents were silent.

"When I surfaced he held me under. I couldn't breathe and swallowed a lot of water. I thought I'd drown." Maggie leaned her head into her hands, describing her experience. She tried to rub the tension out of her neck with her hand. "I thought of screaming for help, but I didn't want Rudy to hear me. I was afraid he'd come back. So I hid under the raft. I managed to breathe through a knothole."

"You say you didn't want Rudy to hear you. Where was he at this time?" Hank reached for one of her hands and squeezed it.

"I saw him swimming toward shore."

"Had you talked to him at any time since that night you went with him to the dance?"

"Not once. The last time I saw him was yesterday afternoon. Remember, Hank, we both saw him on our way back from sailing."

"Maggie, I had no idea that you were in danger. As usual, you kept a steady head." He looked at her parents. "You have a brave daughter."

Maggie touched her sore eye again. "Do you think this will turn black? I seem to come out with black eyes each time I try to help you. Maybe I should consider it a hazard that comes with the job." She smiled, a note of buoyancy sounding in her voice despite her fear.

"No, Maggie. You don't deserve it."

Dr. Brenner spoke up, "It could have ended much worse."

"Thanks be to God; she's all right," Mrs. Brenner said.

"Sorry to do this to you, Maggie," the detective said. "I want you to be invisible for a few days."

Their eyes met. Maggie read concern in his. "I wish you could stay, but I know you can't," she said resigned to Hank's schedule.

Turning to her parents, he asked, "When are you leaving the lake?"

"We planned to leave Friday," Dr. Brenner answered. "Now I'm thinking we should leave earlier."

"Did you get the lab report on the lamp base?" Maggie asked.

"Not yet. I should have it soon. I have a deputy assigned to patrol this area. I'll give you his number. Call him if anything suspicious comes up. Just stay away from the windows, Maggie."

Dr. Brenner said, "Rudy should be arrested for assault and battery."

Hank answered, "That's an option. I'll write a report and discuss it with the district attorney before I leave for Milwaukee in the morning. I need to see Amelia Mercken." He rose to go.

"I'd rather go with you than stay here." Maggie got up from her chair. "How long will it take you to do your business?"

"I should be back here tomorrow evening. Remember you said you'd stay inside."

"If I wore sunglasses, no one would notice my eye," Maggie persisted.

"I think you need to get some rest." He glanced at Dr. Brenner. "What do you think?" he asked. "It's a possibility."

"It might do Maggie good to get away," he answered.

"I'll be leaving very early, about six."

"I'll be ready." Maggie brightened, showing signs of recovery from her ordeal. "You forget I'm used to rising early. We rose at five o'clock."

"Good, I'll be here at six.".

The detective left the Brenner cabin and drove to the Green Apple.

When Butch saw him enter, he picked up the deck of cards on the counter. "Want to play cards, Lieutenant? We need a fourth."

Hank thought a moment, loosened his tie, and sat down with Al Steger, Butch, and Ted Bryson.

"Want a beer?" Butch asked.

"Sure," Hank said.

After they drew cards for the deal, Al set the deck in front of Hank. "Your deal, Lieutenant."

Hank picked up the cards and dealt. He remembered euchre was a popular game often played in bars.

"Too bad about the Brenner girl," Al Steger said as he picked up the cards and sorted them. "I heard she's missing."

"What happened to her?" Butch asked.

"One can't be too careful in this lake with all the undercurrents." Hank trumped the first trick and collected it. Drinking from a bottle of Schlitz, he led a card from his hand.

No one walking into the Green Apple would have noticed a difference in the players. Hank sat in his shirtsleeves, chewing on a toothpick, his collar open. He shoved the brim of his straw fedora up on his head. Intent on the game, he hoped to catch some detail on the whereabouts of Rudy or at least not to get "euchred," the term when a bid in the game wasn't made.

"Rudy's been out there looking for her since he heard about it," Al said.

"I didn't know he was back," Hank lied. He put his bottle of beer down and rocked his chair back to the wall, waiting for Al to lead his next card.

"Rudy came down from Madison yesterday." Al leaned over to take the next trick. "I made my game," he said as he collected the cards for the next deal.

Jim Adams entered the Green Apple. He walked over to the card players.

Hank stood. "Jim, take my place. See you all later."

Collecting his coat, he left and drove to Elderberry Lane where Rudy stayed with his uncle, Al Steger. A scrawny-looking terrier barked when the detective drove up. Hank leaned over from the open door and petted his head. The dog quieted and sniffed his shoes. After knocking at the door several times, Hank heard groans and thumps from the second floor. A not-yet-wide-awake Rudy yelled, "Who is it?"

Entering the unlocked door, Hank called up the stairway, "Lieutenant Kummer here."

"Who?"

Hank repeated and heard more creaks as Rudy bound out of bed. Appearing at the top of the steps, dressed in undershorts, an unhappy Rudy trotted down. He laced his fingers through his disheveled hair and brushed several days' growth of beard around his chin. "What do you want?" He sounded concerned, almost contrite, as if he expected bad news.

Was he concerned or was he playacting? "Are you expecting news?"

"Not really. Why are you here?"

"I'm investigating the murder of Sam Mercken. I want to ask you some questions. Can we sit down somewhere?" Hank looked through a doorway. Newspapers spread across a bare floor in front of a faded sofa that faced a television. The program *I've Got a Secret* blared to an absent audience.

"Do you want a beer?" Rudy offered.

"No thanks."

"Mind if I do?"

"Suit yourself." He turned off the television and sat on a lumpy, threadbare chair.

Rudy returned with a bottle of beer from the refrigerator and sat before the darkened screen. His position in the middle of the sofa seemed to say, you're intruding on my space. "Why are you asking me about Sam Mercken? I live in Madison. I wasn't near Sam's house that night."

"How well did you know Sam?" The detective took out his little book.

"Just seen him around when I came down to the lake."

"Were you in Madison the night he was murdered?"

"No."

"When did you arrive at Orchard Lake this trip?"

Rudy looked out the window as if he had to figure out the day. "I came last night."

"Oh, so you hadn't heard about the Brenner girl?"

"What? She drowned? She was such a good swimmer. I seen her swimming to the raft several times. What was her name?"

"Maggie."

"Right, Maggie."

"Rudy, what kind of work do you do in Madison?"

"I get pickup work with a building contractor when he needs me."

"Did you work yesterday?"

"No, I knew I'd be coming here." Rudy stretched his head up and looked toward the window as though he was expecting someone.

"What time did you arrive?"

Leaning back on the chair, he answered, "I got to Orchard Lake about six last night."

"And what did you do when you came here?"

"Not much. I met a few friends at the north end of the lake. Sometimes, we go fishing. Yesterday, I saw Josh. We played the pinball machines at the arcade."

"To what time?"

"About midnight."

"Tell me a little about your background. Where did you go to school?"

"Wisconsin High. I graduated in 1947."

"That's ten years ago. Then what did you do?"

"I went to work for Sawyer Dairy Processing Company. My job was in the cheese department, wrapped it after it aged."

"How long did you work there?"

"Hmmm." Rudy looked out the window as the sun was going down. "Must have been two years." He rubbed his eyes as though it was hard to think then reached for the funny papers from the floor and placed the sheet on his lap, concentrating on *Mary Worth*.

"Then what?" Hank ignored Rudy's flagrant lack of attention.

"Picked up work, here and there."

"Well, Rudy, so far you've got a few facts wrong. Because of truancy, you never graduated from Wisconsin High. It's true you worked for the processing plant, but you were fired and charged for theft. You were brought to court and served seven months in the county jail."

Hank saw Rudy's fists ball; his body tensed as though he'd been tricked and got caught.

"If you knew all this, why are you asking me these questions?" he whined, scratching his unruly hair.

Without answering Rudy's question, the detective continued, "And I saw you yesterday afternoon diving from the raft. I happened to be sailing on the lake."

Rudy looked stunned. He didn't volunteer any more information.

Lieutenant Kummer closed his black book and placed it inside his coat. "From now on, I want the truth. You put yourself in an awkward position, Rudy, when you lie to a law officer. I can make it very difficult for you. You can refrain from answering my questions, and I'll record that. Now you'll have to convince me what you say is true." Hank went out letting the torn screen door slam behind him. The dog picked himself up and followed him, his tail between his legs. A gusty wind came up blowing dried leaves from last season.

Lieutenant Kummer had one more stop to make before leaving Orchard Lake that evening. He returned to the Mercken house to collect some papers. Across the road, he saw Maggie's bedroom window darkened. One light remained in the kitchen. He hoped Maggie was resting well.

40

Maggie shut off the alarm, so her parents wouldn't waken. After brushing her teeth, she stared into the mirror. Did it make any difference to Hank if she wore cosmetics, or not? The sun had given her a natural freshness making her feel like a native. Did Hank think nine years difference in their ages was an obstacle? The way he reacted to her, he could just as easily call her Sister Camille instead of Maggie. So far, it had been the investigation that kept them together

At her age, most of her friends were married and had children. She hadn't gone to college as a young girl. She hadn't joined a sorority to learn social graces, or dated. And she had no money but would have to borrow money to go to school, to buy a winter wardrobe, maybe a car. Maggie was surprised how many items she needed. Her dad insisted that part of the money she brought home be used for health insurance. Insurance had never entered her mind.

Maggie was ready when Hank drove up. The rising sun spotlighted a stand of trees on the farther side of the lake. A few cottages showed lights. They passed an angler with a pole over his shoulder and his dog heading toward the lake. The German shepherd loped along, sometimes running ahead pricking his ears when he caught a scent around a log or among the weeds.

"What is your plan for today?" Maggie asked.

"First, I have an appointment at the Lincoln Guarantee Insurance Company. After that, I want to see Amelia Mercken," he said as they left the lake village.

Maggie nodded. Ted Bryson mentioned a burglary during his interview. Of course, an insurance company would be involved.

Forty minutes later, they entered the large Lincoln Guarantee Insurance office in Milwaukee. It occupied the first level of a multistory office building. Maggie looked up at the decorative, high ceilings, the huge crystal chandeliers. Black-and-white-veined marble counters lined one wall. After Hank spoke to a clerk, they were ushered down a hall to an office. Daniel Cavanaugh, Investigations was printed on the door.

This is real life. Maggie tried to imagine a day in an investigator's life. It had to be exciting.

Inside, Hank introduced himself. "Lieutenant Henry Kummer, Dade County Sheriff Department. This is my assistant, Miss. Brenner."

Maggie smiled at the new title. Did she look the part dressed in a multistriped, gathered skirt and red knit top. The office personnel wore suits or dresses. Hank might have introduced her as his secretary but he didn't. This pleased her.

"I'm interested in examining a report your company made on a jewel-robbery claim by Samuel Mercken in 1932." Hank presented a warrant he brought to access personal information.

The investigator rose and shook their hands. "Name is Dan Cavanaugh." He looked at the warrant and handed it back. "I've read about that claim, though I didn't work here at the time." He pressed a lever on his desk to request the file. A few minutes later, a secretary entered the office with it. Mr. Cavanaugh opened it. "That was twenty-five years ago." Reading further, he said, "Investigator Charles Darint handled that case. He's no longer with us, retired a few years back."

"Would you have his address?" Hank asked.

"I can get it for you. He's living on one of the lakes near Madison." The investigator closed the file. Looking up through his bifocals, he handed it to Hank. "You're welcome to examine it, Lieutenant. What causes you to review the case?"

"Samuel Mercken was murdered last week. I want to review some of the old claims and the contacts involved in it."

Mr. Cavanaugh leaned back in his seat, fingering the mustache on his upper lip. "That could put a different slant on this case. We'll be interested in your findings and will assist you in any way. You can use one of our offices to examine the file." The investigator again signaled for his secretary, who appeared. "Show Miss. Brenner and Lieutenant Kummer to an office where they can work."

"Thank you, Mr. Cavanaugh." Hank stood and shook hands. "If I come up with anything significant, I'll let you know."

Maggie and Hank followed the secretary to an office where they sat at a long table. Hank opened the file and read through the case findings. He passed them along to Maggie. All seemed innocent enough. Then he spread out reports beginning with the summaries written by Samuel Mercken and Charles Darint and the declaration of stolen property. He read aloud, "Lincoln paid one hundred fifty thousand dollars in 1933 to Samuel Mercken, who claimed that a quantity of jewelry disappeared from his vault on November 27, 1931."

"Whew!" Maggie blew through her lips. "One hundred fifty thousand dollars is a lot of money."

"It was a lot more in 1933 than today." Hank laid the jewelry declaration on the table for Maggie to see.

J AND M JEWELRY STORE
4369 FIFTH STREET
MILWAUKEE, WISCONSIN

1 Matching set: amethyst/diamond ring, bracelet, medallion necklace. Total: Diamonds 20 carats, Amethyst 50 carats set in 18K.
Amber bracelet, 30 stones. 33 points each.
18K Watch and chatelaine with Hogarthian enameled miniatures.
Sterling Silver necklace set with 6 Montana agates and comb similarly set.
18K Double flower brooch set with brilliant diamonds 20 carats set in silver.
Set: 18K necklace, earrings, bracelet and ring set with opals and emeralds 10 carats.

18K Georgian pendant, with central large diamond inset, 5 carats

14K Fob chain 3 inches long with a heart ornament on the end.

18K Twin brooch set with rose diamonds and pearls connected with 8 inch chain.

18K Locket set with pearls and sapphires.

18K Ring with a cluster bezel of rubies and pearls.

18K Chatelaine with ivy leaves, grapes and cherubs.

18K Gold Ring, one round vvs. diamond, 1.02 carat.

30 Inch pearls, 8 mm, pink rose.

"That's quite a collection. I've never seen any pieces like these," Maggie said, looking down at her hands. She tried to picture how one of the rings of that much value would look on her fingers.

Hank continued to sift through more reports from the file. "Not many of us have. Today, they'd be museum pieces."

"Why would J and M Jewelry Store have an inventory of this value?" Maggie said, studying the list. "That was during the Depression."

"All of these pieces were purchased in the early to late twenties before Sam inherited the store. Customers who bought these kinds of pieces did well until the crash of '29."

"That makes sense. It's interesting that each of the four men you interviewed had purchased a piece of jewelry. I remember they each said Sam had made them available for a cheap price. Al had bought a ruby ring; one had gotten a diamond bracelet; Butch had earrings, and there was another piece."

"That's a good point, Maggie," Hank said. "Now let's see what course of action Lincoln Guarantee Insurance Company took. Here are the summaries Sam wrote about the robbery."

"Would Al have been Sam's accountant then?" Maggie tried to recall the interview scenes in Sam Mercken's house.

"He might have been. It's hard to tell."

Maggie picked up the summary sheets and laid them side by side. "Why are they handwritten instead of typed?"

"The insurance company requires handwritten copies. There's a certain authenticity in a handwritten document," Hank answered.

Maggie read Sam's summary.

From: Samuel Mercken,
J and M Jewelry, 4369 Fifth Street, Milwaukee, Wisconsin

To: Lincoln Guarantee Insurance Company, 2655 Kilbourn Avenue, Milwaukee, 17 Wisconsin

Under policy #365798 issued to Samuel and Amelia Mercken on April 10, 1919 and renewed in April 1924. Total insurance was for $150,000. For our theft I claim $175,000, because more jewelry items are missing.

The robbery occurred between 9:00 PM December 3, 1931 and 8:30 AM December 4, 1931 at J and M Jewelry Store, 4369 Fifth Street, Milwaukee, Wisconsin.

On December 4, 1931 I arrived at my place of business at the J and M Jewelry Store, 4369 Fifth Street. At 8:30 AM I entered my store from the alley between Fifth Street and Sixth Street to find a broken window. Opening the locked door and on entering I found the vault door open. A collection of antique heirloom jewelry, many consisting of matching sets of necklace, earrings, bracelet, ring and lavaliere set in precious stones and metals were missing. Boxes that held them were scattered on the floor.

I called the police and my Lincoln Insurance Agent, Michael Banning immediately.

We have never suffered a loss by burglary, or theft. Enclosed is the list of missing jewelry. There are more items than stated on the original policy. Also enclosed are photos of the exterior and interior of the store.

Any other information that may be required will be furnished. I understand this does not waive any of the rights under the said policy and in case of any recovery of the property, we agree to turn over jewelry to Lincoln Guarantee Insurance Company.

Signed: Samuel Mercken,   December 29, 1931
            Amelia Mercken,   December 29, 1931

Submitted by: Charles Darint, December 15, 1931

On June 18, 1924, Policy #365798 was issued to Samuel and Amelia Mercken of, J and M Jewelry Store 4369 Fifth Street, Milwaukee 21, Wisconsin. Samuel Mercken hereby makes claim for $150,000 loss of jewelry. Samuel Mercken wants to go beyond the limitation of the original scheduled policy claiming more jewelry was taken in addition to the 1924 policy. The policy has a business deductible of $100.

On December 3, 1931 between nine in the evening and eight thirty in the morning on December 4 a theft occurred. The claimant, Samuel Mercken parked his car in the alley behind the J and M Jewelry Store between 5th and 6th Streets. I visited the site and found a double hung window had a hole in the lower pane near the lock. Inside the premises I found a sharp edged rock the size of a baseball on the floor and broken glass. A footprint below the window on the ground, and fingerprint smudges on the window indicated forced entry. The exterior door on the alley was still locked with a Yale combination additional to a dead bolt. The dead bolt on the front business entrance was open, which provided a point of exit. Inside the vault door stood open. On examination I found no visible marks of forced entry on the door or combination lock. Mr. Mercken reported the theft to the police at eight forty. The police responded in ten minutes. I asked the insured what he did in that ten minutes. He responded he called Lincoln Guarantee Insurance Company and didn't touch or move anything.

I asked Samuel Mercken if all the missing items could have been carried out by one person or if the burglar dropped any items? The insured described that one person carried all the items on the scheduled policy, none were dropped. Only a few less valuable pieces were left behind which led me to believe the burglar knew their value and had access to the vault combination.

When I asked about damages to the building, the insured stated that was covered by another insurance carrier.

The store had no alarm system, nor window bars, or a night guard. The owners relied on the services of the police who checked locks at night. The location on Fifth Street is in a low risk area. The surrounding stores sell bona fide services and products. I examined his mortgage and found no delinquent payments. His business records show no outstanding debts. His marriage to Amelia Mercken nee Paradyze seemed sound. They had no children. Gilbert Paradyze, a nephew lives in the city. Samuel Mercken, age 43 claimed to be in good health as well as his wife Amelia, age 40. They seemed to be hard working owners taking no vacation, saving all their profits to put back into the store. Their part-time accountant, Alfred Steger was visiting family in Switzerland. There was no additional departmental staff. He alone with the owners knew the combination of the vault.

There are a few puzzling features. If the storeowners didn't take vacations how was their part-time accountant able to afford a paid Atlantic Crossing to Europe. According to Mr. Mercken Albert Steger had received a telegram that his father was in poor health.

I suspected an insider and secured the services of the special investigator department. Included are photos of the alley door, front business door, interior and exterior of the store, the vault, door handle and window lock, and a statement from Samuel and Amelia Mercken.

Signed: . . . . Charles Darint . . . . January 15, 1932.

Maggie and Hank shuffled the papers back and forth. Hank took notes while Maggie watched.

"This is interesting." Hank smiled as he gathered the sheets and inserted them into the file. "Let's go and see Amelia Mercken now. We have a lot to do."

41

Amelia Mercken met Maggie and Lieutenant Kummer at the door dressed in a fashionable chemise style that hung straight down from her bountiful bosom. When she sat down, the hem slid up exposing her legs. She tugged at her skirt to bring it down. Leaning over, she looked down at her legs, smiled, and looked over at Hank. She also wore a large amethyst ring and earrings.

Amelia exclaimed, "Lieutenant, how is my husband's case developing? Have you found out who killed him yet?"

"Not as fast as I'd like, Mrs. Mercken, but we're making progress. After I talked to you last week, I wondered if you remembered anything else. Do you know of anyone who had a grudge against your husband? Someone who may have felt he didn't get his fair share of the insurance settlement after the jewelry robbery?"

Maggie watched Amelia. Hank may have hit on a sensitive subject.

Amelia shook her head. "I can't think of anyone who could complain." Her answer sounded more like a question than a statement. She stared at the detective in disbelief. It was the first time the burglary reference came into his questioning.

"Who were your employees at the time of the robbery?"

"Only Al Steger, our accountant. He was young and fresh out of Marquette Accounting School. We treated him like our son. But I remember he was out of the country at that time. He had gone to visit his parents in Switzerland." She nodded, thinking back to that time. "We didn't mind. Business was slow."

"Was Al born in Switzerland?"

"No, he was born in the United States. His parents had come over earlier, but they decided to return to the old country during the Depression. It was hard to get work here. Al was in school then and didn't want to go back with them. He often stayed with us." Amelia smoothed out a fold on her dress and glanced at her legs again.

Maggie liked to see the fit of a new dress too and would turn sidewise in the mirror to check the fall of the fabric over her back. Was the skirt the right length when she sat down, etc. Maggie stopped daydreaming when she heard Hank ask, "What do you remember about the robbery in 1931?"

"I know very little about it. My husband's father, George Mercken, had purchased those valuable sets of jewelry in the early twenties. When Sam inherited the business after his father's death, many of our customers couldn't afford those expensive stones. I remember there were several sets that included a matching necklace, bracelet, earrings, and a ring. But they weren't any use to us and stayed in the vault. Once in a while before a holiday, Sam used to put a few pieces in the display windows for the customers or passersby to see." Amelia took a deep breath as if yearning for the old days.

Hank nodded, not wanting to interrupt her flow of thought.

She continued, "We had an opera-length string of pearls that was valued at five thousand dollars." She held out her hands wide to indicate the length. "You can imagine what they'd be worth today. Solid nacre they were. Not like the cultured pearls we get today that are produced by adding irritants into the oysters. They have only a few layers of nacre.

"I used to beg Sam to let me wear one of those sets while I was in the store. But he wouldn't allow it. He was always afraid something would happen to them, or that the customers would think we living high on the hog." Her smile gone, she said, "What we needed was a less costly stock our customers could afford."

"When did Sam's father die, Mrs. Mercken?" Hank asked.

"George died in January 1930. I often thought the crash finished him. He was sixty-three years old. It seemed he didn't have anything to live for after Naomi, Sam's mother, died. That was four years earlier. Then he'd been ailing, too." She looked up. "The business was going downhill when Sam and I rescued it."

"What was the cause of death?"

"His heart!" Amelia's eyes widened at the memory. Her voice increased in volume. "He had a massive heart attack and died within minutes."

Hank waited a respectful moment and then said, "I want to know more about the robbery. Do you remember how many pieces were taken and their description?"

Amelia's eyes looked glazed when she turned back from a window where a hedge of blooming red roses grew. "I know there's a list someplace. Perhaps the insurance company has it."

Hank continued, "You received a sizable settlement from the Lincoln Guarantee Insurance Company, one hundred fifty thousand dollars."

"Yes." Amelia nodded. "We always kept our premiums up to date even though it was hard for us. Often we did without little pleasures to make ends meet. We never took a vacation."

All sorts of ideas were going through Maggie's mind. Amelia sounded too sure of herself. She wanted to ask her what Sam did with the settlement money but remained silent. Hank would have a more tactful approach.

The detective continued, "The claim was paid off by Lincoln Guarantee Insurance in 1933, twenty-six years ago in the middle of the Depression."

"Yes. It helped us update our inventory with pieces our clientele could afford. We also purchased resale jewelry," Amelia said. "At that time, many jewelry ads appeared in the newspaper by those caught in the crash."

"When did you buy your house in Orchard Lake?" Hank asked.

"It was," Amelia looked up toward the ceiling fixture, "it was either 1935 or 1934." Her head went up again. "Now I remember. It was the same year we put in the tile floor in the store, 1933."

Hank asked, "Going back to last week when Sam died, did you see anything peculiar in his personality, in his actions?"

"No, nothing."

"Any new acquaintances or an old acquaintance that recently showed up?"

Amelia shook her head as though she might have missed something. "No, Lieutenant, I can't think of any, but if I do remember, I'll let you know."

Amelia asked, "Will you be staying in Milwaukee all day?"

"Yes, we're trying to finish our business here today." Hank glanced at his watch and nodded to Maggie. They both got up from their chairs.

"Why don't you come back for dinner tonight? Gilbert will be here, and maybe I'll think of something else."

"That's very generous." The detective looked at Maggie and saw her smile. "We accept your invitation. What time would you want us?"

"About six thirty?"

"Thank you, Mrs. Mercken. We'll be here." They left.

Maggie asked after they got settled in the car, "Where to now?"

"I thought we'd drive by Merckens' jewelry store on our way to the passport office. Just idle curiosity that goes with the job."

They drove past the old Mercken store where they saw a remodeled storefront and customers inside. The new owners retained the name "J and M Jewelry." It was printed in calligraphic style in black and gold on the show window.

Maggie scanned the display. Jewelry had been the last thing on her list of needs. Someday, she thought, I might own an exquisite piece. It'd be a ring to replace the signet ring she received as a bride-of-Christ symbol when she made her profession of vows. Looking at her hand, still bare, she rubbed the callous in her palm.

Maggie said, "Amelia looked like she was expecting someone special. And she didn't once talk to me, even to ask about her cat, Smudge. I don't believe she thinks about him or cares what happens to him."

"Why didn't you ask her?" Hank asked, directing his attention to a turn in the street.

"She seemed so distant; it didn't seem like the right time to bring up the cat. I'd never have recognized Amelia if I saw her walking down the street. She doesn't seem to be in mourning at all."

"I agree, and she never talked about going back to Orchard Lake either." Hank parked on a side street near the Pfister Hotel. "We'll stop here for lunch."

They walked through the lobby, past elegant sets of matching lounges and chairs that looked comfortable and inviting. A large chandelier with thousands of crystals dominated the high-arched ceiling. Colorful oil paintings of Wisconsin pioneering days stretched from panel to panel on one side of the room. She complimented Hank for his first-class choice. She wondered if he always ate at expensive places.

Over a shrimp cocktail, she asked, "What do you think is behind the change in Amelia? Do you suppose it was a stormy marriage, and she's relieved Sam Mercken's gone?"

"It's difficult to tell at this point."

"This is very tasty, Hank." She almost said this was the first time she had shrimp but caught herself. She was beginning to sound like a broken record with her first-time accounts. "Here, let me give you a taste." She forked the dainty silver prongs into a large shrimp, dipped it into the sauce, and held it to his mouth.

Hank bit the shrimp off her fork, like bait from a hook. He savored the shrimp. "So far it looks like she's keeping house for Gilbert and plans to stay."

The detective looked at his notes and took a pencil from his coat to compute some figures he had written. He estimated, "Amelia would have been about twenty-one when they married."

"And another thing," Maggie said, "you'd think Amelia would have been sorry to lose these exotic pieces of jewelry. But it sounded to me like it was the best thing that happened to their business."

She hooked her fork into another shrimp. "This is close to blessedness."

Hank looked up from his notes and smiled at her description.

Maggie said, "Now, Gilbert, he's another mystery. Have you ever had a chance to talk to him?"

"Only at the funeral. I want to interview him again. We'll have a chance to see him tonight. I also want to stop at the county tax office. We have a lot to do."

After their lunches, they drove to the federal building. Hank learned Al Steger had applied for a passport on November 27, 1931. It had not been renewed.

"Next we'll check the county tax office to see if his taxes are paid up." Hank announced looking at his watch. "It's only two thirty. We're making good time."

"What do you expect to find out at the tax office?"

"Do you remember Al Steger told us Sam bought two cottages in Orchard Lake? I want to check the location of the second one. I have a hunch I know who lives in it."

"Really, Hank?" Maggie waited for his answer, but Hank remained silent, pulling away from the street where they parked.

At the county office, the county clerk assisted the detective to delve back into tax files from the 1930s. He found out Samuel Mercken continued to pay the taxes on the two properties through the current year. One cottage was located on Highway 64 where the Merckens resided, the other on Elderberry Lane.

"Just as I thought," Hank remarked, his voice low.

42

When Maggie and Hank returned to the car, he said, "From the information we received from Lincoln Insurance and the tax offices, do you see a pattern?"

"I do, Hank. But it looks too simple." It was the first time Hank asked her opinion about the case. She, a mere amateur in the ways of the world, considered it a compliment. In her past, it was always, "Yes, Mother; no, Mother," never an opinion nor a discussion.

Hank started the motor and looked at his watch. "It's only two forty. We still have a few hours before we're due at Gilbert's house. Would you like to stop for a drink?"

"Sounds good to me," Maggie said. "Where to?"

"Let's go back to the Pfister House where we had lunch."

"Good. It's so palatial and beautiful."

Seated on a maroon leather sofa in the walnut-paneled lounge, Maggie took in the surroundings. A piano with an extension around the curved end sat near them in the lounge. Maggie knew pianos. She noted the manufacturer's name as they pass it. Would someone play it later? Her hands were itching to try the ivory keys.

Men dressed in business suits and ladies in dresses and suits sat on similar sofas under soft lights. Some sat on high stools at the ornate mahogany bar looking into a mirror. The languid blue gray smoke from their cigarettes spiraled upward like miniature smoke signals. Maggie caught herself sitting with her hands in her lap. Like a nun, she thought. Imagining the look of a cigarette in her hands, she raised her arm up imitating a patron at the bar. Would it look smart? She turned toward Hank, put her elbow on the back of her seat, and crossed her legs. The ambiance would be ruined if she had a fit of coughing. Maggie decided to use a few cuss words to throw people off from suspecting her past life. She looked at Hank and thought, no, not with him.

Coming out of a cloister brought heavy baggage. Maybe people would think she was dull, not worth making a friend. Or that she'd be prejudicial, or pass judgment on them because she had lived such a strict life. Friends were what she wanted most. As yet, she hadn't had a chance to make any except Hank.

"Getting back to your question, Hank, from what I read on the summaries, I wouldn't be surprised to hear Al Steger lives rent-free in that second cottage Sam Mercken purchased. Al must have done something special to be treated so well all these years."

Hank opened a pack of Lucky Strikes. When he offered her one, she declined. She'd practice smoking by herself where there'd be no draft and no embarrassment if she had a fit of coughing.

"That's interesting, Maggie." He requested a cocktail menu when the waiter appeared. "I'm listening. This is a place where you can order any kind of a drink." Flipping through the leaflet with colorful pictures of mixed drinks, Hank leaned toward her.

"Black Russian, bullfrog, and here's captain's blood. They don't sound all that good," she said.

"Let's go down the list." He pointed. "This is a martini. It contains gin and vermouth with an olive garnish. A Manhattan is bourbon, a little vermouth with a cherry. Then there's just plain scotch. Some brands of liquor are better than others, so you have that choice too."

Maggie raised her hands in a helpless gesture. "I don't know any of these drinks. Dad and I've had 7Up and bourbon, but mostly I drink beer. It would be fun to try something different. What is a Singapore sling? That has a nice ring to it."

"It's a tall sweet drink." He read, "Made with gin, cherry brandy, fruit juices, and a dash of bitters."

"That sounds yummy. I'll have that." Maggie gave her order to the waiter, unaware an escort usually placed the order.

Hank followed with his choice. "Dewer's scotch on the rocks."

Maggie hesitated to ask about rocks, deciding to wait to see his drink. She didn't want to appear stupid. Every day more descriptive words were added to her vocabulary.

After drinks were served, Maggie took a sip. "This is very good," then she continued with their discussion. "Wasn't it timely that Al Steger had a valid passport before the robbery?"

Hank nodded. "Mr. Darint, the Lincoln Insurance investigator, wondered how a part-time accountant could afford an ocean-crossing voyage. I'll be interested to talk to Mr. Darint. He lives near Madison. I'll have a chance to see him."

"This is like drinking Kool-Aid," Maggie took another sip. "If Al Steger disappeared from this country away from the reach of the law, do you suppose he carried the jewels with him? If he did, he'd have to be on a ship for Switzerland before the robbery was discovered.

"He'd have no trouble fencing them in Switzerland then return to the United States with a sizable cache."

"Then Sam Mercken would have the one hundred fifty thousand dollars insurance settlement plus the profits Sam brought back. That would make 'ole Sammy smile." Maggie giggled.

Hank finished his scotch. "It's hard to believe Amelia Mercken doesn't have a clue, or she's a mighty good actress."

"If Sam Mercken gave the cottage to Al Steger as a reward for what he accomplished, what would be Al's motive to kill Sam? He should have been grateful. Think of the money he saved all these years with a house tax and rent-free.

"If we knew that, we'd have the case solved." Hank picked up his briefcase and pulled out a copy of Samuel Mercken's bank application.

"Another thing that bothers me is, if Al killed Sam, what role does Rudy play?"

Hank put down the paper. "These cases are rarely simple, like mystery novels, but involve complex issues between the murderer and the victim."

"And if it isn't Al Steger. Oh, Hank, I feel dizzy. I better not finish this." She pushed the glass away and leaned back on the sofa, resting her head on the back of the sofa.

"I should have warned you that drink has a powerful kick, but you seem so ready to try new things. Do you think you can make dinner tonight at Amelia's? We can cancel it."

"Aw nooo. I'm fine. I'll be all right."

"I was just thinking. Now that we'll be staying for dinner, it'll be much later when we leave the city. I can make reservations to stay here tonight."

Maggie didn't respond.

"I'll make the reservation then I'll call your parents and tell them we're staying here."

"Uhhum."

Hank disappeared down a corridor. Minutes later, he returned. "Maggie, our rooms are ready. You better go up and rest."

"Sounds good to me, Hank." Maggie got up and stumbled, grabbing the arm of a nearby chair. Hank took her arm and guided her toward the elevator.

"I'll be all right. You don't have to help me." Maggie caught his eye and winked then snuggled closer holding his arm tight. When the elevator reached their floor, Hank led Maggie to her door and unlocked it.

Maggie looked at her surroundings. "This is pretty swanky." She flopped down on the bed. "What time is it?"

"It's four thirty. Why don't you lie down?"

"Okay." Echoes of the slang word resounded in her ears. She twisted her body around. A few minutes later, Maggie was dreaming Hank looks like Jimmy Stewart.

Hank removed her shoes and noticed Maggie had thrown up on her blouse. She had no clean changes and couldn't return home this way. He unbuttoned it and slipped the blouse off along with her skirt without a struggle from Maggie. Disappearing through the adjoining door, Hank brought back a cover and put it over her and called housekeeping.

*   *   *

Gilbert answered the door when he arrived. "Come in, Lieutenant. Amelia's almost ready. Would you like a drink?"

"No thanks."

"Hello again, Lieutenant. Where's that cute girlfriend of yours?" Amelia bustled into the room wiping her hands on an apron embroidered with apples and oranges. "What's her name again?"

"Maggie. She was tired and stayed back at the hotel. You remember the Brenners. They have the cottage across the road from yours. Maggie is their daughter. She's taken a special interest in your cat and has been feeding him."

"Oh dear, I've neglected Smudge. I'm glad he came back. Be sure to thank her for me. Now I'll have to plan what to do with him."

Gilbert spoke up, "You know I'm allergic to cats. He can't come here."

Hank said, "Maggie and Smudge have struck up a friendship. She said she'd take him."

Gilbert answered, "That's settled then. Are you ready for us?"

Amelia led the way and removed a place setting. "You sit here, Lieutenant."

*   *   *

Maggie awoke and got out of bed. She pulled the drape back from the window. A bright billboard advertising Schlitz beer lit the dark sky. Headlights of shadowy cars streaked on the street many floors below. Her head throbbed, but it was clear enough to take in her surroundings and to see her skirt on a hanger. Did I hang it up? Where is my blouse? Is this what it felt like to be drunk? Will Hank tell my parents? Had he already told them? They'd have so much advice. How can I face Hank? Maybe he won't want me along again.

She switched on a light to read two twenty on her watch. Did Hank go to Amelia's? With her ear to the adjoining door, she listened but couldn't distinguish any movement. She turned the knob, and the door opened a crack. Hank's rhythmic breathing sounded so peaceful. Maggie closed the door.

Massaging her aching head, Maggie thought about Sister Cecilia, her novice mistress who would suggest offering up her headache for the poor souls in purgatory. Maggie could never figure out how the poor souls could profit from someone's headache or other pains. But now, there was nothing else to do. It seemed to release the grip of her pain, and she drifted off to sleep.

A female voice called, "Laundry."

Bright sunshine filled the room. "Just give me a minute, please." She put on her skirt and put a towel around her shoulders then laced her fingers through her short curls.

Maggie opened the door. The maid handed her a blouse.

"Thank you." Maggie closed the door and clasped it to her. Oh my God. What happened? Did I soil it? Did Hank take it off and send it to the laundry?

She put it on quickly.

Another knock sounded. Opening the door, a uniformed waiter stood behind a steaming breakfast cart. Hank towered behind him. Maggie stood aside, so they could enter.

"Good morning, Maggie." Hank grinned as if nothing had happened out of the ordinary. "How did you sleep?"

"Like a baby. What a nice surprise." After the waiter left, Maggie massaged her forehead. "My head feels twice the size, but I'll be all right. Was I drunk?"

"Of course not, you just lost your equilibrium. But you'll need to be careful about your drinks. No more Singapore slings."

"I'm so embarrassed. Did you see Amelia and Gilbert?"

Hank nodded. "Let's sit down now and eat." He pulled two chairs around the small table and handed her a platter of hotcakes.

"I'm anxious to hear what you learned. What's Gilbert like?"

"From his appearance, I'd say he enjoys expensive clothes. He wore sharkskin suit and white shirt with gold cuff links, engraved with his initials. And he smoked English cigarettes. After dinner, he took off his coat and rolled up his sleeves. You could see USMC tattooed on his arm." Hank took a bite of the sausage.

Maggie poured coffee. "Had Gilbert ever worked at the J and M Jewelry Store when he was young?"

"Good question, you may remember the interview with Jim Mooreside. He was the one who heard the gunshots and called the sheriff. He told us Gilbert had been a guard at the United States Embassy in Peking. He was taken prisoner after the attack on Pearl Harbor."

"I remember. The Japanese guards decreased his rice portions each day."

"After VJ Day, Gilbert was released and returned to the States. With his GI money, he went to college in Milwaukee and got an engineering degree. Since then he's been employed with Klusner, Brown, and Holt engineering firm. They have offices in the United States and abroad."

"Let's see. Gilbert would have been fourteen or fifteen at the time of the robbery."

Hank said, "Once in our conversation, he call Amelia, 'Mom.'"

43

On the ride back to Orchard Lake, Hank made no reference to Maggie's blouse. She tried to concentrate on clues they had gathered from the tax office and the insurance investigator, but found herself thinking at least she has on as much as a bathing suit.

Hank said, "First, we'll go to Elderberry Lane to see Al Steger. Is that all right, or would you rather go home first? I can go back later."

"This is your case, Hank. You make the decisions."

Al was outside tying a line on his fishing pole when the car pulled into the yard. Hank rolled down his window. "Going fishing?"

Al set the pole against the fence and walked over to the car, looking up at the eastern sky. "Don't know yet, Lieutenant. Looks like it might rain." Leaning his elbow on the open window, Al pulled out a bag of tobacco from his pocket. He jiggled grains on a thin square of paper and tied the sack strings tight with his teeth before putting it back in his pocket.

Hank looked toward the sky and nodded. "Guess the farmers would welcome that. I have a few questions to ask you."

Maggie could smell whiskey on Al's breath.

Al rolled the cigarette then jerked his head toward his cabin door. A dirt path edged with weeds and overgrown brush led the way. "Want to come in, Lieutenant?" He struck a match on his shoe and drew on the cigarette, exhaling a cloud of smoke.

Maggie watched Al's casual motions. Was it a deliberate act to camouflage his fears?

"No, this won't take long. You mentioned at our last meeting that Sam and Amelia Mercken were arguing the day Sam was murdered. Just how well did they get along? You knew them better than the others."

"They had their differences about money like any other married couple and also about Gilbert."

Hank asked, "Did Gilbert ever work in the store?"

Al blew out a cloud of smoke, then brought his voice down as if he were about to divulge an international incident. "Gilbert's name was never spoken aloud in the store or at their house."

"Can you explain?" Hank said.

"Gilbert was Amelia's son." Al straightened, waiting for the detective's reaction. He flicked the ash from his cigarette continuing. "She had him out of wedlock before she married Sam. And for her one mistake she had to pay. Gilbert was never allowed to visit Amelia in Orchard Lake or in Milwaukee. I remember hearing Amelia plead with Sam to let him come for a special holiday. But stubborn Sam wouldn't let him. He always referred to Gilbert as a bastard, and he wasn't going to let any bastard ruin his business or interfere with his life. He didn't want any of his customers to know Gilbert existed, afraid the scandal would hurt his business."

"Where did Gilbert live?" Maggie asked.

Al ducked his head to the side of the window to glance at Maggie.

"He was raised in the Waukesaw County Orphan Home in Milwaukee."

"How terrible." Maggie shook her head and turned toward the lake to avoid the pesky smoke.

Al continued, his cigarette bobbing up and down between his lips, "I knew about Gilbert because Amelia told me."

"Where did he go when he was eighteen? They usually have to leave the orphan home then," Maggie said.

"He joined the marines. Part of his tour of duty was spent in China. He was taken prisoner by the Japs after the attack on Pearl Harbor. When he came back, he was in bad health and had to stay an extra year in the marines until he passed the physical. With his GI money, he went to the university and graduated with a degree in engineering. Later, he built his home in Milwaukee. He never married."

Al continued, "I always felt sorry for Amelia. She took the brunt of all their arguments. I often thought Sam mistreated her. Once, Amelia came to work with a black eye and tried to hide it with makeup. Amelia never said a word to me about it.

"She kept in contact with Gilbert without Sam's knowledge. I was the go-between. After his house was finished in Milwaukee, he wanted his mother to move in with him." Al removed the cigarette from his mouth and turned to spit. "Now that Sam is gone, Amelia's free. She suffered enough for that one mistake. As you can imagine, Gilbert had no love for Sam."

Hank said, "We've uncovered some information this past week. I know you were employed by Sam Mercken at the time of the robbery and had gone to Switzerland."

"Went to see my dad. He hadn't much time left for this world."

Hank said, "Six months later, you returned and acquired this cabin. How did it happen that Samuel Mercken purchased two cottages at Orchard Lake?"

"I don't know. I didn't handle that." He threw the butt out and toed it into the dust.

"You were his accountant."

"Sam and I were friends. I helped him out with little glitches all the years I worked for him. I was good with a hammer and saw too." Al shrugged and lit another cigarette. His hands shook.

Hank continued, "Lincoln Insurance Company kept records of the J and M Jewelry robbery and a description of the pieces taken in the robbery. I'd like you to take a look at the list. Would you say this was accurate?"

Al squinted through a puff of smoke. He took his time before taking the paper from Hank into the light. After studying it several minutes, he handed it back, shaking his head. "I can't remember. Sam inherited a lot of that expensive jewelry when his father had the store. I remember some of the pieces, but I don't know if this was all of it."

Al looked at Hank as if to question how could he be expected to remember that far back, then added, "The robbery was over twenty years ago."

"Where are you going now that your cabin is the sole property of Amelia?"

Al frowned. He looked down at the ground, scraping his foot back and forth across a loose pebble. When he raised his eyes, Maggie saw the color drain from his face. A look of desperation replaced his cocky attitude.

"I don't know; something will turn up. Rudy and I are working on a deal." Al stood back from the car as though he was finished with the interview.

Maggie thought, did he say too much? She wondered how Rudy would share in the deal.

"Don't leave the area, Al. I'll be in contact with you soon."

After they left, Maggie said, "I think Al's worried. But I remember when you interviewed him before he said he 'bought' his cabin years ago when prices were cheap."

Hank nodded.

"What else did you learn, besides the fact that Al lied, and Sam was generous with his help and mean as a skunk to Amelia?"

Maggie raised her hand to rub her forehead, where a starched band had rested when she was in the cloister.

"Did you see the ring Al wore?"

Hank nodded as he parked by the Brenner's cabin. Boxes and suitcases were stacked in the entrance, ready for their return to Georgetown.

After Hank left, Mrs. Brenner said, "That was some outing you had with Hank. It's time you stop playing detective and get on with life in the real world."

Maggie didn't reply. Would her mother be impressed if she divulged the important information Hank got from the insurance and tax offices? It would be revealing confidential information that would be better left unsaid. She said, "This is a murder investigation. Hank had to see Gilbert. Waiting to see him after work saved him a trip back to Milwaukee."

Her mother continued, "I wanted to leave Orchard Lake early this morning. Now your dad wants to wait until tomorrow. I'm going to miss my culture-club meeting. I won't have time to get my nails done." She looked down at her fingers, pushing back the cuticle with a fingernail.

"What did you do in Milwaukee? Did you and Hank have separate bedrooms at the hotel?"

Maggie looked down at her freshly ironed shirt. "Of course we had separate rooms. What do you take me for anyway? After Hank saw Gilbert, he thought it was too late to start out for Orchard Lake." Maggie wondered why she had to defend his decision. She wouldn't mention that she had slept through Amelia's dinner and the meeting with Gilbert or that she had soiled her blouse.

"What is Gilbert's connection with Sam's murder?" Mrs. Brenner asked.

"Gilbert is Amelia's illegitimate son. He grew up in an orphanage. Sam never allowed Gilbert in his sight."

"So Amelia got herself in trouble before she got married. Let that be a lesson for you, Maggie. Be careful when you're out with men."

"One thing I know are the facts of life, Mom. Amelia can't have her cat in Milwaukee because Gilbert is allergic to cats. She said I could have him."

Mrs. Brenner frowned, shaking her head. "Cats are nice, but they belong outdoors."

"Smudge is an outdoor cat. It would only be until I start classes in August. Would you mind if I brought him here until then?"

"How do you think you can manage a cat at the university?"

"I'll manage. Now, what can I do now to help you to ready the cabin?"

"You can try on the flower-printed skirt. I need to see how the waist fits. The blouse is finished. I'll be glad when you have everything ready for school, then I can get my breath. It hasn't been much of a vacation for me with all the sewing, and you're not even here to help. You've spent so much time with Hank."

The Brenners left Orchard Lake the next morning, leaving their cabin furniture covered and winterized until the next vacation. Before they left, Maggie and her dad went over to the Merckens' to find Smudge.

With him snug in her arms and purring in her ear, Maggie found it hard to leave. She wasn't sure how her relationship with Hank would continue in Georgetown, then to Madison either. With so many lingering questions about Sam Mercken's murder, Maggie couldn't put it out of her mind. She worried she'd have no part in the rest of the investigation, which had turned out to be more interesting than swimming and getting a tan. However, it was time to take her next step. That was to move out of her parents' home and get an apartment or a room in Madison as soon as possible.

Back home in Georgetown, Maggie explained her plans, "I'll get a job as a salesclerk until the fall term begins." She folded each of her new garments into a suitcase.

Mrs. Brenner watched, her face drawn. "You don't have any money. How do you think you can live in Madison without money?"

"Don't worry. I'll get a loan from the bank. It'll be just a month early instead of waiting till September." Maggie lifted the rose wool jacket from the bed and tried it on. Standing in front of the mirror, she held the matching skirt in front of her. "This is beautiful, Mom. You did a lot of work for me, and I'll never forget it."

"You don't have any experience at that kind of work," her mother continued.

"It's only six weeks until classes begin. What can I learn at home that would make it easier to wait?"

"You should be practicing for your audition. You could still be a concert pianist, Magdalena." Mrs. Brenner clamped her lips in a straight line.

"I didn't leave the cloister to become a concert pianist. Anyway, I'll still have a chance to practice at the music school."

"Maggie wants to move to Madison now and play detective with Henry Kummer. That could be dangerous," her mother told her husband when he came in.

Dr. Brenner said, "I'll go with her to find lodging."

It was settled. Maggie sighed with relief.

She and her dad made the rounds of rooming houses from addresses Maggie found in the newspaper. She wanted to locate a room near the music school. Some of the houses looked old and unkempt. Maybe it was because the bedrooms were stripped in preparation for the fall student enrollment. "A bedroom always looks better with curtains and a made-up bed," she told her dad.

Dr. Brenner discussed the rent with the housemothers and asked about the meals. He bounced around on mattresses, remembering the routine when he was a student. They settled on a boarding house that served an evening dinner. The housemother, Miss. Shelley, pointed to the rules posted on the wall. Absolutely no cooking in the rooms, students had the use of a pay phone at the bottom of the stairs, and three students shared one of the two bathrooms. Dinner reservations had to be made the evening before. Maggie could move in the following week.

"One more question, Mrs. Shelley," Maggie said.

"I'm Miss Shelley, Miss Brenner."

"Sorry, Miss Shelley. Do you suppose I could bring my cat?"

The housemother shook her head. "We don't allow cats."

Dr. Brenner said, "Smudge can stay with us. He seems happy to be in Georgetown."

"I heard Hank say he had a cat once. Maybe he'll take him," Maggie said.

Armed with a teaching-assistant application from the music school and a loan application from the bank, Maggie and her dad returned home.

It was too early to register for classes. Filling out the applications made Maggie nervous. What would she put down? Even the simple requests such as name, address, and telephone numbers were new to her. She tried to act experienced when she talked to those in charge. Instead, she felt alarmed and couldn't complete the forms in their offices. How could she explain that in the past twelve years, she had never filled out an application? She wondered what to write for past employment or the lack of it. Also, there was the problem of a different name on her transcripts from Saint Andrew's College.

Her dad insisted, "You can fill this out here, Maggie."

"No," she whispered, "I want everything to look ordinary. I need more time."

"Oh, that again. You'll have to come to terms with your past one of these days. You can't hide it, Maggie. Anyway, what's to hide?"

44

Maggie and her mother drove down Oxford Street in Madison, arriving at Miss. Shelley's around two in the afternoon. Mature trees and large green lawns fronted the framed two- and three-story homes built in the twenties and thirties. Many had large porches graced with a swing or a glider. Next to Miss. Shelley's boarding house, children chased through a sprinkler causing shrieks of laughter and water arches bending in all directions.

Mrs. Brenner reminded her daughter, "We can go to the bank now if you hurry. We still have time before it closes."

"Don't worry, Mom; I'll open the account tomorrow."

"Be sure to get that one-thousand-five-hundred-dollar check deposited. You'll need to write checks on it right away. How much cash do you have in your purse?"

Maggie sat on the bed and counted out $65.72.

"You'll be okay." Mrs. Brenner looked at her watch. "I'll be going. Don't lose that check,"

Maggie flung the large suitcase on the bed to unpack. Her enlarged wardrobe included clothes given by friends and relatives. It seemed everyone she met wanted a part of remaking Maggie and had clothes to offer her. Today, she wore a strapless bra, a gift from her classmate, Betty Lou. Betty had said strapless bras were more comfortable because they didn't cut into your shoulders. Maggie turned sideways and caught her uplifted reflection in the mirror. At least, she still had a good figure with a marked waistline.

She fondled the smooth satin slip that felt so soft. After her years of wearing homemade muslin sixteenth-century underwear, the luxury of these fitted garments still seemed risqué to the point of daring. She had to remind herself that this was normal and ordinary.

After she fit everything neatly in the chest of drawers, Maggie sat on the bed and studied the university catalogue. What will my adviser think of the courses I took at Saint Andrew's College? The transcripts still had "Sister Camille Brenner" on them. Why am I in a position to have to explain it? The registrar said having my religious name on it wouldn't be a problem. I'll write to the president of the college to see about a name change, or this transcript will follow me when I need to get a teaching position. Maggie could feel tension build.

She arched her fingers as if they were posed on a keyboard, drumming them on the cover of the catalogue. Tomorrow, I'll go to the music school and practice. Lord knows I need it to audition with the piano department head in a few weeks.

Further on in the catalogue, she read the course offerings in the psychology department. "This is what I need most," she whispered to herself and continued to read the prerequisites. With her undergraduate courses, it looked like she could qualify for the master's program in psychology. If she changed her major from music to psychology, her mother would have a fit. Would it be worth it to have another conflict with her? Maggie answered "yes, yes, yes" and read further.

Alone for the first time, she felt a chill, a lost feeling, and tightness in her chest. Her hands tightened into a fist. I just have to get used to being alone. In the cloister, the sisters, though often silent, were always nearby in the chapel, the refectory, or at recreation. Even in their tiny eight-by-ten-foot cells where they practiced silence at all times, a sister occupied a cell on the other side of the partition. It was just so quiet now; she could hear her heart beat. It would be better when the university students returned in August.

Later that afternoon, Maggie met Mildred, a boarder who came from work. Mildred had short frizzy, graying hair and gray eyes made smaller by corrective lenses. She wore a simple print dress and oxfords. Mildred said she worked at the university library. She seemed to distance herself from the university students. Downstairs before dinner, Maggie met Pat, another boarder.

"Hi, you here for the fall term?" Pat asked.

"Yes. I came early to get a part-time job."

Pat tore open an envelope from the mail table. "This is from my boyfriend." She flapped it against her chest. "He misses me, and I miss him." Her eyes sparkled. Her beautiful brunet hair curled like a picture in a beauty-salon advertisement. "Eddie and I graduated from Worthington High last June. I'm studying at Vernon's School of Beauty Culture."

"You look beautiful, Pat. You'll make a great beauty operator."

Pat smiled. "Thanks, Maggie. A student worked on my hair today." She twirled around. "I'll be a model for the show next Friday." Her eyes widened with pleasure, pleased with the results.

Maggie found everyone had stories so curious, so different from hers. Like someone who had been left on a desert island; she was alert to every new experience and what she could learn from it.

After dinner, Pat took her aside. "I know everyone here. Linda, Peggy, and Donna will be back. Have you met Mildred?"

"I did earlier."

"What did you think of her?"

Maggie shrugged her shoulders wondering where Pat's questioning led. Before she could answer, Pat giggled. "We call her 'the religious one.'"

Maggie copied Pat's giggle. "You do? That's a riot." The outdated slang from her high school years slid back into her vocabulary as easy as soft custard. If the girls ever found out her background, Mildred would pale in their eyes as the religious one. From now on, she had to learn how to smoke. She'd buy a pack of cigarettes tomorrow when she went to the bank.

Back in her room, she turned on the bedside radio her dad donated from his office. The classical station played the D Major Mozart Piano Concerto. She had studied and performed it with Dr. Sutton at Saint Andrews in fulfillment of her BA degree. Listening to the cadenza, she compared it to the one she composed and played. After that movement ended, she hummed along with the melody in the slow movement.

The school catalogue stated the university orchestra would perform some of the Mozart concertos that year. Would she have the courage to play with an orchestra? Her stress level rose along with her indecision to change her major.

When the last note of the concerto came to an end, Maggie wished she had a tranquilizer, or at least a bottle of beer that was always so handy in her parent's home. She hadn't realized her beer supply would be missing here. A glass of beer would lift her spirits and help her to sleep that evening.

It was still light when she walked down the street and stepped into the Silver Zephyr bar. Maggie sat on a stool near the door.

When the bartender asked her, "What'll you have?" she replied in her disciplined voice, "I'd like a bottle of beer, please." Did she sound like an addict who had to have a drink? A moment of truth flashed. Maybe she was dependent on tranquilizers.

The bartender picked up a bottle opener.

"Don't open it! I want to take it with me."

"Sorry, miss. We don't sell bottles of beer to take out. You'll have to drink it here."

Maggie broke into a sweat and felt dizzy. She twisted her head and looked around the smoked-filled atmosphere. Truck drivers and farmers and one girl who wore a tight sweater and a cowboy hat all focused on the blaring television where a frenzied prize fight flashed.

She nodded to the bartender, who had left her to tend another customer.

"I'll drink it here."

"Schlitz, Coors, Budweiser, or Hamms?" he recited in an automatic monotone, his eyes never leaving the TV screen.

"I'll have Schlitz."

"Bottle or tap?" he asked, still absorbed with the fight.

The announcer's voice shouted, "That was as clean a blow as you ever want to see. He's got a bleeding cut over his eyes. He's groggy! He's down for the count!"

Maggie detected impatience in the bartender's voice. A flushed feeling rose from her neck to her ears. She asked, "What's tap?"

The bartender's arm rested on one of the spigots. He lifted it and pointed to it. "Right here."

"I'll take . . . tap beer. How much is it?"

"Two bits."

She pulled a quarter from her purse and laid it on the counter. When he placed the stein of foaming, cold beer in front of her, she said, "I'd like a package of cigarettes too."

The barkeep pointed to the cigarette machine. "Over there." He left her and returned to the end of the bar to watch the fight.

Out of the corner of her eye, she saw a patron wave an empty beer bottle to the bartender, who replaced it with a fresh one. He looked familiar. Afraid to turn her head for fear of showing interest, Maggie decided to drink the beer as fast as possible. It didn't even taste good. I don't want to stay here, but I need this. She drank up and went over to the cigarette machine to read the directions, checked her change, and saw her lack of coins. The bartender had been hassled enough without her asking him for change.

Outside, she calmed herself. The effort to get a beer made her fearful of taverns, not because of the smoke and liquor odors. They smelled good, but how was she going to survive?

Back at Miss. Shelley's, the familiar face at the bar haunted her until, "It was Rudy," she said aloud. Her breath became shallow. That Rudy lived so close made her shiver. "He's someone I don't want to see," she whispered. "As if I don't have enough worries, now he's in Madison."

Maggie knocked on Pat's door. Pat appeared wrapped in a towel. "Where do you go for a beer around here?" She needed another one.

Pat said, "At the supermarket."

"Thanks, Pat. I'll go there tomorrow. Is there anything you need while I'm there?"

"Naw, I go by there every day. You can keep your six-pack in the frig."

Of course, a six-pack, the best way to buy beer. Why didn't I think of that? What a dope I was to go to that bar alone.

That settled, she wrote a list of chores for the next day and wondered if Hank would ever call. How would he get her phone number? He didn't even know she had come to Madison. She thought about their time together at the lake. Did Hank like to have her with him because he needed her help? Of course not. Did he just tolerate her assistance? She questioned further. Was her feeling for him love or a simple crush? Crushes were for teenagers. She imagined herself telling him little details of things that happened that week after she left Orchard Lake. Maggie decided to stop thinking about Hank and got ready for bed. If she had more years experience, she'd know what to expect.

What was happening to the Sam Mercken murder case? Tomorrow she'd buy a newspaper to see if anything was reported in the Madison news. She added that to her list and left her room to check the phone book. First, she looked for the number of the Dane County Sheriff Department. She ran her fingers down the column of services listed: coroner, administration, detention division, forensic, patrol division, and technical services. Then she saw Criminal Investigation Bureau and jotted down the number. Next, she looked in the residential section and found Kummer, Henry, his phone number, but no address. She went back to her room with both numbers. It would be a good thing to have these telephone numbers handy. Maggie went to bed hoping to get to sleep.

Was she getting neurotic, or worse, psychotic? Maggie remembered Dr. Raymond who was so helpful in encouraging her to leave the sisterhood. If only she could talk to him. But that meant going back to Stone Hill, and she didn't want to go there. Around midnight, she managed to fall asleep.

The next morning, with her head tall, she went to apply for a job at the Pot Deli Bell. After that, it would be close to ten o'clock when the bank opened. She wore a coral-flowered sundress with spaghetti straps fit for a warm July morning. It fit close from the waist up with a flared skirt. Her makeup consisted of a tinge of rouge beneath her short blond ringlets.

Mr. Rinehardt, the proprietor of the deli, looked at her resume and smiled. "So you've been a teacher for how many years?"

Maggie said, "Nine years." So far, she was doing well with her interview, an experience that others would consider ordinary. They sat in a crowded nook off the kitchen with just enough room for his cluttered desk and a chair.

"And you plan to stay in Madison for how long?" he asked.

"At least a year. I hope to get a master's degree."

"Have you ever worked in a kitchen or bakery?"

"Yes," Maggie said, thinking of her experience in the kitchen at Saint Clotildes. She hoped he wouldn't ask where.

"Can you begin Friday?"

Maggie agreed and walked out on the street with a smile. She had a job that paid a minimum wage and a loan from the National Bank in Georgetown. With a room and one meal a day at Miss. Shelley's, she could live on a dollar a day. If she announced that meager plan, her parents would think her abstemious. Besides convincing them that she could follow this plan, she'd probably have to explain the meaning of "abstemious," a religious term for frugal.

At ten, Maggie walked into the First National Bank.

45

Maggie Brenner was first in a line when the First National Bank opened at ten the following morning. The teller asked for the usual family names and birth dates. He didn't ask about her previous banking history. With the new record book and temporary checks tucked into her purse, Maggie walked out the exit heaving a sigh of relief. This much was accomplished; now she had a bank account and a job.

Her contented thoughts were obtruded. A car swerved into the curb next to her. A man jumped out and grasped her in a chokehold. Stunned, Maggie struggled to balance herself and began screaming.

"Shut up. Get into the car," a voice yelled.

She felt hard metal behind her ear. When a hood was placed over her head, she resisted with her free arm.

"Please," she blurted as she was pushed, stumbling over her feet. "What are you doing?"

The gun was in her back. She screamed, "Help. I'm Maggie Brenner from Georgetown." Every word came back to her under the heavy hood. Maggie heard no voices, just feet shuffling, nor did there seem any reaction from police or people on the street. Pushed into a car with the motor running, she fell to the floor with someone on top holding her down.

"Go," her captor yelled to the driver.

"I'm going, I'm going," the driver said as his gears screeched, and the car jerked ahead then took on speed.

Maggie thought the voice sounded familiar. No one spoke. She tried to keep calm and tried to estimate how long the car went straight by counting, one, one thousand two, one thousand three. The car made an abrupt right. At the next turn, it seemed to be another right, a left, then a U-turn. Confused, she stopped counting seconds between turns. Where were the police? Why didn't she hear sirens? Someone must have witnessed what had happened and taken down the license plate number of the car. Her captors had eluded anyone who followed. After the car crossed railroad tracks, Maggie detected an oily odor. Were they near the railroad yard?

The vehicle came to a sudden stop. The door opened.

"Get out," an angry voice screamed.

Grabbed by the arm, Maggie was pulled out on the street, stumbling to her knees. The car sped off. Maggie was pushed up an outside flight of steps to a second story, another clue she wanted to remember. At this point, she didn't know if anyone else was around.

"I can't breathe. Take off the hood. Please!" She heard something crash to the floor and break.

The hood was jerked off. Though it was dark, Maggie could see the room was narrow. She stood against a bed. The room had one window covered by a shade. A tiny hole in it cast a long sunbeam to the floor. A chest of drawers sat against the opposite wall. She couldn't read the expression of her abductor, who still wore a ski mask. What would he do to her? Would she come out alive? She pulled up the spaghetti straps on her dress that had slid down.

"I haven't done anything to you. Why am I here? Think of your family. Think of your mother. What would she think about you?" She wanted to keep talking, stalling for time with the hope the police would come. It would be easy to get hysterical. She tried to keep a cool mind and took a deep breath. I must stay calm.

"Shut up! This will shut you up." He pushed her down on the bed and stuffed a rag in her mouth.

She gagged, choking on it.

"Will you shut up?"

Fearing the menacing sound of his voice, Maggie didn't want to aggravate him. She tried to stop coughing. The cloth was yanked out.

Relieved to have the rag out, she still couldn't get her breath and continued to cough, doubling up on the bed with her fists clasped to her chest.

Her assailant reached down, placed both hands around her neck, and squeezed. "This will stop your coughing."

Maggie stopped breathing. After he let go, she struggled to say something but couldn't get her breath and coughed again, throwing up her breakfast. A swift blow to her head stunned her into a comfortable world. She longed to remain in that relaxed state for an instant more, but standing next to her was an armed man. When his hand pulled up her skirt, her wits returned. She sprang to her feet. Trapped in a deserted house with no help, she would survive. She had to escape. Another blow slid her once again into the peaceful oblivion of a dimensionless void, until she felt his hands tug at her panties. She had to shake the mists from her head. He was ready for his final insult. After he finished, would he cut her up into pieces like the evening newspaper reported about a recent series of rape crimes?

He pressed the gun to her temple. "I'll shoot you."

Maggie felt the cold metal. Don't panic. It was possible the gun wasn't loaded. "Go ahead! Shoot!" She waited, alert to his next move. The window! If she could get to it. He laid the gun down to unzip his pants. That was her moment. She was at the window, her fist slid under the shade. Glass shattered like thin ice.

Maggie screamed, then opened the window, and crawled out. She hung from the sill covered with glass shards planning to drop to the ground. If she broke a limb that would be better than getting raped or shot. A door slammed. Where was her attacker? He hadn't followed her to the window or slammed the window down on her hands. If he came close, she'd jump. Maggie hung on longer, listening. Hearing stillness, she raised herself over the sill back into the room, crouching in a corner.

She heard running footsteps on the stairs and crawled under the bed. A woman yelled, "I called the police."

Waiting a little longer, she crawled out to meet whoever was there.

Maggie saw blood dripping from her nose and more blood from her wrist and hand.

Someone grabbed Maggie's wrist, compressing the blood vessel, holding the wrist high. Did someone call the police, or were they just trying to keep her calm for further assault? Her assailant might be standing among them.

More footsteps pounded on the stairway. When a uniformed officer walked through the door, Maggie fainted.

After the policeman applied a vial of spirits to her nose, she came to and broke down crying in front of everyone. The officer applied a tourniquet on her wrist.

"We'll get you to emergency. What's your name?"

"Maggie Brenner," she mumbled.

"How did this happen?"

46

"You're lucky to be alive, Miss Brenner." The doctor sutured her wrist. "A couple of millimeters to the left and you would have severed an artery. If that had happened, you wouldn't be my patient."

Maggie didn't react. She couldn't even if she wanted to. The artery wasn't severed, so why worry about it? If she had gone to the bank when her mother suggested the afternoon before, if the gun had been loaded. It was the "ifs" that haunted her. Her future seemed so fragile. It had been a rocky beginning since she had left the cloister. "You were brave, but it was risky to break the window with your hand," the doctor continued.

Maggie stared at her wrist as he finished stitching. She felt no pain from his needle. "Is that all you have to do? Am I finished?"

"No. See this X-ray?" He pointed to the wall.

Maggie looked up at the lighted pictures on the wall.

"You have a sprain here." He touched the sensitive spot on her wrist. "Does this hurt?"

"A little."

"We won't have to cast it. A bandage will protect it." He paused, then his eyes moved to her neck. "How did you get those red lines on your neck?"

Maggie touched the tender area. "He tried to choke me." She spoke in a matter-of-fact tone. It would be easy to get hysterical if she dwelt on it, but would that help? Maggie hesitated then said, "He put both hands around my neck and squeezed. I couldn't get my breath." Her voice trailed to a whisper. "He almost succeeded."

"You seem to have trouble talking."

Maggie nodded. "It feels sore here too where he tried to gag me." She pointed to the corners of her mouth. "He did that before he hit me."

"Are you having dizziness?"

"A little."

The doctor probed her neck. "Does this hurt?"

"A little."

"Do you have someone to stay with tonight?" he asked.

"I have a room at Miss. Shelley's boarding house," Maggie mumbled. "I moved in yesterday."

"You've got quite a shiner. Did you know that?"

Maggie's hand felt around her right eye. She winced.

"I think you'd better stay in the hospital tonight for observation."

"I'm so scared." Maggie sat up from the table, her fists clinched. When the hospital gown slid down from her shoulder, she lifted it back in place. "I'm so worried he's still out there looking for me."

"What about that, Officer?" Doctor called to the policeman who sat outside the door.

The officer who brought Maggie to the hospital entered the examining room. "An officer will be here tonight, ma'am. You'll be safe."

Maggie closed her eyes trying to feel secure. "I have a friend, Hank Kummer, in the sheriff's department."

"I know Lieutenant Kummer," the officer replied. "Ma'am, if you want, I can send him a message you're here."

"Yes, please." Maggie smiled. Those were the sweetest words she had heard all day. Some of the tightness in her throat left.

*　　*　　*

Hank came that evening carrying a package under his arm. He wore a detective's face as she watched him walk first to the window to estimate the drop to the ground. Maggie didn't say, "Hi, Hank," or "I'm so glad to see you." Instead she said in a hoarse voice, "I don't want to talk about it."

"You're going to have to tell the police to help reconstruct your kidnap," Hank said. "You've got guts."

"I'd rather talk to you if I have to talk to anyone."

"Are you lisping? Are you having trouble with speaking?" Hank asked.

Maggie nodded. "He tried to choke me. It made me sore here. And my throat keeps making sounds. I can't seem to control it. My neck is sore too." She turned her head in a modified arc. Maggie slid her injured hand under the covers for warmth and comfort.

She felt Hank's unwavering eyes and looked away, allowing him to continue his examination from her head down to her feet as if he were making a detailed report. It left less for her to explain.

"Sorry, this isn't my jurisdiction. You can do it. A news reporter is sitting outside your door waiting to ask you questions."

"What? Don't let him in. That's all I need." Her head sank to her chest. "My mind keeps repeating the details scene by scene like a bad movie, with me in it. I don't want to recognize that person. I feel like it's happening over and over again. I'm so afraid, Hank." Maggie's good hand flew to her face to wipe tears.

He reached for it and held it. "You have a good reason to be scared, Maggie."

"My life in the cloister was so protected. I'm wondering if I made the right choice to leave all that security."

He shook his head. "You didn't belong there, Maggie. I knew that when we investigated the mother superior's murder." His velvety brown eyes deepened and held hers. "There wasn't anything you could have planned or predicted when you went to the bank this morning. You were in the wrong place at the wrong time. There was nothing you could have done about it."

Maggie looked into Hank's eyes and felt his caring and gentleness. "Do you think I was a target?"

Hank nodded and continued to massage her good hand with his long tender fingers. Maggie's facial features relaxed, enjoying his touch. Looking up, she thought how handsome he looked with his trim mustache. Feeling unsure of his affection, she pulled her hand away. "Hank, there was something familiar about the voice of the driver in the getaway car. I've been asking myself where have I heard it before? If only I wasn't blindfolded.

"I remember my dad once made a remark about a man's voice being adenoidal. It was like that. I think it was Rudy."

"Did you tell that to Officer Greening?"

"I told him." Maggie's facial muscles tightened.

Hank said, "Officer Greening left me his number, so I could keep abreast of the case. I'll be in touch with him. Did the hospital call your parents?" Hank turned to pick up the package.

"I think they did. A nurse asked me for their phone number." She made an audible sigh. "Oh dear, they'll have so much advice. My mother will scold I should have gone with her to open the account yesterday as she suggested. Who would have thought I was in danger just by walking out of a bank?"

Hank opened the bags with the name Manchesters' imprinted on them. "The police have taken your clothes, so I've done a little shopping. These will tide you over until you get back to your room. Where are you staying?"

"At Miss. Shelley's boarding house on Astrid Street."

Hank pulled out a green sweatshirt and pants, with white socks, tennis shoes, and panties.

Maggie smiled, holding up the pants and shirt. The lifting made her wrist and some of the cuts on her hands smart. "Oh," she moaned, dropping the shirt and holding her good hand to the sore spot. "If I hadn't worn that sundress with the spaghetti straps. That's another one of those 'ifs' that keeps going around in my mind." This time, she grinned. Maggie looked up to see Hank grinning. Their eyes met and for a second, it seemed like old times.

"Thanks, Hank, for the clothes. I'm grateful to you. I hadn't planned what I'd wear after I was discharged." She noticed a missing bra but didn't comment.

"Why is the doctor keeping me in bed?"

"Hospital procedures, Maggie. You've had severe trauma. Lie back and enjoy the attention the nurses give you. Have you looked in a mirror?"

Maggie nodded. "I've seen my black eye." She grinned again. "It reminds me of the time Zelda pushed me into the closet, and I hit the concrete steps."

Hank handed Maggie a card. "Here's my telephone number. Keep it close by you. I'm here to help you in any way." He bent over and kissed her forehead. "Keep up your courage, Maggie. I have to go now."

"I wish the doctor would give me a tranquilizer."

"I'll tell the nurse. She'll be able to help you." Hank walked toward the door.

"Wait, Hank." Maggie raised her aching shoulders, leaning on her elbows. "Don't go yet." She wanted to say I need you. When will I ever feel your strong arms around me? Instead, Maggie said, "I know you're busy. Thanks for bringing the clothes."

Hank turned around again. He heard her pained breath.

She asked, "What's happening with the Samuel Mercken case? I haven't seen you since we left Orchard Lake, and I don't know what's happened."

"All in good time, Maggie. We'll have time for that later after you get some rest."

"Please, Hank. It will give me something else to think about. Is Amelia still in Milwaukee with Gilbert?"

Hank nodded. "I don't think she'll ever go back to Orchard Lake. Since I saw you, I've met with Mr. Darint, the investigator for Lincoln Guarantee Insurance Company who investigated the robbery in 1931."

"I remember. He retired soon after the jewelry-heist case. What did you find out?"

"Charles Darint lives a peaceful life on Lake Mendota and spends much of his time fishing and reading. He remembered the jewel robbery. Said he always thought Samuel Mercken worked in collusion with his accountant, Al Steger, but he could never prove it."

"That leads us back to where we started." Maggie eased back on the pillow. "Where do we go from here, Hank?"

He reached into his inside coat pocket and took out a worn blue leather booklet with loose strings hanging from the binding. Handing it to Maggie, he said, "I found this in Sam Mercken's safety deposit box. Take a look at it."

She opened the soft cover. On the first page, a handwritten title read, "Special Collection," with George S. Mercken's signature, dated April 23, 1927. "Hank, what is this?"

"It's an old receipt book of Sam's father, George Mercken. When Sam inherited the business, his father must have kept special pieces of jewelry listed here in a special collection. None of these were included on the insurance form at the time of the robbery."

"Are these more heirlooms?"

"From the accurate descriptions of each and the distinctive identification mark of George Mercken, I believe these are worth investigating. His mark, GM enclosed in a square, was engraved on each one. Look at this page."

Maggie took the book and read, "Bow-shaped brooch of platinum lacework set with five-baguette cut diamonds, 1 carat each, VVS, White." She looked up at Hank, "I can just see it in my mind."

"Read the next page," he said.

Maggie turned to it. "Bracelet, 16 carat gold, 10 diamonds, total wt. 5 carats, SI, white."

"Notice the name penciled on it?" Hank pointed.

"Ted Bryson! And here's Al Steger's name next to the ruby ring." She leafed through the small booklet and found Jim Mooreside and Butch Merdoc's names penciled in and dated next to the jewelry each had purchased from Sam Mercken. "There's a total of nine pieces listed in this book. Were none of these pieces described in the insurance investigation?" Maggie asked.

"Nope. Now notice the date on the book, 1926. It's before the robbery. There are still five possible pieces unaccounted for."

Maggie's eyes widened. Looking up from the receipt book, she nodded, forgetting her pains. "What happened to them? We have to find them."

"What do you mean, we? You're staying right where you are, in bed. I know you're safe here."

"But I won't be here long. How are you going to look for them? What's your next step?"

"Because of the accurate descriptions and the identification mark of George Mercken, I've telexed the descriptions to all the police precincts and sheriff offices in Milwaukee, Madison, and in Dane County. Next, I'll also send it to the pawnshops. After that, I'll go back to Orchard Lake and talk to Al Steger, Ted Bryson, and Butch Merdoc. I have the feeling we don't know all that they do." Hank smiled. "Now will that give you enough to think about?"

Maggie's lips drooped. "Wait. What about Gilbert? I think he's holding out on us. There's more to him than just being an orphan and a marine. It's kind of interesting that Gilbert was in an orphan home and Rudy was too. Do you think there's a connection? Were they in the same orphan home?"

"Now you have time to work that through." Hank smiled and opened the door just as her parents rushed in.

Mrs. Brenner ran to her daughter's bedside. "Maggie, we've been so worried about you." She straightened the top sheet on her bed.

"Oh, Mom, I'm getting to be an old hand at getting hit on the head. First, at the Chateau and now here." Maggie almost laughed, trying to keep it light.

"It's all that detective business you did with Henry Kummer in Orchard Lake. I still can't believe all that happened since Sam Mercken was murdered. I just bet this had something to do with his murder."

"Well, that's not an unusual idea, Mom."

Her dad leaned in next to his wife checking out his daughter.

"How are you feeling?"

"I feel fine, Dad. I don't know why I'm in bed. I should be up, getting practice at the music school. My fingers still work." Maggie wiggled them in the air to allay their fears.

"Uhhum, and what else?" He joked. "Mow the lawn?"

"Well, I have a job at the Pot Deli Bell. I'm supposed to start work as a cook Friday. I'll have to get word to Mr. Rhinehardt."

"A deli?" her mom asked. "Couldn't you find a better job than that? I thought you'd be a clerk in a nice couturier dress shop."

"It's a respectable place. Mr. Rhinehardt seemed nice."

"Why don't I stop there on our way out of town and tell him what happened to you? I'm sure he'll understand," her dad said.

"No. Wait. I still have three days before Friday. I'll be out of here by then. I need this job. It'll be good for me. I need something like this to get my mind off what happened." She didn't want to tell them more details of what happened after her kidnap. No need to alarm them more.

Her father said, "I talked to your doctor. He said you had a wrist sprain, and he's keeping you in bed in case you had head injuries."

"Then I'll be getting out of here soon. How is Smudge?"

"He caught a mouse yesterday." Her dad sounded pleased.

"Inside the house?" Maggie asked glancing at her mom.

"Not in the house." Her mother looked affronted. "In the garden."

"I wish I could have Smudge at Miss. Shelley's house. Give me a little more time, and I'll see if we can work him in. She has a cat."

After her parents left, Maggie had another visitor.

"I'm Detective O'Keefe. I'd like to ask you a few questions."

"Yes, I expected you would," Maggie answered.

"You'll be glad to hear Martin Crothers, the man who abducted you, was taken into custody late this afternoon. A witness came forward and identified him. We'll have the driver soon."

Maggie's eyes grew saucerlike. She was unable to respond and wanted to feel relief. That reaction would take time.

"He's confessed to everything, to abducting you with the intention to rape."

Again, Maggie stared with no fixed focus.

"Have you been examined here for seminal fluid?"

"I wasn't raped, Officer. I told the doctor that when I was brought in. My injuries are from broken glass and punches. My dad just left. He found out from the doctor I had only a wrist sprain."

"Did the abductor touch you?" he asked.

"Of course, how else could he knock me out?"

"It's surprising how quickly you recovered from a knockout. It takes about fifteen minutes."

"Maybe I wasn't knocked out, just stunned," Maggie said.

"Then what did he do?"

"He threatened to shoot me."

"And?"

"I said go ahead, shoot. I sensed a delay, and that's when I got away from him and broke the window."

"You thought the gun wasn't loaded?"

"It was possible. He may have carried it just to scare me."

"For your information, ma'am, that gun was loaded."

Maggie closed her eyes. She wanted to shut the whole experience out of her mind.

The officer continued, "Fortunately for you, he had to lay his gun down and unzip his pants. Sometimes it takes two hands. I'm not surmising this; he told us when he was cross-examined." He eyed her bandaged hand. "You were fortunate you didn't bleed to death after you broke the window."

"Yes, the doctor told me, when he stitched my wrist."

The detective got up and went to the door. "I'm just concerned that when you were knocked out, he may have raped you."

Maggie shook her head. She wished he'd get off that subject. "Officer, I think I'd know if that happened."

47

Maggie sat in front of the mirror at Miss. Shelley's applying powder base to her black eye, now turned to greenish yellow.

After the telephone rang in the downstairs vestibule, Pat, another boarder, called up. "Maggie, it's for you. He sounds nice. Is he your boyfriend?" Pat said after Maggie came down.

Maggie smiled. "He's a good friend." Then into the receiver, "Hi, Hank."

"How are you? When did you leave the hospital?"

"Yesterday afternoon. I spent the night there."

"How do you feel?"

"Let's say I'm mending nicely. As Sister Bernadette used to say, 'I'm able to sit up and take nourishment.' No, better than that, I just came back from having a hearty breakfast at the diner. It was my lunch too."

"Did you sleep?"

"Very well. Thanks to the sleeping pills the doctor gave me to take home. Have the police found the driver yet?"

"Not yet. They're working on it. You knew your abductor was taken into custody?"

"Yes, Officer O'Keefe told me."

"Have you started working at the Pot Deli Bell?"

"Monday. I can't see any reason not to. In fact, I'm looking forward to it. Mr. Rhinehardt postponed my starting date. Dad told him I was in the hospital. I have the weekend free."

"Do you feel well enough to do some investigating with me?"

Maggie stood taller. Being with Hank made her feel better. "Today?"

"Yes. Can you make it?"

"I sure can. Have you found something that relates to the little blue book?"

"We'll go over that when I see you. It's ten o'clock now. I have a meeting at eleven. I'll pick you up at one thirty."

"Sounds good to me. See you then."

Maggie returned to her makeup applications with more care. Since the spaghetti-strap dress was still held at the police station, there were two other dresses to pick from her summer clothes. As far as she was concerned, the police could keep that dress. It had too many bad memories.

Later, when the doorbell rang, Maggie looked at her watch, 1:10. Hank's early. She took a deep breath, relishing the thought of seeing him. Her world was back in normal focus again. She opened the door to Rudy.

"What are you doing here?" Maggie gasped.

Rudy grinned. "I read about your kidnap in the newspaper and wanted to see if you were all right."

"I'm fine. How did you know where I live?" Her shoulders hunched.

"I live in Madison, too. Just down the street. I've seen you. And sometimes I eat at Miss. Shelley's too. The food's pretty good."

Maggie wanted to slam the door in his face. He had some nerve trying to find her. Is he crazy?

He said, "Do you want to go dancing tonight? There's a good band playing at the Union."

"I'm busy tonight and every night." Maggie put her hand to the door as if to close it. She didn't ever want to see him again. Madison was too small a city for her.

"Just thought I'd ask. Didn't I see you at the Zephyr the other day?"

"Zephyr?" Her eyes pinched. "Where is that?"

"Yea, the Silver Zephyr, the bar down the street. I saw you there, drinking beer."

"Oh." The uncomfortable experience came back. She remembered thinking one of the men at the bar looked familiar.

"You didn't stay long," he continued.

"No, and I have to go now." Maggie looked at her watch. Hank would be arriving any minute now.

"Just thought I'd ask." Rudy turned on his heel and left muttering, "What a broad."

Maggie closed the door and sat on the nearby settee against the staircase. With her head bent over her clasped hands, she prayed, Dear Lord, help me.

If Miss. Shelley or Pat sees me praying, they'll think I'm the religious one instead of Eleanor. She crossed her legs and leaned on one arm then continued her prayer in a less prayerful posture. I can pray standing on my head if I want to.

How many times has Rudy appeared in my life? First on the raft, the practice date, on the raft a second and third time, the time he had tried to drown me, in the bar, and now here. Am I getting psychotic? Is he worried the Sam Mercken case is getting too close to him? Has he been observing my actions? What does Rudy have to gain?

Interrupted by the doorbell, Maggie looked up. Through the frosted glass with an etched design of a cozy house scene centered in a wreath, she saw Hank's unmistakable outline. Maggie jumped up and opened the door. "I'm so glad to see you!" She wanted to wrap her arms around him. Instead, she asked, "Did you see who just left?" She leaned past him to look both ways on the street.

Hank stepped out and followed her glance.

Frustration tightened her voice. "It was Rudy!" Maggie's eyes darted back and forth down the street again. Rudy was nowhere to be seen. She rubbed her temples to relieve her ache.

To her surprise, Hank put his arms around her and held her.

"He said he lives close by and has seen me walking to the diner. Do you think I should find another boarding house?"

"Don't rush into moving yet. We know where Rudy lives."

"He's such a . . ." her voice trailed off.

"Say it, Maggie. Let it out. You've held in your feelings too long."

She laughed at his suggestion. "It isn't that important."

Hank waited, urging her with his eyes.

"He's such a shithead," she said, snapping her head forward and laughing at her forcefulness.

"That's better." Hank released her. "Come on. Let's go."

They got into an unmarked car. "Remember I told you I telexed the pawnshops in Madison with a description of the five pieces of jewelry listed in the blue book? I got a call from one on the east side. We're going there now."

"I remember. You said George Mercken had a distinctive identifying mark on each item of jewelry. Nine were described, five unaccounted for."

Hank nodded.

"And remember the matchbook Smudge brought out of the wall? What was the name of that pawnshop?"

"That's exactly where we're going. The pawnbroker has a ticket with a signature of the person who pawned three of these pieces."

They drove in an easterly direction for about twenty minutes and pulled up in front of Eastside Loan Office Pawnbrokers. Under the sign, Maggie read, "Largest Pawnshop Jewelry Inventory." A Chinese symbol was printed next to it. To her, they were mysterious places with sinister overtones. Even though her life was becoming complicated, she was getting an education.

The lighted glass case displayed rows of sparkling jewelry. Hank flashed his badge to the owner, a small middle-aged Asian who in turn bowed. Hank introduced Maggie.

She wondered, did the broker ever care about a person down on his luck? He must have heard many a tragic story about each piece of jewelry in his showcases. Something about him spelled hard cash, not feelings.

Mr. Won brought out three selections from inside the glass counter. From the description in the blue book, Maggie recognized the platinum lacework brooch set with baguettes, the flower clip of rubies and pearls with a drop diamond, and the gold necklace with an octagonal pendant set with garnets embellished by pave diamonds.

After the clerk handed a jeweler's loupe to the detective, Hank passed it to Maggie. "Look, Maggie, at the distinctive mark of George Mercken. We're lucky he was particular about his identification."

Maggie squinted through the loupe. "I see GM in a square. These must be the pieces, Hank. Do you have the blue book?"

He pulled papers from his coat. "Here are copies of it." He spread them out and pointed to the exact description and placement of the mark on each piece in front of them.

The pawnbroker went to his files and returned with a ticket. Hank handled the card by the edges. Maggie looked over his shoulder.

It was dated, June 16, 1957, with a brief, handwritten description of each piece of jewelry. Maggie noticed it was one day after Sam Mercken was murdered. For the brooch the pawnbroker gave the customer seven hundred dollars, for the flower clip, five hundred and fifty dollars, and for the necklace, three hundred and seventy-five dollars. Alfred Schuster's name was signed at the bottom of the pawn ticket, no address.

"Can you describe Alfred Schuster?" Hank asked.

"He was Caucasian, about five feet ten, thin, with balding gray hair. His complexion same color as mine." At this, Mr. Won chuckled. "He had big Adam's apple."

"Was he wearing a ring?"

"He wore ruby baguette on gold band. Must be five-carat ruby."

"Thank you, Mr. Won. I'd like to put a hold on these three items. They may be evidence." Hank slipped the ticket into a plastic envelope.

"Okay, Lieutenant. I most anxious to assist." He bowed, and Hank nodded.

As they walked back to the car, Maggie remarked, "Alfred Schuster. It doesn't sound like anyone from Orchard Lake."

He said, "We'll go back to my office to compare the handwriting to business documents and inventories we retrieved from Sam Mercken's house."

Maggie thought going to the sheriff's headquarters was another new adventure. She found each step in solving Sam Mercken's murder logical and encouraging. Now, it was the jewelry heist. What would be next?

She looked at the photos on the rolltop desk in Hank's office while he disappeared down the hall. In a black-and-white photo, a young girl in shorts stood with Hank by a prewar Ford sedan. Fishing rods stuck out the back window. He stood behind the girl with both arms around her waist. Turning the picture over, she read, "Virginia and Hank, June 1949" . . . eight years ago. He would have been thirty-one then, her age now. His pain must have been great when she was killed in an auto accident. Hank said he never met another girl he wanted to marry. Except for his trim mustache that made him so handsome, his looks hadn't changed.

Maggie put the picture back and picked up one of a baseball player. The autograph of Stan Musial was scrawled over it. From under a clutter of magazines and papers, she saw a baseball glove and ball autographed by Mickey Mantle, another side of Hank's life other than crime investigating. Would she ever become a permanent part of it?

Hank returned. "We got another call from Midtown Pawnbrokers. This time, it's close by. Come on, we'll go there."

The pawnbroker said, "The customer came here smelling of whiskey. Here is the collection he brought in." From inside the showcase, he lifted a velvet display form holding a matching necklace, bracelet, and earrings set in diamonds and aquamarines. He placed it on the counter in front of them.

Maggie refrained from expressing a muted oooh as she eyed the brilliant display. Hank didn't seem as impressed with it as she. In a methodical way, he examined each piece, finding the distinctive GM etched in a square then passed it on to her.

"May I see the customer's ticket?" Hank asked as he reached in his pocket for a cellophane bag. Aldous Scribner signed the ticket and received nine hundred dollars for the complete necklace, bracelet, and ring set.

"How would you describe the customer?"

"He wasn't as tall as you, probably weighed a hundred and fifty pounds, a wiry build with gray balding hair. He wore faded jeans and a work shirt. I noticed a mole on his neck, about ten millimeters, and a ruby ring on his finger. I asked if he wanted to pawn it. He declined. I offered two hundred and fifty dollars for it. Said he planned to keep that ring. I've seen him around before, playing pool at Duke's tavern near here."

Hank directed the pawnbroker to put a hold on the display.

They returned to Hank's office and placed the tickets side by side. "See the similarity in the signatures. They should have the same latent prints, but before I send them to the lab, I want to compare the handwriting and the prints with Mercken's account books."

The evidence storage shelves were filled with boxes, parcels, and bags from the floor to the ceiling. A deputy stood behind a half door to check out items to them.

After Hank secured what he wanted, they went into a small cagelike area with a table and chairs. Hank opened Mercken's accounting books. Taking a loupe from his pocket, he first studied the writing in the books. He said, "Two distinctive writing styles are evident in these entries." Hank held the pawn tickets to each writing style in turn. "Look at this."

Maggie leaned over. She didn't need a loupe to see that the same person wrote some of the handwriting in the business books. "The writing on the ticket resembles the script on this page. You can tell a lot about a person just by looking at how the letters in his signature are formed. Sister Michel was interested in graphology. She taught me how to read signatures."

"That's interesting, Maggie. What would you forecast?"

"It's not a forecast, or anything like fortune-telling. It shows personal characteristics. For instance, if the writing is slanted to the right, it means the writer shows his feelings and takes an active role in life. If it slants to the left, the writer tends to hide his feelings and have a passive attitude. Then if the letters are straight up and down, upright, the writer shows poise and self-reliance. There's a lot to it."

"Go on. I heard the police in Chicago use graphology in building a case."

"When Sister Michel studied a signature, she placed the writing into three zones. Let me show you." Maggie picked up a requisition card from the checkout counter and placed it below the upper third of Aldous Scribner's signature on the ticket. "This is the upper zone where the upper loops of the *l*'s and *t*'s are formed. If these loops are large, it shows little business sense or confidence. The lower zone." She moved the card down to the line, which exposed the lower third of the signature. Broad loops of the *p*'s, *y*'s, and *z*'s means a good business sense. Of course, there are exceptions."

Hank placed the second plastic envelope with the ticket in front of Maggie. "What do you see from this signature?"

"From the little I know, and from the way the writing slants to the right, I'd say both writers took an active role in the business. It must be someone who is desperate for money."

Hank picked up the protective envelopes containing the tickets. "When they come back from the lab, we'll have an indisputable case." He looked at Maggie. "We need to make one more trip to Orchard Lake." His smile reflected success. He pulled out two tickets from his pocket. "But first, here are two tickets for tomorrow's baseball game."

"Who's playing?"

"The Milwaukee Braves and the New York Giants. Would you like to go with me to Milwaukee?"

"I'd love to. It's a long drive."

Maggie was surprised he could switch from his investigation to baseball as quick as an eye blink. She was still thinking of the handwriting.

"We'll have to leave early in the morning. I'll pick you up at eight."

The following morning, he suggested, "Let's leave shoptalk back in Madison; I've looked forward to seeing the Milwaukee Braves this afternoon. They've got Hank Aaron and Eddie Matthews, who are great hitters, and the pitcher, Warren Spahn, who has a fifteen-to-four record. You'll be seeing baseball at its best."

"It will be an event. I used to play left field on the Georgetown High School team." Maggie smiled.

"With your height, I bet you were a good runner."

"I could catch, too. Do you think the Braves have a chance at the world series?" Hank maneuvered the car into a parking space at county stadium.

Seated in the second tier behind home plate, Hank asked, "How do you like the seats? I was lucky to get them. One of our secretaries had to cancel and offered them to me."

"Tell me about Hank Aaron. I heard my dad speak of him."

"Hank Aaron is a talented and versatile ballplayer. When he connects to a fastball pitch, you know it's going to be a home run. He leads the league in homers." Hank sounded pleased and spoke as though he himself had trained the famed player.

"Wait!" Maggie said, her voice taking on a sharp edge. "Do you see that man, two rows down?" She hunched her shoulders together and leaned closer to Hank. "It's Rudy." Her short breath cut off her words. "He's following me."

Hank followed her gaze and then placed his arm around her. "Relax, Maggie. We won't let him disturb the game. Remember, no shoptalk." He pulled her closer.

48

Maggie and Hank rode down University Avenue out of Madison toward Orchard Lake in light Sunday-morning traffic. After a rain shower during the night, the air felt crisp and clear. The humidity had gone down a few degrees.

Looking down at her new pair of jeans, Maggie smiled. She sensed Hank liked them too by the look he gave her. He didn't look a bit troubled or anxious about the meeting in Sam Mercken's house, rather he acted like they were going on a holiday instead of to a showdown of key players in a murder case.

He asked, "Were you notified about your preliminary hearing?"

"Yes, it's next Thursday. I'm so scared. I dread the thought of facing those kidnappers. How do I know they won't come after me again?"

Hank reached over and touched her clinched fists. "If it will make you feel better, in my experience, it isn't likely. I've known of only one case where that happened. Will your folks be there?"

"I hope not. I don't want them to come."

"I'll go with you. What time is it?"

"It's set for nine thirty." Maggie turned toward him. "I appreciate your taking time off. I feel better already." She managed to smile.

"Then relax." His hand, still on hers, massaged her fists until they opened.

"We must talk, Maggie." Hank kept his eyes on the road as he maneuvered a turn onto the highway.

She detected a change in his voice from the subject of the trial and asked, "What about?"

"Us," Hank said, waiting until he shifted into high gear to regain his speed. "How many years were you a sister? For some reason, you never want to talk about it."

Maggie was unprepared for personal questions. She felt the meeting this afternoon in Orchard Lake was crucial to solving the case. Why did Hank want to talk about her? Or was he hinting at something else?

After an awkward silence, Maggie said, "About twelve years," not at all sure where his questions were leading. She wanted to change the subject. Her reasons for leaving St. Clotildes were complex.

"How does it really feel to be away from there after all those years?"

She looked into his deep brown eyes. How much do I tell him? "Hank, this may sound strange to you, but I don't know. I'm not familiar with my feelings. I had to suppress and regulate them for more than a decade. In the monastic environment, feelings were viewed as a weakness. It was as though we weren't supposed to feel. We never talked about it. When a bell rang, the community moved to a spiritual exercise, and I moved with them. I had no practice making choices because every activity, even our thinking, always concentrated on the rule, the constitution, the schedule, or the superior's requests.

"I'm not bitter about spending my time there, even though I was enveloped in a long black habit that was supposed to numb my sensuality. I never earned a paycheck. Now at the age of thirty-one, I'm just starting. I no longer cling to the myth that God was always in danger of being offended."

"You have everything going for you, Maggie. Life is just beginning. You're young, beautiful, and very special." He looked over at her. "This year, you'll be involved in activities at graduate school, meeting men your age. You must be excited about that."

Maggie rubbed her eyes, thinking, *Was this all he wanted to know, and I gave him all this monastic jargon stuff?* "I am. My first goal is to get my degree. Then I have to get a job to support myself. I have to borrow money for everything, not only for my education, but also for health insurance plus all the extras, even a toothbrush. I can't be dependent on my folks forever." She shrugged her shoulders. "Dating and having fun sounds great, but I wonder if I'll even have time. Another thing, if I major in music, piano majors have to give two solo-performance programs to fulfill the requirements of a master's program. This is going to take a lot of practice time." Maggie paused. "But I've been looking at the psychology prerequisites. I could qualify for the master's program in that field. That interests me too."

"You're all work, Maggie. What about taking some time for fun? Don't you plan to see the Wisconsin football games? I have season tickets." Hank leaned toward her. "You think you'll be so busy studying that you can't go with me to the games? Wisconsin is in the Big Ten Conference."

She shook her head. The Big Ten meant nothing to her. "Football games never entered my mind."

"Then it's a good thing this Mercken case happened during the summer because you wouldn't have had any time for me after your classes began."

Maggie took a deep breath. "Oh, Hank," she laid her hand on top of his on the steering wheel, "I'll always have time for you. I thought you might sign me off after the Sam Mercken case." She hesitated. "I don't believe I could stand that." She squeezed gently on his hand and saw him smile.

He said, "Let's stop for lunch somewhere. If you see a good place, let me know."

"How about pizza?" Maggie asked. "I never had it until I came home."

"Sounds good to me." Hank spotted a pizza sign, pulled in, and parked. "There's something I want to ask you. I've hesitated because of our age difference. I'm forty. You're so much younger." He stopped. "I love you, Maggie."

"Oh, Hank, I love you too." She slid to the middle of the seat and kissed his cheek.

"I want to introduce you to many new experiences." He turned and wrapped his arms around her. "I've wanted to do this for a long time."

Maggie sank into his embrace responding to the warmth of his body. She closed her eyes and nuzzled her nose and lips across his face, nibbling his rough cheek until she found his mouth. The taste of his lips on hers ripped open a sensation pent up too long. She felt her body go limp.

Time melted into minutes, then longer minutes. She loved the feel of his hands as they caressed her.

Finally Hank released her. "Maggie, I think I've loved you ever since I first met you at the Chateau. Then I felt guilty because you were a nun. Now I've found you again. And this time I refuse to feel guilty."

"I had feelings for you too." She gazed into his loving eyes. "But I had to test myself. I didn't want to make another mistake. That's why I waited five years to make the decision to leave. It took me that long to realize I became a nun for the wrong reasons."

She kissed him again. "Now, I'm sure of myself."

49

Hank looked at his watch. "As much as I'd love to prolong this, the meeting at Sam Mercken's house is at two o'clock. We have to keep moving."

Hank glanced into the car mirror and wiped the lipstick from his cheek. Maggie pulled out a tissue to wipe it again before leaving the car

Looking over the pizza selections, Maggie asked, "Has Sam's assets been distributed?"

"Not yet. It's still in probate. That usually takes a minimum of four months."

"I've forgotten. Did he leave much to Amelia?"

"Yes, she received the major portion of the estate. Virgie Pinski was also remembered."

"Virgie? Was she the beautiful blond I saw at the funeral? I remember she stood under a tree a distance from the gravesite."

Hank nodded. "She's the one."

"Hum." Maggie paused to consider if she should pursue the subject then said, "I remember Amelia never spoke to her at the reading of the will. Was Virgie Sam's mistress?"

"Yep."

"Do you think Amelia knew about it?"

"Probably," Hank said, studying the menu.

Maggie could see he wasn't concerned with the issue.

After they gave their order, Maggie asked, "Who's coming to the meeting?"

"I've included Jim Mooreside, Ted Bryson, Butch Merdoc, Al Steger, his nephew Rudy and Amelia and Gilbert."

"Rudy! He seems to be every place I go." Her voice took on a challenging tone. "We'd better pick up a can of coffee. I remember there wasn't much left the last time."

"Okay. There'll be eight altogether plus a couple of deputies."

"Deputies? This sounds like an Agatha Christie novel." Maggie looked surprised.

Hank smiled. "I hope so. Here comes our order."

*   *   *

After Hank twisted the key into the Mercken's front door, Maggie entered. Her eyes glanced toward the bloodstains and taped outline still in place on the brown flowered carpet. The upright Chickering piano stood in the corner, covered with an embroidered scarf of red and yellow roses and family photos of a bygone period. Next to it stood a bookcase.

Maggie went into the kitchen to measure coffee into the pot and arrange cups on a tray while Hank set nine chairs in a semicircle in the parlor. After the phone rang, Hank answered it. From the doorway, she watched him nod his head then hang up. He smiled and walked toward her. "That was Officer O'Keefe from the Madison PD. A witness has identified the driver of the kidnap car you were in."

"Was it Rudy?" Maggie's eyes widened; her back stiffened.

Hank nodded and put his arms around her. "Don't worry. He'll be here this afternoon, and he'll be watched."

"I feel safe when I'm with you."

They were interrupted by the doorbell. Al Steger, the former part-time accountant of the deceased, entered. He appeared not to have shaved for several days and took the chair closest to the door. He rolled a cigarette and lit it. Then he filled his lungs with smoke and let it all go in a big cloud.

Maggie tried to put aside her fears and concentrate on the murder. Did Al look guilty of murdering Sam Mercken? So much evidence pointed toward him. She'd try to keep an open mind.

Next Rudy, Al's adopted nephew, came in and sat without greeting his uncle. Maggie made a face as if she had a bad taste in her mouth and stepped back into the kitchen to avoid eye contact. She leaned her head against the cupboard and closed her eyes. Besides Rudy's collaboration in her kidnap, he had wanted to kiss her and have sex in his truck and play pinball machines like an adolescent. Pieced together, the scenes read like a cheap novel, with Rudy as the central figure. The experiences did give her a fast, rude education.

What would the sisters say if they knew? They had nothing good to say about her anyway after she left. She focused on her friend, Sister Angelica, who was a model nun. She was what most people expected from a sister who had professed the vows of poverty, chastity, and obedience.

Ted Bryson and Jim Mooreside came in next. Jim lived across the road, next to her parents' summer cottage. After he found a chair, Maggie saw him clasp his hands then turn them over as if studying his cuticles. Was he the guilty one?

Ted, who lagged behind Jim, had been a friend of Sam's from Milwaukee before he had retired to Orchard Lake. She remembered he had stood by the door until Hank invited him to sit at the table

Behind him came Butch Merdoc, the bartender at the Green Apple Deli and Bar. His bloated face was expressionless, and his purplish skin was stretched to a point where it could pop. The chair creaked as he sat down. It barely fit his body.

Though the four of them often played cards at the Green Apple, they didn't greet each other as old friends nor indulge in backslapping jokes.

The last to enter were Amelia, Sam's widow, and Gilbert. They came from the farthest distance, Milwaukee.

Hank stepped forward to shake hands with them. "Glad you could make it."

Amelia took hesitant steps into her house where she had lived her retirement years. Her eyes darted toward the outline on the rug where Sam's body had lain. When dishes rattled in the kitchen, her head jerked in that direction like a cat claiming its territory. Then Amelia recognized the familiar faces of her neighbors sitting in the circle. She didn't greet them; instead, she stopped and looked back at the door, as if deciding to stay.

It was clear Amelia wasn't pleased to be back in her house. Her pinched face looked much older than the gay Amelia, with the short skirt they had visited in Milwaukee before. Was this the first time Amelia had returned to her house since the murder? There must have been something in the house she would want to keep. Hank guided her to a chair near the desk.

After the coffee finished perking, Maggie brought out steaming cups. As each adjusted their coffee preferences with the cream and sugar, their silence and inquiring eyes seemed to shriek, why am I here? How is this meeting going to end?

After serving everyone, she returned to the kitchen, poured herself a mug, then sat at an angle where she could see and hear but couldn't be observed. Glancing around the kitchen, she remembered the day she heard Smudge, Amelia's cat, meowing, trying to get free from inside the wall behind the sink. So much had happened since then, coming to Madison, getting a room at Miss. Shelley's, her abduction.

Maggie took out her little notebook to double-check which hand each one used to pick up their cups. Gilbert was a new entry. She jotted "clear-cut lefty."

Hank addressed the group, "Thank you for coming. I invited you here because each of you had a connection with Samuel Mercken, and each of you had an opportunity to kill him."

Butch hooted, "Whoa there."

"Not so fast, Lieutenant," yelled Gilbert.

"You'll have to prove that," Jim piped up.

Al Steger shouted, "Not me!" He blew a cloud of smoke that made him less visible.

Hank ignored their comments and waited a few moments for them to settle down. "All of you had dealings with the deceased. I've called you together to discuss your activities and motives. Who stood to gain from Sam's death?"

This time, they remained at attention, as if any movement or sound might signal a guilty plea or bring the detective's attention to them. They sat, heads up, holding on to their coffee cups like a cast of players in a play.

What was he trying to do? Provoke them? He must know who is guilty. Hank was so smart. Just looking at him made her forget everyone else in the room. She felt his warm lips, his caressing hands. Taking a deep breath, she allowed these sensual feelings to flow through her, down to her toes. These would have been called "impure thoughts" and would have had to be confessed as sins. Now, she could wallow in these feelings if she wanted to. It made her want to get finished with the meeting, so they could be alone again.

Maggie heard Hank addressing Rudy. She refocused her attention.

"You had familiarity with arms. A gun was found in your truck. When your parents were killed in an auto accident, you lived in an orphanage until your Uncle Al took you in. Then you were pretty much your own boss. You're twenty-eight years old and haven't held a steady job. If problems arose with your boss, you quit, never working out solutions. There was always good old Uncle Al in Orchard Lake where you could run for help."

Rudy was on his feet. One side of his mouth turned up. Maggie knew he'd have a smart-alecky remark. Instead, he shouted, "That not fair! It's not even true!"

Hank held up his hand, waving him to sit.

"You visited Orchard Lake the weekend Sam Mercken was murdered and had knowledge that a gun was thrown into the lake. The gun was found. Lab tests proved it to be a .32 automatic Remington, the same kind that killed Samuel Mercken."

Rudy stood up again. Hank ignored him. "You went to Sam's house that night. You didn't intend to hurt him. You just wanted cash. When Sam resisted your demands, you hit him over the head with a ceramic vase. That was not part of your plan. You saw him on the floor. You were stunned and panicked. You worried he'd point a finger at you. Did you decide to finish the job?"

Rudy shouted, "You're out of your mind. What makes you think I wanted to kill that old man? He meant nothing to me. I wasn't near Sam's house that night. I don't—."

"I want to know," Hank interrupted, "how you knew the gun was in the lake."

"I didn't know. Honest, I didn't. I always go diving for treasures at the bottom of the lake. You'd be surprised what the summer people drop overboard. I've found beach umbrellas, cameras, sunglasses, and a whole bunch of other stuff."

"Rudy, you've told so many lies. Why should I believe you now?"

"Because it was none of your goddamn business!" His face and neck strained showing veins in his neck. Beads of sweat spilled out on his forehead. Rudy stomped out of the house.

Al jumped up, "Want me to bring him back, Lieutenant?"

Hank shook his head. "He won't go far." As he watched Rudy leave, Hank's eyes followed him toward the door.

"Jim Mooreside. You heard the gunshot the night of June 15 and called the sheriff. You didn't know Sam Mercken until he moved to Orchard Lake in 1948 but you, like the rest here, purchased a valuable piece of jewelry from him that year." Hank paused to read from his notes, "An eighteen-carat-gold lavaliere with three diamonds, one half carat each."

Without raising his voice, Jim lifted his hands palms up in a gesture that asked what of it. "I bought that for my wife. It came from Sam's father's store. When Sam retired, he brought heirloom pieces with him to Orchard Lake and made this piece available to me at a reasonable price."

Amelia stirred in her chair. "I didn't know anything about that. Sam never told me he still had that jewelry. I thought it was all taken in the robbery."

Gilbert leaned over and laid his hand on her arm.

Hank continued with Jim, "You also played cards with Butch and Al at the Green Apple until ten the night of the murder."

Jim ran his hand over his cheek. "What of it? We play cards there every Saturday night."

Hank looked at his notes, "Butch, you also played cards. How come you closed so early that night? Isn't it usual for bars to stay open until two?"

Butch answered, "It was a slow night. Elaine had left her prescription pills by the cash register and called me to bring them over to her house."

"From Samuel Mercken's heirloom stash, you bought a pair of black pearl earrings, 12-mm cabochons."

Maggie noticed the circle remained silent, each looking from one to another as if to ask, what did you buy? She glanced at Ted Bryson. He looked lifeless, not moving a muscle. Was he guilty?

"And Al bought a ruby ring," Hank continued.

The words echoed in her mind. Yes! Yes! That was it. Both pawnbrokers described a ruby ring on a man who brought in jewelry to pawn. She saw it on his left hand now.

"What I'm wondering is," Hank said, "how it happened you all got such a good deal from Samuel Mercken. What drove Sam to keep these valuable gemstones all those years he and Amelia owned the J and M Jewelry Store in Milwaukee then liquidate them to you, folks, in Orchard Lake? Why? He could have sold them for 100 percent profit."

"That's easy to explain, Lieutenant," said Al Steger, stretching his head and shoulders tall as if any idiot should know. "Sam retired in 1950. Maybe he didn't realize these pieces of jewelry were still in storage."

Maggie thought, not a good answer.

"Humph!" Amelia uttered her disgust. "He's lying."

"Yes, Al, you would know more about the business than anyone else in this room except Amelia." Hank nodded respectfully in her direction. "You were Sam's accountant from 1930 to 1950. You moved to Orchard Lake about the same time as Sam. How did that come about?"

Al shifted back in the chair, moving his head from side to side. "Over the years, Sam and I became good friends." He smiled, folding his arms across his chest.

Maggie nodded; Al seemed too sure of himself. He talked like his friendship with Sam cleared him of all suspicion.

"Sam bought two houses and offered the second one to me. He wanted it as an investment."

"That was a generous offer; don't you think, Al?" Hank said. "Who owns the house you live in now?"

"It's part of Sam's estate." Al answered, as though he was asked the day of the week.

"Do you pay rent?"

"No," Al answered.

"So you've lived in your house rent-and tax-free for how many years?"

"Since '50, nine years this September. I often tried to buy it, but Sam always said he wanted it for an investment. And for this, I did every damn little job he wanted done and was loyal 'til the day he died."

Died? An understatement, Maggie thought. Sam didn't die; he was murdered. What was Al trying to say? Did Amelia know about the arrangement with his house? Amelia's eyes were closed.

"You must have done something special to get such a handsome reward," Hank persisted.

"Well," Al started to say something else and then closed his lips.

Gilbert stood tall and turned toward Al like a captain giving orders. "Yes. What did you do for Sam? I've always wondered."

Hank cut off Gilbert's question. "Al, you were the last one to see Sam alive that night. Did you return to Sam's house after you played cards at the Green Apple?"

"No, I went straight home." Al's hand brushed his nose with the back of his hand, his lips tightening into a straight line.

"What size shoe do you wear, Al?" Hank asked.

"I wear a size 10D, Lieutenant. What's that got to do with Sam's death?"

Maggie remembered the cast she and Hank had made of Al's footprint in the mud. Did that casting match the partial bloodstained footprint on the carpet? Hank had never told her if a successful cast had been made.

"It could mean a lot," Hank said. "We secured a plaster cast of a size-10D footprint on the rug in here and outside this front door. Do you have a registered automatic pistol?"

"Yes, I do." Al wiped his bald spot with a handkerchief.

"We know that a shell found in this room came from an automatic pistol."

"Not mine!" Al refolded his arms in front of him, looking annoyed. He continued to move his head side to side as if the whole idea was preposterous.

Maggie's gaze shifted from Al to Ted Bryson. He sat like a whipped puppy. Would he be next on Hank's list?

"Gilbert," Hank said. "Where were you between midnight and two the night of June 15?"

"I was home in Milwaukee."

Butch interrupted, "Nooo, you weren't. I saw you in Orchard Lake late that night when I came back from Elaine's."

All eyes turned to Gilbert waiting to hear his explanation.

Gilbert raised his voice, "It wasn't me. You must have seen someone else."

"It was, too." Butch jumped up, his heavy jowl swaying. "I saw you driving your silver Merc on Highway 69 heading toward Main Street."

"Do you drive a silver Mercury, Gilbert?" Hank asked.

"Lieutenant." Gilbert's color grew ashen. He smiled out of the corner of his mouth as if annoyed then stood up with his hands in his pockets. "If I were you, I'd find out why Al Steger went to Switzerland after the robbery in 1931."

"Let me hear your version," Hank said.

"It was Sam who staged that robbery to claim the insurance his father had on the jewelry store." Gilbert paused to let that bit of information sink in. "In addition to the payoff from the insurance, Al had taken what Sam claimed were stolen gems to Switzerland. There he fenced them and brought back a sizable sum of money; I heard him brag about it one time when he had too many beers. That's why he was handsomely rewarded with a rent-and tax-free house all these years." He sat down again and reached for his coffee cup.

"You'll have a damn hard time proving that," Al said.

"That may be. But when the truth comes out, Sam's just lucky he won't be around to take the consequences."

"What about you?" Al asked. "What were you doing here that night? You haven't given a satisfactory answer."

Gilbert gulped on his coffee and shook his head. He looked around the circle as if looking for an answer. In a soft voice, he said, "Butch was right. I was in Orchard Lake that night. I did come back. I lay in bed unable to sleep the night before. I said to myself, I had enough of the way Sam Mercken mistreated Amelia. So I decided to confront him and demand that my mother come to live with me."

Heads turned toward Amelia.

Maggie jotted a note in her book.

"Amelia is your mother?" Butch asked.

Amelia said, "It doesn't matter anymore." Her fingers fluttered at her throat.

Gilbert patted her arm. "It's time you all knew. Sam made my mother suffer her entire married life because I was her illegitimate son. I was never allowed to visit her. Any communication we had was done in secret, even when she visited me at the orphanage. I could have been a big help in Sam's business, but he never let me near it or near my mother."

Maggie thought about Amelia, who as a young girl had gotten herself into trouble and had to live with her secret all these many years.

Gilbert said, "On my eighteenth birthday, I left the orphan home and joined the U.S. Marines. After the war, I got my accounting degree. When I got a good job, I wanted my mother to come and live with me." Gilbert stood up and looked around the room. "My mother deserved a better life than what Sam gave her. He was an unfeeling son of a bitch bent on making a fortune at everyone's cost!

"Yes, I went to Orchard Lake that evening to see Sam. I knew he wouldn't recognize me. I just had to stand inside the door of Sam's house and say, I'm Gilbert Paradyze, Amelia's son. He cursed and told me to get out. He tried to push me out the door, but I was bigger than Sam and stood my ground. I told him I knew he engineered that jewelry robbery for the insurance money. Sam pulled a gun out of that desk drawer. Before he had a chance to aim, I picked up a vase from the table and threw it at him. The vase hit his head and knocked him down. I tried to kick the gun out of his hand, but it slammed into the bookcase where he could reach it. So I ran out of the house and got into my car before he had a chance to shoot me.

"That's when I passed Al Steger in his Ford pickup. I saw him drive past Sam's house. That's all I know and all I saw." Gilbert sat down.

Amelia reached over and put her arm through his. A proud smile lit up her face.

All eyes returned to Al Steger. His proud pose changed. All his big talk was turning into smoke. His sunken shoulders made him seem smaller in the chair. How will he get out of this? Maggie heard Hank ask, "Al, have you ever heard of Alfred Schuster or Aldous Scribner?"

"Can't say I ever have." Al's Adam's apple bobbed up and down.

Hank continued, "The initials of these two names are the same as yours, AS."

"So what?" Al took out his handkerchief and patted his brow. Maggie thought she saw his initials on it.

"As an accountant to Sam Mercken, do you remember the identification marks Sam's father had stamped on those valuable pieces of jewelry?"

"Sam never used identifying marks."

How could Al be so stupid? Maggie asked herself as she watched Hank's tactful plan unfold before her eyes. Al was under the gun now.

Hank continued, "You're right, Al. Sam didn't, but his father, George S. Mercken, did. His initials, GM, were engraved inside of a square." He paused to read from his notes. "A necklace, bracelet, and earrings set in diamonds and aquamarines; a flower clip of rubies with a drop diamond; and a gold necklace set in garnets and pave diamonds all had George Mercken's distinctive identification. It seems an odd coincidence that these pieces went into circulation right after Sam was murdered."

Everyone was silent.

"They were taken to two pawnshops, Eastside Loan Brokers and The Midtown Pawnshop, by a man wearing a ruby ring. The brokers said their client was about five foot eleven inches, slight build with gray balding hair, and a noticeable mole on his neck" Maggie remembered that the pawnbroker said the ruby ring was five carats. Al reached up to pull his shirt collar higher to cover a spot on his neck and then scratch his ear. She knew Hank had more evidence, the fingerprints from the tickets plus the handwriting analysis.

Al braced his forehead in his hands. He looked toward the kitchen then to the front entrance. Until that moment, the blame had shifted from one to another in the group. Now it was on him alone. The scene became silent, surreal. Hank stared down at him, waiting.

Al had difficulty swallowing.

"Yes," Al said his eyes evading Hank's stare. He leaned over, crumbling his handkerchief into a ball to cover the initials. Taking his time, he stretched one leg forward and shoved the handkerchief back into his pocket. Al's despairing voice revealed exhaustion. "I went back and found Sam sitting on the floor rubbing his head. The vase was on the floor." Al looked straight at Gilbert as though he had set the scene.

"Sam moaned; he was hurt and couldn't get up. It was my chance. I knew about that special collection of jewelry Sam had listed in a blue book, and I wanted them. I did so much for Sam through the years. I never got enough for doing his dirty work. I risked a long prison term taking that trip to Switzerland. You say rent-and tax-free like it was a bountiful gift. That cabin was a shambles, a pigsty.

"Sam didn't need those heirloom pieces. I had no job and was desperate. If they were stashed in the house, I'd find them. If they were elsewhere, I had to find out where. I didn't even carry a gun.

"Then Sam started to made fun of me just like he used to do. He called me a simpering fool and picked up his gun and waved it at me. I couldn't stand it. I grabbed the gun from him, and I shot him. I went through his pockets and found the key to his safe. It was my passport, my golden opportunity. I didn't even have to argue with him about why I should have those sets of jewelry. It was easy.

"I found the jewelry in the safe and left with the gun still in my hand. I had to get rid of it and ran past Brenner's cabin down to the lake and threw it in." Al looked toward the pantry. "The Brenner girl found it."

Maggie hunched her shoulders together. It explained so much.

No one in the group spoke. It was as silent as a bank vault after closing hours.

Maggie stood and stepped back. Two deputies and Mr. Cavanaugh, the claims investigator from the Lincoln Insurance Company, entered the room.

One of the deputies put handcuffs on Al and led him to the waiting car where he joined Rudy, who was already cuffed and waiting.

Mr. Cavanaugh walked over to Hank, holding a taped reel. "I have it all here. I'll send you a copy."

*   *   *

It was over.

After everyone left, Hank entered the kitchen. "Al and Rudy are on their way to jail."

"That's a relief. Why was Rudy stalking me?"

"It was all about the gun you found in the lake. Rudy was protecting his uncle Al who stood to lose his happy home when Sam died. You had to be punished."

Maggie threw a dishtowel to Hank. "You were brilliant to get them all riled up. She saw his half smile open to a full beaming one, stretching his thin moustache into a straight line.

"My next case is you. It's time we celebrate. He set the towel down and turned Maggie toward him. Looking into her eyes, he touched her face, tracing his finger around her cheek and lips. His hand moved around her shoulders, drawing her close.

Maggie laid her head against his neck. She felt her breasts against his chest. In his embrace, there was much warmth and comfort. A shiver ran up her spine awakening her senses as his lips met hers. With her arms circled around his neck, she said in a muffled voice, "I've been waiting too."

Hank asked, "Do you see a detective in your life, one with a few miles on him?"

She answered, "I didn't leave the cloister to remain a virgin."

The End